RESONANCE

The Resonance Series: Book One

Jennifer Greenhall

FORWARD
PROGRESS
MEDIA

Resonance is a work of fiction. Names, characters, places, organizations and incidents portrayed in this novel are either products of the author's imagination or are used fictitiously. Any resemblance to actual persons, living or dead, businesses, companies, events or locales is entirely coincidental.

Copyright © 2018 by Jennifer Greenhall
All rights reserved, including the right to reproduce this book or portions thereof in any form whatsoever.

Published by Forward Progress Media, Inc.
Printed in the United States of America

ISBN-13 (paperback): 978-0-9998166-0-8
ISBN-13 (e-book): 978-0-9998166-1-5

First Edition

Cover Design by Gabrielle Prendergast
Author photograph by Dean Bradshaw
Formatting by Polgarus Studio

To my little ones:
May you realize your hearts' desires
and fill your lives with joy.

ACKNOWLEDGMENTS

Sharing what I've written with the world took a leap of faith, a leap I could finally take because of the loving support of my family and friends. I'm grateful to all of you for helping me reach this goal and for contributing to my life in countless positive ways.

Many people spent significant time and energy providing me with valuable feedback and edits. For these efforts, huge thanks go to Kim Floyd, Stephanie Green, Celena Jacques, Leanne Gaspar, Joanna Mitchell, Jennifer Hollander, Susanna Pang, Susanna Finnell, Nancy Gutierrez, Barbara Green, Ellen Stiefler, Stephanie Walker, Jeanie Haddox, Mignon Hilts, Ahren Crickard, Alicya Astudillo, Jordan Greenhall, and Ann Lumley.

For technical advice, my thanks go to Matt Domsalla, Sean Evans, Paul Lebidine, Cara Seekings and Rachel Teagle. I'd also like to thank Deborah Halverson for editing an early version of the manuscript, Dean Bradshaw for taking my photograph at Torrey Pines State Beach, Scott Green for creating a graphic art version of the cover, and Gabrielle Prendergast for the final cover design.

I want specifically to thank my sister, Stephanie, brother-in-law, Jim, and my parents, Barbara and Bob, for their endless feedback, on-the-spot editing advice, and unconditional love. I couldn't have done it without you. To the kids in my life, you are truly loved and make everything worthwhile.

PROLOGUE

Scorched paper drifts through an acrid haze pierced by stains of clear blue sky. A deafening boom rattles the earth. Cries. Screams. Desperate feet sprint to escape the chasing clouds of dust and rubble. Briefcases shield bodies from the pelting debris . . .

A kiss on my forehead and a soft caress wake me. As I blink my eyes to greet the morning light, my mom's ashen face and grief-stricken eyes tell me something's terribly wrong. "It's your dream, Sophia. It's New York."

We rush downstairs to join my twin brother, Thomas, already watching the nightmare unfold on TV. High above the skyline, fire and smoke billow out of huge, gaping holes in identical monoliths.

"How could anyone do this?" my mother cries. The TV coverage shifts to another wreckage. "God, not the Pentagon too?" None of us can truly believe the images of destruction and death flashing before us. We stare and listen in dumbfounded horror.

The minutes tick by. A sick dread settles into the pit of my stomach as a realization dawns on me . . . the people sprinting. Those buildings are going to fall. "They have to get everyone out!" I yell, just as one of the skyscrapers disintegrates before our eyes.

I sink into the couch and cover my face with both hands. I don't need to see the tragedy unfold on screen any longer. I'd seen those people running for their lives, their screams bleeding into the choking smoke over and over again in my dreams. I didn't know where it would happen, though, or when. I thought the dreams meant the big earthquake might finally hit, taking out San Francisco, my beloved home . . . but I was wrong, so wrong. Even for a psychic, the future is rarely clear.

My mother breaks down into sobs when the second tower collapses. Thomas, who'd been sitting as motionless as a statue, leaves the room. He can't deal with our anguish any longer on top of his own. He'll be consumed if he doesn't focus on protecting himself.

Tears stream down my face, collecting on the rim of my jaw before dropping into my lap. *All those people . . . could I have tried harder to understand my dreams, to solve this puzzle? God, could I have prevented this from happening?* A part of me knows that no one important would have listened to a nine-year-old girl, but another part still feels responsible. *A precious gift has been wasted on me.*

Catching a glimpse of the future isn't a blessing. It's a curse.

The ghost-like wails echo through my mind. The guilt, the pain, the sorrow are beginning to suffocate me. I press my fingers hard into my temples and struggle to slow my breathing. While counting the lengths of my inhales and exhales, something shifts inside of me and spreads like a chain reaction throughout the fiber of my being. *I have a purpose.* Though I don't know why I can do what I do, the obligation of it is now clear. Next time, I'll be ready. I *will* figure it out. Next time, and every time. Nothing like this will ever happen again if I can help it.

CHAPTER ONE

Two heavily armed men patrolled the nondescript corridor. Neither sensed me as my consciousness passed between them and into the room they were protecting. I could already see the elusive trace of pink light emanating from a long glass tube. *Jackpot.* Another pair of menacing-looking guards stood sentry at the interior entrance while a few technicians in yellow protective suits wandered around the room. Condensation trickled down cooling pipes. Thick acrylic glass with radioactive warnings separated bulky stainless steel equipment from the rest of the room. The laser rested on an optical table emitting short intermittent spurts of air, and the Korean phrases I'd been trained to identify confirmed its function. I studied the setup and the gauges of the instruments and phased repeatedly back to my body to sketch the room's layout and jot down any Korean I could find.

My boss, Roger, and our client asked me then to search for certain security features not included in my official debriefing. Once they were satisfied, I relaxed and withdrew into myself, recalling my consciousness or whatever part of me escaped into the ether to hunt down this dangerous nuclear technology. Uniting my thoughts with my heartbeat, my mind and body merged into a whole again, my skin tingling slightly as always. I focused on the rise and fall of my chest for a few breaths before opening my eyes and bringing my notes over to the men. We reviewed the recording of my spoken observations of the journey and confirmed some finer details. When the C.I.A. representative left, he was ready to take action.

After spending the last eight days sleuthing at sixty different facilities, Roger and I were relieved to have this assignment behind us at last and hopeful it would decrease the chance of a nuclear war. I was going on my fourth year as an astral projection specialist in the Psi Solutions division of San Diego Consulting Corporation, better known as SDCC, a large, mostly government contractor. Though psychic abilities were recognized as legitimate in the late '90s and proven by scientists to have increased throughout the population over the last thirty years, SDCC was the first and still one of the few companies to hire psychics openly. They cleverly privatized what the military and intelligence agencies had covertly recruited for years.

Since I'd been working extra long hours and had no urgent case, Roger insisted I wait until Monday to start my next project, barring any emergencies, of course. After retiring from the military four years ago, Roger joined SDCC to set up and oversee the Psi Solutions division. He interfaced with our often top-secret clients, coordinated and set our agendas, and obtained any training or resources we might need, though he also had to assist personally in some projections to relay intelligence to and from our clients. He sported a salt and pepper crew cut, an athletic physique, and a habitually business-like manner. Roger was a devoted family man with a wife he adored and three kids in college. He was a good man and a great boss.

It was Friday and only lunchtime, which meant I could spend a leisurely afternoon wrapping up my paperwork, and still easily make my "family" dinner with Thomas and the Reeds that evening. Dr. Harry Reed was our Psychology professor at UC San Diego (or UCSD for short), and was the leading expert and media figurehead for any and all things psychic. In our freshman year, he began teaching a class on Parapsychology, the scientific study of paranormal phenomena. Though psychic or *psi* abilities had been accepted as fact, this course was the first of its kind to be taught at such a scientifically rigorous institution (and not without controversy, as we had to wade through shouts of "devil-worshipers" on our way to class). Thomas and I met some of our closest friends here and for the first time truly grasped that we weren't the only freaks on the planet.

My stomach growled, and my hands trembled slightly, making obvious that I desperately needed to refuel. I locked the folder in my desk, grabbed my purse, and walked over to the cubicle of one these friends. Diana was a strong telepath, though not as impressive as Thomas. She was tall, slender, and beautiful, and her Indian-European mix imparted an exotic flare. We were both twenty-five, but her telepathy and genteel upbringing lent her a worldly sophistication that often made me feel like her kid sister. We'd started at SDCC together right out of college and sometimes joked that we were a superwoman duo working to save the world. Diana was reading on her computer when I peered over her divider.

"I'd love to grab lunch." Her eyes sparkled with glee and mischief. "Do you just want to hit the café downstairs?" she asked.

Though she already knew my response, this time she patiently waited for me to speak, pretending to make up for her *faux pas* of answering a question in someone's head before it's voiced.

"Ha, ha. You *know* I want to go to the café," I replied. Apparently, I was even more exhausted than I realized. I rested my arms on her cubicle, shut my eyes, and visualized my mental fortress, an automatic protection for my thoughts unless I'm mentally fatigued. Growing up linked to a telepathic twin, I had to learn to shield my thoughts to give him peace and myself privacy. I possessed a touch of telepathy as well, at least as far as Thomas was concerned. We could communicate by thought over more than a few thousand miles, the farthest we'd been apart, but with other people, I had to be physically close and focus intently to receive or send any thoughts. Since I experienced firsthand how difficult my brother's life was growing up, I never had a desire to develop my telepathy. I already had too much to deal with.

When my shields felt intact again, I opened my eyes and grinned at her. "I'm glad you're back. It's been lonely around here. Are you ready to eat?"

"Definitely." Diana closed her laptop and pulled her red alligator Chloé purse out of a drawer. As we strolled toward the elevator, she counted on her perfectly manicured fingers. "That makes it the fifth time I've caught you with your shields down. You could have made my day if you'd been thinking about something more salacious than a turkey and avocado sandwich." She smiled but searched my face, eyes concerned. "Tough morning?"

Depending on the situation, my job could be more than just physically and mentally draining. Finding missing persons, helping with hostage crises, and delivering ground intelligence during a battle included some of my more stressful and emotionally charged assignments. Recovering from those experiences took me a while sometimes. Fortunately, this project had been uneventful.

"No. We've just been working for eight long days without a break, but we finished at last."

"Good girl, Sophia, just in time for my party."

The elevator doors opened, and we stepped aside to let the passengers out. Diana was barely suppressing a mischievous grin. She was obviously chomping at the bit to tell me something.

"What's so funny? More gossip about the catfight on the fifth floor?" I asked while pressing the button for the ground level.

"No, just some news I heard when I came in this morning. An old friend of ours started in the new Psi Solutions group today."

"Really? Who?"

"Nate . . . Nate Barclay."

"Oh." My stomach dropped a little along with the elevator. Nate had been the best friend of my ex-fiancé, Brian, and had actually introduced the two of us. Nate and I had been close, but when Brian and I broke up in the spring of our senior year, I severed ties with all of his friends. It was too awkward and painful, and at the time, I didn't know what else to do.

Diana frowned slightly, clearly expecting a different response. "You two were good friends before the big breakup. Couldn't you be friends again . . . or *more*?" she prodded.

"Diana." She was at it once again. My pathetic dating life never ceased to call out to her altruistic yet meddlesome side. "You know we were *only* friends. He was your friend too. Maybe *you* could become something more."

"Hey, I'm only trying to help. You don't need to get defensive every time I try to set you up." With the ring of the elevator door, we stepped into the reception area, and her mild annoyance disappeared. In fact, her smile began to creep back, which made me wary. "Last I saw, Nate definitely had the tall, dark and handsome thing going on, but even if I weren't already involved, he could never be my type. My telepathy made him uncomfortable. I caught him checking out my boobs once, and when I laughed, he realized I'd heard his thoughts. After that, he was still friendly but a bit standoffish. Come to think of it," she said, trying to sound as if her comment was unplanned, "I do remember him appreciating your boobs as well."

"You'll never stop, will you?"

Diana dared to look innocent, which was funny because innocent she was not. I gave her the smile she wanted, but it faded quickly. I began fidgeting with the strap of my purse.

"Diana, I don't know what he thinks of me after what happened," I said, my voice sounding small. "Nate might hate me. Brian certainly does, or at least, he did."

"I can't see Nate holding irrational grudges, but this discussion is probably moot since the ladies were all over him in college. He's most likely married or in a serious relationship with someone. Still, if he isn't, he's worth taking a chance on. Hot psychics don't fall out of the sky every day."

"I know you find it lacking, but I really am happy with my life."

"So you say."

As we made our way into the café, we noticed that our topic of conversation was sitting in a booth with David, his team leader, receiving the informal office scoop. I tried to look away before Nate recognized us, but we caught his eye. He cast us a bright smile and a nod, and we waved and smiled in return. Seeing him sent a surprising jolt through me. Maybe it was nerves, but I'd also forgotten how attractive he was. Thank God Diana missed my reaction, otherwise I'd never hear the end of it.

The Psi Solutions division at SDCC originally started as one group of six people covering three areas of psychic ability — telepathy, astral projection (also called remote viewing), and psychometry (sometimes known as touch clairvoyance). Over time, the number of contracts increased to a point where we couldn't keep up. Six months ago, SDCC began recruiting psychic talent for a second group of six. Nate was their third member. He could astral project like Jack and me, which would help pare down our backlog of projects. Finding psychic talent proficient enough to do our jobs wasn't easy.

"I guess we'll be learning soon if he's married or involved," Diana whispered.

I elbowed her to keep quiet and ordered my sandwich.

"Come on." Diana bumped my hip.

I smiled and bumped her back.

"I'm just looking out for you, you know. If it weren't for me, you'd have been celibate these past three years. You're young and beautiful, Sophia. Enjoy it now before age shrivels you up."

"Ha. I think you missed your calling as a motivational speaker."

"Point well-taken. Truce?"

"Truce."

As we ate, we shared the unclassified bits of our lives that we'd missed over the past week. I could hardly believe how serious Diana was getting with John, her latest guy. They were pushing a record-breaking two months. For as long as I'd known her, Diana's always had an attractive male in her life, but because of her telepathy, she couldn't usually stand a man for more than a few weeks. To avoid complications, she began to keep her love life separate from her friends during our first year of college. In fact, I'd only met a few of her many boyfriends in person.

Nate and David finished their lunch, and Nate excused himself. I sensed him moving in our direction. I didn't know if it was Diana's teasing or the fact that we hadn't spoken since I'd broken up with his best friend, but my hands were sweating.

"Hey, you two. How are you?" Nate asked, flashing us his heartfelt smile, one that had never failed to bring out my own. I'd forgotten that about him too.

We replied, "Great!" and "Fabulous!" as we stood up to greet him.

Diana gave him a hug, and I followed her lead, still feeling a bit anxious. In the warmth of his embrace, though, my nervousness eased. I found that I was genuinely happy to see him.

"Sit with us while we finish eating," Diana suggested.

"Sure. I have about ten minutes before I have to head back upstairs."

"What have you been up to since graduation?" I asked as we sat down.

"I was working at a biotech start-up in Palo Alto, but our funding ran out this summer."

"I'm sorry," I said.

"How'd you end up at Psi Solutions?" Diana asked. "It's a big change from biotech."

He looked at me this time with a shy, boyish smile that emphasized his dimples, the same first smile he'd given me long ago and the one that had instantly told me we'd be good friends. "Hardly anyone's hiring right now, especially someone with only a B.S. in Molecular Biology and three years of experience. My choices were to work here, for the military or the C.I.A., or go back to school. I still might apply to medical or graduate school, but I thought I'd give this gig a shot first. Do you like it here?"

"I enjoy it," Diana replied.

"So do I," I added. "I love that we can help make the world safer and see history unfold firsthand. The work can be draining, but they treat us well."

"The telepaths have to travel a lot, but it's fun and easy as pie," Diana said.

"Does Thomas work here too?" Nate asked.

"No. He's studying for his Ph.D. in Marine Biology. He still prefers to hang out with the ocean and sea animals rather than people."

Nate laughed. "I guess I'm not surprised."

Using telepathy, Thomas was deciphering dolphin communication. He'd introduced me to some of his research subjects on a few occasions. It was fascinating to see the dolphins react to him as if he were one of their own. Another researcher told me that they could sense Thomas nearby long before he came close to the water.

The conversation fell into a short and slightly awkward silence as Diana and I both took large bites of our food at the same time.

"So . . . what part of town do you live in these days?" Nate asked.

"I've got a beach house in La Jolla," Diana piped up. She had that look on her face. I knew she'd have elaborated more, but she was too busy extracting everything that passed through Nate's head.

"I have an apartment not far from UCSD," I added, picking up from Diana and hoping to cover for her, "and Thomas lives in graduate student housing within walking distance of his favorite surf spots. Have you found a place to live yet?"

"Sort of. I'm subletting an apartment in Pacific Beach near some friends until I decide on something permanent."

"PB, huh? Enjoying the rowdy nightlife and the cute little undergrads?" Diana teased.

Nate furrowed his brow and quickly changed the subject. "Uh, no, not really. What are you two doing tonight?" he asked.

"Thomas and I are having dinner with the Reeds," I replied.

"Wow, you still keep in touch with Harry? I haven't seen him in years. How is he?"

"He's doing great, and so is Irene. They've kind of adopted Thomas and me. We see them fairly often. Harry's still the passionate academic trying to educate the world about psychic abilities and how to improve them."

"Well, I have a date tonight," Diana interjected, "but tomorrow I'm throwing a party for my birthday at a club downtown. You should come, Nate! Both Sophia and Thomas will be there, though there *is* a dress code. You must come prepared to disco."

Nate and I looked at each other and laughed. He must have remembered from our college days that Diana loved to throw themed parties. I didn't know if it stemmed from her patrician heritage (she claimed that all her mom ever did was plan spectacular events), but it was one of her favorite pastimes.

"That sounds fun. I'll be there." Nate glanced at the time on his phone. "I better go upstairs before I make a bad impression. Can you text me the details of your party? What are your cell numbers?"

After the exchange, I watched Nate walk away with a sense of relief and something else I couldn't quite name. He didn't seem to resent me for Brian's sake. In fact, it had been so long since we'd hung out that I'd almost forgotten how close we'd been. Nate was the first person I'd ever met who shared my specific abilities. That had forged an instant connection and an easy comfort between us. I was really glad we'd be friends again.

"It was great seeing Nate, don't you think?" Diana asked as we threw away our trash.

I could feel her scrutinizing me. "Yeah, it was. It'll be nice to have him around the office."

"Really? Nice? That's it?" Diana punched the elevator button, a sure indicator that she didn't get anything out of my response. She didn't always take kindly to not being able to see inside my head. "Your poker face is too good." After a moment of hesitation, she asked, "Would you like to know what he was thinking when he saw you?"

I could feel my face giving me away now. I was surprised to realize that I genuinely wanted to know, but another part of me didn't at the same time. It wasn't ethical to know to his unspoken thoughts. Over the years, my brother had painstakingly convinced me of that. Thomas always tried to tune people out, but it was impossible to do so all of the time. In high school whenever I asked him if a certain guy liked me, he'd give me the same retort, "If I hear anything that impacts your safety or well-being, I'll tell you. Otherwise, it's none of your business." He referred to it as his "credo," and I had to live by it.

Diana didn't abide by the same rules though she occasionally tried to for my sake. She simply enjoyed knowing people's secrets and gossiping too much, though she'd never reveal information she shouldn't about her work. As I vacillated, my indecision apparent, she seized the opportunity. "I'll just say that he was happy to see you. He noticed you weren't wearing a wedding ring and was relieved that you're having dinner tonight with Thomas and the Reeds because that likely means you're unattached. He's also available," her lips spread into a wide smile, "and hopes to do the horizontal mambo with you at some point."

"God, Diana," I whispered, my cheeks reddening. I hastily looked around to see if anyone had overheard. "Why did you tell me that? I'll be uncomfortable around him now."

"I told you because you wanted to know, even if you won't admit it." The doors opened, and we stepped into the vacant elevator.

"You may be blocking me, but I can tell you're happy to have him back in your life, even if he's only a friend. Maybe it could be more this time. Just let yourself live a little. You never let anyone in." She saw me starting to object so she continued. "Yes, you've dated and had the occasional short relationship, but nothing in a long while. Look, I promise to stay out of it from now on, but give Nate a chance or at least give yourself a chance with someone soon. Please."

I'd grown increasingly annoyed with her meddling over the years, but she was right that I kept my distance from potential romantic entanglements. Diana might drive me crazy sometimes, but she had what she thought were my best interests at heart. I'd lay down my life for her and knew she'd do the same for me.

"Okay," I said, "if it looks like he might be interested, I'll give it a try, but don't act all pleased with yourself. While I do appreciate your concern, promise me you won't interfere again unless I ask. Agreed?"

"Agreed." She squeezed my hand. "We're going to have so much fun at my party! I can't wait to see you all dolled up. Remember, you promised to wear more than just your usual mascara," giving me a pointed finger and a faux stern look as we parted ways.

I finished writing up the day's experiences and my summary of the entire project by five o'clock. Though I loved my job, I appreciated being able to go home at a normal time. I gathered my things, upbeat about the relaxing weekend ahead. On my way out the door, Diana ran after me.

"Sophia, come and meet John. I know you'll see him tomorrow, but he's been bugging me about meeting my friends, and you, especially. Come." She pulled me by the hand out the front door towards a new, black Mercedes.

A tall, handsome blond with fashionable sunglasses stepped out of the car. He was impeccably dressed and muscular, exactly Diana's type. Smiling, he came over to us and kissed Diana in greeting, wrapping his arm around her waist.

"John, this is Sophia, my best friend in the world."

"It's nice to finally meet you, Sophia. Diana talks about you all the time."

Diana beamed as we shook hands.

"It's great to meet you as well. Did you just drive down from LA?"

We exchanged other pleasantries and discussed our evening plans before saying goodbye. He was whisking Diana off to an early dinner followed by a theatre performance, an ideal evening in her book. As I walked to my car, I glanced back at them. John opened the car door for her and kissed her sweetly. She gazed into his eyes with a raw intimacy and trailed a finger down the rim of his jaw. I'd never seen Diana look that way at anyone and had to wonder whether John might be the one.

CHAPTER TWO

At half past six, I packaged the dessert and donned a sweater to ward off the cool evening. It always surprised me when people complained that San Diego didn't have seasons. With the weather being close to perfect most of the time, maybe they had to find something to grumble about. While San Diego didn't have the stark contrasts of most cities, the distinctions were there and were made more special by their subtlety. It was October, the cusp of fall. I could feel it and smell it in the air. In the evenings, the coastal breeze was beginning to leave a hint of a lingering chill, and the darkening days promised that the chill would strengthen. I took a deep breath of the fresh air and left my apartment to pick up Thomas.

When I was a few blocks away, I thought to him, *"I'll be there in a minute. I'm taking a left onto La Jolla Shores now."*

"Okay. I'll head down into the parking lot," he answered back.

His apartment was nestled among eucalyptus trees and overlooked the Pacific Ocean. Though it had some maintenance issues, I couldn't imagine a more idyllic spot for graduate student housing in the country. As I pulled up in my hybrid, Thomas was coming down the stairs. *Telepathy can be so convenient,* I thought to myself.

"It has its advantages," he answered.

When we communicated telepathically, our thoughts lay open to each other, mine more so than his since my ability was puny in comparison. When I focused a thought at him, he "heard" that thought more loudly than the others bouncing around in my head, but he could still pick up what I might not want to share. I usually closed the link automatically the moment we finished conversing. Realizing I'd left myself exposed, I reflexively started thinking of things I wanted to keep private, mere moments before I could close our connection. *Jeez, both Diana and Thomas in one day.* I really was exhausted.

Thomas folded his tall body into my car and closed the door. "So . . . not to pry, but Nate will be working with you now, huh?" He buckled up and shook his dark, wavy hair out of his face.

"Yeah, he started today in that new group they're putting together." I tried to sound like it was no big deal and eased my car back into traffic.

"That's great for you."

"What makes you say that?" I looked at him suspiciously. *Was he conspiring with Diana?*

"Since he's a projector, your workload should improve. Considering the amount of energy your job zaps out of you, you work way too much."

He could see that I was about to become defensive. "Hey, I know you're passionate about your job. I get it, but I have to agree with Diana. It could be good in other ways too. He's a cool guy, and he did have a crush on you when you first met. After you started dating Brian, he was disappointed but as a loyal friend, moved on — though I think the relationship did get to him at times."

"Aren't you breaking your credo? I didn't know he had a crush on me."

"Come on. I'm not breaking it if anyone else could tell. You must have been too blissed out on Brian to notice at the time, but, back to my point, you and Nate were good friends. When you and Brian called it quits, you cut yourself off from that friendship. It'll be good for you to reconnect, even if you're only friends."

"When did you start channeling Oprah?"

Thomas gave a wistful smile. "I may not have a huge amount of personal experience with relationships, but I have a *lot* of perspective from the world around me." He looked out the window. "I can't remember the last time we talked about stuff like this. Thank God, you've got Diana for that, which I'm sure we both prefer."

Thomas was the best person I knew, a truly good and kind soul. We were extremely tight, even for a pair of twins. With his telepathy, we couldn't survive together and not be. For a long time, we shared every thought, but luckily for me, I couldn't hear the noise that constantly bombarded him.

When our unusual gifts began to make life difficult in elementary school, my mom tried to improve our mental control with meditation and yoga. She added martial arts training to our regimen after some punks gave Thomas a black eye and a couple of bruised ribs.

In middle school, my mom took us to a quaint Victorian village in New York State called Lily Dale, a community of spiritualists that offered workshops on meditation, mediums, and spiritual healing. Using our meditative practice as a springboard, a woman there taught us how to visualize and create strong mental shields so that my brother could block out the world of voices and my mom and I could gain some mental privacy. You'd think we could have found a good psychic mentor at home in San Francisco, where you could barely throw a rock without hitting a Ouija board, but awareness of the increasing prevalence of psychic abilities only began to surface in our last few years of high school. It was an encouraging time, but until we went to college, Thomas and I never fully appreciated our abilities. We fought simply to control them.

I turned on some music to prevent any further speculation on my love life (or the lack thereof) for the rest of the drive. When we pulled up in front of their house, Harry and Irene were waiting at the door with smiles on their faces. Harry was a beatific man in his early sixties with a jolly disposition and a cheerful belly to boot. While his feelings flitted openly across his face, those of his beautiful wife remained carefully concealed except to those closest to her.

Irene came over from China as a college student over thirty years ago, met Harry, and stayed to make a life with him. She was a talented artist with shows throughout the west and taught classes at several colleges and universities. Harry and Irene couldn't have children, but the lack of kids didn't hinder their relationship. They were the most in-love older couple I'd ever met. Since my parents weren't so fortunate, I often looked at them with awe and hope.

We hugged all around and settled down in the living room with a mellow *chenin blanc* Vouvray, one of Harry's favorites from his wine collection. Harry was the main reason Thomas and I chose to attend UC San Diego, and he became the first true mentor we'd ever had. The Parapsychology class he taught and the friends we met there truly helped us understand ourselves. Harry had precognitive (also known as prophetic) dreams and visions like my mom and me, and Irene was a rare telekinetic, often employing her ability in her sculpting and painting. Together, they helped us eventually embrace our abilities.

Harry trained me in the skill of lucid dreaming so that I could control the direction and discriminate better between standard and prophetic dreams. He taught me techniques to wake myself at the end of a dream and to recall more accurately the important features. In precognitive dreams, I was always an observer, and they tended to be more rational and realistic than a regular dream. Yet, since most of my dreams were fairly nonverbal, more glimpses and experiences than actual conversation, distinguishing between the future and imagination continued to be difficult.

Astral projection was my more troublesome gift. When I was young, I occasionally found myself in strange places in the blink of an eye. In one moment, I'd be sitting in class, and in the next, I could be in a prison in Bangkok, surrounded by emaciated people in shackles and the stench of urine, or worse. My only consolation was that no one could touch, see, or harm me. I was like a ghost floating in the air. Meanwhile, back in reality, my classmates would be in an uproar over my seemingly comatose body, which my mom cleverly explained away as narcolepsy. Ah, those were fun days . . . poor, little Sophia, the narcoleptic. Our time in late elementary and middle school was a social nightmare. My mom, the physician, even made things worse by insisting I wear a helmet to prevent head trauma. After a few days, the whispers and pointing upset me, and the helmet conveniently disappeared. As I grew older, my meditative practice began to provide me with some control, enough to get through high school without a single "episode," but Harry's guidance helped me own it so that I now only visited the places I chose.

Harry helped many students, but Thomas and I were the only ones to remain close to him after our class ended. Maybe he filled our need for a father figure, and as like-minded people, the age difference didn't hinder our friendship. Over time, Harry and Irene transitioned from mentors and friends to being like part of our family. As such, we attempted to get together for a "family" meal at least once a month, but we were in touch more often than that. If I had a disturbing dream, I'd call or meet Harry to analyze it, and on the weekends, I sometimes kept Irene company in her studio. As she worked, she taught me techniques to improve my sketching, which was invaluable for my job, and expanded my artistic repertoire.

"So, Harry, how's your latest book coming along?" I asked.

"Great." He sipped his wine. "I recently finished the introductory section that discusses the differences between psychics and mediums but also shows their common foundation in compassionate meditation. For the past month, I've spent most of my time writing the practical portion of the book, describing techniques to develop and master psychic skills. I emphasize that everyone is born with some innate psychic capacity and that there are more people with extraordinary gifts around now than ever before in history. Though the percentage of the population seems to have peaked and leveled off with your age group, our world is going to change forever. People are finally realizing the potential implications of having a growing number of psychics in the world."

"Do they still believe the reason for the increase is a change in the earth's electromagnetic frequency spectrum?" Thomas asked.

"That's the dominant hypothesis. Since the sun rises in the east every day, people forget that the universe is constantly changing. We live in a sea of environmental exposures we can barely fathom. Scientists will have a hard time determining the exact cause. We can measure more now than we could thirty years ago, but the lack of data in the past makes it difficult to compare. Even so, our instruments may still not be advanced enough to pinpoint the important difference. The cause could be an infinitesimal shift in the earth's magnetic field, or a cascade effect due to a comet passing through the inner solar system decades ago or even a faraway supernova thousands of years ago. I doubt we'll ever find the answer. However, we do know two things — that to have psychic abilities as strong as yours, the EMF change had to occur prior to your development in the womb, and that there's a definite genetic predisposition since those with impressive abilities come from families already showing minor hints of psychic talent."

Harry drank another sip of wine when his eyes suddenly enlarged with excitement. "Oh! I just received a device that makes achieving a deep meditative state easy. With it, people will be able to harness the full potential of their abilities with minimal effort. It's a breakthrough but will make some of my practical instructions obsolete."

"Interesting. What's the story?" Thomas asked, putting his glass down and stretching out his long legs.

"A telepath named Dante Lombardi developed the device on the side while finishing his Master's degree at MIT. He calls it the 'GammaBeat' and built a company around it. Since he was a fan of my books, he sent me a beta version to test."

Harry's brows knit together, and he paused for a breath. "Yesterday, I just realized that Dante's the son of a friend and colleague from the East Coast who died a few months ago. She and her husband died in a car accident." Sorrow creased his forehead, and he looked lost in thought.

"I'm sorry, Harry." I'd never seen him sad, and it pulled at my heart.

"They were a nice couple, both quite gifted," he said, still distracted. Irene squeezed his hand to share some of his grief.

"So, how does the GammaBeat work?" Thomas prompted, trying to pull him out of his reverie.

"Well," Harry raked his fingers through his wavy gray hair and shifted back into his professorial mode, "research has shown that when Buddhist monks enter into a compassionate meditative state, they emit high frequency brain signals called gamma waves. The more experienced the monks, the more intense and synchronous their production of these waves. As you know, attaining a deep meditative state is essential to using and controlling most psychic skills. When more gamma waves are produced, the meditative state deepens, which can allow us to reach our true psychic potential."

"Are gamma waves the ones heightened in near-death, out-of-body experiences?" Thomas asked.

"The exact ones. Very good, Thomas." Harry smiled in approval. "Sophia, you might recall that these are also the same brain waves implicated in lucid dreaming." He rubbed his hands together excitedly without a trace of his former melancholy. "I'm sure you've both seen some of those meditation headsets on the market. Most try to increase your production of alpha waves, which only helps some people attain a relaxed mental state. This headset is the real deal for enhancing psychic abilities because it focuses on increasing the quantity of gamma waves your brain makes. The device has two modes: one that teaches you to make gamma waves on your own, and another mode that stimulates with a mild 40 Hertz electrical current to entrain your brain to make even more gamma waves."

"What do you mean by entrain?" Thomas asked.

"Well, think of it as a way to nudge your brain cells into resonating at the frequency of the current, which is within the gamma frequency spectrum."

"So, when more of your brain cells resonate at this gamma frequency, psychic abilities can become even stronger?" Thomas asked.

"That's the theory, at least, and it really does work."

"Does it hurt?" I asked.

"No. The current's low. You won't feel it, but the tight fit did give me a minor headache after an hour. There haven't been any long-term studies since this is only a prototype, but Dante said that he and his team have been using different versions for over a year without other side effects. We can't know for sure, of course, but it should be safe. Buddhist monks tend to have long lifespans and make more gamma waves than anyone else, but someone with migraines or a seizure disorder should proceed with caution. Just think, by using the GammaBeat consistently, a process that takes decades to master can be conquered in a matter of months. It really is a breakthrough. It's in the other room if you'd like to try it," he suggested with a gleam in his eye.

"Sure," Thomas and I said in unison.

"Wonderful," Harry said and left the room to retrieve it.

"Harry has been acting like a child in a candy store since he first received this device," Irene smiled, her face full of affection. "I have to say, though, that it works quite well. It helps me focus my telekinesis so I can move larger objects. The other day I was able to lift the mahogany coffee table four feet off the ground."

Thomas and I were both impressed and curious since we'd never seen her move anything that massive.

Harry presented the device with a flourish and placed it on my head. The GammaBeat looked a bit like an ancient Roman headdress with three bands. The first went across my forehead and settled behind my ears. The second spanned the top of my head from ear to ear, and the third stretched across the top in between. Harry tightened each band to fit my skull and turned it on. Immediately, I felt the electrodes project many small, blunt metal tips flush against my skin.

"Okay. I have it in the basic mode. When I press the start button, it will emit occasional beeps. The lower the pitch, the deeper the meditative state," Harry said. "When you begin to generate a strong pattern of gamma waves, you'll hear three low beeps in a row, indicating that you've crossed the required threshold and can consider yourself in the gamma zone. If you start to leave this state, there will be three beeps again but higher in pitch."

"Okay," I said. "I'm ready."

"Get comfortable first and then close your eyes."

I adjusted in my chair so the back of my head rested against the top edge.

"Now, meditate," he said as he touched the button.

As I transitioned into a meditative state, a short occasional beep sounded that lowered steadily in pitch, with only an occasional rise when I became distracted. I found the instant feedback on my progress helpful, and I attained a deep meditative state slightly faster than normal. I reset and then tried it again with the electrical stimulation. This time, I went into the gamma zone almost immediately.

After I finished experimenting, Thomas had a go with it. Though he was even faster at shifting into the gamma zone than I was, the assistance was useful to him as well.

"Dante also created a phone app where you can visualize and record the comparative levels of gamma waves you're making in order to track your progress. If you prefer, you can have the app provide you with live audio feedback instead of the device's beeps."

"I want one," I said. "It would be great if it could make remote viewing less tiring. Are they on sale yet?"

"Not yet, but I'll ask if I can get you one. I've been trying to use it to harness my precognitive abilities," Harry said. "I've read about precogs who can direct their visions of the future. My experiences have always been sporadic, like yours, Sophia, and I've had no luck. I can't figure out how to tap into it. But with your greater natural ability, maybe you'd be able to do it."

"Gosh, I wouldn't know where to start either. My visions just sort of appear and then evaporate, as if manifesting out of thin air. With nothing to mentally grasp, I doubt I could turn it on or off at will. When I astral project, the process is almost physical. I can control it, mold it, tweak it. I've never felt that way with any of my precognitive experiences."

"Well, think about it," he said. "It could come in handy."

"I will," I replied.

Though I paid careful attention to my precognitions so I could help people, I'd never sought them out because I'd never thought it possible. To be honest, the idea that I might be able to see them at will scared me. A day rarely passed where I didn't have to push the burning towers out of my mind. Thankfully, I hadn't foreseen a tragedy of that scale since then. Most of my visions were local and impacted fewer people, though I did once save an entire apartment complex from dying of carbon monoxide poisoning and helped in smaller ways as well, like rescuing my neighbor's dog from being run over and preventing an eight-year-old girl from being abducted. Though, since the police never caught the kidnapper, I worried that my interfering had led to a different child's abduction. People who wanted to know the future had no idea what kind of hell they were asking for. I felt powerful while astral projecting, but usually powerless when seeing the future.

"In your book, do you discuss any of the research trying to understand how psychic abilities work?" Thomas asked.

"A little. I emphasize that though scientists haven't figured out anything definite, research in neuroscience, quantum mechanics, and wave theory have produced compelling hypotheses. Speaking of which, Sophia, have you given more thought to going back to school? There aren't enough researchers focusing on the interplay of quantum physics and psychic phenomena. I know you're probably better at astral projection than anyone on the planet, but does that challenge your mind? Is that advancing our knowledge of how the universe works?"

During almost every visit, Harry, who'd served as a co-advisor for my senior honors thesis, encouraged me to pursue graduate studies in Physics. I did consider taking that path, but the far-off and elusive reward of deciphering the universe's mysteries wasn't tangible enough for me. I needed to make a direct impact and had committed myself long ago to do what I could to save humanity from itself. The intelligence community had tried doggedly to recruit Diana and me, but because of our government's lies about weapons of mass destruction to justify the Iraq war and leaks proving our country had spied on its own citizens, neither of us wanted to work for them directly. We wanted to have control over our own lives. When we learned that SDCC was hiring for a new Psi Solutions group, Diana and I jumped at the chance. Though much of our business ultimately came from the Defense Department, at least we weren't going to be owned by them.

"Harry, you know I love my job. I can't imagine doing anything else. But I am saving my money, and I can always pursue graduate school later if something changes."

Harry frowned a little, but Thomas came to my rescue. "Another one of your students started working at SDCC today," he said.

"Which one?" Harry asked.

"Nate Barclay," Thomas replied.

"He was working at a Biotech that folded," I added.

"Ah, I believe he had skills similar to yours, Sophia, if I remember correctly." I nodded. "He was a nice young man. Please give him my best," Harry said.

A buzzer sounded in the kitchen. "It's time to eat," Irene said as she stood up. "Make yourselves comfortable at the table. I'll serve the food."

"I'll help," I said, following her. I enjoyed watching Irene in the kitchen. She reminded me of one of the fairies baking in *Sleeping Beauty*. The oven door lowered on its own, and Irene took out two casserole dishes. A drawer opened and a few serving spoons flew across the room, easing into the dishes as if they had a mind of their own. A bottle of salad dressing floated over to Irene where she dressed and tossed the salad. I carried one dish to the dining room, while Irene carried the other. The salad bowl preceded us, hovering toward the table. Seeing Irene in action never ceased to entertain me.

"When's your next art exhibit?" Thomas asked Irene.

"Oh, I am glad you asked because I have one next Friday, and I meant to invite you. I will email you both the details, but it will be a small group exhibition with a mix of different pieces at the Museum of Contemporary Art in La Jolla."

"Wow, Irene, that's impressive! I can't wait to see it," I said. Thomas added his congratulations as well.

The ever-composed Irene blushed. For some reason, she felt embarrassed whenever anyone made a fuss over her and her talents. Harry patted her hand and picked up the conversation.

"Sophia, what have your dreams been like lately?" he asked.

"I haven't had any interesting precognitive dreams in quite a while. The last one was about a week ago and involved a finch singing on my terrace as I ate breakfast. How about you?"

"I haven't been dreaming lately, which is strange." Harry sounded uneasy. "But, it's probably nothing, just that I'm overtired. I have been working late."

After dinner, we ate the flourless chocolate cake I bought from my favorite bakery and then relaxed in the living room once again. During the conversation, Irene noticed me glancing at their piano and encouraged me to play. I was hesitant since I hadn't played in a while but eventually caved. I couldn't resist running my fingers over those beautiful keys. Harry was the proficient here, as talented at the piano as Irene at her art. I started playing Beethoven's "Moonlight Sonata," uncertain whether I'd remember the entire piece. For some reason, Beethoven had always plucked at my heartstrings. His music had a way of reaching inside and gripping my soul.

"That was beautiful, with real feeling," Harry observed. "You should get a digital piano for your apartment. Good ones aren't that expensive these days, and you'd enjoy the distraction."

"I do miss playing. I'll look into it when I have a chance."

Harry's eyelids were drooping. He really had been pushing himself too hard. "Harry, you're worn out. Thomas and I should leave you two in peace."

Harry tried to dissuade us, but Irene had also noticed Harry's flagging energy. After gathering our belongings, Thomas and I hugged them goodbye.

"Thanks for having us. Dinner was delicious as usual, and we always enjoy spending time with you."

"Yes, thanks for putting up with us," Thomas said with a wink.

"You both know we would love to see more of you. Sophia, do come visit me in the studio to paint soon. You'll both come to my exhibition opening on Friday?" Irene asked.

"Of course," Thomas said.

"Unless an emergency comes up, I'll be there," I said.

* * *

By the time I arrived home, exhaustion had overtaken me as well. I threw my sweater over the back of the couch and went directly to my bedroom. Days of projecting with repeated phasing had caught up with me. After hastily preparing for bed, I grabbed my iPhone and a favorite book and snuggled under the covers. I'd barely read the first few pages before my eyelids began succumbing to gravity. I placed my iPhone on top of the book, opened it to the voice memo app and turned off the light.

I'm on the beach, and the sun is glorious. It's that time of day when the sun hasn't yet touched the ocean, and the clouds are glowing orange and pink. I'm in a thin, flowing sundress that's billowing in the wind. Ahh, I love dreams where I can unwind. An attractive man shuffles his feet in the sand about thirty yards away. Other than the two of us, it's completely deserted. He's wearing khaki pants and a button-down shirt, half open and flapping in the breeze. He catches my gaze and smiles. I return his smile with a shy one of my own. I notice then that though it's abandoned, the gate to the Ocean Beach pier is open. I've never walked its full length so I make my way to the boardwalk, climb up to the pier and begin to explore.

The café is closed. As I wander along the wooden deck, seagulls cry softly overhead. The walk to the end takes longer than I expect but is serene and utterly peaceful. Since the sunset is off to the left, I veer towards that end of the T-shaped pier. I have a strange feeling that I've just chosen a critical path on a journey that will change my life. God, this dream feels so real. The remaining sunrays warm my skin while the slight chill of the ocean breeze raises goose bumps on my arms. There's a bench at the end of the pier, a perfect spot to watch the ocean envelop the sun. I sit and relax, breathing in the cool air. A sense of peacefulness radiates through me. I could stay here for an eternity.

The sound of footsteps catches my attention. The man from the beach sits down beside me and smiles again. I smile back, surprising myself. Being skeptical of men and a little paranoid in general, having a lone stranger so close should make me anxious, but he seems harmless. Besides, this is a dream, and I'm in a happy place. I won't begrudge him this magical experience. Ah, the sun finally collides with the ocean. I'm exhilarated but a little sad at the same time because once the sun hits, it descends quickly, forewarning that this enchanting moment is drawing to a close. He sighs. Was he thinking the same thing?

We turn and study each other. He appears to be in his late twenties, with olive-toned skin and wavy dark hair that dangles slightly below a masculine chin. He has the broad, welcoming smile of someone truly happy to see you. As our eyes meet, I see his are a warm hazel, lit with reflections of the sun and filled with an intensity I can feel in the pit of my stomach. I force myself to look back at the sunset. What a bizarre dream . . . but I still feel sublime. As the water engulfs the sun, the breeze takes on more of a chill. I shiver. He scoots closer and wraps his left arm around me. A small part of me is uneasy, but in this instance, his touch just feels right, and my tension dissipates. The sun's almost gone. I'm hoping for that elusive streak of green. Ah, there it is. I sigh and instinctively put my head on his shoulder. What perfection.

I woke up and reached for my iPhone. After stretching and rubbing my eyes, I pressed record. "This was a sunset dream at the beach . . . quite realistic, but ethereal at the same time." I continued recording until I'd recounted every detail of the dream. After 9/11, I began to keep meticulous logs of my dreams in the hope that I could prevent another disaster. I learned lucid dreaming techniques from Harry to help me wake up at the end of a dream and developed an ingrained routine to record them, though over the years, my methods evolved along with technology. In the morning, I'd use a voice transcription app to convert the audio to text and then sync with my laptop's ongoing digital log.

When I finished describing it, I analyzed the dream. "It felt more real than any recent dream. I'm certain it wasn't precognitive, but it didn't feel like a standard dream either. It had a weird vibe. Who was the guy? Have I seen him walking around? It's odd that I felt comfortable with a stranger, especially a mysterious man in a secluded location. It was like part of me knew or trusted him. He was attractive, definitely my physical type. . . . Maybe he just represents something, like me coming to terms with my difficulty in trusting men? Hmm. I've only seen the Ocean Beach pier in person twice and walked no further than the café. I wonder if there's a bench where we sat. I'll find out. If the reality matches, it could be more than a regular dream." I stopped recording and checked the time. It was only two o'clock in the morning so I turned over and went back to sleep.

CHAPTER THREE

Thomas and I arrived at Diana's party early as planned Saturday evening and found her working on the decorations. She was an almost perfect replica of a young Diana Ross, complete with gigantic Afro and five-inch hoop earrings. She gave us the once over and approved of our costumes. Thomas sort of looked like a pimp from the '70s. His shirt was buttoned quite low, exposing not a small amount of his chest, and a gold peace sign necklace dangled halfway to his waist. I wore a wacky, colorful disco dress with white go-go boots and a moderate amount of makeup. The dress emphasized my petite frame and ample enough attributes, and the platform heels raised me three inches above my five-foot-four, giving me the height I'd always wished I had.

John was out running a last-minute errand for Diana. I got to work placing party favors and battery-powered lava lamps on the tables while Thomas assisted the D.J. with the karaoke machine and sound system. The disco ball was twirling, and the dance floor looked like a trip back in time. Diana had outdone herself again.

Nate arrived just after we finished decorating. Diana must have told him to come early since Thomas and I would be there to help. Thomas was talking with him when Diana and I interrupted.

"Hey, guys, let's order drinks before I'm distracted by other guests," Diana suggested.

The bartenders were decked out in humorous disco gear as well and chatted with us as we ordered. Having everyone dressed up added to the festivities. Diana knew that wearing costumes helped people come out of their shells and mingle with strangers.

As we walked to a table carrying our drinks of choice, Diana asked offhandedly, "So, Nate, you live in PB near some friends. Anyone we know?"

"No, just some guys from high school."

Silence hung in the air while we sat, sipping our drinks. I took a deep breath and gathered the courage to address the subtext behind Diana's question. "Are you still in touch with Brian?" I asked.

"Yeah," Nate replied, letting out a breath he'd been holding. "We lived in the same apartment complex in Palo Alto and saw each other a lot."

"How is he?" I asked, attempting nonchalance.

"He's good. He's finishing up medical school this year, and . . . um . . . he's actually getting married next month," Nate replied.

"Oh, wow . . . that's wonderful news," I said. The looks I received from Thomas and Diana told me that my attempt at feigned happiness hadn't concealed my shock from them.

Thomas attempted to salvage the conversation. "So, Nate, what language will you be learning?"

"They want me to study Russian as my primary, but I have to get up to speed on the basics of Arabic pretty quickly too. Sophia, your primary is Arabic, right?"

"Right."

"Are you fluent yet?"

"I'm close. I can understand it well most of the time. They'd planned to send me to a language boot camp, but I've been too swamped to go since the day I started. They did hire a tutor during my first few months, but I've mostly learned from the computer programs. Projecting is frustrating when you don't speak the language."

"You're lucky Mom sent us to a bilingual English-Spanish elementary school, and then you picked up German in high school and college. I'm sure that's helped," Thomas said.

"Yeah, I've used the Spanish, and knowing both languages has made it easier to pick up others, but I still wish I'd learned more when we were younger. I've had to learn bits of Farsi, Pashto, Mandarin, Russian, and Korean for specific jobs. I'm supposed to focus on Russian once I've mastered Arabic. I'll help you with Arabic, if you'll help me with Russian."

"Sure," Nate said.

"Have you met Jack yet, the other projector?" I asked.

"No."

"He's a nice guy. He started about a year ago and is fluent in Mandarin. Unless he's too busy, he'll handle those jobs. Have they scheduled any sketching classes for you yet?"

"Not yet, but I'll need the help. Drawing is not my forte."

"Don't worry. You'll get better with practice, and if we need a high quality, detailed sketch of a suspect, they'll bring in a forensic artist to draw from our description."

Diana spied John approaching and lit up. "John, come meet some of my college friends. You've met Sophia already. This is Thomas, her twin brother . . . and Nate." After shaking our hands and some small talk, he leaned over to kiss Diana on the cheek and whispered something in her ear.

My God, she blushed! I'd never seen Diana blush and frankly hadn't thought it possible. Although I'd not yet formed an opinion of John, her reaction was so cute that I began to like him.

Diana and John left to greet the arrivals. Thomas got up shortly afterwards to introduce himself to an attractive woman who looked like she felt out of place. I gave Nate a somewhat strained smile. I couldn't think of anything to say. I was still digesting his announcement.

After an awkward lull and several sips of our cocktails, Nate broke the silence. "I'm sorry if the news about Brian upset you. I thought it might, but I didn't want to ignore the elephant in the room any longer. I want us to have a real conversation like we used to, not just pleasantries or work. I'd like to be friends again. If you want, I'll answer any questions you might have about Brian."

Surprised by his straightforward manner, I pushed some hair behind my ear, one of my nervous habits, but his open and kind face relaxed me. "I'd like to be friends too, but I don't feel like talking about the past right now. So, what should we discuss that isn't work-related or merely polite conversation?"

He tilted his head and scrutinized me. "Well, you seem quite at home here drinking your mojito. Do you often go clubbing these days? Is that what you do for fun?"

His ridiculous question made me laugh. He'd known me too well to believe that. "I haven't changed *that* much. I'm still your basic homebody. I rarely go clubbing, but when I do, I drink mojitos because they're refreshing." The tension began to lift. Nate smiled and clinked his glass with mine.

"So, what *do* you do with yourself when you're not working?" he asked.

"I mostly hang out with friends or practice yoga or kung fu, and I do the usual things like read or watch a movie or a TV show. Occasionally, Thomas convinces me to surf with him. I do love the ocean and the exercise, but I have a hard time persuading myself to plunge into ice-cold water early in the morning and can't get rid of a nagging suspicion that sharks are lurking beneath the surface waiting to eat me."

Nate choked on a laugh and nudged me with his elbow. "Now *that's* the Sophia I remember."

As we began to settle into our old, easygoing banter, Thomas returned to the table with a plate of appetizers and the woman he'd met. "Sophia, Nate, this is Nadia, an old family friend of Diana's."

Nate and I greeted her, and they sat down with us. Nadia was a pretty blonde, dressed up for the night. Her hesitant and quiet demeanor signaled her shyness. Besides Diana, she knew no one else at the party. They'd been friends since toddlerhood. Even though they went to different private schools, they managed to stay close. We all shared some of our amusing stories of Diana, and Nadia eventually relaxed and seemed to enjoy herself.

While immersed in this pleasant conversation, Diana announced that the dancing would begin. Fog began to creep onto the dance floor, and the lights started shifting colors. The four of us joined the crowd as "Staying Alive" began to blare. Diana and John disco-shuffled over to us, and we all danced like we were channeling *Saturday Night Fever*. John Travolta would have been proud. My sides hurt from laughing at everyone's inventive disco moves. Between songs, Diana and John bounced around to other groups, bringing a new disco dance move to each circle.

I knew Thomas could dance since I'd forced him to learn while we were growing up, but I was surprised and impressed by Nate. He was such a guy's guy that I didn't expect him to be comfortable on the dance floor. He moved to the music with ease and confidence, not the typical awkwardness of a suburban white boy. His shirt was only partially buttoned like Thomas's, and when it gaped open exposing his chest, a wave of attraction hit me like a physical blow. The smattering of hair peeking out of his shirt drew my eye to his toned pectoral muscles. I couldn't deny his sensual appeal. Despite Diana's innuendos, I realized then that I'd never thought of him sexually before. Of course I knew he was good-looking. His tall, muscular body and handsome face would satisfy most women's dreams, but I must have considered his appearance in an objective, intellectual sense in the past, never letting it affect me because he was Brian's best friend. Nate caught me staring. I looked abruptly away, my cheeks flushing in embarrassment.

The next thing I knew, his hands were on my hips pulling me toward him. I must have had a surprised look on my face, but Nate seemed amused, even mischievous. I didn't withdraw. He led me in an improvised combo of ballroom dancing and disco and made me laugh when he morphed a rumba into spinning arms and disco fingers. He was having fun playing but stayed in command, and I fell under his control as he whirled us around the dance floor. Nate sent me out in a wide spin, and as I spun back into him, the sudden impact of our bodies caused our fluid dance to falter. Pressed against him from hips to breasts, my stomach fluttered. My breath caught in my throat as heat replaced humor in his eyes. He kept me close and began a sort of salsa, changing the tenor of our dance. As we twisted and turned, his fingers sliding over my skin left a tingling warmth behind. His touch was like a caress, a caress I craved. The longer we danced that hypnotic rhythm, the more attuned to each other we became. Each touch heightened my senses, my body responding to his slightest movements. My breathing matched his, and he held me tighter with each song. An almost tangible electricity began to hum between us. We were sharing something much more intimate than a mere dance. I couldn't tell if it was from physical attraction or exertion, but my heart was beating fast. When his cheek lightly skimmed mine, his scent aroused me even more.

I hardly noticed the pauses between songs. We shifted beats but never stopped moving, never stopped touching. Out of the corner of my eye, I sometimes spied others watching us, but my attention never left Nate. My body continued to flow with his. He dipped me over one arm and rested his hand momentarily on my lower stomach as I let my head tilt back. My knees began to feel weak as the hand glided slowly down to my hip. He then pulled me up quickly and tightly against him, and my breath hitched once more. The music ended. Even in the dim light, I could feel Nate's eyes boring into mine. Our lips were only a finger-width apart, both of us still struggling for breath. My stomach tightened as he leaned in for a kiss, his top lip barely touching mine, when suddenly Diana's voice over the loudspeaker broke the spell, and the ceiling lights began to brighten. The focus of the party was switching to karaoke for a time. Dancers began to disperse and drift to tables. Our bodies continued to press together a few moments longer, but his lips pulled away from mine. The loss felt like an ache in my chest.

Nate smiled and grasped my hand, caressing it as he led me off the dance floor, but our hands separated when we sat down at the table with Thomas and Nadia. They must have left the dance floor well before us and were engaged in an animated conversation, barely noticing our return. I wasn't offended. The rest of the world could have exploded while Nate and I were dancing, and I might have missed it.

Nate watched me over his water bottle as we quenched our thirst. My cheeks reddened at the thought of our interaction on the dance floor. *What was happening between us? Had I always found him this alluring but repressed it, or maybe it had just been too long since I'd had sex?* I saw appetizers circulating about the room and waved a waiter over as the first karaoke singer started her tune. I glanced away from Nate, feigning attention to the singer. I needed to collect myself. My mind and senses were in a jumble, and I was at a loss as to what to do or say next.

About halfway through the song, Nate cleared his throat. "So, to continue our earlier conversation, where was your last exotic vacation?" he asked.

Relieved he'd broken the ice, I thought a little teasing might help even more. I looked at him suspiciously as I swiped some *hors d'oeuvres* from the waiter. "Hmm, so it's twenty questions now, is it?"

"No," Nate laughed. "I'm just trying to catch up."

"Okay, but you'll have to answer my questions too," I challenged. He nodded his agreement and popped a sushi roll into his mouth.

"I don't know if I've ever had a truly exotic vacation. My last trip was a short one to San Francisco to see my mom and to visit some old friends and my favorite haunts. In the summer, Thomas and I spent a week in Texas with my mom and grandparents. It was peaceful, though I doubt the suffocating Texas heat could be considered exotic. Hmm . . . well, the best vacation I've ever had was after Thomas and I graduated from college. My mom took us on a European tour for a month. It was fantastic."

"Nice. I've projected all over Europe but haven't yet made a trip there in person. My family spent most of our vacations camping and hiking in national parks. What countries did you visit?"

"We have relatives in Greece and Germany so we spent a good deal of our time there, but we also visited Italy and France." I paused to chew the sushi roll I'd stuffed in my mouth and could feel myself relaxing again even after the interlude on the dance floor.

"What was your favorite place?" he asked.

"Hmm, it's hard to choose. Each place had its charms, but if I have to pick, I think my favorite place was the Tuscan countryside in general and a terrace overlooking it in particular. I felt a strange serenity and connection there I didn't expect. I'd go back in a heartbeat." I was lost in the past for a moment, remembering the sun setting over distant hills and cypress trees but snapped back to the present and smiled. "Okay, enough about me. What do *you* do for fun these days?"

"Lately, I've just been hanging out with my friends in PB, visiting the bars in the area, but that's not how I usually spend my time. In Palo Alto, I hiked a lot, hung out with friends, read and watched TV and movies. I try to run most days and practice taekwondo when I can, though I haven't yet found a place in San Diego."

"You didn't mention surfing. If I remember correctly, you used to be pretty good."

"I sold my boards when I graduated. I haven't had time to pick out a new one since I've been back, but I'm hoping to buy one tomorrow."

"I'm sure Thomas would love to surf with you again. The water's already too cold for me, but I'd be happy to cheer you on."

Nate smiled. "I'll take you up on that."

"Where did you go on your last vacation?"

"I went to Kauai in the spring with my ex-girlfriend, Sarah. We snorkeled, hiked, and enjoyed swimming in the warm ocean water. It was beautiful there."

"How long were you and Sarah together?"

"About nine months. I met her at work. We had a lot of fun, but we weren't serious enough to take it to the next level. We broke up in July. What about you? Have you dated anyone recently?"

"Not really," I glanced across the room, pretending distraction and hoping for a change of subject.

"What does 'not really' mean?" he persisted.

I looked him in the eye and sighed. "It means I've dated several people since Brian, but nothing has lasted for more than a few months. If it weren't for Diana, I doubt I'd have gone out with anyone. I guess I should thank her, or maybe not since none of them worked out. Even though some of the guys were great, that special spark just wasn't there."

"Why wouldn't you have dated anyone without Diana's help?" he asked.

"I don't know. I guess I haven't had much desire to pursue it on my own. I love my job, and I work a lot so I don't have a lot of free time, but it could be a convenient excuse. Diana says I'm too guarded. She introduced me to all but the last guy, and I probably wouldn't have gone out with him if she hadn't convinced me to give him a shot. Pretty pathetic, huh?"

"No, not pathetic, but interesting. You didn't used to be so cautious. When you first met Brian, you didn't need any encouragement."

"That was a long time ago."

Diana came over and thankfully saved me from the uneasy path our conversation was taking. "Sophia, I have a birthday request. I know it's mostly a crowd of strangers to you, but I want you to get up there and sing karaoke with me. You're probably the only person at this party talented enough to share the stage with me."

I laughed. "You don't need to flatter me. I'd be happy to sing with you."

"Ah," she smiled. "I love it when a plan comes together. Let's go, girlfriend! We've got to get this party rockin'!" Hearing Diana speak even a little street was comical. I couldn't help but smile and followed her lead.

Diana positioned me on stage and handed me the mic. When she winked at the D.J., the music began. Music resonated with a part of my soul that stayed hidden away most of the time. I didn't often let it loose so I relished it when I did. We finished 'Dancing Queen' to loud applause and then sang 'I Will Survive' with as much tough feminine moxie as we could muster. Afterwards, Diana rounded up the next performers, and I returned to my table.

"You two were great! Brian said you could sing and dance, but I'd never seen you perform. It was like you transformed into a different person," Nate said.

"Thanks," I smiled and took a deep breath, "I think the only time I ever completely open up to the world is when I sing and dance. It's freeing."

"Can I get you another drink? You must be thirsty."

"Water would be great, thanks."

As Nate headed to the bar, a friend of Diana's from high school introduced himself to Thomas, Nadia, and me and sat in an empty chair to my right. With his strong jaw and blue-blooded pedigree, Troy clearly considered himself the ladies' man.

"You and Diana were terrific on stage," he flattered.

"Thanks. It was fun," I said.

Nate returned with the drinks and looked at Troy with suspicion. I thanked him, grabbed the water, and gulped it down, trying to avoid any more conversation, but Troy didn't relent.

"You and your boyfriend were also quite impressive on the dance floor. You must have taken a dance class or two together."

"Oh, Nate's not my boyfriend. We're just old friends," I said instinctively but regretted saying it the second the words tumbled out of my mouth. I wasn't happy with the direction of the conversation and could tell that Nate had stiffened his back. He pretended to drink his water and pay attention to the karaoke, but I could tell he was listening to every word. The tick in his jaw gave him away.

Troy's eyes became predatory and his voice dropped in pitch. "Well, then, since I'm not stepping on any toes, I'd be honored if you'd dance with me when the floor lights up again. I promise not to disappoint you." Thomas almost choked on his drink.

Nate shifted in his chair but didn't look at us, though his jaw muscle ticked again. Normally, I would have danced with Troy the polite amount, hoping he didn't expect a similar experience to the one he'd witnessed, and would have then moved on, but it felt wrong saying I'd dance with him with Nate sitting right there. We'd had a moment, actually a long series of moments on the dance floor, and I think we were now more than friends. I'd never had such a swift change in my perception of someone. The problem was I didn't know what we were. I was confused and flustered. Escape seemed the best option.

"Thanks," I replied, "but I'll probably leave before the next round of dancing. If not, I'll find you. If you'll all excuse me, I need to freshen up."

I grabbed my purse and headed for the restroom. When I returned, I was relieved to see that Troy had left our table. Nate's hackles were no longer up, but he looked like the wind had been taken out of his sails. I was sure that my comment about us being merely old friends was the cause, but I didn't know what to do about it.

"Sophia, you're a coward," Thomas grumbled. "Would you really prefer to leave early just to avoid that snake? We're having fun, and you know Diana will be disappointed if we duck out before the party's over."

"He caught me off-guard. I was only trying to be polite to Diana's friend. Besides, you know I don't like to stay out late. With the karaoke and the cake, it'll be after midnight before dancing starts again. We won't miss that much." Thomas just shook his head.

"I can drive you home so Thomas can stay longer," Nate offered.

"Thanks," I replied, sounding unaffected even as my heart rate sped up. "I might take you up on it, but let's wait and see how the night unfolds." My eyes challenged Thomas, but he rolled his eyes at me in response.

Nadia distracted us from our sibling quarrel by telling us some sad yet inspiring stories of teaching inner-city elementary kids in South Central LA. She apparently came from money and could have had a lucrative career as a stockbroker, but she found that life to be vapid and chose instead to help poor children start out right in life. She exuded caring and idealism. Needless to say, I liked her and thought she could be good for Thomas.

Later, when the karaoke wrapped up, the D. J. led us in a rendition of "Happy Birthday." Diana preened with the attention, then made us laugh pretending her Afro had caught fire while trying to blow out the sparkler candles. Amid cheers and hugs, the wait staff passed out a variety of tasty desserts. As we finished the last bites of our treats, the dance floor started queuing up again. It was already past midnight. I was ready to go, but Thomas was enjoying himself with Nadia. I didn't want to make him leave.

"Nate, are you sure you don't mind driving me home? I know I'm completely out of your way." I tried to sound nonchalant, but the prospect of being alone with him made my stomach flutter.

"Of course I don't mind. Let's get our jackets and say goodnight to Diana."

I knew Diana would make a face when she realized Nate was driving me home, but at least she wouldn't give me a hard time for leaving early. I hugged her, wished her a happy birthday, and congratulated her on another outstanding party.

"Well, I do love a good party," she said. "I'm glad you came, Nate. And, Sophia, thanks for humoring me with the karaoke. If we decide to leave Psi Solutions behind, we could go on the road together."

Diana began to turn back to her other guests but stopped herself. "Oh, guys, tomorrow John's going to grill up some barbeque at my house in the afternoon. Why don't you both swing by around two? We can relax on the beach or just hang out while he's cooking."

"I'll be there. You know good barbeque can lure me anywhere," I said.

"Count me in. I'd only planned to buy a surfboard and watch football," Nate added.

"Great! I've got a decent surf break behind my house, and I'm not far from Windansea. Bring your new board to test it out." She hugged me again and whispered, "I want details."

Nate and I walked toward his SUV a few blocks down the street. The air was damp, and the humidity from the ocean hung in foggy layers. He opened my door for me, but before I could climb in, he pulled me toward him and brushed his lips lightly against mine. He drew back to gauge my reaction and then kissed me again, parting my lips with his. I kissed him back and felt almost dizzy from the sweet, gentle kiss. I didn't want the kiss to end. His hands held me tighter, and the kiss deepened, rousing something deep inside of me. All of a sudden, he stopped and smiled. After a quick peck, he walked over to his side of the car. I was dumbfounded for a second, not quite sure what had happened, but I regained my senses and climbed in. As he started the car and pulled out into traffic, silence reigned. I had to say something.

"Thanks again for driving me home."

"No problem. I'm glad we're friends again, Sophia."

"Me too." I looked at him, wondering if he was being facetious. He sported a tiny smirk so either he was teasing me or he was feeling self-satisfied about my reaction to his kiss or both. Several blocks passed before Nate spoke again.

"Even though we haven't hung out in years, I think I still know you pretty well. I remember that blue's your favorite color. You also enjoy eating good food and can surprisingly pack away a lot of it, despite your small size."

I frowned a little. "That's not a particularly flattering memory." He elbowed me and smiled, lightening the mood.

"I also remember that you're shy but love to laugh. That's how Brian won you over. He doesn't have a shy bone in his body and can crack up anyone." We sat in silence for a few moments both caught up in our memories of the past.

"Can I ask you a question?"

"Sure," I said.

"Do you think of me *right now* as just an old friend?"

I wasn't prepared for his directness. "Well . . . um . . . I don't know," I stammered.

"I don't want to scare you off, but I'd like to be more. I really enjoyed dancing with you. Did you like dancing with me?"

My palms began to sweat. I was surprised at how self-assured and confident he was. When we first met as freshmen seven years ago, he was somewhat shy like me. I knew he had climbed out of his shell and had certainly developed an active dating life, but having never been someone he pursued, I didn't anticipate this side of him. Although uncomfortable, the best approach was to be up-front and honest. What had happened on the dance floor was too obvious to deny. "Yes. I enjoyed it very much. I've never danced with anyone like that."

"Neither have I. We have chemistry, Sophia, and neither of us is dating anyone. Give me a chance to be more than a friend this time. Date me. Let's spend time together and see where it leads us."

Concerns over ruining our newly re-established friendship surfaced in my mind, but I found that I really wanted to spend time with him, and part of me definitely wanted to be more than friends.

After a moment of hesitation, I asked, "So, will our first date be Diana's barbeque tomorrow?"

"Maybe," he smiled and grabbed my hand, caressing it with his thumb. "I'm glad you liked our dance. It was pretty amazing."

"We moved together seamlessly. Where did you learn to dance like that?"

"I've taken some ballroom dancing classes with girlfriends over the years. I've always enjoyed dancing, especially with a beautiful woman."

My cheeks blushed at his comment, but I tried to keep the conversation light. "I'm impressed you learned to dance. The only reason Thomas can dance is because I was a ruthless taskmaster. I wanted someone to dance with me, and since we often kept to ourselves growing up, that meant Thomas was my partner. He was willing but didn't appreciate my high expectations. I probably sapped any joy out of it for him."

"He seems to have survived your tyranny unscathed." Nate squeezed my hand.

"So . . . where will you shop for your surfboard tomorrow?"

"There's a great place up in Encinitas on the 101 with a lot of selection. I'll buy one and then swing by to pick you up for the barbeque, if that's okay with you."

"That sounds fine. What will your friends be up to tomorrow?"

"They'll probably spend the earlier part recovering from their hangovers and then watch football the rest of the day. I love those guys, but I don't think they've grown up much. Life is still one big frat party for them."

"What's your apartment like? It must be pretty rowdy with all that partying nearby."

"It's a one bedroom and a bit dingy, but it's within walking distance of the beach. I'm wrapping up the lease for a friend. There's less than two months left. The nights *are* noisy, but I'm a good sleeper so that hasn't bothered me. I have loved running on the beach in the mornings, but I don't think I'll renew the lease. The traffic getting in and out of PB every day is brutal, and the bar lifestyle is too pervasive to ignore. I will miss being able to walk over to my friends' apartments to hang, but even though we're the same age, those guys make me feel old."

"Where do you think you'll live?"

"Probably somewhere closer to work, assuming my first week goes well. I'll have to start looking soon. Speaking of places to live, we're getting close to your exit. You live near UCSD's campus, right, but where exactly?"

"I live in the Villas near UTC mall. Do you know it?"

"Yeah. I lived near there when I was a student. What's your apartment like?"

"I have a two bedroom, which gives my mom a place to stay when she visits. It's fairly peaceful and more than enough space for me. Since I'm on the top floor, I don't have to worry about loud neighbors much."

I pointed out the specific building to him, and he pulled into the garage and parked the car. "Can I walk you to your door?" he asked.

"Sure."

We climbed out of his car and walked toward the security gate enclosing the anteroom for the elevator. When the doors closed, Nate pulled me to him, his chocolate brown eyes searching mine. He kissed my lips gently again, easing into it. I kissed him back slowly while my pulse quickened. The kiss held a seeking, a questioning, a yearning. He teased my lips and then opened them with his tongue, kissing me more forcefully. The intensity of that kiss rapidly escalated. A passion for him began to erupt inside me when the elevator beeped to let us know we'd reached my floor. We reluctantly ended the kiss and stepped out holding hands.

When we stood before my door, I looked up at him and sighed. "Nate, I think we should say goodnight here."

"Whatever you want," he said. Nate leaned in and continued the kiss, rekindling the fire that had just begun to smoke. Each kiss begat another one more passionate than the last. I didn't want to stop and started instinctively kneading his back and sides, pulling him closer and closer, needing him close. God, he was well built. My mind clouded with sensation . . . the velvet of his tongue, the softness of his lips, the hardness of his chest and the strength in his arms. As he grabbed my hips and pulled me flat against him, the evidence of his arousal nearly undid me. He started to move his hands restlessly up and down my sides, glancing the sides of my breasts, but when they began to caress my butt and lift my dress, I forced myself to end the kiss, still panting heavily. I looked up at him and smiled. "Goodnight."

I stepped back and fished my keys out of my purse. As he caught his breath, he watched me open the door and then grabbed my hand and kissed it when I turned around.

"So, you'll pick me up tomorrow for our first official date?" I asked.

He leaned in then and kissed my cheek, intertwining his fingers with mine. "Yes, I'll pick you up around one-thirty or call you if I'm running late, though now I'd say that *this* is our first official date. Tomorrow will be our second," he brushed some hair out of my face, "but I'd like to have a date with only the two of us soon. If you leave yourself free next Saturday, I'll try to arrange something fun."

"I'd like that."

Nate smiled and kissed my hand again. "Goodnight, Sophia."

I smiled at him one last time as he looked back before turning the corner in the hallway. Once I was safely alone in my apartment, I leaned my head against the door, still somewhat shocked by the abrupt change. *How in the world had this happened?* In a matter of hours, Nate had transitioned from someone who'd been a friend, someone whom I'd cared about as a friend, to someone whose close presence made me want to jump his bones. *Did this passion truly start with our dance that evening? Could it have been there all along, only carefully tucked away?* I hadn't been aware of it if that was the case.

"God, what a crazy night!" I said aloud. I hastily prepared for bed and turned off the lights though my mind didn't readily succumb to sleep.

CHAPTER FOUR

I woke up to sunlight filtering through my drapes. As I stretched, I reached for my iPhone and saw that I'd recorded only one dream. One was less than usual for me but not unprecedented, and the dream didn't have any unusual qualities.

After yoga class, I realized that I'd missed several calls from Diana with four increasingly impatient messages. As I was backing out of the parking lot, she called again. I answered it over my car's speaker system.

Before I'd finished saying, "Hello," Diana interrupted. "Sophia, I can't wait any longer. Tell me *everything* that happened. Is he still there?"

"No, no. He didn't stay the night, but I guess we're dating now."

"I saw the two of you dancing. Whew! I thought you were gonna get laid right there on the dance floor."

"Diana!" I chided as she laughed at my expense. "The dancing wasn't that bad, was it?"

"Relax. I'm exaggerating. But clearly, there will be sex. The question is, has it been had yet?"

I described the unfolding of the evening to her in vague terms, ending with us deciding to give a relationship a shot and sharing a kiss goodnight. I knew she craved the details but taunting her by omitting them was too fun to pass up.

"That's it?" Her disappointment rang loud and clear.

"That's it."

"Seriously? But there had to be heat!"

"Intense heat. God, it took all of my will power to tell him goodbye at the door."

"Why did you end it there? After what I saw on the dance floor, it could have been a truly magnificent night."

"Diana, we've only been in each other's lives again for less than forty-eight hours. You have to admit that's probably too fast, even for you."

"Well, thank you for that."

"Look, he's a friend, and I wouldn't want to screw that up by doing something rash. I haven't had sex in over six months. My body wasn't acting in my best interest so I had to use my head." I took a deep breath. "Okay, we are not talking about me any longer. How are things with John? You two seem happy."

"John's great," she sighed. "You like him?"

"Yes. He seems to adore you."

"The feeling is mutual. I don't know how I got so lucky. He's smart, funny, confident, sexy as hell, and extremely talented in bed. We're having a lot of fun. For the first time, I'm not getting bored. The only strange thing about him is that his mind doesn't sound like the average person's. He knows about my ability and claims to have none of his own, but his thoughts aren't garbled and free-associating like everyone else's. They're clear and simple when I can read them. It's as if he has some innate shield, and I can only read him when he's focusing hard on a particular thought."

"Hmm, that might make him the perfect match for a telepath."

"We'll see, but I love that my ability doesn't bother him. It's liberating to be open about what I can do with someone I'm dating. He's fascinated and tests me from time to time to see if I can really hear his thoughts. It's so cute. I also told him about what the rest of you can do, and he thinks it's awesome. Well, anyway, you guys are still coming today, right? Thomas said he'd be here, and Nadia's staying at my house."

"Nate's picking me up. Do you need us to bring anything?"

"No, nothing at all. John's been marinating the meat since yesterday. I'm about to run to the store for a few last-minute items."

* * *

After breakfast and a shower, I dressed for the beach, pairing an azure sundress with a white cardigan and strappy sandals. I found myself looking into the mirror more than usual, observing myself from different angles. After one day of being involved with Nate, I was already feeling more self-conscious about my appearance. *Jeez, I'm such a girl.* Embracing that fact, I painted my toenails and caught my reflection again. *Oh, treacherous libido!* I'd originally thought I'd picked the dress to accentuate my eyes but now suspected that I subconsciously chose it to highlight my breasts. Since I didn't plan on having sex with him, the dress might be kind of cruel. I contemplated changing, but I felt comfortable and confident. I had to face it. I wanted to look good for Nate. I put on some sunscreen and a bit more makeup than usual, though still not that noticeable.

Nate called a little after one to let me know he'd found a board and was on his way. The time passed slowly. I kept finding excuses to check the mirror. I brushed my teeth again, reapplied lip gloss, then added a little powder and a hint of perfume. My cell phone finally pinged with a text that Nate was in the garage. I took the elevator down and saw him standing next to his car, admiring the new surfboard strapped on top.

"What do you think?" he asked.

From my years of board shopping with Thomas, I'd learned a bit about surfboards. I ran my hand over it. "The quality seems good, and it's attractive. Going with a fish was a good call. It should provide plenty of float for a guy your size and pick up the waves nicely, but if you haven't surfed in over three years, are you certain you're ready for Windansea?"

"Well, I want to try . . . and speaking of attractive," he entwined his hands with mine and pulled me toward him. "You look wonderful." He kissed me lightly with soft lips, lingering a little. "Are you ready to go?"

His brief kiss awakened the sensations from last night, making me a little dazed. "Um, Sure."

I gave him basic directions to Diana's place after we buckled in, and he reached over to hold my hand as he drove. I had to sneak surreptitious glances at Nate since I didn't want him to catch me staring. The change in our relationship had me seeing him in a new light, noting intricacies in his features I must have overlooked in the past. Heat rose in my cheeks when his thumb traced a circle on the palm of my hand. I was beginning to feel uncomfortably warm. Either I needed to take off my sweater or ask Nate to turn up the AC. At first, I couldn't decide which made my predicament more obvious, but I dropped his hand and took off my sweater. He looked over at me, and I could tell that I'd made the wrong decision. Without the additional cover of my cardigan, my breasts were more prominently displayed, and he noticed. His hand found mine again. After a few minutes, our hands were becoming warm and sweaty. He turned up the AC. The sexual tension was suffocating, and neither of us seemed comfortable speaking. I wracked my brain for a way to cool us off and stumbled upon a topic I wanted to broach that would certainly stop the escalation.

"What is Brian's fiancée like? Is she good for him?" I asked.

"Do you want the truth?"

"Of course I do."

"Stephanie's great. She's a medical student in Brian's class at Stanford. She's smart, fun, pretty, and a good person. I think they'll be happy together."

"That's good," my voice trailed off. Part of me was a little sad that he'd moved on so definitively, but a larger part was glad he'd found someone he loved that much. It gave me hope for myself.

Nate turned onto La Jolla Boulevard, not too far from Diana's. "Okay, where do I go from here?"

I navigated us to a parking space one street over from Diana's. Parking was always at a premium near the beach. Nate grabbed his board and wetsuit, and we walked towards her place.

"Nice location," he said as he glanced out at the ocean.

"Wait until you see the view from the second floor," I said.

Diana's house was right on the beach. Her father was a billionaire, and her house reflected that. Several years ago, he'd renovated it to perfection, adding a modern twist of glass and stainless steel to the pervasive southern California stucco and clay tile roof.

Diana's gate was open, and she greeted us with hugs. "I'm so glad you're here. Nadia and Thomas are in the back with John. Nate, you can put your surfboard out on the back patio. Would you guys like anything to drink? Wine? Beer? Water?"

"I'll have a glass of white wine if you have some open," I said.

"I'll just have water for now," Nate said. "I want to surf, and I'm afraid of being pummeled to death on my first day back in the game."

Diana and I laughed. "Well, the surf's not that good right now. It's the typical afternoon wind chop, but it should improve later in the day." She handed both drinks to me since Nate carried his suit and board.

"Your place is incredible," Nate complimented.

"Thanks," Diana said. "It was one of our family vacation homes, but when I decided to work in San Diego, my dad gave it to me. He still takes care of it financially, though, since he doesn't think I make enough money." She motioned us toward the open sliding doors. "Enjoy the sun and the smell of John's cooking. I'll be out in a second with a plate of appetizers."

"Do you need any help?" I asked.

"Not at all. Go relax or take a walk on the beach. I've got it covered."

As we went outside, Nadia and Thomas stood up to welcome us, and John waved his greeting from behind the grill. I placed the glasses on the table and hugged them.

"I'm glad you both made it," Thomas said. "Nate, you're surfing today?"

"I'm going to try," he said.

"Cool. I can help you. This cove can get some great swells and is more private than Windansea. We won't need to go over there to compete for waves."

"Great." After he gently placed his new board and wetsuit on the patio, Nate glanced out at the ocean. "What a gorgeous day. Do you guys mind if Sophia and I take a short walk on the beach first?"

They assured us they didn't mind, and Nate tugged my hand and led me across Diana's yard to her back gate. When we were out of earshot, I poked him in the chest with my finger and teased, "You didn't ask *me* if I wanted to go for a walk."

"Sorry. We arrived at Diana's before we could finish our conversation about Brian. There's something I want to ask you." We left our shoes on the edge of Diana's yard. Nate hopped down into the sand first, then helped me down, and held my hand tightly in his as we walked.

"Okay, go ahead," I said warily.

"Will you tell me why you and Brian broke up? You don't have to if you don't want to, but Brian would never talk about it. The only thing he ever said was that you didn't love him enough. None of us were sure what that really meant."

"I can't say I *want* to talk about it, but I will. I think I finally understand what happened since I've been psychoanalyzing it for years. Brian might be right. I did love him, but I realized several months ago that I didn't trust him enough to commit to spending the rest of my life with him. Brian knew I had psychic abilities, and that you, Diana, and Thomas did as well, but I don't think he ever fully grasped the extent of it. My dad was a psychic null, like Brian, or at least pretended to be, and he couldn't handle our abilities. He deserted us. He called his own children 'freaks' and wanted nothing to do with us. I haven't seen him since I was seven years old." I buried my foot in the sand and spread my toes.

"Obviously, I wasn't over that and probably never will be completely, and since Brian's a psychic null too, I think I subconsciously feared he might also abandon me one day, especially if we had kids like Thomas and me. Brian pushed me to set a wedding date, and I resisted. A few months after the engagement, he started to become angry and accusatory, saying I must not love him if I wasn't ready to set a date. I assured him that I did but was simply nervous about the whole idea of marriage because of my parents. When we returned from Christmas vacation, he gave me an ultimatum — that I agree to marry him in June after graduation or we break off the relationship entirely. I wasn't ready."

I didn't want to talk any more. I dropped Nate's hand, picked up a flat rock, and tried to skip it across the water. Before Brian had stormed out, he'd yelled that my father's abandonment had damaged me so much that I'd never be able to trust anyone enough to get married and would always be alone. His words stung. I had trust and commitment issues for sure, but I prayed that Brian was wrong and that he just wasn't the right guy for me. He was like my dad in many ways, which should have been a red flag from the start, but a small part of me still worried from time to time that he could be right. Those were the days when I gave up on myself, gave up on ever finding love again.

"I'm sorry about bringing this mess up." Nate picked up a stone and skipped it four times on the water, his skill vastly superior to mine. "Did you know that the breakup was super awkward for the rest of us? It was as if you'd vanished. You even removed yourself from social media and changed your cell phone number. Brian was a mess. He took such a self-destructive course for a while that none of us dared contact you, or even mention you, and you didn't contact us. It was weird not to see you any more, not to get your dating advice, or hear about your latest physics experiments. We felt like the kids of divorced parents, but as his closest friends, we had to stand by him."

He threw another rock and then continued. "Brian's temper was awful. We had to tiptoe around him for months. I missed seeing you. I caught a glimpse of you walking to class about a month after the breakup. I wanted to approach you, but you looked so depressed, so fragile, that I was afraid I'd upset you. I also didn't know if you'd want to talk to any of us, like we were somehow tainted by association. I thought it best to stay away." Nate grabbed my hand and pulled me to walk further down the beach.

"That was a tough time for me," I said. "Moving on would have been less difficult if we hadn't still cared for each other. I was not only missing him and terribly sad that I'd caused both of us pain, but also wondering if I'd made the biggest mistake of my life. About a month after we broke up, he started sending me so many hateful and nasty texts that I changed my phone number, and though he was hurtful, he helped me get over him because he showed me a side I'd never seen and didn't like. I shut down emotionally for a while, but I came to understand that if Brian had truly loved me or if we had been right for each other, then he wouldn't have forced my hand."

"So, do you think you're completely over him?"

"Yes, I am now. I first started making peace with our breakup when I was in Italy on that terrace overlooking the countryside I told you about. I got my first decent night of sleep in months after communing with nature on that patio. I began to heal from then on, but there's still a small wound, and as you remarked yesterday, I'm not as carefree as I used to be."

"What can I do to help?" he asked.

"You can do this," I said and went up on my tiptoes to kiss him. He kissed me back, soft yet purposeful lips at first, and then the kiss intensified into that surprising and consuming passion from last night, setting me on fire. No matter how deeply we explored, the kiss began to feel insatiable, more and more like it wasn't enough. He pulled me tightly against him, and I could feel his response through my thin dress. The urge to sink into him was overwhelming, but this wasn't the right time or place. I gently ended the kiss and looked into his smiling eyes.

"Mmm, another time," he said. He cupped my right cheek as his piercing gaze held mine and reached deep into my heart. I shivered and then kissed the palm of his hand. He kissed my forehead and hugged me sweetly for a moment, the breeze rustling through our hair. We then started walking again, holding hands.

"Do you remember when we went to the Death Cab for Cutie concert together, just you and me?" Nate asked. "Brian was sick with the flu and couldn't go. He didn't want you to miss it so he asked me to take you for him."

"Of course I remember that night! That was the best concert! We had such a great time."

"It's one of my best memories from college too. I had a bit of a crush on you back then, but I never made a move since you were Brian's. When he first asked me to go to the concert, I tried to talk my way out of it. All of my excuses fell short, though, and he cornered me. I was afraid I wouldn't be able to treat you as only a friend and that all my restraint over the years would have been wasted. When you gave me a hug goodnight, you smelled so good, and I had to exercise all of my control not to kiss you then. I was worried I still held you close for too long. I went home and lay awake for most of the night. I don't know if you noticed, but I wasn't around much for a few weeks. I had to get some distance from you and Brian."

"I never thought you had any interest in me. You almost always had a girlfriend, but I do remember thinking when I went to bed that night that the girl you ended up with would be really lucky." Nate squeezed my hand. We walked a little further in silent thought, when suddenly, something occurred to me that needed to be addressed.

"Uh, Nate, since we're going to date, it would be great if you could work extra hard to develop your telepathic shields as quickly as possible. Going back to the house with Diana and Thomas will be a little embarrassing, but work will be a nightmare. Our private life will be open to all the telepaths there and possibly anyone they talk to. I value my privacy and don't want people at work knowing the details of my love life. Which telepath will be helping you develop your shields?" I asked.

"David. He seems like a decent guy," Nate replied.

"David is nice and discrete but watch out for Carol. She's a nosy telepath who likes to gossip. You'll learn to shield as part of the job, but Thomas and I can help you too."

"I'll do my best. I'd also appreciate the privacy."

"Learning to shield is similar to developing a muscle you've never used or like learning how to ride a bike for the first time. Once you've fully developed it, though, the process becomes automatic and you won't have to think about it most of the time. You meditate to control your astral projections, right?"

"Right."

"To shield, you start in the same way, but instead of projecting out, you remain in your head. I think what we're technically doing is creating some sort of interference pattern, but visualization is what helped me solidify my shields. I repeated to myself, 'Thomas can't hear me,' over and over again while seeing a thick-walled chamber protecting my thoughts, protecting me. Thomas then gave me instant feedback. When it seemed to block him some, I tried to replicate and intensify whatever I was feeling at that moment, all the time linking my visualization with what was going on psychically until I could block him completely. By associating the act of shielding with my image, I created a more mentally tangible way to control my shields." As we walked, I looked around for a comfortable and dry place to sit.

"When I put my shields in place, I imagine my whole body within a cozy medieval fortress that has no doors or windows. It's like a safe room in a magical castle, with arches above illuminated by warm, glowing orbs, a luxurious bed on one side, and a lounge with nearby floor pillows on the other. For all telepaths I know but Thomas, my shields are impenetrable, though I can tell if someone's trying to force their way in. When Thomas wants to communicate, he'll 'tap' and a door will just sort of appear for him."

"Interesting."

"Do you want to give it a try now?" I asked.

"Why not?"

I led him to a clearing in the sand and sat down with him.

"To learn, you really do need the feedback of a good telepath, but it can't hurt to try the visualization. The more real the shields are to you, the better. Feel the rough texture of the stone walls. Push on them and appreciate how solid and impenetrable they are. See the vibrant reds and purples of the drapes around the bed. Note the softness of the lounge's cushions as you lie there staring up at the orbs. Basically, envision whatever works for you, whatever makes you feel protected, and then add details. Okay, meditate for a few minutes first and then begin to picture your shields. We can ask Diana and Thomas if they sense anything different when we return."

Nate closed his eyes and began to meditate. Looking at him, with the damp, salty breeze blowing through his hair, I remembered the sunset dream from the other night. *Could Nate be the guy from that dream?* I tried to picture the face, now a hazy image in my mind. No, although he looked similar, he wasn't that man. *Maybe it was Nate in essence? Maybe the dream symbolized that it was time for me to open up to a man again?* I leaned back, planting my fingers in the sand, and stared at him some more. I found myself smiling and felt at peace. I was enjoying simply being with him. When Nate came out of his meditation ten minutes later and caught me beaming at him, he smiled. The next thing I knew, he'd tackled me in the sand.

"What are you doing?" I laughed, attempting half-heartedly to break free.

"Trying to help you feel better, of course," he responded. He looked at me and then leaned in to kiss my mouth. After a minute, he started kissing down my neck. I couldn't help sighing. Even though the pressure of his body on top of mine was immensely satisfying, I kept my head about me.

"Nate, not that I don't enjoy this, but I think we should get back to the others."

"I'll behave," he promised, taking a deep breath, "if you'll relax with me for a minute and watch the waves."

"Okay," I said as he pulled me to a sitting position.

He settled me in between his legs and wrapped his arms around me. I rested my back against his chest as we gazed out at the ocean. Happiness was seeping into my heart just from being near him and enjoying this beautiful view together. All of a sudden, a dolphin hurled itself out of the water into a flip. I've seen pods of dolphins in the wild many times, where their fins ascend and descend in a defined area, but I've never seen a jump outside of the shows at SeaWorld. Nate and I were so surprised and excited that we instinctively leaped up to see more. We noticed six fins gliding up over the surface and then down below again and waited several minutes in the hope we'd see another jump, but the pod kept migrating further away from shore.

"That was amazing," Nate said.

"It was," I agreed. "That dolphin seemed to jump just for us."

Nate smiled down at me and tucked a strand of hair behind my ear. "I guess we should head back." He seemed reluctant. "I already can't wait until next Saturday when we can spend the day alone."

We playfully dusted the sand off of each other and walked toward Diana's.

"Are you ready for work tomorrow? Have you practiced projecting?" I asked.

"They made me take a proficiency exam to get the job. I had to project to specific rooms around the world containing written messages. That was easy, but I've been practicing anyway. I project to a few different places each day to stay fresh."

"I enjoyed that exam. It was like hunting for treasure." We compared notes to see if the test had changed much over the years.

"The only thing I don't like about the job so far is that they 'frown on' their employees using social media. I guess that's why you and Diana aren't on Facebook or Instagram," Nate said.

"Yes, and you think you don't like it. Diana was a Facebook queen, and when we started, it wasn't just frowned upon, it was forbidden. They started relaxing their stance about a year ago. That policy was almost a deal breaker for Diana. She was constantly posting and tweeting in college. It wasn't a big deal for me because I'd already deleted my accounts when Brian started being hateful. If you want to keep yours, it should be fine as long as you follow the rules, but remind me to tell you a social media secret when you can shield well."

"Okay."

We were almost at Diana's house. "Can you still visualize your fortress?" I asked.

"I think so."

"John's aware of our abilities, but I don't know if Nadia knows so we should keep it quiet. I'll send Thomas a message to see if he and Diana can sense anything different about your thoughts."

As we drew near Diana's back patio, the sounds of pleasant conversation and the smell of delicious barbeque filled the air. John had just finished taking the food off the grill, and everyone was digging in. After eating and chatting a while, Thomas let me know that he and Diana could hear Nate's thoughts and that they didn't notice a change. He also reminded me that it would be impossible for Nate to develop shields in a matter of minutes, especially without any feedback from a telepath.

I closed my door to Thomas's mind and started paying attention to the conversation. John was talking about his job in LA. Apparently, he was in his early thirties, worked in financial management for a big investment firm, and did extremely well, much better than his job warranted in my opinion. I hate to admit it, but I was prejudiced against banking executives and stockbrokers, who created nothing yet siphoned off a large proportion of the world's wealth. I tried not to let John's occupation affect my personal opinion of him. Fortunately, he impressed me with his barbecue skills. A man who could cook well always deserved kudos in my book.

An hour or so later, Nate and Thomas suited up to go surfing, and the rest of us followed to watch. Nate had some fairly severe wipeouts, but after a few tries, he started to get a feel for it again. Thomas, as always, was inspiring to watch. He seemed to know exactly where to be and when to start paddling to catch a wave, as if he had some paranormal ability in this arena as well. Upon our return to the house, we snacked some more and played Cards Against Humanity, where I once again embarrassed myself with my lack of dirty knowledge. Around seven, we said our goodbyes and headed out.

"So, Thomas said the shielding didn't work, huh?" Nate asked as we walked to the car.

"How did you know?"

"I watched your face. I remembered that you look as if you're concentrating hard on something when you communicate with Thomas."

"You're sweeter and more polite than Diana. She takes great joy in telling me I look constipated."

Nate laughed. "That sounds like something Diana would say, but I disagree. Anyway, you had that look and then you seemed disappointed. I promise to make it a priority. I'll practice diligently with David tomorrow at work and make sure we meet often." After a short pause, he asked, "Would you like to grab another bite to eat?"

"No. I might be a little hungry later, but I'm still full. Are you hungry?"

"No," he said, pulling me to face him and looking into my eyes, "but I don't want our evening to end."

"Oh," I murmured, a hitch in my breath, "well, do you want to watch a movie at my place? I could make peanut butter and jelly sandwiches later if we get hungry."

"That sounds like a plan." He pecked me lightly.

As we drove, I began to fret about what might happen at my apartment. The attraction between us was getting harder to control, and I didn't want to have any regrets with Nate. I could already tell that we had the potential for something really special. After a long, awkward silence, I gathered the courage to address what I imagined was on both of our minds. "Nate, I feel really uncomfortable talking about this . . . but . . . I don't want us to have sex tonight."

"Okay," he choked out. "I didn't expect we would, considering it's only our second date, but . . . may I ask why?"

I didn't anticipate the question that and doubted my face could turn a brighter shade of red. "Well . . . it's just that things are moving fast between us. Maybe it's because we knew each other so well in the past, but it doesn't feel like only a second date to me. I just want to take that off the table before we get back to my apartment because I'm afraid my body will betray me once we're there."

Nate was smiling, obviously pleased with my comment. "So, I should listen to you now and not then?" he teased.

"Yeah, I guess so," I said, somewhat flustered. "I'm just not sure I could resist if you tried to seduce me. I know I'm mentally not ready for that, and I don't want to have any regrets with you. Let's watch a movie and enjoy each other's company but not let it get too heated."

"Okay," he exhaled slowly, "but it won't be easy. I want you so badly I can hardly see straight."

With that, warmth flushed over my skin, and I had to look out the window and remember how to breathe. Maybe I was being silly, but I wanted to be sure, and a week or even a day for that matter wouldn't kill us.

Back at my apartment, we decided to watch the fun cult classic, *The Big Lebowski,* to lighten the mood, but it was a good thing we already knew the storyline. I could barely focus on it. The chemistry between us charged the air. I felt sensitized to Nate's physical presence, as if he radiated energy. Like a moth to flame, I had to touch him. While we snuggled on the couch, his kisses below my ear sent a frisson through my core. Sliding his hand slowly down my arm to my hip and back, over and over, heightened my need. Maybe the intensity was ratcheting up ironically because we'd agreed not to seal the deal, but it was almost too much to bear. A few times his kisses carried me away, made me forget myself, but though it pained him, Nate found the restraint to soften our urges. In the end, he topped off a perfect evening with a sweet kiss goodnight at the door. Aside from the burning heat of our attraction, the most important discovery of the evening was that having Nate's arms around me just felt right.

Before I finished my bedtime routine, I checked the medicine cabinet for an old prescription that fortunately hadn't expired. It would take at least two weeks for the birth control pill to become effective, and it likely wouldn't be long before I'd need it. Although necessary to protect against STDs, condoms weren't my preferred form of birth control since my mom became pregnant with Thomas and me using them alone. I took a pill and made a mental note to renew the prescription soon. I continued washing up, and in a matter of minutes, I was in bed, under the covers, my head heavy on the pillow.

It's a bright, sunny day at the zoo and busy as always. I look at the line of people waiting to see the pandas. I haven't seen them in years because of the insane lines, but it isn't too bad today . . . hmm, I'll do it. As I wait, I admire a little girl dancing in a pretty pink dress . . . my dream changes. *All of a sudden, I'm leaning against a brick wall, and Nate is kissing me. It isn't chaste. It's all-consuming as I kiss those supple lips and taste him with my tongue, pressing my body as close to his as I can and wrapping my right leg around his left. I can't get enough of him. He plunges his tongue into my mouth and explores, making a deep, primitive sound. I feel as if I'm drowning of thirst, and I simply can't be sated. His lips then trail along my chin as I breathe heavily trying to catch my breath. He kisses feverishly down my neck, and his warm tongue licks my collarbone until his teeth find my bra strap. His head jerks up, and we look at each other. An expression of shock and surprise covers his face, and mine, I imagine. This isn't Nate.*

I sat up in bed, panting. "What the hell was that?" I asked of the dark. I could have sworn it was the same guy from the sunset dream. He looked surprised too. The dream felt so real, more than some of my strongest precognitive dreams. I put an absent hand to my lips, expecting them to be swollen, but they weren't. I felt like I'd physically kissed him, like my body had strained against his, and I was still raring to go. I had to focus to stay objective in order to make any sense out of this. I grabbed my iPhone, quickly recorded the zoo dream and then moved on to the kiss. After the factual recounting, I began to pick it apart.

"Again, like the sunset dream, it felt very real, and this time, even more so. The guy is so fully formed, so responsive and invested, much more than most characters in my dreams. It seemed like he was actively participating. Holy shit! Could we be sharing dreams? When we looked into each other's faces, I think neither of us expected the person we saw. I thought it was Nate. He must have thought I was someone else. God! I think we were in that dream together."

I pressed pause on the recording, my mind reeling from the possibility. Thomas and I had occasionally shared dreams when we were kids. We usually shared some kind of adventure, but I didn't remember them feeling this intense or real. *Are we really sharing dreams or is this a premonition? Is he someone I'll meet? Who is he?* I was ninety-nine percent certain it was the same guy from the sunset dream, but I wanted to be sure. I picked up my iPhone again and tried to record everything I'd observed about him. "He had dark brown hair, almost black, not short but not too long. I couldn't see his eye color. His lips were full, surrounded by light stubble. He had a symmetric, handsome face with olive-toned skin but nothing unique. He was well built, Nate's height or a little taller, so at least six-two. Hmm. I don't think I've seen him anywhere else but in the other dream." I could remember the act of tasting him but couldn't recall a specific taste or scent.

After adding this dream to the electronic journal on my laptop, I reread the sunset dream again, and the description of the guy seemed to match. I emailed Harry my journal entries for the two possibly shared dreams with a promise to call after work to discuss. One unanswered question from the sunset dream was whether the details of the Ocean Beach pier matched reality. Although I could astral project to answer my question, I wanted to check it out in person during the day. Maybe I could run into this mysterious stranger and put a stop to these dreams. Since it was only one in the morning, I needed to get back to sleep, but I set my alarm an hour early so I could try to swing by the pier at lunch. I laid my head on the pillow, unable to stop wondering how or why I was sharing dreams with this stranger and whether I could do anything to keep him out of my head. *Jeez, get a grip, Sophia. Calm your mind.* I took two deep breaths and then focused on emptying my thoughts, releasing tension, and feeling the rise and fall of my chest. Eventually my worries eased, and I fell back to sleep.

CHAPTER FIVE

I dressed quickly in the morning and hurried into work. After packing away my purse, I reviewed the next three files slotted for my attention. Since none of them required Roger's supervision, I went directly into one of the quiet rooms with my laptop and other necessary items. For the first case, I traveled to where they specified and shortly found what they were seeking. After writing up my observations and the report, I picked up the next file. I finished the two other cases in good time and headed back to my desk. I was a little nervous about seeing Nate. I'd never had a relationship with someone from work. I wasn't sure how to combine the personal with the professional, but I didn't have to wait long for the initial meet.

"Hi, there." Nate leaned his arms on the top of my cubicle and peered down at me.

"Hi, yourself," I said, feeling my cheeks flush at the handsome sight of him.

"Will you have time to grab lunch today?"

"Actually, I came in early so I could drive down to the Ocean Beach pier at lunch. I dreamed about it the other night and want to see if it matches my dream. Would you like to join me?"

"I'd love to, but I only have a thirty-minute break between meetings. We're going over security systems, signs of booby traps, weapons, specific explosives, SWAT and military raid procedures. The list seems endless. You'll have to enjoy the sunshine for me today." Nate rested his chin on his hands and looked down at me with a smile. "So, about our upcoming date, are you free only Saturday or all weekend?"

"I'm hoping to go to Irene's art exhibition on Friday. If you'd like to come, I'm sure she wouldn't mind, and I'm certain Harry would love to see you. I can leave Saturday and Sunday completely open. What are you planning?"

"I'm not sure yet, and I might want to surprise you." He seemed to be enjoying making our weekend plans. "I'll stop by your desk before I leave for the day. Wish me luck with my first projection."

"Good luck." I smiled after him as he turned to leave. That was easier than expected. I didn't even embarrass myself. Having a romance at work might not be so difficult after all.

After wrapping up one more project, I escaped to Ocean Beach. The pier felt different in the harsh light of mid-day. Even on a weekday, the pier bustled with people fishing, meandering, eating at the tiny café and just hanging out. I walked to where I'd sat in my dream, and the bench was in precisely the right spot, same build, same texture, same color. The pier itself was almost exactly as I remembered, but without the people. The minimal graffiti, the seagull droppings, and even the faint smells of fish were there, just more noticeable now. Even so, the pier still had a mystical presence, though more subdued under the bright noon sun. I searched the faces that passed, but none of them were his. Satisfied with my quest but not certain what it meant, I bought some fish tacos at a nearby eatery and headed back to work.

Around six, I gathered my belongings and went to find Nate to say goodbye. He was working on the Russian language program on his computer when I peeked into his cubicle. Although it would be rushed, he convinced me to meet for a quick bite before heading to my kung fu class. I wanted to spend time with him, but I hadn't yet thought about how having a boyfriend at work might affect my daily routine. I should have expected it would.

At the café, we ordered our sandwiches, then sat at a table. We chatted about our day, but the tick in his jaw told me he had something else on his mind.

"Nate, is everything all right?"

"Yes, but I want you to know that I don't mean to crowd you. I know you had a life before I came along."

"Nate, you're not." I reached over to hold his hand.

"I just don't have a routine yet, and I'd prefer to spend my free time with you," he squeezed my hand and gave me his shy, sexy smile, "but you shouldn't feel like you have to share every second with me. So, if you need some space or time alone, let me know, and I'll try not to take it personally."

"I want to spend time with you too. I just didn't think about how having a boyfriend at work might change my life. I've never dated a colleague or gone out much during the work week, but I'm here with you because I want to be." He caressed my hand with both of his and kissed it.

"I like hearing you call me your boyfriend."

"I can skip my class tonight. I don't make it often anyway."

"No. You should go, but for the rest of the workweek, how about this: if we don't catch lunch together, then we try to have dinner. Other than that, our lives are our own. I promise to keep my hands and lips to myself when we're at work, but all bets are off when we're not." He proved his point by nuzzling and then kissing the inside of my wrist.

Our sandwiches were ready, and Nate fetched them for us. "Let's eat fast," he said, "because I've only got ten more minutes with you, and I want to hold your hand some more." We finished eating and walked outside. My heart felt light as we held hands in the twilight and talked. When it was time to go, he kissed me goodbye at my car.

I was more distracted than usual at my kung fu class, but it was a good workout. When I arrived home, I threw down my stuff and dialed Harry, who'd been waiting for my call.

"What do you think, Harry? Could these be shared dreams?"

"It seems likely. I don't personally know anyone else who's experienced a shared dream besides you and Thomas, but the literature describes the two dreamers as being fully developed characters in their own right rather than a figment that reacts to the dreamer's subconscious whims. Most convincing were the facts that no one else was in either dream with you and that he looked shocked when he saw you the second time. To share a dream, one of the people involved must be a telepath. Since your telepathic abilities are weak at best, although they could be much better if you practiced, he must be one. Are you sure you've never seen him outside of your dream?"

"I don't think so. Would he have to live nearby to share dreams with me?"

"Not necessarily. He could be a world away, just as you and Thomas can communicate over thousands of miles. But I'd think that to connect with someone he's never met, if he is far away, he'd have to have impressive telepathic abilities."

"I thought I could only share a dream with someone I'm telepathically linked to, and Thomas and I haven't even shared one since we started shielding. Why aren't my shields keeping this person out now?"

"I don't know. I think you and this person have somehow forged a connection. I wish we knew how or why. From his surprised reaction, it doesn't seem like he's doing this on purpose, but we can't know for sure. What worries me is if he is intentionally pulling you into these dreams, he could try to mentally harm or terrorize you, possibly even hypnotize or control you. For all we know, he may look nothing like your dream person, or he could even be a woman. How did these dreams end? Did you break out of them using lucid dreaming skills or did you simply wake up?"

"The first one ended of its own accord, and I woke up at the end of the dream like I've trained myself. I think the second one ended because we were shocked. If he's what he seems to be, do you think I can communicate with him verbally to ask him to stop sending me dreams?"

"Intentional verbal communication in dreams is sketchy and likely difficult in shared dreams as well. As a telepath, he should have a better chance of communicating than you would. The best advice I have is to work on your lucid dreaming. Practice controlling your dreams by purposely changing what's happening and by making yourself wake up from within dreams at certain moments. You need to be able to pull yourself out of these dreams at will."

"Okay. I'll work on it. Oh, I visited the OB pier today, and it's basically the same as my dream even though I've never seen the entire pier in real life. Could this mean something?"

"That's interesting. The realistic quality you described isn't a typical feature of shared dreams. I wonder if your ability to astral project is somehow involved in the settings. Do you recall where the second dream was?"

"No, it wasn't clear. . . . Uh, Harry, do you know anything else I can do to keep him out of my dreams? I just started dating Nate. I don't want to be dreaming about another guy. I know it's not my fault, but I feel a little guilty."

"Don't be ridiculous. The activity in your dream likely occurred *because* you started seeing Nate. You could try making your shields stronger, but I'm not sure that'll help as they're quite strong already. Has Diana ever been able to read your thoughts with your shields up?"

"No. If I have them up, she can't penetrate them, even if she tries to force her way in. I think trying to make them stronger is worth a try. Could I borrow the GammaBeat? Maybe it could help."

"Of course. If I remember, I'll bring it to Irene's opening on Friday, but I'd like to get it back. I spoke with Dante yesterday. He recently sold his company and isn't certain whether the devices will become publicly available now, which was really disappointing to him. I don't have to return it, but I want to keep it in good condition since we may never be able to order another. Oh, and please bring Nate with you to the opening. We'd love to see him again."

"Thanks, I will."

"Call me if you have more dreams with this stranger. We can try to find more clues."

* * *

The rest of the week passed without a hitch. Nate and I kept things low-key, and although I was tempted to alter my schedule to see more of him, I think it was smart for us to ease into the relationship. Even my workload was light, with no emergencies, pretty regular hours, and an open weekend ahead of me. The one thing bothering me was that I hadn't had a single dream since the shared dream on Sunday. I've only had a few dreamless nights since I started recording them years ago. The last time occurred after Thomas convinced me to run a half-marathon on the spur of the moment without training, but I've never had more than one dreamless night in a row. First the shared dreams, and then no dreams. I wasn't sure what was going on, but I had a sinking feeling that something wasn't right in my psychic universe.

It was Friday, and we had to leave work on the early side to make the exhibition opening in time. Nate came to work dressed for the event since he wouldn't have time to go home. I left to get ready while Nate picked up some take out to bring back to my apartment. When he arrived, I was already wearing my little black dress.

"Wow," he said.

"You don't look so bad yourself. Let's eat. I'm starved."

We ate quickly since I still needed to put on makeup and do something with my hair. Nate read on his phone while I finished up. When I came out, he swallowed audibly, giving me a thrill.

"I just realized that you don't normally wear much makeup. When you do, your eyes really stand out. You look amazing."

"What do I usually look like?" I poked him jokingly in the stomach.

"Don't get me wrong," he laughed, flinching away from my poke and grabbing my hands. "You're always beautiful, but I'm blown away when you dress up."

"I'll take that as a compliment," I said and gave him a peck. His arms encircled me as I wiped the lipstick off of his lips.

"I like your dress, but I can't help thinking that I'd prefer to take it off." He nibbled on my ear and began kissing down my neck.

I could feel his smile against my skin and knew he was teasing me, but still my heart began to race. "Uh . . . Nate," I said somewhat breathy. "We're running late. You know we can't do this now."

"Not now," he smiled at me, satisfied by my reaction, "but soon, I hope."

*　*　*

Nate parked the car along Coast Boulevard, and we stared at the waves in the moonlight. They were crashing fiercely against the cliffs and rocks, but I could still hear the music and chatter wafting from the back patio of the Museum of Contemporary Art. I turned to see its iconic nested boat sculpture on the back of the building. Dozens of people had already arrived for the exhibition opening, and Nate and I hurried inside. Since a large group surrounded Harry and Irene, we found Thomas and discussed our weekend plans. Thomas was looking forward to a date with Nadia in LA. Nate shared with both of us that he'd be cooking me dinner after taking me on a hike at Lake Hodges, which Thomas agreed was one of the better hikes in San Diego County.

Harry and Irene eventually came over to greet us. Irene gave me a hug and whispered in my ear, "You and Nate make an attractive couple." They shook hands with Nate and then bombarded him with questions. They were truly interested in learning about the changes in his life since he was last Harry's student, but I knew some of the questioning was because they were protective of me.

The night went well for Irene. The director of the museum introduced her and described her art and career, and Irene said a few words about the exhibit. She had twelve paintings and eight sculptures on display. Her art was unique. It was elegant and sleek but quite intricate and at the same time possessing a certain soft vulnerability. Yet what really separated her from the rest was that she used her telekinetic ability to work with her media in a way that a normal artist simply couldn't. As the event drew to a close, I walked over to say goodbye to Harry and Irene.

I pulled Harry aside to talk privately, noticing that he looked tired again, even more than the last time I'd seen him. After he dismissed my worries for his health, I shared with him the status of my dreams. "I haven't had a single dream in the last four nights. I checked all my past journals, and I've never had more than one dreamless night at a time. Something's not right."

"That's disconcerting. I haven't dreamt in the past week either, and I have a similar intuition that something's wrong. Have you had any visions?"

"No, but they're rare."

Harry grimaced. "Let me know if you have any dreams or visions, even if they seem mundane or insignificant." He remembered the GammaBeat, retrieved it from Irene's purse, and refreshed me on its operation. "If I figure anything out about our dreaming situation, I'll call you, but try not to dwell on it and have a good evening with Nate. I think he could be a good match for you."

I blushed. "Thanks, Harry. I'll let you know if anything comes up." I went to Nate and entwined his fingers with mine.

When we were in the car, Nate quizzed me about the tête-à-tête with Harry, and I told him about our dreamless nights, leaving out the possibly shared dreams. In spite of Harry's and my concerns, I tried to reassure him that there was nothing to worry about. While he didn't seem convinced, he left it at that. "Can I walk you up?" he asked.

"I'd like that," I replied.

One of my neighbors, a medical student at UCSD, entered the elevator with us. I introduced him to Nate, who had already possessively draped his arm across my hip, and we chatted until we reached our floor.

At my door, Nate smiled down at me while holding me close. "Your neighbor has the hots for you."

"No, he doesn't."

"Yes, he does. Thank you for telling him I'm your boyfriend."

"Well, you are, aren't you?"

"I am." He kissed me sweetly. "Tomorrow, you're all mine," he said in my ear, rubbing his cheek against my skin. "No work, no friends, just us. I'll pick you up around eleven. Dress to hike and leave your worries behind."

"I'm looking forward to it. Aren't you going to come in?" I asked and kissed him again.

"Mmm. Not tonight, but rest well because tomorrow you're gonna need it." With a suggestive grin on his face, he departed.

I closed the door and took a deep breath. I'd waited long enough. We'd known each other for years, and I'd seen him every day for the past week, which probably translated to dating for a month or two in the normal dating world. I suddenly wanted everything that grin implied.

CHAPTER SIX

After waking from another dreamless night, I meditated to try to detect anything abnormal about my mind. Someone had to be screwing with my head and Harry's to prevent our dreams. *But why? Who would do such a thing?* I didn't notice anything different and was about to give up, when I remembered the GammaBeat. I put it on and fell quickly into a deep meditative state, although I bounced out of it more frequently than I'd like to admit. The beeps subsided after several minutes, and I stabilized in the gamma zone. The shared dreams and lack of dreams had to be linked, but my gut feeling insisted that the shared dreams were unintentional. I decided to attempt to reinforce my shields by envisioning them growing thicker, stronger, and more impenetrable. For over an hour, I imagined feeling an increasing massiveness around my mind. When I finally opened my eyes, it was nine o'clock. Thomas was probably still out surfing. I didn't want to kill him by catching him in the middle of a wave, but I figured that was unlikely since ninety percent of surfing was sitting on the board awaiting the next good one.

"*Hey, Thomas,*" I thought, "*is this a bad time?*"

I didn't get an immediate answer and started to worry. I realized then that this thicker wall no longer had a secret door for him. I visualized a small duct-sized opening that connected directly to Thomas while at the same time focusing on the bond that Thomas and I shared.

I repeated, "*Hey, Thomas, is this a bad time?*"

"*Not at all, what's up?*"

"I used Harry's GammaBeat to strengthen my shields. I had to create a new opening to be able to contact you. Can you sense anything different?"

"No. Why are you strengthening your shields?" Just then my thoughts betrayed me. *"Harry thinks a telepath is sharing dreams with you?"*

"Maybe. Can you try to contact me now? I'm closing the connection."

I concentrated on my reinforced fortress and replaced the opening of the tube with stone again. After five minutes of hearing nothing from Thomas, I became anxious. I listened closely and finally heard a small rapping. I then imagined the new conduit opening to him.

"Thomas, did you notice anything?"

"It seems stronger or at least different. My usual method of contacting you wasn't working. I had to concentrate harder on your mind and visualize other ways of getting your attention before you heard me. I don't like that it's more difficult to contact you, but it worries me more that some unknown telepath may be pushing his dreams on you."

"Harry and I don't believe anyone is pushing *dreams on me."* I then shared my conversation with Harry and our concern about the lack of dreams. Thomas didn't like that one bit either. He hadn't noticed anything suspicious, but he'd now be on alert.

I stretched as I closed my mind to Thomas and decided to revive myself with yoga poses. I then turned on some music, made green tea and cooked an egg-in-a-hole. As I ate, my most recent precognitive dream became reality. A goldfinch perched on the rail of my balcony and sang. I stared at the beautiful little bird and wondered if it had any special meaning for me. *What was the message?*

I'd barely finished dressing when Nate arrived with the groceries for dinner. After unpacking the goodies, including a gorgeous tiramisu he'd picked up from a bakery, we drove to the start of a trail at Lake Hodges Dam and got the backpacks out of the car. Nate insisted on slathering me with sunscreen, which I certainly didn't mind, and we were off. The trail was pleasant and greener than I expected for San Diego County, especially after a long, dry summer and a conspicuous lack of fall rain. Flowers even bloomed, celebrating the reprieve from the summer heat and showering the world with one last spectacle before winter set in.

As we walked, Nate taught me the botanical names of the plants we passed along the trail, putting his biology education to good use. Our conversation soon turned from the scientific to the metaphysical as I touched on a topic most precogs had struggled with.

"How many of your precognitive dreams or visions have come to pass?" I asked.

"I haven't kept count, but likely most."

"Do you believe free will exists?"

"I do, but I think changing what we foresee would be an uphill battle," he said. His mood sobered a little, deep in thought, and he tossed a stick into the brush. Most psychics have spent hours upon hours pondering this issue. "I think we can agree that what we see are small glimpses of a future that *could* occur based upon the state of the universe at a particular moment. It's like there are threads that pull events in a certain direction, or like a large funnel or gravity well that draws a ball towards its center. It's not inevitable that the event will happen since something can come along to cut the string or knock the ball out of the funnel, but without some unforeseen external force, they'll probably occur as we see them." He grabbed my hand and turned me to face him.

"None of my visions has been a life or death situation. Most were trivial, like my mom buying M&Ms at the grocery store," he said, placing his right hand on the side of my face and caressing my lip with his thumb. "I had no desire to interfere, and these dreams became reality. Occasionally, they haven't materialized, and I've always assumed that something unexpected must have happened." He stared into my eyes as if trying to find an answer. His soul-deep chocolate browns searching my light blues. After a moment, he tipped my chin up and gave me a sweet peck. "So, I don't know if I answered your question, but I think there's free will. I think we might be able to prevent something we see, but it would take a lot of effort since the momentum of current forces would be working against us."

"I believe in free will too, and I've changed a few of my visions." I finger-combed Nate's hair out of his face and tugged him to continue our walk. "I can't stand the thought that our future might be predetermined or that some ultimate destiny awaits us. Life would be meaningless if everything were pre-ordained."

"I don't think anything is necessarily pre-ordained, but all of our collective past choices that created the current state of the world at that moment point the future in a certain direction. I think that's what we see. Why do you think we have these dreams? Why do you think they're more common in people who can astral project than in other psychics?" Nate asked.

"I think it's because both have something to do with that theoretical astral plane where time and space supposedly lose meaning. All the other names for astral projection — astral travel, remote viewing, etheric projection — they're all terms to try to explain how deeply we access that plane although their distinctions depend completely on who's describing them. When I astral project, I guess I tap into it, but I don't think I've ever really existed or hung out on that plane. At least, I've never been aware of a separate timeless dimension outside of our physical plane. Time doesn't change when I project. I can travel instantly to anywhere on earth, but it's still in my physical world and time. I think precognition taps into the astral plane as well but in a way that exploits the timelessness of it. As to the scientific nature of these abilities, I don't want to get into my undergraduate thesis, but we hypothesized that a specific quantum event was common to both abilities, but we couldn't prove it."

We entertained each other with some of the silly dreams and visions we'd experienced. "Mine mostly seem like a waste of psychic energy," I said. "Although their visions are more vague and symbolic, my mom and grandma only see the future when someone they love is in trouble or experiencing a life-changing event. While my visions are clear scenes of an actual future, most have been trivial. This ability is useless if it doesn't help me protect people, especially my friends and family."

Nate smiled at me and squeezed my hand. "You're a good person, Sophia."

After we passed the seven-mile mark, we found an inviting spot to sit, and Nate pulled out a blanket and a picnic lunch from his backpack. His planning, his thoughtfulness, and the tasty lunch impressed me. As we ate, we absorbed the environment and took pleasure in watching a majestic red-tailed hawk soar high above us, floating on a soft breeze of rising warm air.

On the return loop, we talked, laughed, and simply enjoyed the rest of our time together in the beautiful outdoors. Though part of me felt like we'd always known each other, each story we shared brought us closer still. I wanted to know everything about him.

As we drove back to my apartment, I grabbed Nate's hand. "That was great, Nate. Thanks for showing me one of your favorite hikes."

"It wasn't too long? You'd be up for doing this again?"

"Yes, as long as you promise to teach me about what we see."

"You're on. Do you mind if I shower at your apartment before I start cooking? My legs are covered with dust."

"I don't mind at all," I replied, hoping my poker face concealed my nerves. I raised my lower leg and saw a coating of dirt stuck to my sunscreen. "I see what you mean. I'm filthy as well."

When we returned to my apartment, I set Nate up with fresh towels in the guest bathroom. He didn't seem disappointed, and relief washed through me. I guess he didn't expect to share a shower after all. I went to my room and straightened it, hiding my birth control pills and some feminine items. I took a shower as well and changed into a cute, comfortable dress, with my nicest black lingerie underneath. I blew my hair dry just enough so the rest would air dry okay and painted on a little makeup.

When I came out to the living room, the smell of sautéed garlic filled the air. "Mmm, what are you making?" I asked.

"Just a simple soup," he replied.

"Garlic is one of my favorite smells. Is there anything I can do to help?"

"Would you mind slicing up the vegetables on the cutting board?" he asked.

"Not at all." I grabbed a knife and started chopping away. "I always do the cutting when I help my mom or my grandma cook. Grandma is a genius in the kitchen. She can make anything, and I swear you can taste the love in it. My mom's great too, but she didn't have time to cook much during the week with work. She outdid herself on the weekends, though. Thomas and I can cook fairly well, but it's been diluted through the generations. We don't enjoy it like they do, and since I live by myself, I lack the motivation to cook much more than breakfast on the weekends."

After about fifteen minutes, I finished chopping the vegetables and set the table. Nate then asked me to play a random selection of music from my iPhone. I suspected he was trying to gain some insight into my musical preferences. Putting my library on shuffle, I hoped he didn't scoff at my eclectic taste in music. I had some great bands from different eras, but I also had a lot of Broadway musicals and *Glee* remakes that I liked to sing.

When the music began, he insisted I simply relax while he cooked. He was definitely trying to pamper me. Though I didn't want to disturb his stirring, I couldn't resist giving him a kiss on the cheek. He dropped the spoon and yanked me back for a brief but more exciting kiss on the lips. I then fetched my book from the bedroom and lay down on the couch to read and watch Nate at home in my kitchen. I kept finding excuses to walk around the apartment so I could sneak over and hug him from behind. The smells, especially when he started making a sauce with pancetta, lured me there as well, but having a handsome man cook in my kitchen was downright irresistible.

An hour or so later, dinner was served, a vegetable soup and Bucatini all'Amatriciana. Nate topped it off by lighting a candle in the center of my small dining table.

"Everything smells amazing. Where did you learn to cook like this?"

"From my mom. She's a great cook and wanted to make sure her boys knew how."

"What a wise woman. I like her already." I tasted a sip of the soup and closed my eyes in obvious pleasure. "Nate, this is delicious. Is it your mom's recipe?"

"Thanks. No, the recipe is Sarah's. We used to cook together a lot. She's half-Italian, and her old family recipes are incredible. The soup and the sauce are hers," he said.

"Oh, that's nice," I replied. My smile felt a bit tight and the skin between my eyebrows crinkled a little. Tasting Sarah's soup, I knew I couldn't compete with her in this arena. I wasn't a bad cook, but I didn't like spending a lot of time in the kitchen. I felt a little insecure about this weakness since it had made me less domestically desirable with a past boyfriend.

"Does that really bother you?" Nate asked, amused.

"No, not really," I said, but in a stupid part of my brain, I was jealous.

"Your brow is furrowed."

I smoothed my forehead with my hand, and Nate laughed at me. I kicked him lightly under the table, making him laugh harder, and tried to put myself back in the moment. I tasted the pasta and closed my eyes again to savor it. "Mmm. Thank you so much for cooking. This is divine." Nate seemed satisfied with my obvious enjoyment. I did truly love eating delicious food.

After finishing off the tiramisu he'd brought that morning, we cleaned the dishes together. I washed. He dried.

"Sophia, I have a request," Nate said as he hung up the towel.

"Yeah?"

"Dance with me," he said, grabbing my hands and drawing me close.

My eyes locked onto his. "I'd love to."

As if on cue, the music switched to a remake of REO Speedwagon's "Can't fight this feeling," and we began to sway with the beat.

"How appropriate," he said.

Nate held me close for the most part, the heat building between us, but he still led me in a few moves in the confined space of my apartment. When he pulled me back to him after a turn, our eyes riveted on each other. Even as our bodies moved apart, the almost tangible connection in our eyes drew us back together. As the song progressed, the dancing became more sensual, like foreplay, his hands caressing my arms, my hips, my waist, but Nate's lips stayed at least a breath away from mine. I was mesmerized, so much that I barely noticed the music any longer. Suddenly, Nate leaned in for a kiss. His tongue skimmed my lips and then quickly possessed my mouth as he pulled me tight against him. A burn radiated down from my belly button, and passion erupted in me. I kissed him back hungrily, starved for him, unable to keep my desire suppressed any longer.

"God, Sophia," Nate murmured.

We clung to each other as the heat between us exploded, our lips devouring. My skin came alive at every touch. Our bodies pressed closer and closer, molding against each other, fighting to meld. Nate began to trail luxurious kisses down and up my neck while his fingers tentatively lowered the zipper on the back of my dress. When I didn't protest, he unzipped it all the way, but held me so my dress stayed in place.

Nate kissed me beneath my ear, then whispered, "Sophia, please, *please*, say yes." The need in his words echoed throughout my body.

I didn't *say* yes, but I showed him. I stared deeply into his eyes, exposing my desire for him, kissed him deeply, and used his hands to slide my dress down my body. With his help I pulled his shirt up and over his head. His muscular shoulders and arms shuddered at my touch. Kissing my neck and collarbone, he unfastened my bra. I pulled the straps down my arms and dropped it on the floor. The cool air wafted over my breasts and sent a shiver down my spine. Nate stared at my breasts, hungry, then covered them with his large hands. He lightly touched the tip of my right breast. My breath hitched, and then he bent down to tease it with his tongue. My knees almost buckled. I had to put one arm against the wall to steady myself when he began to ravage my other breast.

Nate brought his lips back to my mouth and pulled me into him. The feel of his chest against my naked breasts was intoxicating. He was solid, strong, and emanated a heat my cool skin craved. His hands glided over my body and then clutched at my hips and butt, pressing me into him. I popped the top button of his pants and dipped two fingers into his waistband, when he suddenly lifted me up and carried me to my bedroom, kissing me voraciously. He set me on the bed and took off his pants and boxer briefs. I couldn't take my eyes off of him. He grabbed an item out of his pocket that put part of my mind at ease while the other part growled at the sight of him. He leaned over me and kissed me, sliding his hands along my hips and slowly pulling my panties down my legs. We finally lay down on the bed together with no impediments between us and kissed and touched in a frenzy. I couldn't get enough of his tongue, his lips, his hands, his body. I wanted everything. I felt him struggle to put the condom on without breaking our kiss, and I opened my legs for him. His fingers found my entrance and eased inside and out a few times, exploring me, stretching me. He then focused on my most sensitive area until my moan broke our kiss.

"Nate, now!" The last week had been like a bout of extended foreplay, and I couldn't wait any longer. He worked his way in slowly, helping my body adapt to the invasion. The feel of him inside me was overwhelming. I couldn't help but moan and arch my back. When he finally filled me completely, we began to move as one. I met him with my hips and tightened around him with each thrust. Our lips united with a fierceness and a desperation. The tension inside me was mounting again.

"Oh, Nate, don't stop," I cried as I nipped his ear. Our bodies fit together perfectly and beat together in an intensifying rhythm. As the sensations escalated, I began to pant and moan until he pushed me over the blissful edge. Nate, who'd been fighting himself for some time, finally let go and engaged me hard and fast. He cried out my name as he peaked, sending me up and over once more, and then relaxed with a deep sigh on top of me.

"Oh, Sophia," he said as he covered my face in kisses and rested his forehead against mine. I inhaled his scent as we caught our breath. I felt protected and deeply satisfied with his warm weight pushing me into the mattress, being as closely connected as we possibly could be. God, I didn't want him to leave my body. After a few minutes, he gave me another kiss, then pulled away to take care of the condom. I lay there, feeling somewhat bewildered and tingly all over. He climbed back onto the bed and nestled against my side, propping himself up on one elbow and dangling the other arm across my waist. He smiled at me and smoothed a lock of hair out of my face.

"What are you thinking?" he asked.

I smiled up at him, feeling like a sated cat. "Well . . . that I want you as close to me as possible right now. Would you spoon me?"

"Gladly," he replied. He moved to the other side of the bed and pulled my back against his heated chest. I sighed and felt what little tension I had left ebb away. I rubbed my hands along his arms and asked him what he was thinking.

"That being with you was better than I imagined."

"Ah, Nate," I turned my head and kissed him.

"Can I tell you about a happy dream I had years ago?" Nate asked as he moved my hair so he could nuzzle my neck.

"Please do," I replied and burrowed myself more deeply into him.

"About two weeks after we met, I had a precognitive dream of us making love."

"What?" I turned again to see his face. "You dreamed of tonight all those years ago?"

"Actually, no. The dream I had hasn't happened yet. What makes me even happier is that the dream tells me we'll probably be doing this again under different circumstances."

"You didn't think I was a one-night stand sort of girl, did you?" I teased, elbowing him.

"Of course not, but I do know that you're guarded now and sometimes push people away. I have a small fear that you'll run for the hills once we get out in the light of day."

I turned, placed my hands on his cheeks and stared into his eyes. "I'm not going anywhere. I definitely want to make love with you again. In fact . . ." I raised my eyebrow at him.

"Give me a few more minutes," he laughed, "and I'm sure I'll rise to the occasion."

"I can help," I smiled. I pushed him onto his back and started kissing down his neck to his chest. His nipples were taut, and I teased them with my tongue. As I kissed and nipped down his stomach, he stirred again. I pretended not to notice. Since oral sex was out of the question until I knew he had no diseases, I kissed his thigh, squeezed my hand over his shaft, and lightly palmed his testicles. Nate grabbed my hands and flipped me over. Though his eyes looked like he was possessed, he kissed me slowly and luxuriously while caressing the tips of my breasts. I lost myself in that kiss. Eventually, his left hand reached away, fumbling for something at the edge of his grasp. Another condom. It warmed my heart that I didn't have to say anything to convince him to use one.

Nate traced circles on my stomach, then my thighs, before settling in the middle. He lingered there until I arched involuntarily, pressing my body against his hand. Nate felt my aching and joined me. He took his sweet time and made our lovemaking last until I was incoherent at the cusp. His control at last abandoned him, and he powerfully brought us both to completion.

* * *

Ahh. I was so relaxed that my legs seemed boneless. Nate snuggled me from behind. I felt cherished, wanted, loved. A smile spread across my face as my eyes closed.

After dozing for a bit, my eyes opened to Nate caressing my hips and then my breasts, cupping them in his strong hands. He seemed fascinated with my body. He turned me onto my back and stared as if trying to memorize me.

"You have the most beautiful breasts I've ever seen." His comment made me blush, and I tried to shield myself with my arms. He seemed amused by my shyness. "After what we've done, *that* embarrasses you?"

I let him move my arms to the side. "Yeah . . . I'm not sure why, but flattery and being scrutinized have always made me uncomfortable. I do appreciate the compliment, though. They're one of my favorite body parts too," I said with mock innocence.

Nate laughed and kissed my chest, rubbing his cheek against me. "Mmm, your skin's so soft. I love that a woman's skin is so much softer than a man's. Why is it that?"

"I don't know," I said, starting to feel a bit unsettled. This remark and the comparative breast comment were leading me to believe that he'd had loads of sexual encounters. He certainly showed expertise. I couldn't let it slide. "You keep comparing me to other women. Have you had so many?"

"What?" he asked, his body tensing.

"That many?" I challenged, analyzing his face.

"Not too many, no, but a conversation like this never leads anywhere good."

I frowned a little but decided to switch to a more practical subject that was never easy to broach.

"Nate, I just started taking the pill, and it should be effective in about a week. I see us," I touched his chest and motioned back to mine, "going somewhere serious. I'd love to be able to ditch the condoms with you, but I need to know you don't have any STDs first. I was clean for everything two months ago and haven't been with anyone in over six months. When were you last tested?"

"A few years ago, but I should be fine," he said. "I haven't been with anyone since Sarah and I broke up in July. I know her doctor tested her while we were together, and she didn't have anything, but I'll get tested soon. Hey," he grabbed my hand and entwined it with his, "I'm glad you're cautious because you should protect yourself, and by doing that you've also protected me. I see us going somewhere serious too." He leaned in to gently kiss my lips then smoothed my hair off my cheek as he looked into my eyes. "The idea that I could jump you anytime, any place without having to worry about condoms is more than appealing."

Hearing him talk about jumping me made my toes curl. *But how many others had he 'jumped'?*

"Nate, how many women have you been with?"

"Do you really want to talk about this?"

"I think I do." I kept visualizing the many attractive, buxom women he'd dated in college. With his good looks and the fact that he played on the UCSD soccer team, women flocked to him. Okay, maybe part of me didn't want to know, but his resistance to telling me his history made me suspicious.

"Sophia," he said somewhat sheepishly. "I don't know what your expectations are, and I don't want to disappoint you. I'm sure I've slept with more people than you have."

I didn't say anything. I wasn't sure what I was feeling at that moment. Disappointed? Jealous? Nate stared intently at me in the silence, sighed heavily, and then said, "Fine. Let's get it out in the open because you're probably imagining my experience to be worse than it is." I looked at him expectantly, and he continued. "I've been with sixteen other women. The first was a girlfriend in high school, eleven were in college and four were in the last three years. It's not that many compared to most of my single friends. I had a one-night stand once and swore them off afterwards." I must have made a face. I didn't know what I was expecting, but that seemed like a large number to me. Nate kissed me on the nose. "Sophia, talk to me."

"Well, you're right, that's a lot more than me . . . but I guess it's not that many for a single, attractive twenty-five-year-old guy," I conceded.

"I'm not single anymore," he said and kissed me gently on the lips.

"What about you? How many men have you been with?"

"Three others. Brian was my first and then two since college."

"You said you'd never dated anyone from work, right?"

I nodded.

"That's good. I wouldn't want to lose my job if an old boyfriend looked at you the wrong way. Thinking of you with anyone else makes me feel kinda crazy."

Seeing him feel possessive of me made me smile.

"Brian was the only person I didn't always use a condom with. How many for you?"

"Just Sarah," he said.

I felt relieved. We had a difficult discussion behind us, and he was likely clean, but I didn't feel in the mood anymore, especially at his having mentioned Sarah a few times.

"Something's still bothering you. What's wrong?"

"I'm not sure. . . . I guess it's Sarah. You dated for a long time. You cooked with her and went to Hawaii with her. I think I'm jealous," I confessed.

Nate smiled, dipping his head to peck my lips. "You have no reason to be jealous. Do you know why I came back to San Diego?"

"You needed a job."

"True, but that wasn't the real reason I returned. I came back to San Diego and specifically chose to work at SDCC to reconnect with you again. I felt something for you from the moment we met, and I had to find out if we'd ever work as a couple before it was too late. Watching Brian plan his wedding made me anxious that you might be doing the same thing. You weren't on social media, and I didn't have your new email or cell phone number. I didn't have a way to track you down except that I knew you worked here. When I asked about you in the phone interview, they told me you were their most productive projector and that their main reason for wanting to hire me was that you were overworked. The fact that you worked all the time gave me hope that you were still single, but if I hadn't tried and you'd married someone,

I would have always regretted not taking the chance."

My heart ached at his words. I framed his face with my hands and looked in his eyes. I couldn't understand how I'd made such an impression on him. He'd cared about me for years and had never stopped. My mood took a definite turn.

"Thank you for not giving up on me, Nate. I'm very happy you're here with me."

I wrapped my arms around him, pulled my body closer and kissed him. As I kissed him, I felt like my body was floating. My entire existence centered around that kiss. Nate kissed me back with an escalating intensity until I could feel him becoming hard against my thigh.

He broke away to reach over the side of the bed for a condom. After putting it on, he whispered in my ear, "Would you mind being on top? I want to watch you and feel you above me."

I kissed him and smiled. Taking all of him inside of me, I gazed down into his eyes. I *knew* him. I *had always known* those kind eyes. Memories flashed back to me . . . the first time I saw him in class, the moment we realized we shared the same special abilities, thinking how lucky the girl who captured his heart would be and how the women he dated were never good enough for him. After another satisfying release for both of us, I collapsed on him and rested on his chest. "You're going to stay with me tonight, aren't you?" I asked.

Nate kissed my head and sighed. "You couldn't force me to leave if you tried."

We prepared for sleep, and of course, I took longer than he did. By the time I returned to bed, he was starting to nod off. I put my iPhone on the nightstand and snuggled into bed in front of him. He wrapped his body around mine and kissed my temple.

"Goodnight, Sophia."

"Goodnight."

CHAPTER SEVEN

I awoke the next morning to dappled sunlight and a ticklish feeling on my arm. Nate was very gently tracing two fingers across it. "Good morning, sleepyhead."

"Good morning." I yawned and stretched. "What time is it?"

"Just after nine."

"I hope you weren't waiting long for me to wake."

"No, not long. You looked like a slumbering angel with your long hair tumbling over the pillow." He pulled me close and kissed my neck.

"I could get used to this," I said.

"I hope you do."

My senses were awakening, but I had a question on my mind. "Uh, Nate, I was thinking about your dream of us. Do you think it's still in the future or do you think it was a past that never came to be? Did we look more like we do now or like we did in college?"

"I can't say for sure. We haven't changed that much," he said. "The dream's also become hazy over the years, but I do remember that you weren't wearing a dress. You had on a black long-sleeved shirt and black jeans. Do you own either of those?"

"Yes, but I've owned them both since high school so that doesn't help."

"The day after I had this dream, you met and started dating Brian. That practically drove me mad, especially since I'd introduced you. Fate seemed cruel."

"Maybe Brian was an unexpected force that altered the course of events. Maybe that dream was our future until he came into my life.

Nate, I'm so sorry. I had no idea you thought of me as anything more than a friend. Brian was so outgoing and persistent that he easily broke through my defenses. If it makes you feel any better, I never should have dated him. That was doomed to fail before it began. I was simply too unaware and juiced up on hormones to realize it at the time."

He ran his hands down my sides and started tracing circles on my stomach. "Speaking of being juiced up on hormones . . ." and he kissed me. His lips and tongue were soft but relentless. I wanted him, wanted him so badly I could feel it in my toes. I wrapped my legs around him as I suddenly remembered an important detail.

"Uh, Nate, do you have another condom?"

"Sadly, no," he grumbled. "Of all the planning, *this* is where I screw up. I thought I had more. I could kick myself."

"Shh," I said. "I should have bought some too." I kissed his forehead and eyelids to slow us down, and moved his head to rest on my chest, his hair against my chin, his body half on top of me. I ran my fingers through his thick hair and settled my heartbeat.

"Mmm. I'm so turned on right now," he said, caressing my body with his. "Would you like me to pick up some breakfast?"

"What?" I laughed at the non sequitur.

"I plan on making a side trip to pick up something else as well," he grinned.

"Not yet. I don't want your body to leave mine."

Nate took a deep breath to calm himself and closed his eyes, a smile on his lips. I kissed the top of his head and continued to finger-comb his hair while lightly scratching his shoulder and arm with my other hand. Holding him felt right, so right. I dozed off for a bit, but my head falling to the side jerked me back awake. Nate wasn't sleepy as the hardness against my leg testified. He lightly tickled my stomach and then my upper thighs. I started to ache for him again and had to intercept his hand.

"As wonderful as this is, we do have an errand to run." I looked him straight in the eye. "I want you inside me again." I think he didn't breathe for a second. He certainly didn't blink. As soon as he recovered, his lips slammed into mine.

When he came up for air, he said, "Let me go alone. I can't bear the thought of you putting your clothes on. Stay here. Keep the bed warm. I'll grab some breakfast as well and hurry back."

"Okay, but take my keys."

He stumbled into his clothes, gave me a hasty kiss, and ran out the door like lightning.

I lay there in bed for a while staring at the ceiling. I felt so good, so happy, so satisfied. It had been a long time since I'd felt this wonderful that I almost couldn't recall having ever felt this way before. I tried to remember back to the early part of my relationship with Brian, especially when the hormones were raging. I knew I'd felt something like this then, but it seemed distant and vaguely unreal. I was impatient for Nate to return.

Since I had to pee, I couldn't stay in bed the whole time like he'd requested. I used the opportunity to brush my teeth and hair and primp a little, but I rushed back to bed so he wouldn't be disappointed. I was certain I didn't dream last night, but I checked my iPhone anyway. No dreams . . . again. *What was going on?* The minutes ticked away slowly. I picked up my book and read the same line over and over again until I finally heard Nate unlock the door. I quickly laid the book down and tried to look luscious though I wasn't exactly sure what that entailed.

He came in with three bags, four drinks, and a single rose. The first bag probably held enough breakfast for four people. The second carried croissants and other baked goods, and the third bag contained the real reason for the trip.

"I see you come bearing gifts. Mmm. Something smells delicious. I didn't realize how hungry I was until the aroma hit me. Let's eat in bed."

"I bought a tea for you, a coffee for me, and two orange juices. Would you prefer something else to drink?"

"No, that's perfect for now, but I think you might be a bit overdressed for breakfast."

He laughed at me and stripped off his clothes. We ate in bed, naked as jaybirds, snuggling under the covers together, munching on egg sandwiches.

After we finished eating, we were licking each other's fingers when my world crumbled.

Harry's sitting in his office at UC San Diego. His face looks like an expressionless mask. His muscles are twitching. Sweat beads on his forehead. He looks like he's straining. It seems like somehow he's being forced to remain absolutely still, and he's trying to resist. A hand in black leather then comes into view, places a gun into his mouth and fires.

"Nooo!" I screamed. Tears ran down my face.

"Sophia, what's wrong?" Nate shook me a little to snap me out of my vision.

"Harry! We have to call Harry! There may still be time." I staggered out of bed to my phone and dialed. No answer. I called again. No answer, straight to voicemail. "Harry, get out of your office! Someone's trying to kill you, someone who can control minds. He'll shoot you in the head if you don't get out of there!" I screamed. I called Irene and at the same time texted Harry that someone was coming to kill him in his office, that he had to get away.

"Hello, Sophia," she said, her voice cheerful.

"Harry's in danger! Someone's trying to kill him!" The words tumbled out of my mouth like a waterfall.

"What? You have seen something!?"

"Get him out of his office! I tried his cell. He's not answering," I sobbed.

She didn't hesitate to believe me and spoke quickly. "I will call his direct line. If he does not answer, I will drive straight there. Call campus police."

I dialed campus police and told them they needed to check on

Professor Harry Reed in his office because his wife thought he'd had a heart attack. I said she was on her way but was afraid she wouldn't make it in time. I knew they wouldn't have taken me seriously if I'd said I'd had a vision of him being shot, and I had to get them there quickly. Nate was putting on his clothes and watching me with sincere concern. I closed my eyes to contact Thomas to see if he could communicate with Harry. Nothing happened. I started to panic but reminded myself that Thomas sometimes ignored my tapping at inopportune moments. I hoped to God he was okay, but if he were hurt, I'd know.

"I can't reach Thomas. Can you drive me to Harry's office?" I asked. My hands and legs were shaking, and the tears were still streaming down my face. "I can't drive like this, and I need to project to his office. I need to know if he's okay."

"Of course, let's get you dressed and go," he said. I hadn't even realized I was still naked.

As I threw on a shirt and pants, I described the vision to him. His eyes lost their shine, but he reminded me that it might not have happened yet. I tried to cling to that hope. While Nate drove, I closed my eyes and tried to project. Again, nothing happened. I tried once more with the same result. "What is wrong with me? What the hell is going on?" I screamed.

I called Harry, Irene and Thomas on their cell phones several times, but no one answered. *Dammit!* When we arrived at Harry's building, two empty campus police cars and Irene's car were already out front. My chest became tight, and the tears burned down my face when I saw them. There weren't any police lines to keep us out and the front doors were unlocked so we ran inside the building and took the elevator up to his floor. When the doors opened, a gun pointed at us, and I saw Irene sitting against the wall, collapsed on the floor in a muddle of shock and grief.

"What's your business here?" the officer with the gun demanded.

"We're here for her," I said, fighting back tears, and pointed to Irene. "I'm the one who called you and asked you to check on Dr. Reed."

"Stay here with her and don't move or call anyone," he said. "I have two officers combing through the building for suspects or witnesses. The paramedics and San Diego police are on their way. I'm afraid your friend didn't have a heart attack." He gave me an angry and suspicious look.

I sat down with Irene and put my arm around her. She was trembling. "Harry is dead, and they will not let me see him." Her silent tears gave way to huge sobs.

Nate was able to project to the office only yards away and told me that it looked like Harry had experienced what I'd envisioned. I had to see for myself and tried to project again, but something was still blocking me. *God dammit!* I just realized then that if I'd driven instead, Nate could have projected from the car and might have been able to see the killer.

It wasn't long before the San Diego police and paramedics arrived. They collected our separate statements, including our personal information, the details of our arrival at the scene, and which cars outside were ours. I also told them about my vision and about my ruse to get the campus police to come. I could tell they didn't know what to think of my story. The crime scene was starting to bustle with people. They'd rounded up the few graduate students in the building on a Sunday and were noting their personal information and taking statements from them. Apparently, no one had heard or seen anything unusual. The paramedics took their leave after about thirty minutes. They confirmed Harry's death, and the medical examiner was on the way. Irene took a deep breath and didn't want to be held anymore.

She walked over to the officers. "I have to see my husband."

"I'm sorry, Mrs. Reed, but we can't let you in there. We've already explained this to you."

Irene turned to look at me with pleading eyes, hoping I could help convince him.

I walked over to the officer. He'd already placed himself far from Irene. "Please, let her see him," I begged. "She needs to see what happened to him. She needs to say goodbye."

"I'm sorry. It's against police procedure, but trust me, she doesn't want to see him right now. I need the three of you to go downtown to give your statements again, anyway, and it's best that she leaves this place. We can have a patrol car drive or escort you to the station. Your boyfriend seems like he's stable enough to drive, but not you or Mrs. Reed. Would you mind conveying this information to her for me? She'll take it better from you."

I told Irene the situation and that it was time to go. I rode in the back seat of the car with her while Nate drove us to the station. She stared out the window and didn't cry or say a word. She merely sat there with her hands folded in her lap in her usual perfect posture. I tried not to watch her too closely. I wasn't sure what I could possibly do to help her. Suddenly, Thomas flooded into my head.

"Sophia, what's happened . . . Oh my God." He'd read my jumbled thoughts before I could focus a statement towards him.

"Oh my God," he thought again. *"I had a feeling something wasn't right. I've been trying to contact you for the last several minutes, and you just weren't there. I had to be more forceful to get through to you. My God, Harry. . . . Poor Irene. What can I do?"*

"Could you drive down to the main police station? We're headed there for interviews."

"I'm driving back from LA, but I'm not far from San Diego. I'll head straight there."

When we arrived at the station, a seasoned officer and a young man that looked like a college student brought Irene to one room for questioning and placed me in another. Nate waited his turn out in the hallway.

While I waited for my interview with the officers, I tried again to project to Harry's office. This time it worked. They hadn't yet moved his body . . . the blood, his destroyed head, those sightless eyes. *Oh, Harry.* I was back in my vision, seeing him alive and resisting in one second, and an empty vessel in the next with precious parts of him scattered across the room. *So fast. How could everything change so fast?* I couldn't wrap my small mind around the fact that life could be over in an instant. It didn't seem possible. Harry was there, and then he wasn't. Seeing him like that was so wrong . . . the carnage offended me on a primal level. Some part of me wanted to gather everything up to see if I could put him back together again. No one should ever see a loved one in such a state. No one should ever see a loved one die and be unable to stop it. This vision of Harry would haunt me for the rest of my life. Tears ran down my face, with no end in sight.

I was jarred from my internal thoughts when I heard the detective and medical examiner on scene discussing whether it was more likely I'd had a vision or that I was involved in killing him since the description I gave them matched the scene. *What the fuck?* My pulse began to thud in my temple, but they decided in the end that I'd probably had a vision since I was a verified psychic who used her psychic abilities in a professional capacity.

"Didn't do him much good, though," the medical examiner remarked.

I flinched. No, it hadn't. I had failed him.

I said my last goodbye to dear Harry in that office and came back to the interview room. I wished I could tell him how sorry I was, so sorry I wasn't able to help him. Tears continued to pour down my cheeks as I watched the minutes tick away. I stared at the door, the ceiling, the table. I started to feel numb. The tears lessened. I then heard a light tapping at my shields, and Thomas let me know he was waiting outside with Nate. *Thank goodness.*

After what seemed like an infinity of time, the officer and the young man came in and sat across from me.

"Hello, Miss Walsh. I'm Detective Jones, and this is Mr. Schwartz, a consultant. I'm sorry about your loss and the wait, but we needed to take your statement ourselves. First, I'd like to confirm a few details. Your name is Sophia Walsh, age twenty-five, UCSD graduate, former student and close friend of Professor Harold Reed."

"That's correct," I said. Schwartz was staring at me intently, like he was trying to will something out of me.

I realized what was going on and looked at him. "You're a telepath, aren't you?" I asked.

He glanced at Jones, who nodded to him. "Actually, I'm an empath with weak telepathic abilities, but I'm getting nothing from you. I can usually sense feelings and emotions clearly. I can hear pieces of actual thoughts if I'm really lucky. Do you have telepathic shields? I've never met anyone with shields like yours."

"Yes, I do. My twin brother's a telepath, and I learned to shield years ago. If you want, I can lower them during the questioning. I have nothing to hide." I closed my eyes and removed my shields. "I'm a weak telepath as well so you might be able to get more than just feelings from me. Ask away," I said.

"Miss Walsh, could you please tell us how you came to be at the crime scene today?" Detective Jones asked. He apparently would do the questioning while Mr. Schwartz listened.

"My boyfriend and I were at my apartment. We were just finishing breakfast when I had a vision of Harry being murdered." I described the vision in as much detail as possible, recounted the phone calls, explained the lie I told to campus security, and finished with our exit from the elevator. Schwartz asked me to recall the vision as slowly as possible so he could try to see what I saw. It wasn't pleasant, reliving it over and over, but I did as he asked. They asked me about my psychic abilities, my work at SDCC, and my relationship with Harry as a student, mentee, and friend.

"Is there anything else you can tell us? The crime scene is still being analyzed, but there appears to be no overt evidence of a second party. On the surface, it looks like a suicide."

At the mention of them potentially ruling it a suicide, my jaw clenched, and tears started to track down my face again. "I saw him murdered. It happened! Harry would never commit suicide. He's one of the happiest, most content people I know. God, he would never do that to Irene! My brother, Thomas, the telepath I told you about, can verify that Harry wasn't depressed or suicidal. He's outside in the waiting area if you'd like to speak with him." After saying my piece on that, I thought back to my final conversation with Harry.

"I last spoke to Harry on Friday at Irene's exhibition opening. He looked tired and was concerned that neither of us had been dreaming lately. Harry and I have occasional precognitive dreams and visions so we pay close attention to them. I normally have about three dreams a night, and Harry's number is . . . was similar." I started choking up and had to pause for a few moments. "We both had an uneasy feeling that something wasn't right. I think now that it's possible someone was interfering with our dreams intentionally."

"Why would someone interfere with your dreams?"

"I have no idea . . . but maybe since we both possess a precognitive ability, they were trying to prevent us from foreseeing his murder. The murderer must have known about what we can do and didn't want us to stop him."

"That seems a bit far-fetched. How can someone prevent your visions or dreams from happening?" asked Detective Jones.

"I don't know."

"If you have a vision, can you change it? Can you change the future or prevent a vision from happening?"

"Well, anyone can try, and if you know what to do enough in advance, sometimes you'll succeed. Unfortunately, this wasn't one of those times." My jaw quivered and more tears ran down my face. I couldn't speak for a few moments.

I was trying to collect myself when a thought came to me. "When I first had the vision about Harry, I couldn't astral project or telepathically communicate with my brother. It wasn't until Thomas pushed his way into my head about an hour ago that I was able to project again. It felt like something had trapped me in my head. Stress and depression can diminish psychic abilities, but they don't usually stop them completely. I think whoever prevented Harry and me from dreaming, prevented me from being able to use my other abilities today too." Detective Jones tapped his pen on his pad of paper. He wasn't sure what to make of my ideas.

"Why would anyone want to murder Harry?" Jones asked.

"I don't know. He was loved by his students and was a kind and caring man. Harry had a prestigious academic career and was about to finish another book. Though I think some religious-right activists don't like that he teaches about and promotes psychic abilities, I can't imagine why anyone would hurt him."

They didn't have any more questions for me, but I had a small one for them.

"Not that I care much at the moment, but is it legal to have an empath in questioning without the interviewee knowing?"

"For now, yes, although the testimony of psychically acquired information holds no weight in court. But, on the job, the information an empath or telepath gives us is invaluable. He can easily distinguish between true suspects and unfortunate bystanders and those telling the truth from those covering something up. We waste a lot of time and resources following useless leads. We're lucky to have Schwartz consult with us right now. His father's a cop, and he wanted to make some extra money while going to college. Sadly, once he graduates from SDSU and decides what he wants to do full-time, I can't imagine we'll be able to afford him."

Schwartz grinned sheepishly at Detective Jones.

"Well, thank you for your time, Miss Walsh. We appreciate your coming downtown to talk with us. If we have any further questions, we'll contact you. If you think of anything that might be useful, or have another vision, here's my card. Be careful and call anytime."

When I went out into the hallway, they closed the door behind me. Nate was sitting patiently with his head leaning back against the wall, looking up at the ceiling. When he saw me, he walked over and surrounded me with his arms. I needed that hug. I needed him. His warm embrace gave me comfort and helped replenish my waning strength. I held on to him with no foreseeable intention of letting go. He kissed the top of my head and brushed my hair out of my face. "How'd it go?"

"Not bad," I sighed. "Schwartz is an empath and a weak telepath, but don't worry. I think it's helpful because he knows we're telling the truth."

"That's interesting." He pulled back to look into my swollen eyes and cupped my face with his hands. His thumbs caressed my cheekbones. "Thomas just took Irene home. She'd like for you to stay with her. I can bring you there when we finish."

"How's she doing?"

"Not well. Her face looked like stone. She was showing zero emotion. She's a strong lady, but she's suffering and in shock, I'd guess."

Just then, the door opened and Detective Jones asked Nate to speak with them. He kissed me on the cheek, squeezed my hand, and went in. Although I felt numb, I couldn't sit. I paced the hallway impatiently. I didn't want to be there any longer. I looked at my cell phone to see if I had any voice or text messages. None, but I needed to talk to Diana and figured I should give her the bad news. She answered after three rings, and I started crying the moment I heard her voice.

"Sophia, what's wrong?" she asked.

I told her everything. She couldn't believe it. "So, whoever killed him tried to make it look like a suicide?" she asked.

"Apparently."

"God, I'm so sorry, Sophia. Poor Irene. How can I help?"

"I don't know, but if I think of anything, I'll call you."

A bit later, Nate came out, and the police cleared us to leave. When we arrived at Irene's house, I could see that a breakdown was imminent. Irene became frantic that her car had been left in a tow away zone in front of Harry's building. I convinced her to give me her keys and told her that Nate and Thomas would bring her car back. We all offered to stay at her house, but she only wanted me. Thomas and Nate gently pointed out that it might be prudent if one of them stayed as well, seeing that the murderer hadn't been found. Irene agreed that Thomas could stay if he didn't read her thoughts. I made her lie down in her room and told her I'd be back with something to eat and drink.

I closed the door and went to Nate and Thomas in the living room.

"Thomas and I are leaving to get her car. I called Detective Jones, and he said it'd be okay to retrieve it. Would you like me to pick up anything from your apartment?" Nate asked.

"Yes, please." I quickly mentioned what I needed and handed him my keys, rising up on my tiptoes to kiss him goodbye.

After locking the door behind them, I made Irene some chamomile tea and toast with almond butter. I doubted she'd want to eat anything, but I wanted her to have something in case she felt up to it. I certainly had no appetite. I brought the tray to Irene and saw her lying on her side, tears quietly trickling down her face. It was impossible to watch her and not cry, but I tried to remain as silent as possible in order to avoid upsetting her more. I sat behind her on the bed and rubbed her back. "I brought some tea. You should drink it once it cools a bit. If there's anything you want or need, please let me know. If you want complete privacy, I won't be offended. I'm here to help you in any way I can."

"Tell me everything you saw, Sophia. I have to know what happened to Harry." I inhaled a deep breath and described my vision. I mentioned that Thomas might be able to send her the images from my mind if that's what she really wanted, but she shook her head.

"Just stay here with me for now," she whispered when I'd finished.

We rested for about thirty minutes before I heard Thomas softly tapping at my shields, letting me know he was at the front door.

"Thomas is here with your car. I'm going to let him in," I said.

She gave a slight nod. By the time I returned to her room, Irene had decided she wanted to try to sleep or at least lie more comfortably and was taking out her pajamas.

"You and Thomas are welcome to sleep in the guest bedroom or the bed in the office tonight. Make yourselves at home."

"If you need anything, Irene, at any time, get me."

"I will."

When I walked into the living room, Thomas was sitting on the couch reading on his iPhone. He was researching the stages of bereavement and trying to learn what we could do to help Irene. We were out of our league, having never suffered a personal loss like this before. We also didn't want to impose on her. She had other friends she might prefer to help her over us.

Harry had a brother in the Midwest, but Irene didn't have any family in the States, only a sister in China. We figured they'd have to be told soon, but it didn't seem like Irene was ready yet. As soon as people went to work in the morning, Harry's entire department would find out, if they hadn't already heard about it on the news. The barrage of visits and phone calls would then begin for Irene.

Thomas decided to call our mom. She was a psychiatrist at the University of California, San Francisco, and although she technically wasn't a therapist, she'd have good advice. As he talked with her, Nate arrived with my things and some takeout for an early dinner. I was so glad to see him that I wrapped my arms around him before he had a chance to put the bags down.

"I missed you," I said.

"Likewise." He kissed the top of my head. "Where do you want me to put your things?"

"Let's put them in the guest bedroom."

When we got to the room, I closed the door and looked at him, feeling my strength on the verge of crumbling. "Nate, will you just hold me for a little while?"

"That's all I've wanted to do, but I shouldn't stay long. We need to respect Irene's wishes."

I nestled into his arms on the bed, not wanting to talk or think. After a while, Nate broke the silence. "Sophia, how are you doing? I can't imagine how I'd feel in your situation. Talk to me."

"I don't know." I took a deep breath. "I don't want to close my eyes because I'm afraid of seeing the vision again or seeing Harry's lifeless face. Maybe sleeping is safe since I haven't been dreaming lately, but I don't know that I can."

"You need to try," he said.

"The worst," I said, as my voice started to crack, "is that I failed Harry. I couldn't help him. I've been keeping track of my dreams and visions for years so that I could help people. I failed him." The threads of sanity that had been holding me together began to fray, and I broke into deep sobs. Nate smoothed my hair back, kissed my temple, and squeezed me tightly while my shoulders shook.

"Sophia, you did everything you could. You're here helping his wife through the most difficult event of her life. You didn't fail him. He'd be thankful and proud of you."

I took several steadying breaths and tried to pull myself together. "We have to find out who did this to him and why. I can't stand the thought that his death might be ruled a suicide."

"What do you propose we do?" Nate asked.

"I don't know, but I know there's more here than meets the eye. I can feel it in my bones. He was murdered, and whoever murdered him also interfered with my abilities. Maybe it was only to get at Harry, but maybe I'm next."

Nate's arms flinched around me. "What?" I could almost hear Nate's brain working overtime. "It's natural to be shaken and even paranoid after someone's murdered, but you're jumping to conclusions. Why on earth would anyone target you?" He was trying to sound reassuring, but I could tell there was a trace of worry in his voice.

"You're probably right, but why would anyone target Harry? Let's go talk to Thomas and see what he thinks."

We brought the bag of burritos to the kitchen table and shared my concerns with Thomas. He basically gave me the same response as Nate and thought I was overreacting. Again, I felt like he was trying to convince himself as much as me. I still wasn't hungry but watching Nate and Thomas dig into their burritos made me want to try eating too.

"Okay, maybe I'm not at risk, but we've got to do something," I insisted. I unwrapped the paper and foil around the top of the burrito and took a small bite.

"What can we do? We're not investigators, and it's illegal to interfere with the police investigation. Honestly, I wouldn't have the slightest idea where to start. We can, of course, be hyper-vigilant of our own safety, and especially yours. I could try to scan areas specifically around you for malicious intent every so often, but I can't scan 24/7," Thomas said.

"I know what we can do. Maybe I'm not the next target, but how did they find out about me or my abilities? They must have had Harry under surveillance. Maybe we can find some bugs."

"I'll see if the internet can tell us how," Nate said and pulled out his phone.

"The police department will know how to do it," I said.

"But to them this appears to be a suicide. Why would they bother?" Thomas asked.

"It can't hurt to ask them to look at the crime scene. I think the police believe my vision or at least believe that I think it was real. They might humor me."

I called Detective Jones and begged him to check for surveillance equipment. After he gave me several reasons not to do so, Thomas used some mental persuasion and the detective finally relented.

"Well," Nate said while reading from his phone, "it says here that you need special equipment and that you should never mention your intention to look for bugs in a suspected area. Apparently, the more sophisticated surveillance transmitters can be turned off remotely. So, if the murderer has the most expensive stuff and this house or your cell is under surveillance, then we'll probably never find them because they've just been turned off."

"That bites," I said, "but isn't there a physical piece of electronics they can find?"

"Yes, but it could be the size of a needle's point. If the police are only scanning for a transmission signal and not physically looking, we could be out of luck. But, again, maybe the bugs can't be turned off remotely. It depends. If the killer had significant resources, it might be impossible to find the physical bug, but if lower-end models were used, the police might find them."

I frowned. I couldn't think of anything else we could do to find the killer right now. I wondered if Irene knew whether something Harry was doing or writing about in his book might have made him a target. I couldn't imagine raising this subject with her right now, although I hoped the police had asked.

"I better get going," Nate said. We walked to the front porch and closed the door for some privacy. "I'll bring breakfast around 7:30. Do you need me to stay with you tomorrow? I want to help you."

"I know you do," I reached up to place my hands on his cheeks and a quick kiss on his lips. "Breakfast sounds great, but I'm sure Irene won't want much company tomorrow either. Besides, it probably isn't a good idea to take off work so soon after starting a new job."

After Nate went home, I left a message on Roger's voice mail to tell him I wouldn't be at work tomorrow, but to contact me in case of an emergency. I knew he wouldn't mind since I never took sick leave and had a lot of unused vacation time.

Irene hadn't stirred in her room. Thomas and I read and talked, waiting to see if she'd need us. Around ten o'clock, we decided to try to get some sleep though doubted we'd succeed. I snuggled under the covers and felt lonely without Nate. I yearned to feel his arms around me and really needed that extra security just then. I tossed and turned for what seemed like hours before eventually dozing off.

CHAPTER EIGHT

I blinked my eyes at the faint early morning light, not remembering where I was for a moment. When I realized that yesterday had truly happened, that Harry's murder wasn't a figment of my imagination, a fresh wave of grief hit me. The shock and horror passed through me again, and I cried until the tears ran out. Saying goodbye to Harry was like losing a father all over again. I scolded myself for my self-indulgence. *You're twenty-five, for God's sake. You shouldn't feel like an abandoned seven-year-old.*

I dressed for what would be a long and difficult day. I tiptoed by Irene's room, listening for any movement, but heard nothing. While I was making tea in the kitchen, Thomas came in with the Reeds' newspaper.

"It looks like the morning paper only has a small blurb about a professor dying from a gunshot wound at UCSD last night. There's no mention of Harry specifically. It's the same as what I found on the internet."

"Thank goodness for small favors."

"His name's going to come out soon. He's a well-known public figure, especially in the psychic world. The local media's going to play it up."

"Let's keep the TV off. Maybe the reporters will keep their coverage at UCSD and not come here. I hope Harry's address and phone number are unlisted."

"If they bother Irene here, I'll help them decide to leave." Thomas's usually handsome and kind face turned quite fierce. "Don't give me that look, Sophia. It helped you get your bug search last night. You know I don't usually do this." Thomas's outburst told me his nerves were ragged too, and behind his determination, I could see the strain and weariness.

"Sorry. I was just surprised. You're the most moral person I know. You give yourself more rules and ethical codes than a small country. And just so you know, I think persuading them to leave, if they come, is the right thing to do."

As we sat drinking our tea and scanning the newspaper, we heard a forceful knock at the front door. I looked out the side window and saw an officer from yesterday accompanied by two others. I opened the door.

"Good morning, Miss Walsh. I'm Officer Smith. We met at the crime scene."

"Yes, I remember you. Is everything alright?"

"Is Mrs. Reed awake? We found surveillance equipment in both Dr. Reed's office and car. We'd like to check the house and their other vehicle," he said.

"I'll get her. Come in."

I knocked on Irene's door. She didn't answer. I knocked harder and told her through the door what the police had found and why they were there.

"I will be right out," she called.

After a few minutes, she opened the door, tied her robe tightly and headed toward the front of the house.

"Good morning, Officers." Irene cut to the chase. "Do what you need to do. Let us know how we can help."

One officer started scanning the living room with a detector and the others began looking at any and all electronic devices they could find with large magnifying glasses. Thomas and I retreated back to the kitchen to get out of the way while Irene stayed to watch. Nate arrived with breakfast. He again brought much more than we could possibly eat, and it made me smile, reminding me of his special breakfast delivery just yesterday. With all that had happened, it seemed like ages ago.

"I guess they found some bugs?" he asked.

"Yup, and they're looking for more. Thanks for bringing breakfast." I put my arms around his waist and pecked his lips. "Good morning."

"Good morning, yourself," he said and smiled, but then his forehead crinkled with worry. "Did you get any sleep?"

"Some. I still had no dreams, and for once, it didn't bother me."

We ate in relative silence, straining to hear the goings-on of the search.

After only fifteen minutes, Nate had to leave for work. As I walked him out, he squeezed my hand. "I missed you last night. I know it's crazy, but after only one night together, it didn't feel right sleeping without you."

My stomach tightened, and a thrill spread throughout my body. "I missed you too."

When we were at his car, I kissed him lightly on the lips, but he wanted more and pulled me tightly against him. He reminded me that I was still alive. I'd been afraid that in the grief of the past day, any passion I had would be squashed forever, but it wasn't. I could feel his worry and his possessiveness in his kiss. He ached to make me feel better. If he didn't have to work, I don't think he'd let me go. Though my heart was hurting at the moment, the fire still burned between us. We ended the kiss and held each other.

"I'll call you before I leave work to see if you need me to pick up dinner."

"Sounds like a plan," I said. I waved goodbye as he backed out and smiled at myself, feeling like a 1950s housewife watching her husband drive off to work. As I walked back to the house, I noticed Irene watching me through the window. She smiled slightly and turned away. I felt awkward about her seeing me with Nate. I didn't want to make her miss Harry more, and I hoped it didn't seem like I was being disrespectful of Harry's memory by enjoying a moment with Nate.

When I returned to the house, Irene had joined Thomas in the kitchen. Her eyes were swollen, her face gaunt, but at least she was eating. Although you could tell she was a mess inside, having the police here doing something that might find the killer seemed to lift her spirits. I picked at a muffin and listened to the conversation. Irene was telling Thomas what she'd observed while watching the police. "I think they found something on our telephone, and they said they wanted to copy the hard drive from Harry's computer. They are making quite a mess. I will need you two to help me put the house back in order."

"Of course," Thomas said.

"Irene, are there family and friends you'd like us to call for you?" I asked.

She quietly considered for a moment. "Yes, but I need to call Harry's brother, Richard. He should hear the news from me. I have only my sister, Mei, and her family in China. I want to call her too, but no one else right now. I will make a list of friends with their numbers for you."

After breakfast, Irene made the list. Thomas and I split it up and created a discrete script to use as a reference for our phone calls. Irene didn't want anyone to know how Harry had died, only that he'd passed away suddenly yesterday. Thomas suggested that we determine when a funeral might take place before placing those calls. I talked to Officer Smith, who gave me an estimate for the release of Harry's body, and then worked up the courage to approach Irene.

A sketchpad lay on the bed next to her, with Harry's face smiling up at me. Irene was now flipping through a photo album with pictures of Harry and her in their early years. I started to turn around, but she looked up. "Sophia, do you need something?"

"Uh . . . not really . . . it can wait," I said.

"Ask me. Not much is going to be easy for quite a while."

I took a deep breath and began. "Well, before we make these phone calls, I thought we should know if you planned on having a funeral or ceremony of some sort for Harry. The police said that the coroner would be keeping Harry until his evaluation is complete, which could be as long as a week or two."

"Harry always wanted to be cremated and have his ashes scattered on the Pacific. Other than that, I do not think he had any preferences. What should we do?"

"Since you're not burying him, you could have the gathering whenever you prefer, if you want to have one. It would be nice to have a memorial service to celebrate Harry's life."

"Yes, we should do something, but nothing too formal, and I do not want to have it at my house."

"Would you prefer to have it sooner or later?"

"Sooner, I think."

"We could try to plan something for Friday. We should be able to make the arrangements by then."

"Sophia, I may be asking too much, but would you please plan the memorial? I am not in control of myself right now. I cannot handle it."

"I'd be honored to, but would you mind if I asked Diana for help? She's much better at organizing events than I am."

Irene was relieved at my suggestion and gave me a general budget and her credit card to cover the costs. She said she'd ask Harry's brother to conduct the memorial service and that a few of Harry's friends from the department might also want to say a few words. I brought her my list and she pointed out whom I should ask to speak.

"So, you've been drawing Harry?"

"Yes. I want to remember every moment." She picked up the sketchpad and turned it back to the first page. She had already made about fifty sketches.

"This was what Harry looked like when we met. He was very handsome then and so charming. He always radiated an aura of kindness."

"He was handsome."

"Yes, and so good, such a good man. Once I drew this picture, I started to draw other memories of him from significant moments. I drew all night long, but I started having a hard time remembering exactly how he looked at certain times so I grabbed this old photo album this morning." Her right hand reverently caressed the picture of their wedding day, as a tear ran down her cheek.

"I was lucky. We had a good life together." Her chin quivered, and she put her face in her hands. I wrapped my arms around her and held her while she shook and cried her heart out. After a while, she was emotionally spent and wanted to be alone again. When I left her, she was lying on the bed, thumbing through her photo album.

Thomas and I then began making the calls. I would have preferred any other task, maybe even some mild torture, to being the bearer of bad news. Afterwards, I called Diana and asked for her help. She suggested that we contact the Psychology Department because they might provide a venue and pitch in. She offered to take the helm planning the event as her way to honor Harry, and I consented and sincerely appreciated it.

The police officers had finished their search and brought us together to disclose their findings. They identified a bug on the house telephone and a lamp in the living room. They showed us what the bugs looked like and where they were hidden so we'd know how to check for ourselves. The bugs were so small that they almost looked like a tiny wire connected to a fleck of dust and were hard to distinguish from wires that were supposed to be there. They also found GPS trackers on both Thomas's and Irene's cars. These were square and a little smaller than the size of a quarter. Officer Smith claimed that they were all top-of-the-line.

"When we first checked Dr. Reed's office, the scanners didn't detect the bugs because the transmission signals were off. We thought that was the end of it, but after an officer discovered a pricey GPS tracker on Dr. Reed's car, we brought magnifying glasses into the office and finally found them on his office phone, cell phone, and laptop. Miss Walsh, we'll want to check your car as well and may need to check both of your apartments, cell phones, and laptops."

Irene, Thomas, and I looked at each other, blown away at finding ourselves in this situation. *Why were Harry, Irene and Thomas bugged?*

"Do you think we're in danger?" Thomas asked.

"I don't know. We have no idea what we're up against. Maybe it's a right-wing group targeting psychics or a crazed person with a grudge acting alone. We copied the hard drives of Harry's computers to look for clues. We'll check for spyware too, but Harry had the best antiviral and anti-spyware software commercially available. I doubt we'll find anything because our program isn't much better than his."

Not only did we have to deal with Harry's death, but my hands also trembled at the thought that the killer might not be finished. I hoped we could ensure our own safety somehow.

"What can we do to help?" Thomas asked.

"Keep your eyes open and be cautious. If you notice anything unusual or anyone suspicious, contact us immediately."

"We will. Thank you, officers," Irene said.

When the police left, Thomas, Irene and I stared at each other in silence, not sure what to make of the findings. Irene shook her head and then went to her room to call Harry's brother and her sister. I began to straighten up the house. When I was cleaning near Harry's piano, I felt compelled to play the last song I'd performed for him. I needed something to distract my mind.

Irene walked in and sat next to me. I stopped and looked up at her, concerned that hearing Harry's piano might upset her.

"Please keep playing," she said. I picked up where I left off and finished the piece.

"Thank you," Irene said. She looked off into her garden for a while. The hummingbirds were flitting around a flowery bush, unaware of the tragedy around them. "I saw you with Nate. He is sweet and loving to you. You both seem smitten with each other."

I blushed. "We've only been dating a little over a week, but it seems like much longer."

"Are you in love with him?"

"Oh, Irene . . . I don't know. . . . It's happened so fast that I haven't had a chance to put a label on it, but . . . I don't want to be apart from him, and having his arms around me feels right. I can even sense him when he enters a room without seeing him. So, yes, I think I'm falling in love with him, but we're in the 'everything is wonderful' euphoric stage. Whether it will be a love that lasts for months or years, I don't know. I told Brian that I loved him, but I may have been wrong about that."

"You were not wrong about Brian. I saw you with him. You loved him. I think it fell apart because you were not what the other needed, but it does not change the fact that you loved each other for a time. Sophia, you have been putting on a brave, happy face, but I know you have been lonely for the past three years. What you have with Nate may not last months or years, but embrace it. Never waste love. Life is too short."

I gave her a hug, and we held each other for a few minutes.

"Would you like some lunch?" I asked.

"Do not worry about me," she said. "I will lie down and try to sleep for an hour or two."

Thomas and I snacked on breakfast leftovers and educated ourselves on any and all appropriate topics on the internet. Thomas called a friend who's a savvy computer geek to see if he could find any sophisticated spyware on Harry's computer, and if so, what data they were tracking.

"Do you think the killer really set up the bugs? Or do you think it's possible that they're unrelated?" I asked him.

"I don't know. If we consider the principle of Occam's razor, the simplest explanation would be that the events are connected, but it's possible and equally disconcerting that someone else might be monitoring us."

"Maybe the government's been keeping tabs on psychics?" I asked.

Thomas sighed. "That'd be disappointing but not surprising."

Diana called to let me know she'd almost completed the memorial arrangements. "It was easy," she said. "The Psychology Department is understandably upset and wants to help. They booked the Price Center Theater for us at one o'clock on Friday. They'd also like to announce the memorial to their students so that any who want to honor him can come. They said they'd help provide drinks and appetizers. Would Irene mind if students and others come that she hasn't specifically invited?"

"I'll ask, but as long as the whole affair is simple, I don't think she'll mind. She might be touched if a lot of his students show up."

"I ordered some extra food and excellent wine. Harry would be disappointed if we had a party for him without a few good vintages. I'll pick up several flower arrangements and a guest book for people to sign. There will be a table for displaying pictures of Harry and some of his books. All you have to do now is help Irene choose those, write up a program, and coordinate the speakers."

"Thanks a million, Diana."

"How is Irene coping? Have the police told you anything?"

I shared all that we knew with Diana. She was as shocked as we were.

"It's like we're living in the twilight zone," she said. "I'll call you later about the memorial service, but you should start telling Harry's friends the exact time and place to help them arrange their schedules. Keep me updated."

"Will do. Talk to you later."

* * *

Thomas and I had collected the email addresses of the people we'd called and quickly sent off an email with the specifics for the memorial service. We even created a draft of the program based on examples online and our knowledge of Harry and Irene. Most of our work was now finished until confirmations came back. Since Irene was spending most of her time alone, we felt a bit superfluous. The rest of the day passed slowly. Irene was fine with Nate bringing dinner and spending the evening with us, and I was glad to see him when he arrived. We told Nate about the bugs and the plans for the memorial service. Nate was disturbed about the bug on Thomas's car and even more about our suspicion that my car might have one as well.

Irene sat quietly during the conversation, but she finally spoke. "Harry's brother, Richard, and his wife, Barbara, will arrive here tomorrow, and my sister, Mei, will fly in Wednesday morning. You two won't have to watch over me much longer."

"Irene, tell us what you want us to do. We're more than happy to oblige. If you'd prefer to be alone, you won't hurt our feelings," Thomas said.

"I will never be able to convey how grateful I am to you for being here and for all of your help." Her chin quivered as she paused to collect herself. "I love having your company, but you both need to go back to your own lives. Sophia, I think you should go home to sleep. You need to rest. Thomas can protect me from the boogeyman tonight, but if your schedule allows, I would appreciate your company tomorrow, at least until Richard arrives. I need to lean on you a little longer."

"I'll be here as long as you need me, Irene." She gave me a sad smile and retreated into herself again.

After dinner, Nate and I stayed until Thomas returned from gathering a few of his things, then headed home. Walking in, I expected to see a mess from the hasty end of our breakfast, with leftovers stinking up the bedroom, but the apartment was spic-and-span.

"Did you clean everything?" I asked.

Nate nodded. "When I picked up your things yesterday, I cleaned up our mess. I didn't want you to come home to that. I hope you don't mind."

"I don't mind at all. In fact, I'm relieved. Looking at that wasted food would have brought everything back. Thank you." I hugged him. "Stay with me tonight," I whispered into his chest.

Nate hugged me a little tighter and kissed the top of my head.

CHAPTER NINE

The next morning, Nate left for work while I fruitlessly searched my apartment for bugs. I didn't see any, but I didn't have a magnifying glass or any experience finding them. I started tidying up and went to grab the laundry from my closet when I saw the GammaBeat sitting on a shelf. Seeing it reminded me of Harry. He gave it to me just before we shared our last words, before I had my last true glimpse of him alive. I should return it to Irene, but now was certainly not the time. Besides, I wanted to practice with it a little more. My sleep last night was once again dreamless.

I brought some groceries and breakfast over to Irene's. Before we ate, Thomas helped me check my car for the GPS tracker. Since my apartment seemed clear, I doubted we'd find anything. I gasped when I saw the tiny square device stuck to the undercarriage of my car.

"What? They're following me too? Why?"

Thomas stared at the device and then looked away, his jaw clenched. While I took a picture with my phone, I heard an almost inaudible curse from Thomas. He was pissed but didn't want me to know how much. "There's nothing we can do about this now," he said. "Let's eat."

When we were clearing the breakfast table, the police again knocked on the front door. Detective Jones, the lead detective on the case and one of the cops that had interviewed us, came to update us on the progress of the investigation. We sat together in the family room to hear his thoughts.

"Mrs. Reed, again, I'm sorry for your loss and know this is a difficult time for you, but I'd like to go over our impressions and what we've found so far. Well, ahem," he cleared his throat, "at first, the cause of death appeared to be self-inflicted."

"My husband did not commit suicide. He was murdered," Irene spat at him.

"Yes, yes, we believe that to be the case now, but the perpetrator intended the death to look like a suicide. Your husband died of a gunshot wound to the head, and the gun showed only his fingerprints. The gun also had a silencer and was unregistered. The blood splatters showed that the gun was fired while in his mouth; however, the medical examiner found no pockmarking from gunpowder on Dr. Reed's hands, which means that his hand wasn't holding the weapon when it was fired. Someone else had to pull the trigger. Also, his happy personal and professional life and the lack of a suicide note hinted at foul play as well. At your urging, Miss Walsh, and I'm still not certain how you convinced me, we searched for and found electronic surveillance devices in Dr. Reed's car, office, and home and on Mrs. Reed's and Mr. Walsh's vehicles. We're still analyzing the bugs, but I don't think we'll be able to gather much information from them."

"We also found a tracker on my car this morning," I added. "We left it there so we didn't disturb the evidence. I checked my apartment. I didn't see anything, but I don't have a magnifying glass."

Detective Jones frowned at this new information. "Thank you for not touching it. You did the right thing."

After a moment of hesitation, he continued, "The case is being ruled a homicide. It's clear that the murder was well planned and intentional. The extent of expensive electronic surveillance suggests that possibly a group may be behind the killing instead of a single individual. Since there was no physical sign of a struggle, we think it's plausible that the murderer has psychic abilities, specifically the ability to control and hypnotize others, as Miss Walsh's vision suggested, but this is conjecture. We spoke with other faculty members about Dr. Reed's books and whether they were controversial or antagonized any group of people. The most we could gather from those conversations was that he was an active proponent of developing everyone's innate psychic talents and was very good at teaching gifted individuals to improve their skills. I know we talked about this the other night, but have you been able to think of any reason that someone or some group might murder your husband?"

"No, I still cannot think of a reason, although he did get the occasional email or letter from the religious right claiming he was a Satanist or some such thing. Harry's books were not that controversial. He did receive a lot of questions from readers, but I believe he answered all of them and tried to give helpful advice. Mostly because of those questions, his latest book has a larger portion devoted to practical aspects of improving psychic skills than previous books. As far as I know, he never had any disgruntled students or colleagues."

"We're still searching the contents of his work and home computers and going through his email and phone logs, but so far, we've not come up with any solid leads and didn't find any spyware. We put a notice in today's edition of the UCSD paper and the San Diego Union Tribune to see if anyone noticed a strange person or anything unusual around the time of Dr. Reed's death. The UCSD campus police will be sending out an email to the entire UCSD community."

"How can we help?" I asked.

"Just keep thinking. Try to recall anything that might have caused a group of people to hate or fear him. The religious right is a possibility, but it appears that the murderer may have been a psychic himself, which then doesn't make much sense." Detective Jones looked quickly at his watch and let out an exasperated sigh. "I have to head out. Call if something comes to mind. We'll extract the tracker from your car before we leave, Miss Walsh. We should also arrange a time to check both of your apartments. We need to know why someone is tracking all of you and whether you're at risk. You need to be careful. I can't stress that enough."

We set up times for the police to search our apartments and then saw Detective Jones off. Irene closed the door and rested her back against it. The lines of her face were set with determination, and her eyes contained venom. "The killer must be caught. I want him to suffer." Her hands were trembling.

I wasn't sure what to say in response so I went to her and held her. She cried quietly for a few minutes, then settled and let me go.

After a short reflective silence, Thomas changed the subject. "Irene, I have a friend who might be able to find spyware on Harry's computer, if it's there. He has better resources than the police and could swing by today to check it out."

"Please, have him come. If he needs to take the computer with him, he may. Excuse me, I need to make a phone call."

* * *

Trevor came over about an hour later. He was a tall, thin guy of Russian descent, who lived and breathed computers. He and Thomas, both loners in their own way, were roommates during their first two years at UCSD and had become fast friends. He wasn't psychic, but he had a definite talent. In college, I'd named him the "White Knight Hacker" since he'd committed himself to fighting against hackers who preyed on people. Thomas told me a few months later that the name had struck a chord with Trevor, and he'd started using its abbreviation as his online alias. Trevor sat down at the computer and began to rummage through his bag.

"I'm sorry about your friend. If there's anything on here, I'll find it. I've got just the right medicine." He pulled out a pink thumb drive with rhinestones on it. Thomas and I looked at each other and smiled.

"That's some fancy medicine you've got there," Thomas kidded.

"Oh, it's my girlfriend's. I met her at DEF CON a few months ago. She's killer. I'll have to introduce you some time."

"I'd love to meet her," I said.

I was happy to learn that our Trevor had finally blossomed. He was so shy around girls when we first met that he didn't speak more than two words to me during those first few months unless we were playing

Magic: The Gathering, an old constant from our childhood.

After about two hours in deep concentration interrogating the computer, Trevor re-emerged into our reality. "I did find some military-grade mojo that's siphoning data. There's something weird about it though, and I can't figure it out right now. I can squeeze more out of it, but it'll take time. If I can bring the computer home with me, I'll play with it over the next few days."

"Thanks, Trevor. I owe you one."

"No worries, man. I love a challenge." He and Thomas packed up the computer, and he left.

* * *

Thomas and I finished tidying up the office and the guest room as Richard and Barbara arrived. Irene was relieved to see them and clutched onto Richard. After Irene, Richard was the next closest person to Harry. The two brothers were best friends their entire lives. Richard looked shaken, but he and Barbara seemed comforted that Irene was functioning. I felt a little intrusive, observing such a personal moment. I could tell that Thomas felt the same way. Irene must have noticed because she turned to introduce us. Richard and Barbara were clearly tired and grief-stricken, but they made an effort to be kind and welcoming. It was hard not to see Harry when looking at Richard. They had similar mannerisms and looked quite a bit alike. I was probably trying to see more of Harry in him than there actually was and had to remind myself that Harry was gone. I couldn't conjure him back to life.

We embraced Irene and said our goodbyes. Since Richard was going to lead the memorial service, we left him with everything he needed. Thomas and I were thankful that more experienced reinforcements had arrived.

I headed into work with the hope of accomplishing something that would lift my spirits. I stopped by Nate's desk on my way in and was disappointed not to find him. It seemed that my days were already starting to revolve around seeing him. The project I picked up was military. They were looking for a stash of weapons in nineteen potential locations. Luckily, location number six appeared to house the weapons. I wrote up a detailed report and spoke with Roger to schedule the observed astral projection with the military liaison. It was close to the end of the day and too late to start something new, so I packed up and walked by Nate's cubicle on my way out. I was happy to see the top of his head peeking out and had to restrain myself from giving him too warm of a welcome.

"Hey," I said. "Are you almost finished?"

"Almost. What do you have in mind?"

I moved close to him to avoid prying ears.

"I haven't planned anything specific, but I could go for a warm bath by candlelight and some dark chocolate," I whispered.

"That sounds perfect. I need to run home first to grab some clothes. Would you like me to pick up dinner?"

"No, I'll handle it and meet you at my place."

It felt wrong not kissing him goodbye, but I winked at him instead and took off. I went to the grocery store to restock my barren refrigerator and then picked up dinner from my favorite Italian place nearby, checking in with Irene while I waited. When I got home, I stared at my front door. I stood there, my arms weighted down with groceries, and hesitated. I didn't want to open it. At that moment, I realized that after finding the tracker on my car, I was afraid to go into my apartment alone. *What if Harry's murderer was waiting for me?* My pulse quickened, but I had to get a handle on this. I knew how to defend myself and refused to let paranoia rule my life. I put the bags down, quietly unlocked and unhitched the door and kicked it hard enough to smack and expose anyone behind it. The door banged against the wall and shook on its hinges. I walked in, scoped out the great room, grabbed the bags, and quickly locked the door. My hasty action left a scar on the wall and a dusting of drywall on the carpet. *Damn, I'll have to pay for that.*

After I inspected the rest of my apartment, I put the groceries away and arranged our dinner on plates. The normalcy of setting the table helped lessen my worry, but I stayed silent in the openness of the great room, still feeling ill at ease, and watched the minutes tick away. My stomach growled. The delicious aroma of our dinner began to lure me from my concern. I hoped Nate would arrive soon because I wasn't sure I could wait much longer. Within seconds of thinking I might actually start tasting my food without him, Nate knocked on the door. Before I could say "Hello," he was on me, kissing me hungrily. I kissed him back but was torn between letting the heat progress and eating the food I'd been salivating over.

"Uh, Nate, dinner's getting cold."

"I don't care," he said as he kissed down my neck. His hands caressed my breasts under my shirt. "I want you *now*. I've been visualizing you in a warm bath for the last hour-and-a-half. I can't stand it anymore. Make love to me, Sophia. Let me make love to you. Here. Now."

His eyes held a dark, wild stare that penetrated to my core and mesmerized me like a prey caught in the gaze of a predator. I forgot the food and kissed him. Nate continued where he'd left off, but even with his urgency, he catered to my needs first. He brought me close to the edge with his fingers, donned protection, and only then allowed himself to engage. He pumped me hard and fast, and we experienced that magical and often elusive simultaneous orgasm. We grasped each other tightly as the spasms echoed through us and continued clinging to each other as we began to collect our breath. My body felt complete entwined with his, like they should never be parted. Nate looked at me, and his eyes brimmed with emotion. Mine must have looked the same. I'd never felt so connected to anyone. He kissed my eyelids and sighed.

"Do you want to take a bath first or eat?"

"Eat. I'm starving," I replied.

As we ate and talked about the day, Nate worried about the GPS tracker on my car, stabbing his fork into his food. Diana called as we finished eating. She'd just landed in San Francisco for work after a long flight from New York and wanted to check in.

"Hey, Sophia. What's the latest?" I told her what we'd learned that day. She was surprised and concerned as well.

"I can hear someone in the background. Are you enjoying an evening with Nate?"

"Yes, I am."

"Good for you," she said. "Ah, that makes me miss John. He's been on a business retreat in the Himalayas and has been completely off the grid."

"Jeez, a business retreat in the Himalayas? That's just wrong. Investment bankers have the life, don't they?"

"Yeah, it's a bit appalling when you think about it, but he was excited about the trip. Have a good evening with Nate."

When I hung up, arms encircled me from behind and Nate whispered in my ear, "Come with me." He led me to the bathroom where candlelight glowed. Chocolate and glasses of red wine rested on the counter, and bubbles multiplied in the bath.

"Beautiful," I said.

"You are indeed, but I believe you're a bit overdressed."

I smiled, remembering when I'd used that phrase a few days before.

We helped each other undress, and I stepped in. Nate handed me a glass and the chocolate and followed, but my bathtub wasn't the right size for a two-person soak. We scooted around until we found a semi-comfortable position, with him sitting in back and me using him as a warm and cozy chair.

"You'd think that with my physics degree, I could have predicted we'd barely fit." I turned off the water with my foot since the bath was already near to overflowing now that our bodies occupied most of the space in the tub.

"I'm not complaining. I've got a very sexy blanket."

I leaned my head back and smiled. "I'm a little scrunched, but my back is warm and you're a pretty good pillow." We sipped our wine and soaked up the warmth of the water and our physical connection. I broke the chocolate in half and shared it with him.

"I want to go on a trip with you. I want to take you to a nice hotel with a luxurious bath," Nate said.

"That'd be nice."

"You know I'm going to Brian's wedding next month."

"Are you his best man?"

"Yeah, and I told him yesterday that we were dating. He said I could bring you. So, if you want to come along, you're welcome, but I completely understand if you're not interested."

"I can't believe he's okay with me being at his wedding. Would his *fiancée* be okay with it? I don't think I'd want my future husband's ex-fiancée there."

"She won't like it, and I don't know how she'd behave towards you. It would also annoy her that no matter how fancied up she gets for her wedding day, you'll still be more beautiful."

I kissed the palm of his hand for that sweet comment. "What do you want me to do?" I asked.

"Well, I love the idea of traveling with you and having you at the wedding with me. My parents will be there, and I'd like you to meet them. I also want Brian to get used to you being mine . . . but . . . your relationship ended badly. I could tell it surprised and bothered him that we're dating, and I don't think he thought it through when he encouraged me to bring you. Honestly, I don't think seeing him at his wedding would be good for either of you."

"So, to summarize, you don't think I should go, but you want me to know that I can if I want to. Tell me this, is your ex-girlfriend going to be there?"

"She's not in the wedding party, but I think so. We used to double-date a lot with Brian and Stephanie."

"I see. That changes things."

"You're jealous?"

"Of course I am. You dated her for nine months. We've only been together for a whopping week and a half."

"I've already told you there's no reason to be jealous, but I have to say that I do enjoy you feeling possessive of me. It's nice to know I'm not the only one with that particular issue." He finished his wine and then slid his hands down my sides to my hips. "So, what do you think? Do you want to go?"

"Though I'd enjoy taking a trip with you and meeting your parents, my going is a bad idea. Just promise me that you won't dance with anyone. Because of the way our relationship started, imagining you dancing with someone is almost as bad as you having sex."

"Okay. I'll feign a sore ankle or something."

"Do what you have to do," I said and teased him with a kiss. I then cocked my head and narrowed my eyes at him. "Is there going to be a bachelor party?"

"Of course," he said.

"And will this bachelor party include strippers?"

"That's the plan — dinner, drinks and a good strip club."

"How does one define 'good' when referring to strip clubs?"

"Boy, you are cute when you're jealous," he kissed me quickly on the nose and smiled. "In my humble opinion, a 'good' strip joint, is a cleaner, more upscale one with better looking dancers."

"Are these places you visit often? You sound like a connoisseur."

"God, no, Sophia. I've gone about five times, for bachelor parties."

"I don't like the idea of strip clubs. They make it acceptable to openly lust after and salivate over women, which I guess is fine if you're not in a relationship, but if you are, I think it's almost like cheating. Lap dances definitely cross the line."

"I had no idea you were so uptight about strippers."

"Uptight? That's a nice turn of phrase. You don't see anything wrong with it?"

I started to push away from him, but he pulled me back and chuckled. "Sophia, please don't be angry. Uptight was the wrong word. Maybe I should have said opinionated or extremely moral."

I turned to face him. "It wouldn't bother you if I went to a male strip club, got turned on by a guy and slipped a few dollars into his silken thong. I could even pay extra for him to gyrate above me or sit on my lap with an overly muscled, oiled, and sweaty body."

He frowned. "Okay, I wouldn't like that, but I'm surprised it bothers you so much. Guys think of it as a rite of brotherhood that most women simply accept. I'm in charge of the party, and they're expecting a strip club. I can't change the plans now, but I can promise that I won't have any lap dances. Even if the guys try to push one on me, I should be able to avoid it since Brian will be the center of attention."

"That's reasonable, but in future, I'd appreciate it if you'd avoid strip clubs while we're together. I don't know if I'm different than other women, but I think people in committed relationships should steer clear of them. It's like the first step on a slippery slope to infidelity. Maybe it's because my dad had an affair, but I'm sensitive to any form of cheating, and strip clubs come close." I was still annoyed at having to defend my stance and maintained my distance from Nate. He noticed and pulled me against him.

"Sophia, you're all that I want." He tipped my chin up so he could look directly into my eyes and rubbed his thumb over my lips. "I don't intend to give you any reason to push me away. I won't dance with anyone or have any lap dances. I haven't made my plane reservations yet, but I'll likely stay an extra night with my parents in San Jose. They'll be at the wedding in San Francisco, but I doubt we'll have much time together. I still want to introduce you to them. Maybe we can plan a romantic trip to Napa, and then I could bring you to meet them."

"I'd love that. I've never had a romantic getaway before."

"Hmm. I look forward to being the first to pamper you." Nate kissed me tenderly and stared into my eyes. "Do you want to shower off before we get out? I'd like to wash you."

"I could use a good cleaning."

After we helped each other up, I opened the drain and turned on the shower while Nate lathered his hands with soap. He started by massaging my shoulders and nipped my neck in the process. The pressure of his hands and the warmth of the water began to melt away some of the knots and tension from the last few days. He then cupped my breasts, gently teasing the tips between his fingers. I gasped and pressed my body back against his where I could feel him growing hard and full. I shuddered at the thought. Nate slathered more soap across my stomach and arms. I was prepared and eager for him to start cleaning more exciting areas, but he stopped there and let the water beat down on my torso while he tilted back my head to wash my hair. *Ooh, I could purr.* After conditioning my hair, his hands roamed over my breasts, made circles on my fluttering stomach, and turned me around for a passionate kiss.

Though tempted to let the moment escalate, I wanted a turn to play so I ended the kiss before it got out of control. "You're still dirty. I need to clean you too."

"Cleanliness is next to godliness."

I poured the soap in my hands and smoothed it over his chest. Nate had just the right amount of masculine hair, and it covered some very sexy pecs. They weren't the gigantic steroid-induced kind. He simply had good genetics and was strong, fit, and healthy. His stomach sported defined and distinct abdominal muscles without a ridiculously bulging six-pack. He was perfect.

"You're beautiful," I said.

"What?"

"Your chest and stomach are so sexy, though I think this might be my favorite part." I played with the hair on his stomach that led downward.

"My happy trail?" he laughed.

"I don't know what it is, but seeing a handsome man's happy trail just does something to me."

He raised an eyebrow. "Any handsome man?"

I smiled coyly. "I guess I have a general weakness for it, but for yours especially. Turn around." I avoided a certain area as he had with me. I assumed the goal was to get clean first and then let things progress. I massaged his back and shoulders the best I could with my shorter stature and then focused on his butt. It was divine, all solid muscle. *Maybe this was my favorite part?* While massaging it, I pressed my breasts against his back and heard Nate sigh. It was satisfying to know that my body affected his as much as his did mine.

"Turn around and on your knees," I ordered. He obeyed though it couldn't have been that comfortable. I had him lean his head back as I washed his hair. My breasts hung down above his face as I bent over him. His eyes were closed, but he opened them as I was rinsing out the conditioner. He was surprised at first and then laughed.

"I like the view," he said. The next thing I knew he was sucking on my breast, pulling my body against him. He kissed the other one and gave me a hungry look. "You're still not completely clean."

I took me a second to remember where I was in washing him, but I regained my senses. "Neither are you. Up," I commanded. I lathered the soap and slowly slicked it over his testicles and behind and made my way up the shaft, which was taut and ready.

After I made my way back down a few times, he lightly grabbed my hand. "I'm clean enough, but you're still dirty."

Nate gathered a little soap and started playing with my pubic hair. He began at the top and washed the outer areas until he reached my behind, and then cleaned again in progressively smaller circles, ending on a small sensitive area. He massaged over and over and brought me to a screaming climax. The water turned off and the curtain opened. I felt the cool bathroom air before I realized we were getting out. Nate scooped me up into his arms and carried me toward the bed as we dripped water across the floor.

"You like carrying me."

"You're right. I do. I have this weird urge to cradle your small body in my arms and protect you. Does it bother you?"

"No, I like it. You make me feel safe."

We kissed and lay down on the bed. Even though we knew each

other's bodies fairly well now, the excitement of kissing and touching each other kept increasing as we pushed insecurity and hesitancy aside. We made out like that until our bodies started to instinctively want more. My legs opened to him and he started to come close, when he pulled back and reached to the nightstand for a condom.

"Let me put it on. I'd like to try a new position," I said. He handed it to me, looking intrigued, and I tore open the package and rolled it on. I helped him cross his legs under me, and I slid on top of him and wrapped my legs around him.

"Mmm, being inside of you feels so right."

The talking ceased, and at first we just stared at each other as our bodies moved together, our breath playing seductively on our skin. I rubbed my nose and cheeks along his face and then kissed him lightly, letting my top lip linger. Slow, intimate, deep. He looked into my eyes with a gaze that pierced my soul, exposing parts of me never laid bare before. It was almost too intimate, too intense. I smiled and licked from the corner of his jaw to his ear, ending with a little love bite.

"Mmm, Sophia," he said and then kissed me deeply. Each kiss strove to bring us closer together, and we sped up the tempo. Nate was getting close and could tell I wasn't there yet because he slowed down and used his fingers to help me along. In less than a minute, I started moaning and contracting and Nate pumped as fast as he could. When he finished climaxing, we held each other tightly with my cheek against his.

After our breathing calmed, he kissed my cheek and turned me to face him. His eyes searched mine, raw with emotion. "Sophia, I'm falling in love with you."

A happiness I didn't think possible filled me. No fears or reservations held sway over me. "Nate, I'm falling in love with you too." I kissed him gently and hugged him. He then toppled us over onto the bed. We smiled at each other and giggled in our state of euphoria. I had found love again.

CHAPTER TEN

I awoke the next morning to the ringing of soft bells from my alarm clock. I quickly turned it off and grabbed my iPhone. I had three dreams, back to my usual pattern. *Thank God.* None of the dreams were particularly interesting or of any consequence, but they meant that my life was returning to normal. For Harry, unfortunately, that wouldn't be the case. I flashed back to my last vision of him and shuddered. *How could someone do that?* I had a hard time believing I'd never see him again. A few tears fell from my eyes. Nate stirred next to me and a large hand pulled me close.

"Good morning," I said.

"It is now." He kissed my cheek and noticed the wetness. "Are you crying?"

"Yeah, I was just thinking about Harry . . . but on a positive note, I had three normal dreams last night. Did I wake you when I recorded them?"

"No. I told you I'm a deep sleeper."

"That's great. I was worried I'd have to change my dream routine." I kissed him briefly on the lips and reached to turn on my reading light. "We better start moving if we're going to get dressed before the police arrive."

"There's no time to make love?" he whispered in my ear.

"Well, we could, but I'm not exactly in the mood right now."

"I can help you get in the mood."

"I've been crying. It would take diligent effort on your part and probably more time than we have."

"Are you challenging me?" he asked, with a mischievous look on his face.

That look made me laugh. "No, really, I'm not. I think now just isn't a great time. I don't mean to disappoint you."

"No worries," he said, but I could tell he was a little let down. It was the first time that our libidos hadn't been on the same page.

I put my hand on his cheek and looked him straight in the eye. "I promise I'll be in the mood tonight, for as many times as you wish, any way you want. Just because my mind is occupied doesn't mean I don't want you." I kissed him deeply and wrapped my leg around him. After a minute, I was beginning to change my mind. He could tell I was getting into it and pulled back.

"Are you having second thoughts?" he asked in a playful voice.

"I am. My mood changed more quickly than I thought possible."

"Well, I liked your offer, and I'm taking you up on it. You can crawl out of bed guilt-free now." He climbed out of bed to put on his clothes. I felt confused as I watched him dress.

"Did the tables just get turned on me?" I asked.

"I'm not sure, but I think so," he said with a smug look.

"Huh. I'll have to think twice next time before I make an offer you can't refuse." He smiled at me, and I couldn't help but smile back.

* * *

The police arrived at seven to check for bugs. They found some on my home telephone and lamps in my bedroom and living room, but like the others, someone had remotely deactivated them. After the police left, Nate and I drove to work together in silence. I felt violated and a bit freaked out. My home, my sanctuary, had been invaded by a murderer. Thank goodness Nate was driving because I couldn't concentrate, though I could tell he was seething. *How long had someone been spying on me? When did he stop? God, had he listened to Nate and me?*

The police said they'd found almost the same array of equipment at

Thomas's apartment yesterday evening. I called Thomas since I didn't want him in my head at that moment. He'd been waiting to hear what the police found at my place before telling me about his. He was more angry than freaked at the invasion of our privacy. It was a small comfort that Nate's car didn't have a tracker and that all of our laptops and cell phones were clear.

When we parked the car at the office, I received an emergency text from Roger. There was an urgent missing person's case coming in. A seventeen-year-old daughter of a prominent family in Boulder had gone missing. She was last seen walking home from school yesterday but never made it there. Her mother would arrive shortly with photographs of her and several of her most dear possessions. The plan was that Matt, a touch clairvoyant, David, a telepath, and I would work together to try to find her. Missing persons' cases made me anxious because I was successful only a third of the time. Some failures were because the people had already died, but others were because I just wasn't that good at finding strangers in unknown locations. Given geography, maps, and coordinates, I could track down anything, but finding people I had no connection to was difficult, and upsetting when I failed. I had a hard time accepting that I couldn't help a child whose life depended on me.

Nate could see the worry in my face. "Are you okay?" he asked. I pulled him aside and shared my concerns.

"I could help," he said. "I'm good at finding people though I haven't tried to find a complete stranger."

"Let's ask Roger. He'll probably still want me on the case, but unless you have something time-sensitive on your plate, he'll let you join in."

Nate and I looked at a Google Earth picture of the area, scrutinizing homes, apartment buildings, warehouse districts, business parks, and so forth in order to get the lay of the land. The girl's mother arrived, her eyes puffy, red, and consumed with fear. With our shields down, Matt began by holding a small stuffed dog. David sent the images and voices that flashed through Matt's mind to Nate and me. Matt next held Isabella's pillow, followed by her favorite and well-worn T-shirt, and then the photos. David sent us everything and shared any insights with her mother. Lastly, Matt held Isabella's mom's hand and a flood of images bombarded us. Isabella seemed to be a typical high school student who liked to spend time with her friends and thought of herself as grown-up but was still a girl in many ways. She had no secret boyfriend and wasn't involved in drugs or alcohol as far as Matt could tell. Her mom also shared pictures of the school and their home and pointed out several other places on the map.

Nate, Roger, and I went into a projection room together so we could communicate while projecting. We leaned back in our recliners, went into a meditative state and tried to connect with her. I focused on the images of Isabella in my mind and searched for a link to somewhere. Nothing came to me. I then projected to her school and scanned the area from there to her house, still concentrating on her. A few hours passed before I felt a pull.

"Nate, I feel like she's somewhere north of her house." He didn't respond. He was new to phasing between the physical and the projection, which takes practice. I hoped he could hear me.

Finally, he spoke. "I agree. I've already moved out of the neighborhood and across the highway in that direction. I think the draw is getting stronger."

I moved in that direction as well and felt a tug this time to the northwest toward a large brick apartment complex. As I moved closer, the direction felt right.

"I think she might be in the Oaks apartments," Nate said.

I searched for the sign and found that we were homing in on the same complex. "I agree."

"I feel like she's in building J. I'm checking the third floor. You start on the first," he replied.

The tingling on the back of my neck told me we were close. There was no sign of her on the first floor so I moved to the second.

"I found Isabella," Nate said. His voice was strained. "Third floor, apartment 310. She's in the bedroom closet with duct tape over her mouth, wrists, and ankles. She's breathing but is either asleep or unconscious. It's too dark for me to tell if she's been injured. No one else is in the apartment right now."

"Sophia, get there. Double check the apartment for any booby traps or cameras and watch the entrance so we know immediately if the kidnapper returns. Nate, stay with Isabella." The door to our room opened as Roger left to alert the local police department and update her mother.

I didn't find a trap, a camera or even a simple security system. The closet door had an impressive lock but nothing that would trigger an explosion or alarm. No weapons were lying around. Though I could peak into drawers in my noncorporeal form, I couldn't open them, and it was often too dark inside to see much. I'd be surprised if he didn't have a gun somewhere, though it might be with him. Roger relayed our information to the police, and we waited on full alert. The apartment was sparse and clean. No personal photographs or decorative pictures hung on the walls. It looked like no one actually lived there.

After about twenty minutes, the police and Isabella's father arrived, broke into the apartment, and rescued her. She sobbed in her father's arms, which sent tears down my cheeks. She had some obvious scrapes and bruises, but I didn't want to learn more of how she'd suffered. My knowing wouldn't change the past and could sometimes be hard for me to deal with. Since she was safe, I returned to my body and breathed slowly in and out for a few minutes before opening my eyes. Nate was still in the projection so I let him know I was leaving and closed the door.

In the conference room, Isabella's mom was crying on the phone with her daughter, telling her how much she loved her and that everything would be okay. After a few minutes, Nate came in and gave me a small smile though his eyes were troubled. We did it, and although it was a team effort, I felt that he was the hero of the day. We wouldn't have found her as quickly without him. Roger came over and shook our hands and those of David and Matt. Together, we saved an innocent girl. She was alive and back with her family. My job didn't get much better than that.

After tears and many thanks, Isabella's mom left for the airport to catch a flight back to Boulder. She had flown out here on a slim hope that we could help her, and she couldn't have been more thankful that she had.

Nate and I grabbed an early lunch downstairs to recuperate before starting our next assignments. Relieved but subdued, we were quiet for a while, deep in our own thoughts.

"You know, I've never found anyone that fast, not even when Jack and I projected together," I said. "You're really good at finding people. I had better intuition about where to go with you. I didn't have to constantly second-guess myself. If I practice finding people with you, I might learn to trust my instincts more."

"I'm glad I could help. You're much faster than I am at finding exact locations. It's nice to feel I can pull my weight in one arena." He chewed his sandwich but looked lost for a moment. "I hope Isabella pulls through this okay. It won't be easy, but she has a great family. That will help." I squeezed his hand and shared his sentiments.

Back upstairs I spent the rest of the day finding and eradicating meth labs. From what I'd observed through my cases, methamphetamine seemed the most evil of illicit drugs. It took people over and turned them into pathological, toothless liars, destroying their lives completely with almost no hope of return. I tracked down three different labs and vetted their security and weapons stashes in preparation for simultaneous SWAT team assaults. After a few hours of coordination, the operation was successful, suffering only a single drug-dealer casualty. A bit tired but satisfied, I stopped by Nate's cubicle. He looked up from his computer with a smile when he heard me turn the corner.

"You'll be happy to hear that they arrested Isabella's kidnapper," Nate said.

"Thank goodness." What a rewarding end to the day. A young girl was safe, a bad guy was off the streets, and hopefully some poor kid wouldn't become a slave to a drug habit.

As we drove back to my apartment, Nate offered to make dinner while I went to check on Irene. In the garage, I gave him the keys to my apartment and security gate and went straight to my car to drive to her house.

When I arrived there, Irene, Richard, Barbara, and Mei were finishing dinner. Barbara had been cooking up a storm, which was apparently her form of therapy. They tried to convince me to eat, but I told them I had dinner plans. I was relieved to see that being surrounded by family had improved Irene's spirits a little. We sat in the living room, and I told them what the police had found in our apartments.

Irene was contemplative, staring at the coffee table. She appeared to be preparing to speak, and in anticipation, the rest of us waited in silence for a time. Whatever was on her mind wasn't easy for her to say.

"Richard brought me to the coroner's today to identify Harry's body and sign paperwork. Richard had kindly offered to identify him for me, but I had to see Harry again. I had to say 'Goodbye.'" She paused, collecting herself. "It was bizarre. I could tell he was no longer there."

"I'm sorry, Irene." I had to widen my eyes to keep a tear from escaping.

"Sophia, I do not want you to think about finding the murderer anymore. I could not live with myself if something happened to you. Harry might have been the only target, but if we delve deeper, all of us could be."

"But how do we protect ourselves if we don't know what we're up against?" I asked.

"Let us hope the murderer never returns. Sophia, promise me you will be careful."

"I promise."

We then went over the program that Thomas and I had created to make sure everything met with Irene's approval before sending it to the printers later that evening. After we finished, they helped me carry the books and picture frames to my car for the memorial. I hugged Irene tightly before I left.

I pulled into my garage but instead of going straight up to my apartment, I walked to the management office and requested another pair of door and gate keys. Thomas had my current spares, and I wanted Nate to have his own keys. When I reached my apartment, the smell of sautéed garlic wafted through the gaps around the door. I opened it to see Nate happily cooking at my stove. We smiled at each other as I entered.

"I thought I'd have to buzz you in. Did someone open the gate for you or do you have another set of keys?"

"I just got another set. You can keep the ones I gave you."

Nate swept me up into his arms and kissed me. "Thanks. Are you hungry? Dinner should be ready in about ten minutes."

"Mmm. It smells great."

I sat down at the dining table and glanced at Nate's open laptop. I was more than shocked at what he'd been researching. I didn't think he was into kinky stuff.

"Nate, what's this?"

"Oh, that. I'm preparing for tonight. I don't want to waste the opportunity you gave me," he said nonchalantly.

"I see." I suddenly remembering the bargain I'd made that morning. My cheeks felt hot, and I must have been beet-red.

He laughed and closed his browser. "Relax. I'm teasing. I couldn't resist seeing that scandalized look on your face."

"Not funny."

He kissed my forehead, and then headed back to the kitchen.

I opened the refrigerator to get some cold water and saw whipped cream, chocolate syrup, and maraschino cherries prominently displayed on the top shelf. "Ooh, will we be making ice cream sundaes?" I asked with the excitement of a child.

"Not exactly," he said with a sly grin.

Nate started laughing again so I decided to leave him to his cooking while I freshened up.

When I came back to the kitchen, the table was set with a fabulous home-cooked meal, and Nate was cleaning some dishes. I stared at him amazed, wondering how in the world I'd managed to find a sexy guy who understood me and was a good person, a great cook, and even psychic to boot.

He caught me staring. "What are you thinking?"

"Just that I'm pretty lucky."

He smiled. "Sit down and eat before your dinner gets cold."

I took a bite and closed my eyes in pleasure. "Nate, this is fantastic."

"I'm glad you like it," he smiled and then stroked my hand. "So, how's Irene coping?"

I shared the visit with him, and then we discussed the logistics for the memorial and made plans for the weekend. Nate wanted us to go on a double date on Saturday with his friend Steve and his new girlfriend at the Haunted Hotel downtown, which sounded like fun.

As the food on my plate disappeared, I became preoccupied with what Nate might have planned for me that evening. "Uh, Nate? About our agreement, would you *please* tell me what you have in mind?" I asked.

"Well, I'll tell you step by step," he said. "After we clean up the dishes, I want to dance with you."

A grin spread over my lips. Of all the things I'd begun to fret we might be doing that night, dancing wasn't on the list. It was a romantic gesture and much appreciated regardless of what might follow.

Nate selected a slow, melodic song, and we began a seductive dance. Each time we came close to the point of kissing, he'd pull away, again and again.

"I see what game you're playing," I said.

The sexual tension kept mounting with each twist, turn, and skimming of his hands down my body. The dancing was titillating foreplay that neither of us wanted to end, but I wasn't sure I could hold out much longer. By the middle of the third song, I grabbed his shirt, yanked him towards me, and started kissing him hungrily. He emitted a sort of primal growl as he kissed me and pushed my back up against the wall. He'd planned ahead so we didn't have to abscond to the bedroom. Instead, we tested the strength and durability of my dining table and then my couch. After we were sated, we snuggled naked. I grabbed the throw from the back of the couch and pulled it over us.

"You had me worried about what you might ask me to do. I certainly didn't expect you to be so sweet. I have to say though that I'm surprised you didn't ask me to do something at least a little bit kinky."

"I'm sorry if I went overboard teasing you, but your reaction made it irresistible. You must know I'd never want you to do anything you'd be uncomfortable with, but if you'd like to try the whipped cream and chocolate sauce, I'd be more than happy to oblige."

"Well, we haven't had dessert yet." I went to the fridge and retrieved the toppings, gasping as one of the jars touched my bare stomach. "This might be uncomfortable. Everything's pretty cold."

"But nothing will be on either of us for long. I want to decorate you first." He lifted out a cherry and placed it between my lips. I bit down on it, and he kissed me to share it. Nate then dripped the cool syrup on my chest, and I flinched at both the chill and then the warm touch of his tongue. He was right. Our lips and tongues quickly removed the cold sweetness from our skin. After consuming too much sugar and cream and another satisfying release, we showered to remove the sticky residue and went to bed. As Nate held me close, I ran my fingers up and down his arm.

"Nate?"

"Hmm?"

"I'd like to make one of your fantasies come true. Think about what you might want, and we can talk about whether it's something I can do. It would make me happy to do that for you."

He pulled me close and kissed my neck. "I love you."

I turned my head to look into his eyes. "I love you too."

CHAPTER ELEVEN

On Thursday, Diana finally returned from San Francisco and texted me to meet her for lunch in the café downstairs. She was sitting at a small corner table poking at a salad when I approached. She wasn't her usual jolly self. Her eyes were red and puffy, and she didn't have a smile or even a smirk on her face.

"What's wrong, Diana?

Her chin quivered a little, but she regained control. "It's John," she said. "I don't think he's the person I thought he was."

I sat down and squeezed her hand. "What happened?"

She took a deep breath and exhaled slowly. "I tried to call him yesterday. He was finally supposed to be back in civilization after his Himalayan retreat. When I called, the number had been disconnected. I then tracked down the investment bank where he supposedly worked, and no one there had ever heard of him. I even tried some of the smaller satellite offices, but again, no luck."

"I'm so sorry."

"I feel like such an idiot. Did you know that I only had his cell phone number? I never knew his home address. He said he preferred to get out of LA and stay in San Diego with me over the weekends. Since I couldn't read his mind, he totally blindsided me."

"Why would he do that? He seemed to really care about you."

"I don't know. Maybe he has a wife and kids and was just looking for a good time." A tear fell from her eye, and she quickly wiped it away.

We sat quietly for several minutes as I held her hand and let her recover. It suddenly hit me as strange that John would disappear at the exact time of Harry's murder.

"I know you think he had innate shields, but could he have been psychic and hiding it instead?"

"I guess it's possible, but why would he hide that from me and pretend he didn't have any abilities?"

I didn't respond immediately. I didn't think Diana would appreciate my suspicion about John, but the idea was nagging at me.

"Spit it out, Sophia."

"Well," I hesitated, "in my vision, whoever killed Harry seemed to be controlling him, preventing him from resisting. The killer had to be a telepath. Maybe John's odd mind was how he concealed his abilities. He left for his supposed trip just before Harry was murdered."

"You think he killed Harry?" she asked, pulling her hand away.

"I don't know, but the more I think about it . . . maybe. I've got nothing else," I replied.

"Sophia, that's crazy! Nate arrived on the scene just in time too."

I flinched. "Yeah, but he was with me when the murder took place and is still around. Forget it, Diana." I sighed. "I only brought it up because if John was a telepath, he could be a suspect. I didn't mean to upset you even more."

She took a deep breath and grabbed my hand again, squeezing. "I'm sorry. I'm just touchy about John right now." She attempted a weak smile. "I didn't mean it about Nate. He's an open book, and most of his thoughts are about you." She put her hands on her temples as if fighting a headache. "I'm going home. I'm useless in this state. Oh, did you send the final program to the printers?"

"Yes. Thomas is picking it up tomorrow."

"I'll call you later if there's anything else I need for the memorial." She grabbed her purse and started to get up. Diana always tried to hide any weakness and was trying to quickly escape.

"I'm not letting you leave without a hug. Come here, you need one."

She gave me a teary smile, and I hugged her tightly. She clung to me for a few breaths and then kissed the side of my head.

"I'll be okay," she said. "I'll call you."

Diana and I bickered sometimes but usually in a lighthearted manner. We'd never truly upset each other before. She was hurting, and I put salt in her wound. I wished I could make the pain go away.

* * *

I called Thomas and told him about John going AWOL. I wanted to see if he'd suspect him as well.

"That sucks," Thomas said. "I'd never seen her happier . . . but there *was* something off about him. His thoughts weren't normal."

"How so?" I asked.

"Well, you could tell he was intelligent from talking to him, but his thoughts were simple, like someone with mental challenges. He never had more than one thought going on at a time. Most people's minds bounce from one thought to the next. His never did that."

"Diana thought he might have innate shields and that only if he were thinking intently about something could she hear his thoughts."

"I've never met anyone else like that."

"Do you think he could have been psychic but was hiding his abilities?"

"Maybe," he said. He sighed heavily. "Sophia, I see where you're going with this. I'd like to find a suspect too, but we can't indict John yet. He's definitely guilty of being an ass to Diana . . . though, it can't hurt to find out more about him."

"Diana doesn't have any other information on him, but maybe we could get his fingerprints off of something from her house. Or, even better, if there's an object John touched enough, we could bring it to work, and Matt might be able to use it to extract some information about him."

"It can't hurt," he said, "but don't get your hopes up, and be gentle with Diana. She feels more deeply than she lets on."

"I know."

* * *

When I had a break in the afternoon, I called Diana to ask whether she'd mind if the police checked for John's fingerprints and if we could ask Matt for help. She still didn't believe he could have killed Harry, but she badly wanted to know who he was. She already did a Google image search from one of her pictures of him and found nothing. I called Detective Jones and told him our suspicions. He was skeptical but agreed to arrange fingerprinting that day since there were no other leads. He also thought it would be good to check for bugs since Diana was yet another psychic connected to Harry.

Diana called when Nate and I were about to leave work.

"Hey, Sophia. The police just finished dusting for prints and found several that aren't mine. They'll run them through their database to see if anyone comes up."

"How long will that take?"

"A few hours. They said they'd call if they find anything. They're almost finished searching for bugs. Apparently, my car and the light in my dining room were tapped. This sounds awful, but why would it make me feel better to discover he's a murderer than just a lecherous bastard?" Diana asked.

"Maybe because you've never been deceived by anyone. You'd probably feel less like the cliché young woman duped by a man with a secret life. I don't know, but either way, he deserves to be run over by a Mack truck."

Diana was silent for a moment. I could hear her steadying her breath. "I'll let you know when the police call," she said.

* * *

After eating some take-out, Nate headed to his first taekwondo class, while I went to a kung fu sparring session.

As I was parking my car back in the garage next to Nate's, my cell phone began to play Diana's ring tone. "Hey, Diana."

"Sophia, the police called. They think they found John in their database but wouldn't tell me anything else."

"Wow, that was fast."

"I know. I already emailed them the pictures I had, but they want me to go downtown and identify him. Could you come with me?"

"Of course. Is it okay if Nate comes along?"

"Sure," she said. "He knows what John looks like. It might help to have multiple people identify him."

Nate and I picked up Diana at her place and drove downtown together. An officer we hadn't met before escorted us to a back room with several computers. He pulled up the file with the matching fingerprints. A younger, shorter-haired, more serious image of John in a military uniform appeared on screen.

"Is this your ex-boyfriend?" the officer asked.

"That's him," Diana said, starting to shake a little. Nate and I both nodded.

"I hate to tell you this, but you've been dating a dead man. According to his military record, he was killed in Iraq by a roadside bomb in 2010. His real name is Charles Sinclair. He graduated at the top of his class at West Point and became a highly decorated Green Beret."

"How could he still be alive if the military declared him dead?" I asked.

"I don't know, but with the prints and your visual identification, it's got to be him. He has no living family. He's an only child, never married. His dad was a colonel in the Army and died a hero in the first Iraqi war. His mother passed away from breast cancer while he was in college. Remember, we've only proved he was lying about his identity and haven't yet connected him to Dr. Reed's murder. He's certainly our best suspect, though, especially since he disappeared at a suspicious moment, and isn't dead like he's supposed to be," the officer said.

"I know how we can determine if he's the killer," I said. "We were planning to take a few items John touched to a psychometric to see if we could find out more about him. We could also bring the murder weapon, and he might be able to determine if the murderer and John, er, Charles, are the same person."

The officer frowned at me. "What world do you live in? *You* can't bring the murder weapon anywhere. It can't leave police custody. . . . Still, even though psychometric evidence isn't admissible in court, we might learn if he's our murderer. I'll talk to Detective Jones to see if he'll allow a psychometric to examine the weapon here in the office."

"He can call me if he has questions," I said.

"Thanks for coming here tonight. We'll let you know if we uncover Charles's whereabouts or find any information we can share. If you see him, contact us immediately and *do not* approach him."

Nate and I took Diana home. I think hypothesizing about the fact that John wasn't who he said he was had kept Diana's mind occupied, but finding out his true background unsettled her. She was quiet on the ride home.

As she was climbing out of the car, Diana said to me, "I'll bring a few items John touched to work tomorrow. Will you help me ask Matt to look at them?"

"Of course. Come by my desk first thing in the morning." I grabbed her hand and squeezed. "Diana, you're going to be alright."

She gave me a half-hearted smile and unlocked her gate.

CHAPTER TWELVE

I was preparing for my first case when Diana stopped at my desk. She wore an elegant, black dress for the memorial. Though beautiful, the bags under her eyes told of a restless night.

"I brought a few objects that John touched repeatedly — my brush, the spatula he used when grilling, and the TV remote."

"Your brush?"

"Yeah, it was one of the sweeter things that he did. He seemed to love brushing my hair." She looked so lost that I got up to wrap my arms around her.

"Diana, I'm so sorry. I've been more focused on Harry's death than your loss. I'm a wretched friend, and I'm sorry."

"No, Sophia. You're the best. My loss is nothing compared to Harry. I just thought John and I had something special . . . I'd never felt that close to anyone, and it turns out, I didn't know him at all. Let's just get this over with."

We told Matt about Harry's murder and that we thought a man who had touched these objects, a person Diana had dated, might be responsible. He agreed to help.

"We'd appreciate any information you can give us because the police have nothing recent. The military said he was killed in Iraq in 2010. He told us his name was John Taylor, but his real name is Charles Sinclair. He has blond hair and blue eyes."

Diana showed him a picture from her phone. Matt took off his gloves and held the brush in both hands. He closed his eyes and was mostly silent for several minutes. He made an occasional incomprehensible murmur and a few facial tics as his eyes darted back and forth under his lids. "He's a powerful telepath with some kind of mission. . . . He's not alone. He's part of a group working toward a common purpose. . . . He *has* killed people and will do so again if necessary, but he's not a senseless killer. He has some higher justification for what he's doing. Hmm. Okay, that's enough," he said. Matt opened his eyes with a furrowed brow and a worried expression on his face.

"For what purpose? Did he kill Harry?" I asked.

"Can you tell us where he is?" Diana pressed.

"I didn't get anything specific about the purpose or the people he's killed, and frankly, I don't want to know. But he's dangerous. In good conscience I can't help you anymore. Don't try to find him. You're both young. You have the rest of your lives ahead of you. If anything needs to be done, let the police handle it."

"Please, Matt," Diana pleaded.

"Look," he said, "I personally can't afford to get involved in anything risky. I'm not a coward, but I have a pregnant wife and two young children who rely on me. I've learned the hard way to stay out of trouble, to keep a low profile. Harry is dead. I can't say for sure that your boyfriend killed him, but I don't want his group to come after us. I have to stay alive for my family."

"But we need to bring a psychometric to the police. We need to confirm that this man and the killer are the same person. You're the best. Nicole just started and isn't nearly as good as you are. I don't feel comfortable bringing her to the police."

He looked at our insistent faces and shook his head. "Well, you'll probably regret this, but if you want more information, see Mike Williams at Psychic Investigators in Mira Mesa. He's a talented psychometric, and he might extract something different from me, but for your own benefit, give Mike's contact information to the police and stay out of it. You're putting yourselves in danger."

Diana and I slipped into an empty projection room and checked that the recorder was off. "Did you get anything else out of his head?" I asked.

"No, he shields almost as well as you do. We should have asked him to lower them."

"It makes sense that John's a strong telepath. He had to be to fool you and Thomas, to prevent Harry and me from having precognitive dreams, and to immobilize Harry when he killed him. It fits. I'll call Psychic Investigators to see if we can make an appointment with this Mike. I want to meet him first to make sure he's good enough to send to the police."

"Yeah," she mumbled. Diana had drifted off into her own world, and her hazel eyes appeared haunted.

"Diana, are you okay?"

She snapped back to the moment. "Hmm? Yeah . . . I guess John really might have killed Harry then, huh?"

"I think so. It's too much of a coincidence otherwise."

"I know it's pathetic, but I still held a small hope for him simply being the man I knew, even after all we'd already learned." She searched the floor for composure. "I'll get over it," she said, trying to convince herself as well as me.

"I'm sorry, Diana." I put my arms around her and held tight. She breathed in a few shaky breaths and then calmed.

"I'm okay now," she said. "Thanks for the hug. I needed it."

We put John behind us for a time and discussed the final arrangements for the memorial that afternoon. I thanked her again for taking care of almost everything.

"No problem," she said. "I'm good at it, and it's the least I could do for Harry, especially considering the fact that John may have murdered him."

"Diana, no one would ever blame you. You'll get through this, and as you've often told me, there are lots of other fish in the sea."

"Oh, I definitely know that," she said, trying to rally herself, but she remained contemplative. "I think one reason I'm so bothered is that I'm in uncharted territory. For the first time in my life, my abilities completely failed me. I don't think I can trust myself."

"Telepaths with his abilities are extremely rare, and he was obviously well-trained."

The look she gave me lacked any reassurance.

"Though he fooled you *and* Thomas, you noticed that his thoughts were strange. In the small chance that you meet someone like him again, you'll know what to look for. I believe in you and always will," I said.

Diana glanced down at her watch. "I have to get some work done." As we parted ways, I hoped Diana's lack of confidence wouldn't last long. Diana without confidence was like a song without melody.

Before I dove into my projects, I looked up Psychic Investigators and was fortunate enough to get an appointment late in the day.

* * *

Nate and I left before lunchtime to help Diana set up for the memorial. She always claimed she didn't need help but never missed the opportunity to put us to work. Nate and I were setting up the books and pictures and Thomas was placing the programs when Diana discovered us. She had me help with the flowers and asked Nate and Thomas to grab several things from her car.

Irene arrived with her family about thirty minutes early, and to the table with the books and photographs, she added a framed sketch of Harry she'd started on the night he died. The front row was reserved for them and the speakers, and she sat there inconspicuously until the ceremony began.

Richard's face was solemn when he first settled at the podium, but he steered the tone away from a lament toward a celebration of Harry. He and the other speakers recounted funny memories and told touching stories that made me proud to know Harry. I hadn't realized how far-reaching he was in promoting parapsychological education for the masses. He was an optimist who believed that the world might become a better place if as many people as possible developed their psychic abilities. He felt it could forge connections that might help end some of the misunderstanding and strife existing in the world. Tears crept down my face, and Nate put his arm around me.

After the memorial concluded, Irene accepted condolences with grace and dignity. Over five hundred people took a break from their lives to honor Harry. She seemed deeply affected that Harry had touched so many lives. Friends, family, colleagues, and students shared tales along with food and wine for more than an hour before Richard escorted Irene over to Diana and me.

"Thank you all for planning the memorial. It was perfect. I cannot thank you enough," she said.

Diana, Thomas and I hugged her and assured her that her thanks were unnecessary. Irene's eyes were heavy. The event had taken its toll on her, and she departed soon afterward, followed shortly by most of the guests. Thomas, Nate, Diana, and I stayed until after the caterers left, and we packed up Harry's memorabilia and returned the room to its original state. Since we had about thirty minutes before we had to leave for our appointment, the four of us sat around and sipped the little remaining wine.

"I have some disturbing news," Thomas said. He pulled his chair around so that he straddled it and rested his arms on the back. "I spoke with Trevor. He found not one, but two military-grade spyware programs on Harry's computer. They both monitored his email and overall internet use and copied files concerned with his research, but the most often checked file was an Excel spreadsheet listing every psychic he's ever known with their abilities and contact information. The weird thing is that one of the spyware programs was sending false information to the other program."

"What kind of information?" Nate asked.

"He said that it looked like fake email correspondences, but when he tried to read their contents, they self-corrupted. He's had a hell of a time trying to undo the damage. Trevor's also trying to track down where the programs send their data, but the locations keep bouncing around from address to address. He said he'd keep working on it."

"So, Harry had two people or groups spying on him, and one was trying to trick the other?" I asked.

"It seems that way," Thomas said.

"I think Matt's right. John can't be acting alone. It would take well-funded organizations to create these sophisticated programs," Nate said.

"Maybe we'll find out more from the new psychometric," Diana added.

"I wonder which group planted the bugs on us and how long ago. Maybe they weren't even part of Harry's murder plot? Maybe someone is just spying on psychics?" I asked.

"Who knows," Thomas said, frustration showing on his face. "Hey, you should all come over to my place for dinner tonight. It won't be anything fancy, though, just Mom's spaghetti and meat sauce."

I reached over to give Thomas's arm a little squeeze. "That's a great idea. I could use some of Mom's comfort food right now too."

Nate volunteered to help Thomas cook, and Diana and I planned to meet up with them after our appointment. Our evening arranged, we left then in order to arrive early at Psychic Investigators. We hoped Diana might overhear something that could reveal the quality of the business.

Psychic Investigators was housed in a stylish office building covered top to bottom in reflective glass windows. The waiting room reminded me of my dentist's. The furniture and décor were tasteful and softened by plenty of gossip magazines and pots with life-like plants. I checked us in for the appointment and started filling out the paperwork. While I described the information we were seeking from our three items and the need for a police consult, Diana had her eyes closed and was listening intently.

After a short wait, the receptionist led us into a small, yet comfortable office and introduced us to Mike. He wore circular glasses, had a shy, pleasant face topped by a rebellious cowlick in the front of his dark blond hair, and looked our age or a little younger. He was a little taller than Diana and had a friendly, engaging smile. Diana met him with a smile that I knew meant she was repressing laughter, but thank goodness, he didn't seem to pick up on it. He wore gloves and didn't offer to shake our hands.

"Please sit down," Mike requested. He quickly skimmed the paperwork I'd completed. "Who was murdered?" he asked.

"A friend and professor of ours from UCSD."

"I just graduated from there last June," he said. "Which professor?"

"Dr. Harry Reed," I said.

"What?" he asked, his face paling. "Oh my God. He was my best professor. Why would someone murder him?"

"That's why we're here. We just came from his memorial service," I said.

He looked distraught. "I have to charge you for the visit today since it's on the books, but I'll consult with the police on my own time. You don't need to pay me."

"Thank you," I said.

"You said he was your professor as well. Do you mind my asking whether you're both gifted?"

Diana gave me a discrete nod as I began to speak. "I can astral project and have precognitive dreams and visions. Diana's a telepath. We graduated from UCSD three years ago."

He raised an eyebrow and blushed a little.

"Where do you work?" he asked.

"We both work at SDCC in their Psi Solutions division. One of our coworkers recommended you."

"Matt, I bet. He tried to recruit me."

"What talents do you have in your office?" I asked.

"We've got three psychics, using the old sense of the word. I'm actually the only "psychic." The other two are very talented mediums. Our boss is an ex-cop. He started the company after being amazed at the information he received from a medium during one of his investigations. He's a friend of the family and convinced me to work for him when I graduated. He handles the large, investigative cases and brings us in as needed. We deal with any smaller jobs, like yours, on our own."

I recalled the first day of class when Harry explained the distinction between the past and present definitions of psychics. Scientists now used the term, "psychic," to refer to abilities intrinsic to the person possessing them, coming from her mind and body, whereas being a "medium," which also included the disciplines of shamanism, spiritual healing, and many other fields, was about communicating with outside energies (whatever they might be) and sometimes serving as a vessel for them. Scientists have been more skeptical of mediums since even less is known about how those processes work, but like with psychics, there were more mediums with greater abilities around now than in the past. To me, the ability to communicate with outside energies was a psychic gift, but the distinction came about because mediums were dependent on something other than themselves for their gift to bear fruit. There were supposedly some rare people who were both mediums and psychics, though I'd never met one.

"Is business good?" Diana asked.

"Yeah, we're always busy. You were lucky we had a last minute cancellation or you wouldn't have been able to get an appointment today. I work until seven most evenings, and I'm booked solid for the next three weeks. There are a lot of people with questions, people who don't care if the answers are admissible in court. They come from all over the country to see us." He sat up straight in his chair, proud of his company and his work.

After a few more minutes of getting acquainted, Diana handed him the hairbrush. He placed it on his desk and took off his gloves.

"Can you tell me what John looks like and when he last touched the brush?"

"He has blond hair and blue eyes, and he touched it less than two weeks ago." Diana showed him a picture from her phone. "His real name is Charles, according to the police."

He closed his eyes and touched it in silence for a few minutes before speaking. "He finds you very beautiful, Diana. He loved brushing your long hair, but it's more than just attraction. He has feelings for you . . . maybe not love necessarily, but strong, possessive feelings, and they frustrate him. He hasn't felt this kind of emotion in a long time and didn't expect it. . . . He's not supposed to become attached. . . . His getting together with you was some kind of ploy to come into contact with other people, to do reconnaissance. He's a telepath whose power is greater with physical contact. He's here for a purpose, a purpose he believes is extremely important. He has to be careful to stay under cover so his group isn't exposed."

"What other people? Harry?" I asked.

Diana's eyes were closed, and she was listening and seeing everything that went through Mike's mind. Her face looked troubled.

"I don't know," he said.

"What's this organization? What's their purpose? Did he kill Harry?" I asked.

"I'm not seeing it clearly. It's a secretive group. They have to protect their powerbase and their long-term plan. I think they'd have no qualms about eliminating anyone who got in their way, but I can't say if he killed Harry. Not from this object."

"Are the rest of us in danger?" I asked.

"I don't know." He closed his eyes and concentrated again. After a few more minutes, he put the brush down. "I'm not getting anything new from this," he said.

Diana placed the other two objects on his desk.

He held the spatula and was silent for a minute. "I see both of you and Harry in his thoughts, as well as a few others. He's watching and studying you, but no decision has been made. . . . He actually does like to barbeque."

He next held the remote to see if he could glean more information, but all he could gather was that John did like watching sports and that Diana had an eclectic taste in TV shows.

We agreed to leave the three objects with Mike so he could compare his feelings and impressions from these to those of the person who held the gun. I texted him Detective Jones' contact information. He promised to call the police first thing on Monday and would get in touch with us after meeting with them.

Mike put his gloves back on and walked us out to the receptionist who handled the billing. "Uh, Diana, Sophia, I know you have full-time jobs, but would you be interested in consulting with us on the side? My boss would definitely be interested in your abilities."

"Not officially," I said. "I'm too busy with my job at SDCC, but if you run into a situation where you need my help, give me a call. I owe you one."

"The same goes for me," Diana agreed.

We paid for the consult and headed to Thomas's apartment. Diana was quiet.

"Did you see anything Mike didn't mention?"

"No, he was thorough. His mind was also wide open, and he was extremely visual. . . . Seeing John again was disturbing, especially viewing myself through his eyes. Ugh, I mean *Charles*." She banged her hands on the steering wheel. "Fuck it, Sophia! I'm calling him John! That's what he was to me!"

"Got it. I'll call him that too." I couldn't imagine how she felt right now. The situation was beyond crazy. She seemed to need some quiet, some space to sort things out in her head, so I gave that to her.

After about five minutes of silence, she took a few deep breaths, cleared her throat and restarted the conversation where she'd left off. "Mike is talented. He might be even better than Matt. I think he senses more of the emotions." And just like that, Diana pushed her emotions away.

"Are you really okay? It had to be tough hearing about John's feelings for you. I want to help you. Just let me know what you need."

"I'm confused." She shook her head and made a choked laugh. "God, I'm actually relieved that at least some of what John and I had was real. Isn't that insane? But in the end, he probably killed Harry, and the whole thing was a ruse."

"I'm sorry he used you like that."

Diana shrugged.

She appeared to have reached her limit for talking about John so I changed the topic. "What made you smile when we first walked into the room? You hid it well, but I could tell you were about to burst out laughing," I said.

Diana's lips curved up at the edges, and her spirits seemed to improve a little. "I'll save that story for Thomas and Nate. I think they'll appreciate it. Nate especially."

When we arrived at Thomas's place, the boys were drinking beer and cooking in the kitchen. Nate had upped Thomas's game plan, adding dessert and salad to the menu. He was slicing tomatoes and cucumbers for the salad, while Thomas hovered over his sauce. I rose up on my toes to give Nate a kiss on the cheek.

"So, what did you find out?" Nate asked.

Diana gave them an abbreviated version of our visit. She mentioned that John had been dating her as a way to come into contact with other people. She left his feelings for her out of the summary and gave me a look making it clear that that was all she wanted to share tonight.

Thomas and Nate finished preparing the pasta and salad. Since the table wasn't large enough to eat family style, we set the dishes on the counter and then filled our plates. We all ruminated as we ate, a heaviness hanging in the air. I attempted to lighten the mood since I hadn't yet heard the amusing story Diana wanted to share with the boys.

"Diana, what made you laugh when we first entered Mike's office?" I asked.

A shadow of her usual smile returned. "Well, as soon as he laid eyes on us, Mike started concocting a sexual fantasy. You can't blame him. He's a twenty-two-year-old guy who hasn't had sex in several months when suddenly two gorgeous young women dressed in little black dresses walk into his office. It took him a few seconds to suppress it," she said.

"Diana, that's not nice," Thomas chided, but in a teasing way. He knew she wasn't herself. They sometimes argued about their different ethical approaches to privileged information, but he wouldn't push her tonight.

"That explains why he blushed when he realized you were a telepath. Poor guy."

"Yes, I affect most men that way. They get embarrassed when they realize I know all of their dirty little secrets." Diana smiled a little more. I think reminding herself of what she could do made her feel more empowered. Thomas looked over at her with a conspiratorial smile.

Thomas found the story mildly amusing, but Nate didn't. I put my hand on his and gave him my best reassuring smile. He squeezed my hand and appeared to snap himself out of his temporary funk.

Thomas set out plates and utensils for everyone. "Do you ladies want beer as well or would you prefer wine or water?"

"Beer," Diana and I replied at the same time. After a trying day, a beer seemed to take the edge off more than could be explained by its alcohol content alone.

"What do you guys have planned for the weekend?" I asked. "Nate and I are going on a double-date with his friends to the Haunted Hotel downtown."

"That should be fun. I haven't gone since we all went there together in college," Diana said. "My weekend won't be as exciting but should be good. My parents come into town tomorrow. I can't wait to see them after this horrendous week. The visit will be short, though, since I have to fly to New York for work on Sunday."

"More corporate espionage?" Thomas asked.

"Yup. It never ends, but it keeps me entertained. I love to go into a boardroom as a supposed 'efficiency expert' or 'observer' from the mother company and expose the bad guys. The guilty party is usually a prick who's not only screwing over the company but his wife as well. It'll be good to get away. It might help erase the past two months from my brain."

"Thomas, what are you doing?" I asked.

"The waves should be overhead tomorrow, so I plan on surfing in the morning and then heading up to LA to see Nadia again."

"Is it getting serious?" I asked.

"I don't know," he said. "We have fun and share a lot of the same views, but there's not much electricity."

"Ah, Thomas, I thought she might be the one for you." I put down my fork and folded my arms in a sulk.

"Please, Sophia, I'm not sure there's a particular one for anyone, but we've had fun. We'll see how it goes this weekend."

"You're not going to love her and leave her, are you?" I asked.

"First of all, it's none of your business, and second of all, you know I wouldn't do that. I don't think she feels an overwhelming chemistry yet either. We're just exploring the possibilities to see if something develops. You should give me more credit, Sophia, especially considering how easy it is for a telepath to be a sexual predator."

"What do you mean?" Nate asked, digging into his food.

"Well, it wouldn't be hard to talk almost any woman into bed if I used telepathy."

"Using suggestion or by hypnotizing her?" he asked.

"Neither. I wouldn't have to be that blatant. I'd only have to say exactly what she wanted to hear when she wanted to hear it."

"You haven't tried this, have you?" I asked Thomas.

"Not to trick anyone into bed. That was my point, but I have tried out a sentence here or there. It definitely attracts a woman's attention."

"That's true for men as well," Diana added, "but they always want to have sex with you so making the effort is a waste of time."

After dinner, Thomas insisted that Diana start watching *Game of Thrones* since he already had the DVDs for the first few seasons. Thomas, Nate, and I were die-hard fans and had watched every episode. None of us minded watching them again and thought it might help Diana escape her troubles for a little while.

On our drive home, Nate seemed deep in thought, likely about the situation with John and his group, but he'd also been in a funk after hearing Diana's story.

"Did Mike's brief fantasy bother you?"

He sat up straighter in his seat, and his jaw clenched a little. "I was that transparent, huh?"

"Kinda."

"It did bother me but only for a moment. You're beautiful, Sophia. I can imagine that any guy who sees you might have a sexual thought, but imagining and knowing are two different things. It took me a few seconds to process. I guess I just want everyone to know that you're mine. I don't typically think of myself as a caveman type of guy, but my instincts told me to pummel him and carry you away on my shoulder."

He glanced over at me to gauge my reaction. "Don't worry. I'm not usually the jealous type. The hormonal surges from falling in love are mostly to blame. The jealousy will fade with time."

"Hmm." Knowing that the jealousy would decrease was encouraging, but it seemed like he was implying that his feelings for me would also fade. That, I didn't like. I eyed him suspiciously.

"What? I took a Psychology of Love class in college and learned a little about the subject. Men have hormonal changes that can trigger intense possessiveness. Did you know that the experts compare falling in love to having an addiction?" He raised his eyebrows at me, daring me to challenge his knowledge on the matter.

I laughed. "I can't believe you took that class. I thought only women took it."

He blushed. "Well, you were dating Brian. I'd heard it was a great place to meet women. There were only three guys in the entire class, and it worked like a charm."

"So, you ended up dating a girl from the class?"

"Two, actually. One during the class, and another a few months after the class ended. It was very educational," he teased.

He looked at me a second, noticing the frown on my face, and then pulled into the garage and parked the car. "Now who's jealous? You can't be mad at me for dating people in the past when you were with Brian."

"I know. I know," I said as I got out of the car. "I guess I'm a bit hormone-addled as well. I'm sure women notice how hot you are every day, and the idea does *not* make me happy."

I opened the gate and pressed the button for the elevator a bit aggressively. It beeped open, and we stepped inside. I looked up at Nate. "Although I guess I wouldn't mind losing some of the insecurity and jealousy, I don't want to lose all of the other exhilarating emotions."

"I don't either, but in about six months or so, our feelings will be tamed. If we do things right, something deeper, more permanent should take its place." He rubbed his thumb on the back of my hand and pulled me into his arms, his eyes latching onto mine. "I love you, Sophia. I don't think that will ever change."

He sought my lips gently, sweetly, but I wasn't in the mood for reserved. What I felt at that moment wasn't yet tamed. I jumped up, wrapping my legs around him. He had to take a step back, but he caught me. The surprised look on his face quickly changed to something more dark and feral. He kissed me while hurrying us into my apartment. Nate sort of stumbled and staggered as he carried me to the bedroom, pushing my back into walls and doors on the way. He threw me on the bed and hastily removed my dress while kissing, licking, caressing and occasionally nipping whatever bit of skin he could find. The animal in me was roaring to life. I ripped open his shirt, sending buttons flying across the room, and licked a long line up from his navel to his chest. After unbuttoning the waistband of his pants, I stuck my hands inside to grab his muscular butt. He groaned and quickly helped me rid him of the rest of his garments.

In the next second, his knee opened my legs wide, and his hips began to press into me when he froze, then abruptly pulled back and grabbed a condom. The sex was rough and primal, and God, it was amazing. I screamed his name with the thrust that pushed me over the top. He cupped my hips in his hands, raising me up, and rammed me hard and fast a few more times, grunting and shouting a few choice phrases. We held each other tightly, breathing hard, sweat trickling down Nate's forehead. I wrapped my legs around him and trailed my fingers through his damp hair.

"I almost didn't do the right thing."

"What?" I asked.

"I almost couldn't make myself put that condom on. It was like a primitive impulse possessed me. My body wanted to mate, *truly mate*, with yours. That's never happened before," he admitted.

"I'm not sure I could have objected. I wanted you so badly I wasn't thinking." I kissed his lips and searched his eyes. "I can't wait until you return from your trip. The pill will definitely be effective by then. Assuming your test results are clean, we won't have to use condoms anymore."

Nate smiled and dipped his head to kiss me. "I'm glad to see I'm not the only one who's impatient."

CHAPTER THIRTEEN

The week had tired us out, and we slept late on Saturday. It had been the longest week of my life. We'd closed the blinds the night before but had forgotten the drapes, and the light eventually woke me. I turned to face Nate and watched him sleep. He looked so peaceful lying on his side with his arm tucked under the pillow. His dark brown hair fell forward over his eyes. I carefully moved the strands of hair out of his face. He didn't stir. His left arm rested in front of his stomach, completely relaxed, but you could still tell how strong and toned he was. His chest was pure sexy. Staring at it made me want to see more, to touch more. I lifted the covers slightly to gaze at the rest of him. I hadn't really had time yet to scrutinize his equipment and had never observed him unaroused.

I looked up at his face for any sign of waking, but his muscles were slack, and his breathing as soft and even as the minutes before. I scooted down in the bed just a little to get a closer view and confirmed my long-held notion that male anatomy was truly bizarre. I couldn't imagine having those parts dangling from my body, especially something that could change shape so drastically. It started to stir. I quickly glanced up at Nate's face and was relieved to find him still sleeping. I wondered what dream was causing this change. It continued to grow larger until it looked so taut it might burst. The transformation never ceased to amaze me. I looked for several seconds and decided that it seemed proportional in size to the rest of his body, which was substantial. It certainly did a damn good job.

"Do you like what you see?" Nate asked. I jumped at the sound of his voice and pulled the covers over my head. I felt like a kid caught with her hand in the cookie jar. I prayed he hadn't been awake the entire time I was checking him out. I remained quiet and still, hoping the moment would pass so I could regain my dignity.

"Sophia, are you there?" He pulled the covers away from my head, gripped my waist and with a big smile dragged my body to his.

"I'm sleeping," I said.

"Oh, is that what you were doing?" he teased. "Forgive me. I thought you were doing something else." He pressed himself up against my side and began to kiss my neck.

I was still feeling flustered and thought maybe I could talk my way out of my embarrassment. "Nate, do you worry that someone might be spying on us? I know they removed the bugs that were here, but should we check sometimes to see if new ones pop up?"

"I wouldn't say I'm worried, but I guess we should be more cautious. We could check now and then. I just hope that Harry was their only target and that they'll leave everyone else they were spying on alone. He was the only public figure. I can't see a reason for them to spy on any of you except for your connection to him."

"Maybe the bugs weren't even planted by them? Do you think the government could be keeping tabs on psychics?"

"That's a disquieting thought, but my car wasn't bugged. At least it doesn't appear to be all psychics. I wonder if anyone else from work is being monitored."

"We should check. Most of the time, I forget that someone actually invaded my home, but other times, I remember, and it creeps me out."

"You know I don't mind staying the night here with you." He began kissing my neck again.

"Ooh, I don't mind either. Can you believe we've only been sleeping together for a week? Doesn't it seem like much longer?"

"Wow, you're right," he said, rubbing his scratchy face against my shoulder. "Not that it's getting old. It just keeps getting better, but it feels like our bodies have known each other for a long time."

"When we sleep, my body fits into yours like a missing piece. Your arms feel like they're supposed to be around me, holding me tight."

"And when we make love, it feels like I'm coming home, like I'm supposed to be inside of you."

"I know," I said, "and when you're there, I don't want to let you go. I want you to stay joined with me like that forever."

"I've never had this kind of physical connection with anyone before," he said. "It's physical but more than just physical attraction."

"I've never experienced this before either," I said.

"Really?" he asked. "Not even with Brian?" His face was guarded, like he didn't believe it could be true.

I put my hand on his cheek and said, "Really." His lips opened into his wide, dazzling smile, and he bent his head down to kiss my lips. The kiss grew in tempo and heat until we explored the intensity of that connection yet again.

"Has anyone ever told you that you're a generous lover? Most men don't give women the extra attention they need to reach the end game, so to speak."

He kissed my nose. "How can I possibly answer that question without getting myself in trouble?" I elbowed him, and he laughed.

"I just want you to be as involved as I am, to enjoy it as much as I do, though I have to admit, I'm not totally selfless. That Psychology of Love class I told you about had a section on sex, of course. Every time we orgasm with each other, it binds us closer. It may require a little extra patience and restraint on my part, but I want our lovemaking to increase my pull on you, not just your pull on me."

"You're an amazing lover so I'll crave you more and more?" I smiled and kissed him. "I think that's a reasonable trade-off."

* * *

Nate cooked the eggs and bacon, while I made some toast and tea. Although he was usually a coffee drinker in the morning, he'd begun to appreciate my taste in teas and as a typical male enjoyed the high-tech sophistication of my tea maker. After breakfast, we decided to spend some time by ourselves before meeting back up for the evening's events. I wanted to catch a kung fu class and make it into the yoga studio for once. He was again out of clothes to wear and wanted to make a trip back to his apartment to wash some laundry and go for a run on the beach while he waited.

When I was about to leave for kung fu, Roger called me to help with an emergency in the Middle East. Since he hinted that the job might take a while, I texted Nate to cancel our evening plans with his friends at the Haunted Hotel. Nate had been looking forward to introducing us so I felt bad about canceling and was disappointed myself, but emergencies at work were true emergencies. Roger and I pulled into the parking lot at the same time, and he briefed me on what he knew. Terrorists had kidnapped three Marines six hours earlier without a trace. Our goal was to find them before the soldiers became part of the next sensationalist beheadings. Though captives were sometimes held for months, their tactics had changed of late, making it impossible to predict how long they'd be kept alive.

We brought our computers into the projecting room. Roger established a live link with the military to relay any information I could report while under back to them. I would be checking out several suspected places within a 50-mile radius of the last known location near the Syrian border in Iraq. I familiarized myself with the first target, plugging the latitude and longitude into Google Earth, and compared the images to the latest drone photographs.

After memorizing the pictures of the missing and a few potential insurgents, I placed a sketchpad and pencil on the chair's swivel table and relaxed into the soft, leather recliner. I settled into a meditative state and sent my consciousness on its journey.

Sand, lots of sand. A nearly full moon outlined the encampment in the desert darkness. Six canvas-walled structures stood around a central fire, where three guards talked softly in Arabic. Two others patrolled the perimeter. Among the tents, I found supplies, weapons, lots of sleeping men, and a few women, but no sign of the missing.

Roger and I regrouped to investigate the next target and then more. The places varied from almost normal-looking houses, mosques, warehouses, and office spaces to seemingly abandoned rubble-strewn buildings. After five hours, we took a bathroom break and grabbed vending machine food and water.

"Should we bring in a family member? They wanted to avoid alerting the families of the situation if we could just find them by location, but they believe they can get one to us in about five hours."

"Maybe, but personal connections are harder the farther away they are, at least for me. It could help to bring Nate in like last time."

"He does seem to be good at finding people. I already have Carol and Matt on standby."

"Let's give this another hour before they call the families. Maybe it's wishful thinking, but I feel like we're getting close."

This time I travelled to an outdated office building. Filing cabinets and desks laden with clunky computers and old, bulky monitors filled the rooms. This office floor was deserted, but indistinct male voices and a woman's scream pierced the air. I moved down to the basement through a circuitous hallway and found them.

"Fuck!"

"Sophia, what is it?"

I swallowed. "Two of them are dead, Johnson and Turner. Their heads are propped up on newspapers in the corner near four assholes playing a fucking card game!" I swallowed again and tried to slow my rapid breathing. My job was to respond intellectually to the situation but not react emotionally. *Keep your head in the game, Sophia.*

"I don't see West. She has to be the one who screamed. I'll try to find her."

Roger made sure our military contacts received everything I'd said. They began to make plans while I anxiously searched, listening for her. *How big is this goddamn place?* This lair extended well beyond the confines of the office building's exterior. Each hallway led to another with more rooms and occasional people but not the soldier I sought. Another scream, and there she was. Alive, but barely. Her face was a bloody mess, with one eye swollen shut. The other bloodshot hazel eye stared at the ceiling with a grim determination. She was being raped and had been repeatedly by the look of her battered body and the crowd praying around the man defiling her now.

"Sabaya," he repeated over and over as he thrust into her. *Slave.* To these sick, sadistic barbarians, if they considered her a slave, their raping of her was conveniently considered a religious act, bringing them closer to Allah. It allowed them to justify their lucrative sex slave trade and helped to recruit more young men.

I told Roger everything, which he relayed in turn. "Stay with her for now."

I couldn't stomach watching it. She didn't fight any more, just grunted occasionally due to the pain of jostled, possibly broken ribs and a clearly broken right arm, likely results from resisting earlier. She lay there immobile, gritting her teeth as a tear silently fell past her temple when the next one took his turn, her mind focusing elsewhere. *These bastards deserved to die.* I felt like I was going to throw up. I distracted myself by studying the faces of the men in the room, memorizing whatever details I could.

"Sophia, we need to know more about the layout of the building. Find all exits, count the men, the weapons. Look for security and surveillance equipment. Sketch it out. They've got intel on the street exterior of the building and the surroundings already."

Though I couldn't help by staying in that room, I still felt like I was abandoning her. *Maybe it would lead to her rescue.* That thought spurred me on. I worked furiously to get Roger everything they needed, phasing back and forth to sketch, over and over again. Some men had moved between rooms, so my counts were in flux but were close enough. Investigation completed, I went back to her room. Not much had changed, only some new faces, some new bruises. I was now free to sketch them, phasing from my sketchpad and back again. I drew anyone I could find until Roger engaged my attention.

"Get to the hallway outside of the east room with the largest number of men. We're incoming in five minutes. I need to know when they're alerted to our presence."

Once at my designated spot, the tension mounted. My hands gripped the armrests of my chair, and my pulse drummed in my ears. I hated the wait before a fight. Time ticked by slowly.

"We're in the building. Did you hear anything? Have they noticed?"

"Negative to both."

"Is anyone in your hallway?"

"No. It's empty," I said.

"We're moving in. Check the next hallway." As he said this, I saw the Marines moving silently toward me. I moved to the next hallway.

"No one."

"Move to the next." The soldiers filed in behind me as I went to the next corridor.

"Still no one." I was at her door. A few soldiers joined me. In an instant, several doors were kicked open in unison, and all hell broke loose. Gunfire, shouting. In her room, the soldiers shot a few men who went for weapons, but the others had their hands up and backed into a corner. A Marine wrapped a blanket around West, placed her gently next to the wall and stood in front of her.

"They're in control, Sophia. Look around to make sure they didn't miss anything before they bring her out."

The terrorists I could find had been either permanently neutralized or captured. I told Roger, and the Marines pulled out, cradling their injured comrade and bringing along the heads and bodies of the two murdered soldiers and some prisoners. Mission accomplished. I helped Roger wrap up the report, then on my way out, I texted Nate, asking him to meet me at my place.

I climbed into my car. Alone and unobserved for the first time in hours, I laid my head on the steering wheel and cried. I cried for the two beheaded men and their families, for the torture and brutal raping of Lt. West, for the violence and bloodshed in general and for myself, for the stress radiating throughout my exhausted body from the entire affair. I loved my job, was glad I could help people, but sometimes . . . it was hard.

I breathed deeply in and out for several minutes until I could pull myself together enough to drive home. I didn't see Nate's car in the garage. I thought about projecting to my apartment to make sure the coast was clear. I'd almost forgotten about my own issues, but I was too worn out to care. After I dragged myself into my apartment, I lay down on the couch and didn't move until Nate opened the door.

"Hey," he said. He studied me, concern in his face. "I brought you some food. I figured you didn't get to eat dinner."

I sat up and rubbed my hands over my face and through my hair. "Thanks. I didn't, but I'm not hungry."

"You don't look so good. Have you had anything to drink? I'll get you a glass of water."

He brought me the glass and sat next to me. I drank half of it and set it down on the coffee table, my hand shaking.

"What happened?" he asked.

"I'm not allowed to talk about it yet, but . . . it was a tough one." I swallowed hard thinking back to it. My chin started quivering as I lost hold of my emotions again. "Just . . . hold me."

* * *

We slept late again on Sunday and spent a relaxing afternoon at the beach, lying in the sunshine reading and strolling in the surf hand-in-hand. Since Halloween had reared its fearsome head, we carved a pumpkin and set it outside. We cooked and ate dinner as we waited for the trick-or-treaters. Although I'd warned Nate that only a handful of trick-or-treaters had visited me in years past, he was thrilled at the prospect of handing out candy. While cleaning the dishes, he began to seem a bit distant. We then picked out a movie on Netflix and started getting comfortable on the couch, but Nate still seemed preoccupied, as if something was bothering him.

"What's wrong? Do you not want to watch a movie any more?" I asked.

"No, I do. . . . There's just something I want to talk to you about."

"What?" I asked and turned my body to face him.

"Well, you know that my lease is up at the end of November. I'll need to sign a new lease soon if I want to find a place to live in time." His eyes had been focused on his fingers caressing my hand but suddenly bored into mine. "How would you feel about us living together? I know it's really early in our relationship for such a move, but I'm spending all of my time here . . . and I don't want to be anywhere else."

"Oh," I said but held back any further words. I hadn't seen it coming. Though I was mostly overjoyed that he wanted to be with me, fear and worry surfaced with just a touch of panic. I wasn't sure which emotion would win out.

Nate hid his feelings, but he watched my face closely. "If you think we're not ready to live together, that's fine. I still plan to live close so I can be near you and work. What do you think?"

After a moment of thoughtful silence, I had to say something. "Nate, I can't imagine a night when I won't want you sleeping next to me, but . . . I'm kind of afraid of 'officially' moving in together. It's a huge step. What if it messes up our relationship? I know it feels like longer, but we've only been together for *two weeks*. Most people would think we're crazy. What if we start to annoy each other? What if we have a fight and need some time apart? What if it doesn't work out?"

"Well, if it doesn't work out, I'll simply find somewhere else to live. Come on. Give it a chance. We have something special. You know we do. Don't think about how it might look to other people or how it compares to an average relationship. What we have *isn't* an average relationship. Sophia, I *know* this is crazy. I know this is a leap for both of us. Honestly, I wouldn't have brought it up now except that I have to find a place to live. I love you. I want to live with you. Do you want to live with me?"

I stared at Nate silently for a moment, trying to figure out what I truly wanted while still keeping my fears in mind. As he waited for my answer, he shifted in his seat, looked away from me, and raked his fingers through his hair in an agitated manner. I placed my hand on his cheek and turned his face back to mine. "Nate, I do want to live with you, but I'm scared, scared it will somehow make everything fall apart."

Nate smiled and pushed a tuft of hair gently behind my ear. "Don't worry, Sophia. I love you more than I've ever loved anyone. We just need to be open with each other. Let me know if you need some time alone, and I'll do the same. If something starts to annoy us, we should talk about it immediately before it festers and becomes a problem. We can divide up bills and household duties however you like."

"You sound like you read up on this."

"I did my research," he said. "This is a big step for me too. I have the same concerns that you have."

I squeezed his hand and snuggled against him. "Nate, if we're thinking of going down this path, we should probably find out if we even want the same things in life. Where do you see yourself in ten years? And we haven't talked about this yet . . . but . . . do you even want to have kids?"

Nate kissed my hand. "I've always wanted children, but I'm not in a hurry. As far as work goes, SDCC has been rewarding and interesting so far, but except for learning new languages, it's not intellectually stimulating. After several years, the astral travel might become monotonous for me. I'm still considering medical or graduate school and have been saving up for that. I guess I don't have my professional life sorted out, but I'm a hard worker, and I'll do what I need to do to support a family. What about you?"

"I want to have kids some day too. When I was young, I always imagined my life being like my mom's — a working mom with two children by the time I'm thirty. I know now that my ideal may not work out, and that the specific scenario was just a childhood dream anyway."

I took a deep breath in and let it out, feeling the color in my cheeks rise as I prepared to reveal what my heart desired more than anything else. "As I grew up, I realized that what I want most of all is a husband that will always love me and be my best friend, someone I can trust completely, who will never cheat on me or leave me, someone I can learn from but also teach, someone I can travel and explore the world with. I need someone who's my equal, someone I can lean on."

Nate looked intently into my eyes. "It seems that we do want the same things in life." He kissed me gently at first, and then the kiss grew more passionate until the doorbell rang. We both laughed. It was as if the kids knocking at the door were a reflection of what our life would be like with kids of our own interrupting at inopportune moments. Nate handed out the candy and came back to me.

"Where were we?" he asked, but before we could begin the kiss again, I interjected, "So, we're really going to live together?"

"It looks that way," he said, happy and smug. "When should I move in?"

After sorting out a few details, we settled on the following Saturday. We'd already made the decision and didn't see a reason to wait. This time I leaned over to kiss him, but again the doorbell interrupted us. "Hmm," he said, "I'm beginning to like giving out Halloween candy less and less." Nate got up and opened the door for the kids, winking at me. He pretended to be miffed, but I could tell he was enjoying himself.

When he came back, we decided to play it safe for the rest of evening and cuddled on the couch to watch the movie, pausing briefly for the trick-or-treaters. When the movie finished, we retreated to the bedroom to celebrate our newly changed circumstances.

CHAPTER FOURTEEN

The workweek started off like any other. Even though it was what I wanted, I was still adjusting to the idea that Nate and I would soon be sharing a home. Life can change so fast. In the last two weeks, Harry had been murdered, gone forever in the blink of an eye, and I had fallen in love, so deeply that Nate and I would soon be living together. I wasn't yet ready to announce the move to my friends and family and was relieved that Diana was out of town for the week. I didn't know whether I was happier to avoid her teasing or her cynical cross-examination. I also planned to avoid Thomas for at least a few days until I felt more comfortable with the situation.

When I arrived home that evening, a message blinked on the answering machine. My mom was one of the few people who called my landline and actually left a message. I pressed play and tried to ignore the sinking feeling in my gut.

"Sophia, I had a strange dream about you last night. Could you give me a call when you get in?"

I cringed. Since I'd volunteered to cook dinner that night, I started to prepare the steak and the acorn squash-goat cheese salad with bacon vinaigrette before giving her a call. Once I had the acorn squash in the oven to roast and the bacon sizzling in a pan, I dialed her number.

"Hey, Mom, you said you had a dream?"

"Yes," she said. "I saw you holding hands with a man I assume was Nate. You looked happy and then you walked together into a building. That was it, but it left me with a feeling that something significant was going to happen for you two. How are things going? Last time we spoke, you said things were getting serious."

Since it had happened repeatedly throughout my life, I should have expected the psychic universe to out me. It was a small consolation that my mom's precognitive dreams were only vague and symbolic, unlike mine, but that didn't make me any more pleased with the situation. Though I would have preferred a few more days of wrapping my head around the idea first, I decided to surrender to my fate and just tell her everything.

"Well . . . as a matter of fact, last night we decided that Nate should move in. His lease is up at the end of the month, and since we're spending all of our free time here, we thought we'd give it a try. I know it's crazy, Mom. We've been together such a short time. It's completely unlike me to do something so impulsive." I felt nervous, uncertain how she might respond.

"So, you're in love with him?" she asked.

Though she wasn't in the room, my cheeks started to burn. "Yes, I am. He's a kind, smart, sweet and all around great guy. He makes me happy. You're going to love him, Mom."

"Sophia, I'm so proud of you."

I dropped the piece of bacon I'd been turning. "What?"

"I'm so proud of you for listening to your heart instead of your head for once. I'm sure you feel anxious. What happened with your father has made it hard for you to take risks with men. Of course, things may not work out, and it's no fun when they don't, but you can't find love if you don't take a chance. You deserve to be happy, sweetheart."

"Ah, Mom. You're going to make me cry," I said.

"I wouldn't want that, but, speaking of crying, Thomas said the memorial went well. How are you feeling about Harry?"

"I'm still sad and shocked from time to time. It hurts to see Irene suffering." We talked a bit longer about Harry, Irene, John, Nate, and the bits of work I could disclose while I finished the bacon and started frying the steak. When Nate came in, he kissed me on the cheek and sniffed quietly about the kitchen. I said goodbye to my mom with a promise that she would meet Nate soon.

"Was that your mom?" he asked.

"Yes. She called because she had a precognitive dream that told her something was happening for us." I removed the vegetables from the oven and set them on the empty burners to cool.

"Wow. You can't hide anything, can you?"

"Welcome to my life."

"She didn't say we were moving too fast, did she?"

"Surprisingly, no. I thought she might. Were you worried about that too?"

"Well, some people still believe you should be married before you have sex and especially before you live together. I know that's rare these days, but you never know. I don't want anyone to make you feel bad. What did she say?"

"She's happy for us and proud of me for taking a chance. She wants to meet you."

As I turned the steaks, he hugged me from behind, putting his arms around my shoulders and resting his head on mine. "That's wonderful news. Have you told anyone else yet?" he asked.

"No, not yet. How about you? Have you told anyone?"

"Yes, but only my friends down in PB. They're going to help us move on Saturday. I've reserved a moving van and a storage space, and I let the apartment complex know I wouldn't be signing a new lease."

"You were busy today. Are you hungry?"

"Ravenous."

*   *   *

On Wednesday shortly after lunch, I was sitting at my desk reading about my next case when my cell phone rang.

"Hi, Sophia. It's Mike from Psychic Investigators.

"Hi, Mike. What's up?"

"I met with the police this morning, and they said I could tell you what I saw."

"What did you see?"

"Well, I held the murder weapon, and long story short, your 'John' was the murderer. It was a little cloudy at first because he was wearing gloves when the murder happened, but he'd held the weapon without gloves at another time. John did use his telepathy to hold Harry immobile. He actually tried to get Harry to hold and fire the gun with him, but he couldn't force Harry to raise his arm, mentally or physically, without producing signs of a struggle. He didn't want to murder Harry, but it was his duty and for a 'greater good,' as he saw it. I still wasn't able to piece together what the 'greater good' might mean. John may also have stronger feelings for Diana than one might expect from him using her as a cover. She came up in his thoughts more than a few times. He didn't want to leave her and was unhappy with the way things had to end."

"Does that mean he's gone for good? Can we assume Harry was his only target?"

"I'm not certain, but it felt like his mission had been completed."

I'd been holding my breath and let it out in a big sigh. "Mike, I don't know how to thank you. I know Irene will rest more easily knowing the killer's been identified."

"I'm glad I could help. I owed it to Harry. He made a huge impact on me in college. God, even though I've seen it, I still can't believe someone murdered him." He struggled to keep his voice level and cleared his throat. "I'll leave Diana's things at the receptionist's desk so either of you can pick them up when you get the chance."

"Thanks again, Mike. We'll try to pick them up in the next week or so. If you need a favor, call me."

So, John *was* the murderer. Knowing for certain gave me some relief, especially if he truly was finished here, but we still didn't understand why Harry was killed or why the rest of us were being monitored. Irene might rest more easily, yet I worried how Diana might take this. I wondered what the police were going to do with the information. I had too many questions running through my mind to concentrate on my work.

I needed to share the news with someone. Nate was in an astral projection. Diana was still out of town, and I preferred to give her the news in person so I could gauge her reaction. I decided to call Irene to see how she was doing and relay the news if the timing felt right.

"Sophia, how are you?" Irene asked as soon as she picked up the phone.

"I'm doing fine. How are you?"

"They tell me I am doing as well as can be expected. I went to a therapy group for grieving spouses yesterday. I am uncomfortable talking to strangers, but I promised Richard I would try it for a month."

"Is your family still there?"

"Richard and Barbara left today. Mei will be here for another week."

"Have you been working? That might help."

"No, but if you join me in my studio this weekend, I will start again. Is there a day that works better for you?"

"Sunday's best." Since I would see her soon and she seemed to be moving in a positive direction, I decided to wait to tell her about John until then.

After we scheduled a time and hung up the phone, I opened my connection to Thomas and called his name.

"Sophia, what's up?" he thought.

I replayed the conversation with Mike over again in my mind for Thomas.

"So it was John after all. That bastard! Jesus, let's hope he really did complete his mission. What sort of greater good could be served by murdering Harry?"

"It doesn't make sense unless Harry was involved in something we don't know about."

"It's possible, but Harry was an open-book. I should have noticed if he were hiding something big. I can't believe he was involved in anything nefarious. They could have killed him for who he was, for what he advocated and represented. There was no subterfuge in him, only a desire to understand and to help people. He could have been set up. Remember, one spyware program was trying to trick the other."

"I'd forgotten about that."

"By the way, congrats on the big step with Nate. Mom was so excited that she had to share it with me."

"Thanks. You don't think we're being too rash?"

"Who am I to judge? But, I do know he loves you, and you seem to love him too."

"Did you peek around in his head?"

"Not purposefully. When I saw him Friday, he still didn't shield well. You know I try to ignore other people's thoughts the best I can, but most of his thoughts are about you, and some of them get through. Unfortunately for me, some of them are more graphic than others."

"God. That's embarrassing."

"I know, I know. That's the burden of telepathy. I'm sorry I brought it up, but you might want him to practice shielding more. Your coworkers may be learning more about you than they care to know."

"Got it."

"Over and out."

I stared at my computer screen for a few minutes more and fought the urge to call the police. I itched to know whether they were convinced by the new information and if so, what they planned to do about it. I knew they wouldn't appreciate my call so I took a deep breath to clear my mind and forced myself to continue working.

* * *

By Friday, there was still no word from the police. My restraint had reached its limit, and I placed a call to Detective Jones and asked him how things had gone with Mike the other day.

"Didn't he talk to you? We gave him the go-ahead."

"He told me that John was the murderer, but I don't know whether you'll be able to do anything."

"The information he gave us isn't admissible, but at least we know that John, a.k.a. Charles, is the perpetrator. I want this guy, Sophia. We're pursuing multiple threads to find him. Your friend, Diana, will undergo hypnotic regression next week to see if she can recall the license plate number of his car. I don't have anything else to tell you right now, but we hope that at least one path of our investigation identifies his current whereabouts soon. When Diana comes in next week, we'll let her know of any progress then if we can."

"Did you tell her John's the killer?" I asked.

"No, we arranged her appointment before Mike met with us. By the way, thanks for sending him. Mike's quite talented, and it helps to know we're on the right track. Bye, Sophia."

"Bye," I mumbled, certain he was trying to get rid of me. I wished they had a lead. Since I'd known John was incognito, I'm not sure what I'd expected. I guess I'd naively hoped that justice would prevail, that the bad guy would be apprehended. Knowing who committed the murder but not being able to do anything about it was frustrating, and I needed some freaking peace of mind. Even if he might be done with us, I didn't like the idea of him lurking around out there, especially when he might have been spying on me. *Okay, Sophia, get back to work.*

By the time I'd wrapped up my day and arrived home, Nate was almost finished cooking another delectable Italian meal.

"That smell is mouth-watering," I said.

I went over to him and stood on my tiptoes to give him a quick kiss hello. He grabbed me around the waist faster than I'd anticipated and pulled me off-balance into a sort of dip. He kissed me deeply and smiled.

"It's good to see you too," I said when I caught my breath.

Dinner was again delicious. I couldn't help eating more with Nate around and made a mental note to increase my workouts if my jeans started to feel tight. As we cleaned the dishes, I told him what the police had to say. He seemed annoyed while I was retelling the story.

"What's wrong?" I asked.

"I thought you weren't going to be involved anymore. Why are you calling the police?"

"I'm seeing Irene on Sunday, and I want to tell her what Mike saw and what the police are doing with that information." I knew this wasn't the whole truth, but to be honest, I wasn't exactly sure why I couldn't just leave it to the authorities. I did find it hard to let it go when the life of a dear friend had been sacrificed, but maybe I also possessed an ingrained obsession with justice, fairness, or punishing wrongdoers. Maybe my job had made me too used to solving mysteries.

"Irene told you she didn't want you to concern yourself any longer. She wants to keep you safe. I want to keep you safe. Please let the police take care of it."

"I'll try to," I conceded, "but Diana still needs my support. After we finish moving your stuff tomorrow, I'd like to go over to her place for a few hours. I want to tell her the news about John in person."

He didn't say anything as he put the pots and pans away, but when he hung up the hand towel, he captured my eyes. "Believe me, I'd like John to be brought to justice too, but I'm afraid for you. Someone, probably John, was also tracking you. What if you're still a target? He messed with your head and screwed with Diana's life. I'd like to believe he's done with the two of you, but my gut tells me he's not. He knows who I am, but I don't think I'm on his radar. If you feel we can do something the police can't, let *me* do it. I don't want you to give him any reason to come after you. Remember, John is supposedly part of a powerful group. We have no idea what we're up against. I think our best approach is to keep a low profile and be cautious."

"You're right. I promise to stay out of it unless I think of something we can do to help. Before I do anything, though, we'll talk about it first. I don't want you to put yourself in danger either." I took a shot at changing the subject since he still seemed annoyed. "So, what do you want to do tonight?"

He sighed and pulled me against him. "I just want to lie naked with you, whether we're learning foreign languages, making love, or talking. I need to feel your skin on mine." He leaned down to kiss me and began to slowly strip me of my clothes. I unbuttoned his shirt and ran my hands over his chest.

"I love you, Sophia."

"I love you too."

* * *

When the morning light streamed through the gaps in my drapes, I woke, stretched, and then stared at Nate. He was like a sleeping Adonis, so peaceful, so perfect. I turned on my side and cuddled my back deeply into him, trying to go back to sleep. He instinctively pulled me close without even waking. My skin was soaking up every bit of him, his essence, his warmth. I couldn't sleep but was lulled into a peaceful state feeling his chest rise and fall as he breathed. I sensed the tension in his body when he finally awoke. His hand trailed down my side, cupping my hip, then my thigh until he brought it back up to my breast.

"Mmm. Sleeping naked with you can be very distracting," he whispered into my ear and nuzzled his face into my hair behind it, breathing me in.

"Good morning," I said as I turned my body to face his, still wrapped in his arms.

"How could it not be when I wake up next to you?" He leaned in to kiss me tenderly, running his fingers lightly down my spine.

I shivered and wiggled in response.

"Did that tickle?" he asked.

"A little."

He smiled. "Hmm. I didn't realize you were so ticklish. I like seeing you squirm." He then commenced a session of very light caresses and soft touches that left me writhing and giggling on the bed until I almost couldn't stand it. Apparently, he was practically beyond a breaking point too, as we began to make love fast and furiously.

Afterwards, Nate cuddled me again and asked about my dreams. I vaguely recalled two, but three were recorded on my iPhone so I played them for both of us. The one I didn't remember was a recurring stress dream where I was on stage about to sing in front of an audience but didn't know the song, and the words and notes kept changing on the sheets of music in front of me. Nate found my dreams fascinating and enjoyed knowing what was passing through my head while I slept next to him.

Within the hour, we had the rental truck and were driving to Nate's apartment. He'd texted his friends once we'd signed out the truck, and they were ready and waiting for us when we pulled up. Being the lone female, I was given the task of boxing up the kitchen stuff and any other remaining loose items, while the five men moved the heavy furniture. It was sexist, but I think I got the better end of the deal. Most of Nate's stuff was still packed in the boxes he'd brought down from Palo Alto, so in good time, his apartment was empty, and we headed for my place.

After unloading all of the boxes and the few pieces of furniture we'd be combining with mine, Nate and the guys left for the storage facility to stow the extra furniture while I started unpacking. It was fun combining our cookware, plates, and what not. Their addition made the kitchen seem like a grown-up's, a place where we might legitimately entertain. I also enjoyed seeing his clothes fill out the space in the closet opposite mine. I guess we really were joining our lives together. Nate called to let me know they were finished and had just dropped off the truck. Since I'd planned on visiting Diana that afternoon, he was going to treat his buddies to lunch and drinks at a local brewery.

Diana knew I'd be stopping by, but I called to make sure the timing worked and picked up some sandwiches on the way. She looked really tired or a little sick when she answered the door but said that the three-hour time change between the coasts always threw her system off.

As we ate our sandwiches at the glass table in her kitchen nook, I worked up my courage and told her that Nate and I had just moved in together. Her jaw dropped and shock washed over her face. I don't think I could have surprised her more if I'd told her I'd given birth to an alien baby.

"Wow, that's a bold move after being together such a short time." She narrowed her eyes at me and scooted back in her chair, her arms crossed over her chest. "Who are you and what have you done with my overly sensible and risk-averse friend?"

"We're in love, Diana," I then leaned in and lowered my voice, "and having the most amazing sex I've ever had. I don't want to spend a night without him."

A sly smile erupted on her face. "So, he's good, huh? I thought he might be, but sometimes you can't tell with these masculine yet sensitive guys. If they're too macho, they're not usually much use in the bedroom, and if they're too sensitive, they're frequently not aggressive enough. Well done, Sophia, you caught yourself a good one."

I blushed. I tried to talk about sex like an adult but still felt embarrassed whenever I did.

"Oh, come on." She threw her wadded up napkin at me. "But seriously, living together was his idea, right? You must have been completely freaked at first."

"Yes, it was his. He wouldn't have brought it up this soon except that he had to find a place to live, but yeah, I was spooked. I've been uncomfortable talking to anyone about it all week. The weird thing is that sharing a home with him feels right, like we're supposed to be together."

Diana stared at me, deep in thought, and finally sighed. "Well, it's a good thing I already got you a housewarming present."

"You did?"

"Not that I knew I needed to." She still looked at me questioningly. Diana didn't like surprises. She got up from the table, and I followed her into her sleek, modern office.

"I captured a great picture of you and Nate dancing at my party. I took several, but this one turned out better than expected. You're both clear even though you were constantly on the move." She handed me an artistic silver frame with a picture in it that sped my heart.

Our profiles were perfect, and you could almost see the electricity between us in our gaze.

"It's like I caught the moment you first started falling in love," she said.

"Oh, Diana, it's wonderful." I grabbed her in a vice-like hug. "Thank you so much. You do realize that you've exposed yourself. Other people will now know that you're more sentimental than you let on."

She gave me a wan smile. "I also know about John. I suspect you came over here to tell me in person, but I found out from Mike myself on Thursday."

"I guess I'm predictable, but I'm worried about you."

"Aside from moving in with Nate, yes, you are and always have been predictable."

"How are you feeling? This can't be easy."

"I'm kind of numb. It's surreal, actually, like I'm living in the world of James Bond. Maybe I should be flattered because I guess that makes me one of the hot Bond girls." Her attempt to make light of the situation failed. Her smile didn't reach her eyes.

"Mike told you that John didn't want to end his relationship with you, right? Are you worried that he might try to see you again?"

"He told me, but I can't imagine John would come back. The feelings Mike described didn't seem overwhelming, and he'd have to be stupid to contemplate it. With his background and how well he played me, I doubt he's that."

"He's powerful, though, and possibly arrogant. Arrogance does breed stupidity."

"Well, let's hope we never see him or his mysterious group again. Let's also hope that the only reason the rest of us were on his radar was our association with Harry. I'm going downtown on Monday to see if I can recall his license plate while under hypnosis, but after that, I don't want to think about him anymore. The person I cared about wasn't real. I'm done with him."

I borrowed some clothes from Diana and tagged along at her Pilates class. Afterwards, we walked back to her house, enjoying the cloudless blue sky and the ocean breeze.

"Has Nate been working on his shielding lately?" Diana asked.

"I don't know. They've kept him busy with projects, and he's spending a lot of time studying Russian."

"Well, you might want to get him to focus on that a bit. I can help him if he needs it."

"Why?"

"Let's just say that your relationship has been widely discussed at work."

"What?"

"Carol's been keeping anyone who'll listen to her informed. She's a sneaky telepath and gossips even more than I do. She told people when you first started dating, when you first slept together, and that the two of you apparently 'mate like rabbits.' I'm sure she's shared more since I've been away all week. I bet they all know you're living together."

"God! Why would she divulge the details of my private life? Why didn't you tell me earlier?"

"How would it have helped? You'd only be mortified for a longer period of time. It takes time and practice to create foolproof shields, and Nate's not there yet. It is what it is. Just make sure he makes it a priority. Besides, most people don't really care. Maybe they receive a little voyeuristic pleasure for a minute or two, but they're much more concerned with their own lives. If you want, I can think of a way to exact revenge on Carol at a later date. She's a telepath who lets her guard down a little too often. I can probably get some dirt on her for you."

"Getting even does sound appealing right now, but once I calm down, I won't do it. God, what a mess!"

"For someone who grew up with a telepath, you're so oblivious. I can't believe you didn't see the strange looks cast your way over the last few weeks."

"You could've shut her up," I mumbled.

"You know if I'd said anything to her, she'd have been even worse. Don't stress about this. You two are in love. That's a beautiful thing. Who cares what anyone else thinks anyway? We're all screwed up in our own way, but if you want some privacy, get Nate to work on his shields."

"Will do, and thanks for the heads up."

"Any time."

"I'll have to see if Nate's up for it, but I'd love to have you and Thomas over for dinner tomorrow evening. You'll be our first official guests."

"Ah, my Sophia's growing up. I'd be honored to help celebrate your new living arrangement. Text me if it's a go, and I'll bring the wine."

*　*　*

I hurried home to help Nate unpack and finish setting up the apartment. When I walked in the door, he was busy connecting cables for his TV and various components.

"Boy, your TV is way bigger than mine," I said. "I didn't realize mine was so small. It's like a mini-me of yours."

Nate smiled at my comment. "The screen is great but just wait until you *hear* the difference." I bent over him to kiss his head and ran my fingers through his hair as he finished installing the devices. He turned around, grabbed my hips to pull himself up and kissed me. He stopped abruptly and said, "Let's see if this works."

Nate put in the first *Lord of the Rings* DVD and turned everything on. The picture was impressive, but he was right, once he had all the correct settings on the wireless speaker system, the surround sound quality was astounding.

"I didn't realize I was living in the technological dark ages." I laughed. "This is going to be fun." He smiled, kissed me briefly, and turned it off.

"Okay," he said. "I've got a few more boxes to unpack in the bedroom. Do you want to help?"

"Sure."

I didn't know where he wanted everything to go so I pulled stuff out and grouped related things together. I came across a picture of him with his ex-girlfriend, Brian, and Brian's fiancée. He caught me looking at it and grabbed it from me. He silently pulled the picture out of the frame and crumpled it up.

"You didn't have to do that," I said.

"That picture was a gift from my ex-girlfriend. It probably isn't appropriate to display anymore and would annoy you. I'm also certain *we both* don't want you to see Brian's face every day."

I was thoughtful for a few seconds until I remembered Diana's gift. "Oh, I've got something to show you. Stay right here." I retrieved the picture frame from my purse and brought it to him. "Diana gave us a housewarming present." I placed the picture in his hands. I watched him as he absorbed it. He was surprised at first and then a deep emotion passed over his face.

"Wow," he said. "It's perfect."

"I know. Diana thought she captured the moment we first started falling in love."

Nate looked at me and then stared back at the picture. I wrapped my arms around him from behind and peeked around his side to look at it.

"You're so beautiful. You look like some sort of goddess." He placed the picture on his dresser and turned in my arms. He kissed me tenderly. "Sophia, I don't exactly know why, but I like seeing our stuff mingled together."

"I felt the same way when I was unpacking earlier today. I think moving in together is the right step."

"I love you," he said. He brought his lips back to mine with an increased intensity, and we distracted ourselves for the next half hour. I laid my head on his chest, with both my leg and arm draped across him. He ran his fingers lightly up and down my leg as I gently rubbed small circles on his stomach.

"What are you thinking?" I asked, angling my head to look at him.

"That I don't think I've ever been happier. What about you?"

"Pretty much the same thing. It's hard to believe that a few months ago, I doubted I'd ever love anyone again, but, God, I really do love you, Nate. I don't know if it's that we're older and more mature, but what we have feels much deeper than what I had with Brian."

Nate quickly turned us so he was on top of me again, and he leaned down to kiss me gently. He stared at me for a second and sighed. "I don't know how I'm going to leave you on Friday."

I was puzzled for a second but then frowned. "Oh, the wedding." I'd forgotten about it.

"I don't know how I'm going to sleep without you. Are you sure you don't want to come with me? I don't like the idea of you being here alone."

"I thought we agreed my presence would be a bad idea."

"Well, yes, but you could still come with me and not go to the wedding."

"What? So I can hide out in the hotel while you go to a bachelor party and a wedding? I'd love to be with you, but I wouldn't enjoy that. Besides, I might need to work, and if not, I can catch up on some girl time with Diana while you're away."

"I see your point." He looked away with a furrowed brow, seeing how ludicrous his request was but wanting it all the same.

"Let's celebrate your move-in by having Thomas and Diana over for dinner tomorrow. I know we have more work to do, and I'll be gone a large chunk of the day, but it would be fun to have guests over at *our* place. We'd be like a real couple."

He laughed at me. "We are a real couple. What do you mean?"

"I don't know. I'm not sure I can explain it. I was looking at all of our kitchen stuff together today, and it made me feel like we could entertain for real, like real adults, it's like we're not just playing around anymore, like the 'we' of our relationship is more tangible."

"Maybe you mean that we've taken a grown-up step, and you feel like we're actual grown-ups now?"

"Maybe. Oh, I don't know. I'm being silly," I said, feeling flustered.

"You're cute," he said as he kissed my cheek, "and I'd be happy to make dinner for everyone tomorrow."

After settling on a dinner menu, we forced ourselves to get out of bed to finish unpacking. I texted Diana to come over at six o'clock and then closed my eyes to contact Thomas.

"What's up?" Thomas asked.

"Would you like to join Diana and us for dinner tomorrow?"

"Sure. And yes, I'll bring a chocolate dessert. Hey, ask Nate if he'd like to paddle out with me tomorrow morning. The waves are supposed to be overhead."

I conveyed the question to Nate, who was up for it. We worked out the where and when, and then I closed the connection.

Nate was observing me when I opened my eyes. "I don't think I'll ever get over how cool that is. Okay, let's wrap it up in here, and then I have a few questions about where to put certain things."

We worked for another hour and decided to store his surfboard in the corner of the dining room, not exactly elegant, but we could possibly play it off as San Diego chic, assuming it didn't fall over on anyone. I made us some peanut butter sandwiches, and we sat on the couch to watch *The Fellowship of the Ring* again, pleased to discover that we were both Tolkien fans.

"Oh, you should know that Diana told me Carol's been detailing our love life to the entire office. Apparently, word on the street is that we 'mate like rabbits.'" I used my fingers to make the same quotation marks that Diana did.

Nate frowned. "That's vile of her. I'm sorry my shields are crap. I promise to work on them more."

"Don't feel bad. I know you and David are working on them as much as you can both fit into your schedules. It just takes time. Just keep an eye out for her."

* * *

When we were getting ready for bed, I scanned the titles of the books in his bookcase. "I didn't know you were a huge comic book fan. I think Thomas has read most of these. I've read some."

Nate gave me a disbelieving look. "You read comics?"

"Sure. You've met my brother. How could I have grown up with him and not have read at least a few?"

"I guess I'm surprised. You don't fit the stereotype."

"What stereotype don't I fit? Thomas and I were always misfits, *smart* misfits, and I've got more than a little weird going on in my life. We were hard-core *Magic: The Gathering* players back in the day. I probably fit the stereotype better than most, especially considering the fact that my life is a freaking comic book. Thomas and I have gone to Comic-Con every year since we've lived in San Diego."

Nate wrapped his arms around me and smiled. "Gold, baby. I've struck gold."

*   *   *

My alarm clock woke me at nine, and I stretched, feeling the chill and emptiness on Nate's side of the bed. I smiled, amused that we already had sides. A few minutes before ten, I knocked on Irene's door. She looked better than the last time I'd seen her. She wasn't as gaunt or as fragile, and her eyes were starting to regain some of their inner steel. Even though her sister, Mei, seemed reserved, she hugged me tightly. She understood English but spoke it brokenly. She thanked me as heartily as she could for helping her sister, and then Irene led me to the back of the house. When she hit the lights, the studio gave me the impression of feeling lonely and abandoned. I'm sure I was projecting, but the room seemed to realize it had been neglected over the past few weeks.

Since I'd only painted with watercolors and acrylics in the past, Irene decided to teach me to paint with oils. She placed a medium-sized primed canvas before me, taught me the rudiments and arranged a still life setting for me.

Irene then sat in front of a much larger canvas, one that she'd started a several weeks ago. I heard a long sigh and looked back at her.

"It feels like ages have passed since I painted this," she said in a subdued voice. She gingerly and lovingly glided her hand over it. "I am no longer the person I was then. It will not be the painting I had intended." She stared it at for a minute, scrutinizing, and then seemed to settle on a plan. Her palette floated up into the air beside her, and she began again.

As I sketched roughly in charcoal and then dabbled with the paints, I updated her on everything — John, Diana, and living with Nate. She didn't comment while I spoke, which wasn't uncommon when she worked. She'd eventually get to a stopping point and then catch up with me. When I finished my one-way conversation, I continued to paint, trying to mix the colors to match the objects exactly. Irene sent her palette and brushes to rest on the counter and came to sit next to me, inspecting my canvas.

"Good progress, Sophia." She smiled and rested her hand on my face. "I am happy for you. Cherish what you have with Nate."

"I will."

She stared out the window for a few moments and then sighed. "So, this John is the murderer," she said and then paused to compose herself. "It is a small comfort to know what happened to Harry, but I want them to punish this murderer and whatever group he represents. I cannot understand why someone would want Harry dead."

"It doesn't make sense. Once they ruled out suicide, I think the police initially believed his murder to be the work of a hate group, some anti-psychic fanatics, but since John's a psychic, that's unlikely."

"I know. The police also asked me if Harry was part of a secret society or whether he did outside contract work. Aside from speaking engagements and tours to promote his books, he worked only as a professor. We had a quiet life. It had to be that tricky computer program, but why would they make up something that would threaten his life? I know deep down that Harry did not keep any secrets from me, but a tiny part of me wonders if I am wrong, and I feel horribly guilty."

"Irene, you have a smidgeon of doubt because this makes no sense. That's natural. We both know that Harry never hid anything from you. Hypothetically speaking, if he had, with the amount of time they spent together, Thomas should have picked up on it since Harry wasn't great at shielding."

"You are right. I am ashamed I wondered, but I need to understand why someone would choose to end his life. I have been combing through his emails for some kind of sign, for any possible clue. I also read the rough draft of his book, but nothing seems suspicious to me."

"Do you think Harry could have offended some psychics with his books? Maybe they didn't like them? At the memorial, one of Harry's colleagues mentioned that he was the biggest proponent of teaching everyone to enhance their natural psychic abilities. Maybe John's organization is a group of psychics that wouldn't want this?"

"That could be, but Harry was not the only one, though he may have been the most well-known. A few other academics actively promote educating the public as well . . ." She froze. "Oh, dear. Sophia, do you remember when Harry said that the parents of Dante, the GammaBeat creator, died a few months ago? His mother — I think her name was Violetta — she was a colleague of Harry's who advocated enhancing abilities in the general population as well. Both she and Harry led the major experiments that proved that psychic abilities were becoming stronger and more prevalent. I met her and her husband once at a conference many years ago. Did Harry say they died in a car accident? What if it was no accident? What if they were murdered like Harry?"

"Hmm. It's possible they're connected, but it could still be a coincidence since people die in traffic accidents all the time. Do you know of anyone else like Harry or Violetta? If another person recently died under mysterious circumstances, then I'd be convinced, though it still seems like a lame reason to me. Wouldn't someone else just step forward to take his place?"

Irene contemplated for a few moments. "I will continue searching Harry's files to see what I can find, and I will write Dante to ask for more information regarding the death of his parents."

"Oh, by the way, I still have the GammaBeat. I'd used it to try to improve my shields, but it slipped my mind with all that's happened. I'd like to try it out some more, and Nate could use it to help him shield. Do you want it back?"

"Keep it for now, but I might want to use it again at some point."

"You know, if our theory's correct, Dante should have been a target. His headband achieves what Harry only promoted."

"True." Irene and I looked at each other, our eyes enlarging at the same time.

"You don't think Harry was killed for the GammaBeat, do you?" I asked.

Irene started to clean some of the paint off of her fingers, considering the idea. "Anything is possible, but if so, Dante would be dead. I believe Harry said someone bought out Dante's company. God, I hope he is alive. He would be about your age. . . . I will find out. Keep the device hidden until we know." Irene frowned. I think she didn't want to consider that another person had been mysteriously murdered, especially someone so young. "Enough talk. We should work for another hour and then have lunch. Mei is making you something special."

After an hour or so, Irene and I followed the delicious aromas to the kitchen. Mei had made a chicken and noodle dish that smelled divine. She served me up a big plate, much bigger than theirs, and we all sat down to eat. Irene laughed. "Mei thinks you are too thin."

Irene spoke to Mei in Mandarin for a few minutes, and then she relayed to me their conversation. "I told Mei that you are in love with a nice young man who recently moved in with you. We were both reflecting on how wonderful it is to be young and in love." I blushed, and Mei smiled at me. "Mei thinks you are very beautiful and have a kind, old soul. She has some empathic or subtle telepathic ability and can read people better than anyone I know who is not a full telepath."

"Xiè xiè," I replied, meaning "thank you" in Mandarin, one of the many phrases I'd learned during my language study for work, though in response to a compliment, I probably hadn't chosen precisely the right phrase. She nodded to me, understanding my intentions. The food was delicious, and even though I'd already had a plateful, I got seconds.

"Sophia, I want you to have Harry's piano. I think he would prefer that you have it. You are probably the only other person who ever played on it."

My brow crinkled, and my eyes became moist. "Irene, I'm honored, but you don't need to do that. Don't you think you'll miss it? I don't even have room for it right now."

"I will keep it here until you have room, but it belongs to you. You are supposed to have it." Irene had a way of making things final with a certain tone of voice. I knew that she had decided, and I couldn't change her mind.

Irene switched subjects and told me stories of when she and Mei were children. They came from a fairly well-to-do family that had two girls and no boys. Although their parents loved them, Irene and Mei felt their disappointment at not having a boy. Mei said it made her resent boys for a long time until she met the right one, but Irene didn't share her disdain for the opposite sex and was constantly courted by them. She never bit, though, until she came to the United States. Her parents were upset when Irene decided to marry an American. "They never gave Harry a chance," she said with some bitterness.

"What about Mei's husband, the young man she finally fell in love with? Did they like him?" I asked.

"Mei's husband wasn't the man she fell in love with," Irene said.

"Oh," I said, a bit embarrassed by my gaffe.

"Mei fell in love with another student at the university. They were in love and very happy, but he was killed. I don't think my parents even knew about him. When Mei graduated, my parents arranged a marriage for her with an older, well-established businessman. He was a kind, good man, but I don't think she was ever passionately in love with him. She grew to love him, though."

I felt my eyes become glassy again. Mei put her hand on mine, rubbed it, and said something to Irene. "She doesn't want you to be sad for her. Her husband was kind and caring and was a good father to her children. It was a good marriage." I still couldn't help feeling sad for her loss. After lunch, I said my goodbyes and promised to visit next weekend.

When I arrived home, Nate was lying on the couch with his laptop open on his lap studying Russian, or trying to at least. Though he'd been home a few hours, he still had that just showered, post-surfing daze.

"How'd the surfing go?" I asked.

"Great, but I'm afraid I won't be able to lift my arms tomorrow. After moving furniture yesterday and paddling today, I'm gonna be sore. Come here."

I sat on the couch next to him and leaned over to give him a kiss. "I brought you some home cooked Chinese food."

"It smells amazing."

As he dug in, we caught each other up on our morning. By the time he'd finished eating, his eyes were starting to drift shut. His head bobbed back on the couch, and he jerked awake, shaking his head to rouse himself. I ruffled his hair and brought his dishes to the sink. He automatically burrowed into the couch, no longer fighting his body's need to sleep.

"Relax with me," he said.

"Your wish, my command." I cuddled on top of him, resting my head on his chest.

"Ah, that's more like it. Mmm. Comfortable."

I pulled the throw over us and snuggled into his warmth, listening to his breathing. . . . I startled awake as Nate shifted.

"Sorry to wake you," he said, running his fingers over my hair. "I guess we dozed off for a while. That was nice."

"Mmm. What time is it?" I asked, rubbing my eyes.

"A little before three."

"I'll have to get moving if I'm going to make my yoga class. Would you like me to pick up groceries on my way home?"

"That'd be great. I'll text you the list."

* * *

When I returned to the apartment with groceries in tow, Nate was lounging on the couch, still working on his Russian, but he was fully awake now and multitasking by watching football as well.

"Let me help you with those," he said, jumping off the couch and grabbing some bags from me. "I can't believe you were able to carry all of this. Are there more bags in the car?"

"No, I got everything. I hate making two trips." We pulled out the groceries and put them away. I was appreciating that Nate had already figured out and adopted my organization, when the football game playing in the background gave me a flashback.

"This reminds me of when I was a little kid. In the fall, my dad always had football on the TV, even if he wasn't sitting down watching it."

"Does it bother you?" Nate asked.

"No, not at all, though I prefer music. If you're interested in the game, though, please leave it on."

Nate started cooking while I took a shower. When I returned to the living room, the apartment already smelled fabulous. I kissed his cheek and hugged him from behind as he slaved away over the stove. He didn't need my help cooking so I set the table. It was fun choosing between our various sets of tableware. Neither of us had anything fancy, but we definitely had more than enough decent stuff now. While Nate stirred and sautéed, I replied to a few emails, paid some online bills, and straightened the apartment. Diana arrived first with the wine. I poured us some to sip while Nate put the finishing touches on the meal.

"So, he's a good cook too? Sophia, I'm impressed," Diana said. I rolled my eyes at her because I knew what additional attribute she was referring to. Nate smiled at her compliment oblivious to her secondary meaning. Thomas arrived shortly afterwards with my favorite dessert, my mom's chocolate cake.

"Thomas, you didn't have to make this!"

"Well, it's a special occasion, right? I wanted to do something nice for my little sister, especially since you let me play with Nate today."

"Hey, don't knock the height." I poked him in his chest, and then he grabbed me in one of those brotherly neck holds with accompanying noogie.

"Thomas!" He let go quickly before my martial arts instincts could take over. Nate and Diana laughed at us.

"I thought the two of you were mature adults, but now the truth comes out," Diana said.

When we sat down to Nate's delicious meal, Thomas toasted us. "To good friends, and to Nate and Sophia, for taking a big step forward."

Nate squeezed my hand, and I blushed as we all clinked glasses. Diana then entertained us with stories of deceit and stupidity from her trip to New York for most of the dinner.

After finishing dessert, we took advantage of having Thomas and Diana there to help Nate work on his shields and brought out the GammaBeat as well. They worked together for almost two hours. Nate was improving and had what Thomas and Diana considered to be rudimentary shields in place, shields that would contain his thoughts but wouldn't stand up to any probing. He still had a long way to go, but it was a good start.

Nate took off the GammaBeat and handed it to Diana to try. None of us believed Harry's murder had anything to do with the device since John hadn't acquired it when he killed Harry and the mission had supposedly been completed, but we agreed that we'd feel better knowing that Dante, the guy who'd created the GammaBeat, was still alive, and hoped Irene would soon learn his fate.

CHAPTER FIFTEEN

Settling at my desk Monday morning, I saw that a new intelligence project had been moved to the front of my cue. Instead of searching in one of the usual foreign targets, this project had American and European destinations to visit on specific dates and times over the next few weeks, including several in the middle of the night and on the weekends. They instructed me to report everything I might observe but didn't explain the ultimate goal.

I headed to Roger's office. "This new project's a little weird. Do you have any more information?" I asked.

"I know only as much as you do."

"Do they really want me to hang out at these places for hours at a time in the hope that something might happen?" I asked.

"They must have intel," he said. "The objectives are clear. Just describe everything, though it would help focus your efforts if we knew the purpose. I'll press them again on that. Since you'll be working alone, you can bring your work computer home to do the late night and weekend ones as long as you deliver your write-ups using the secure link. They want immediate reports after each projection."

"I know our government keeps tabs on people, but is it now seriously spying on its own citizens?" I asked.

"Those citizens could be suspected terrorists, but I don't want to speculate. It must be important for national security, or I doubt they'd spend the money to hire us. Homeland Security specifically requested you, just like the military often does. They have a few of their own projectors now, but they must not be good enough for this project."

"I'll do it, but if it starts to appear that they're trying to bust someone for political reasons, I don't want to be a part of it."

"Let's hope it doesn't come to that, but I'd back you up if that's the case." He sighed. "Put the appointments on your calendar and work in as many projects as you can in your downtime. Don't overwork yourself, but try to prevent our project backlog from growing."

"I'll do my best." Without a clear-cut goal, I had a hard time summoning my usual enthusiasm. I'd never before spied on Americans or Europeans for our government. My work had been my life for the past three years, filling me with purpose, but I had an uneasy feeling about this project and now had nicer ways to spend my nights and weekends.

I re-read the brief and put the dates and times on my calendar for the specified remote viewings. Most were during the day, but one was late Friday night, and another was Saturday afternoon. The timing couldn't have been more perfect since Nate would be away, and I could do the inconvenient ones from home like Roger suggested. There would be several more late-nights over the next few weeks, but no other weekend dates. In total, I had to investigate thirty locations for varying periods of time. Since none were in the next two days, I planned to make quick visits to all of the destinations first. I wanted to sketch out and become familiar with the places ahead of time so I could pay better attention to anything that might occur at the appointed times. The mystery behind the assignment piqued my interest as well, and I hoped the locations might give me a hint of the purpose.

Since Nate couldn't meet me for lunch, I decided to power through it and travel to as many places as I could. I first visited an office on the East coast, which seemed to be an investment bank. The two European destinations were dark and deserted, since it was nighttime over there. I couldn't see much, but they appeared to be sleekly decorated granite and glass corporate offices. I'd have to revisit the European destinations later that night, during their daylight, if I truly wanted to get the lay of the land. After six places, I started to tire. I needed a short rest and decided to buy a drink and a snack from the vending machine. On my way to the break room, I swung by Nate's desk to see if I could catch him. I smiled when I glimpsed his dark hair peeking out over the top of his cubicle. I laid my arms on the edge and peered down at him. He looked up and smiled, but his smile faded a little. "You look tired," he said. "Are you okay?"

"I'm fine. I've just been phasing in and out a lot for a new project. I'm headed to the break room for a snack. Can you join me for a few minutes?"

"Sure. I can spare a few."

I noticed Carol watching us as we walked down the corridor. I gave her the most malevolent glare I could muster. Guilt spread across her face, and she quickly glanced away. Maybe she would consider laying off of us in future.

While I was staring at the vending machine trying to conjure a decision, Nate's arms enveloped me from behind. I instinctively leaned into that hug but then remembered we were at work. I gently patted his hands, and he dropped his arms.

"Sorry," he whispered and sat down.

I made my selections and sat next to him. After swigging a gulp of organic energy juice, I sighed and rolled my neck. I squeezed Nate's hand and smiled. "There's no need to apologize for the PDA. I loved that hug. I guess everyone already knows about us anyway, but we just have to be careful. I'm not sure what's inappropriate at work." I then told him what I could of my new project.

"That's unusual to have times scheduled so far in advance, isn't it?" he asked.

"Yeah, it's odd." I took a bite of the breakfast bar, swallowed, and continued. "I'll need to visit some locations tonight and tomorrow night. At least you won't be bothered by the ones this weekend."

"But I don't like that you'll be running yourself ragged." He rubbed his hand along my arm.

"I'm sure it won't be bad once I'm finished previewing, just a few late nights here and there." His hand found mine, and I sighed. We were having a hard time not touching each other. "I guess we better get back. I'm going to do as many projections as I can today. I might be late, but I'll come straight home. I'll be too tired to exercise."

Nate frowned a little. "Just promise me you'll save a bit of yourself for us. I'll whip up something for dinner." He glanced around to make sure the coast was clear and kissed me quickly on the cheek before heading back to his desk.

I started up again and didn't pause for another break. By half past seven, I'd sketched and described eighteen of the thirty places, although some of them were in the dark. I still hadn't determined the purpose but since most places were office buildings, maybe it was some sort of corporate espionage that affected national security. I was dog-tired and headed home, texting Nate that I was on my way.

The evenings were starting to get a bit cold, and I shivered as I made my way to our apartment. *Our apartment.* It still threw me for a loop. When I opened the door, a savory smell of lentil soup wafted out.

"Welcome home," Nate said. He was serving the soup and laying out a salad.

I kissed his cheek and put my stuff down. "I'll never get tired of this reception. Wonderful scents, good food, and a sexy man greeting me as I walk in the door."

"Good," he said and kissed me briefly. "Sit down. I'm going to grab the bread out of the oven and get us some water. Are you too tired for wine?"

"Yeah," I said. When Nate sat down with me, I sipped a spoonful of the soup. "Nate, this soup is perfect. It's just starting to feel wintry outside. Thank you."

"You're welcome, but you'll have to thank Whole Foods. I picked it up when I got the bread and vegetables. I guess the rest of your day was similar to the morning. You look worn out."

"I am. The food should give me some energy, but I'm not looking forward to viewing again tonight. I might use the GammaBeat. I've never tried it while projecting so I'm interested to see if it will make a difference."

"Good idea. Oh, I saw the look you gave Carol today. I think you scared her off."

"I hope so." I had a few more sips of soup and then asked Nate, "Do you think I'm oblivious to what's going on around me?"

"Do you want me to tell you the truth?" he asked.

I frowned. "Of course I do."

"Well . . . yes . . . ah, sometimes," he modified as my face became less pleased. "I don't think I was that blatant, but I had a crush on you from the moment we met. I still wanted you when you were dating Brian although I did everything I could not to. I dated lots of women and was the best friend to Brian that I could be. And, it wasn't just me. You rarely register when any guy likes you. Brian was the exception. He was so forward, so outgoing and entertaining, that you had to take notice."

"I guess I am oblivious to everything around me then, not just to people who like me. Diana said I should have noticed the people staring at us and communicating with hushed whispers."

"I didn't notice either. We've both been distracted since we started dating, which is completely normal. There's a reason falling in love is described as being 'on cloud nine.' Oh, I almost forgot. I've got something for you."

He picked up a piece of mail lying on the counter, sat back down and slid it to me across the table.

"What's this?" I asked.

"Open it," he said.

Since the envelope had already been opened, I easily slipped the papers out and began to read. Nate had visited a doctor, and the results before me showed that he was negative for every STD you could test for. "This is great news!" I pulled him to me for a quick kiss over the table.

"Indeed, it is, though the timing's unfortunate." It was the placebo week of my pill, and the expected event was in full swing. "When I return from my trip, be prepared. I'm going to ravish you at inopportune moments simply because I can."

"I'd be disappointed if you didn't."

After dinner, Nate and I worked on our language computer programs until eleven when I started projecting with the GammaBeat. I was pleased to find that separating my consciousness and casting it out went more quickly using the device, and phasing in and out didn't seem to drain me as much.

By the time I finished, Nate had fallen asleep on the couch. I tickled his arm to wake him. It didn't work so I kissed his mouth. "Wake up, sleeping beauty," I whispered. He gradually became more conscious, and I tugged him into bed.

The next morning, I packed the GammaBeat into an oversized purse and discretely brought it into work. I didn't believe having it put me in danger, but I wanted to heed Irene's warning, just in case. I finished previewing the destinations so that on Wednesday I could begin my scheduled projections. I had two that first day, and they were disappointing, if not painfully boring. I phased in and out to record the mundane conversations I heard. Wearing the GammaBeat made my day much easier. I was happy to find that I felt much less fatigued than usual by the end of the day and planned to make using the device a part of my routine for as long as I had it.

The rest of the week passed too quickly. Since I'd be working late that night, I felt I could spend longer than usual lounging around in bed with Nate before he left for his trip. I breathed him in, trying to imprint his scent on my brain. My stomach felt unsettled at the idea of him being so far from me. When we finally climbed out of bed, we dressed like we were going to a funeral and then went downstairs to our cars together. Since it was a short trip and he hoped to change to an earlier flight back, he insisted on driving himself to the airport. Nate popped his suitcase into his trunk while I put my bag in my car. When I closed the door and turned, he was there and pulled my hands into his. "I know you have to work some this weekend, but enjoy your time with Diana and Irene while I'm gone."

"I will," I said, putting on a brave face.

Nate smiled, but his eyes told a different story. "I'll call you tonight before we leave for the bachelor party."

"Text me when you land as well. I'll feel better if I know you're safe. Make someone take a picture of you in the tuxedo for me."

"I will," he said. His eyes captured mine. "I love you, Sophia."

"I love you too." I rose up onto my tiptoes so our lips could find each other. We kissed tenderly and sweetly at first, but it rapidly escalated to an all-out hunger that kissing and caressing couldn't satiate. When I unconsciously hitched my leg up around his, I knew we needed to stop. I ended the kiss and disentangled myself but kept his hands in mine.

"Go, catch your plane, before I make you late."

He kissed me once more on the cheek, and our hands parted. I watched him as he got into his car, waving to me before closing the door. I sat in mine, took a deep breath in and then exhaled slowly. I started my car and followed his out of the garage and down the street. When he turned the opposite direction from where I was headed, I felt my chest tighten. I was really going to miss him.

Since depression weakens psychic abilities, my day would have been a waste if I hadn't had the GammaBeat with me. I didn't have any appointments for my main project that morning, and an urgent military one came in, requiring me to investigate several possible coordinates for a terrorist cell in Afghanistan. Before noon, I'd identified the location of the cell and immediately shared my results with Roger. He was on the phone in seconds, and I was off to lunch, feeling quite satisfied with my job. Helping catch the bad guys while protecting innocent civilians was what I lived for.

When I approached Diana's desk, she was on the phone and held up one finger to me. I motioned to her that I'd come back. I hadn't checked my cell phone all morning and wanted to read my texts. I grabbed my purse and started walking back to Diana's desk. Indeed, I had one message. Nate had landed. He'd rented a car and was on his way to the hotel. While I waited for Diana to finish, I texted him back.

Diana hung up the phone. "You'll never believe what that was all about," she said. "Let's grab some lunch while I tell you." She closed her computer and grabbed her purse.

When the elevator doors closed, we were alone. "That was one of my clients from New York. Even though Roger does the negotiating for our contracts, I meet personally with most of my clients and present my findings directly to them. Well, since this guy knew how to contact me, he called to ask me to work on something personal for him. He wants me to spy on his wife, whom he believes is having an affair. Of course, when I was on the job, I saw that he suspected his wife and that he was interested in having me find out the truth for him, but I also saw that he hoped we'd get hot and heavy after I imparted the bad news. It's bizarre. He knows I'm telepathic yet doesn't fully grasp that I can hear every single thought in his head. This happens quite a lot for some reason. People think their craziest, most personal thoughts are somehow immune. Anyway, I told him I didn't perform any work on the side and recommended he either confront his wife or hire a private investigator."

"Is his wife having an affair?" I asked.

"I don't know, but probably. When a spouse gets to the point of suspecting an affair, there's usually been one going on for a while."

"That's sad," I said.

"*C'est la vie*," she replied as we exited the elevator.

We bought our sandwiches and sat down.

"So, how are you holding up? Nate's been gone for what, four hours?" She threw her head back and pressed the back of her hand to her forehead. "Oh, how will you ever survive?"

I frowned at her. "Not funny."

"Oh, come on. It was a little funny. We're on for Sunday, right?"

"Right."

"What are you doing the rest of the weekend?"

"I've got a projection at two AM tonight and another tomorrow afternoon. I promised Irene I'd spend the evening with her on Saturday. Other than that, I'll just occupy myself with yoga, kung fu, language studies, and reading, all the stuff I used to do before Nate came along."

"You, Thomas, and I should hang out this evening, like old times. We could watch more *Game of Thrones* and keep you company. I'll pick up the food."

I quickly contacted Thomas, and he was game. "Okay, Diana, we're on. My place at seven."

*   *   *

I spent most of the afternoon spying for my main project, but I still had no idea why I was there. Nate called to let me know he missed me, and Diana and Thomas showed up at my apartment with pizza and beer right on time.

"I see you're already in your house-fit," Thomas teased.

Of course I was. Whenever I spent an evening or a day at home alone or with my family (and Diana was as good as family), I changed into comfy pajamas or sweats at the first opportunity. When you got dressed to go out, you wore an "outfit," so long ago I termed whatever cozy assemblage I wore at home my "house-fit." Thomas spent a lot of his time outdoors, but deep down he was as much of a homebody as I was. It annoyed me when he made fun of me for being one.

I gave him my *"Really?"* look. "And to think that I was going to give you and Diana the best seats. Just for that, you get to sit in the chair off to the side now."

Diana laughed at us. She didn't have any siblings so our bickering always amused her. As I loaded the show and tried to figure out the correct buttons to push on the different remote controls, Thomas admired Nate's audiovisual upgrades. "You should have moved in with Nate ages ago. Just think of all the lame movie experiences we've had to suffer through watching your TV. They could have been so much better."

Diana and I shared a knowing look. "Men," she said.

By midnight, we'd finished the first season. "I guess we'll start season two next time," Thomas said as he got up to stretch.

"I need to get me some freaking dragons," Diana said. "Daenerys is a badass."

"That, she is," Thomas said.

"Daenerys is the best! Do you understand now why I dressed up as her for your Halloween party in our senior year? Don't forget you gave me crap about that costume because you didn't know who she was."

"My God, you're right!" Diana laughed. "I had no idea. I'm sorry, but the baby dragon perched on your shoulder was odd to someone not in the know. My main complaint though was that you weren't showing enough skin."

"Halloween should be more about cool costumes than a contest of who can wear the most revealing outfit."

"True, but when do we get the chance to wear revealing clothing without being called a skank?"

"She has a great point," Thomas added. "We must preserve every opportunity for women to bare as much as possible and not be ridiculed."

"Funny, Thomas, but do you like my Daenerys costume now?"

"I do. I get it."

"Good." Finally vindicated, though years later, I smiled and turned off the TV. As I walked to the kitchen to put the leftover pizza away, Diana caught me trying to cover up a big yawn.

"We should go, Thomas. Sophia needs a nap before her late night appointment."

After they left, I set an alarm and shut off the lights. The next thing I knew, a loud, beeping noise startled me awake. I splashed cool water in my face and drank a cup of tea to revive myself. I grabbed the GammaBeat and settled into the couch with my sketchpad and phone.

I still had fifteen minutes before the designated time, but I pressed record on my phone, put the device on my head, and sent my consciousness on its journey.

Two men pored over documents at a conference table and spoke rapidly in French, which wasn't one of my languages. I could understand some phrases and common words if spoken slowly, but fast conversation sounded like lovely gibberish to me. My client hadn't requested that I know or learn French for this project, which was frustrating, especially since I already had no idea why I was there. If only I could send a voice recorder out with my consciousness, I might actually be useful.

I tried reading the sheets of paper, but again they were in French. I phased in and out, writing down the phrases exactly as I saw them before the pages were turned. There were lots of numbers, but it wasn't a spreadsheet, just some kind of report with a bunch of data. One of the men then closed his eyes, as if he were meditating. That was strange. *Oh my God, could he be psychic?* The other man waited patiently as if this was a perfectly normal thing to do in the middle of a conversation. After a few minutes, the meditator opened his eyes and shared some information, which the other man wrote down. *Shit, he must be psychic!* I quickly jotted down the writing.

They continued their discussion in a more animated tone. Since I couldn't understand them and they weren't paying attention to the report anymore, I wrote down everything I saw on the title page and tried to sketch them and describe their physical appearance. After about thirty more minutes of discussion, the man who'd meditated shook hands with the other man and departed.

The remaining man left the conference room for his office down the hall and sat in front of his computer. His desktop was in English and looked pretty normal to me, with no suspicious looking folders. He called his wife, I assumed, and told her in American English that he'd be home soon to take the kids to the park. He then opened a safe under his desk and placed the report inside. I watched intently and was able to observe the combination of the safe. After he left his office, I had another twenty minutes of time to pass so I looked at whatever I could find. The nameplate on his desk read Alec Milne, and a picture of his family rested next to it. He had a son who appeared to be about seven years old and a daughter around four or five. I hoped Homeland Security wasn't after this guy. His family would be heartbroken if he'd done something to land himself in jail. I ended the projection, wrote up my report, including pictures of my sketches, and emailed it securely before going back to sleep at five AM.

I woke up at eleven-thirty. I had barely enough time for brunch, yoga at home, and a shower before my one o'clock projection. This one took me to the East Coast, to yet another office building. For two hours, I waited around, and no one showed up. It was your regular Monday through Friday, nine-to-five workplace, and apparently no one worked on the weekend. After I'd spent my requisite time there and wrote up and emailed the report, I headed to Irene's. Nate called me while I was driving, and his voice was music to my ears.

Irene had made a hot and sour soup for dinner. We let it stew while we worked in her studio and by the end of our time there, my painting was nearly complete though in no way professional looking. It lacked richness, a sort of multidimensionality that I couldn't put my finger on. It wasn't bad, but it seemed flat to me. Irene seemed pleased with my progress and gave me pointers on how to improve it. She'd created an impressive surrealist painting during our few hours. According to her, the painting was only in a nascent phase. Later she'd embellish and enrich the colors and use her telekinetic ability to fine-tune the texture. During dinner, Irene told me that she'd sent both an email and an old-fashioned letter to Dante, the GammaBeat developer, but hadn't yet heard back from him. We kept our fingers crossed that he was alive. Before I left, we set a date to work together again in a few weeks.

CHAPTER SIXTEEN

When I pulled into the garage, I realized that I'd become used to having someone either with me or waiting for me at home. My apartment didn't feel as safe with Nate away. *Was that one of the reasons I agreed to live together?* I put that thought aside and projected to my apartment. No one was hiding anywhere that I could see, so I went upstairs, opened the door, and tried to feel at ease. I grabbed my much-neglected book and relaxed on the couch for a few hours until I finally reached the end. An overactive sex life was certainly eating into my reading time, but I wouldn't trade it for the world.

My bed felt cold and lonely without Nate. I sighed. I missed him, and not because of any protection or safety he might offer me. I wanted to see his smile, hear his voice, feel his hands on me. I imagined him handsome in a tuxedo. He was probably enjoying himself at the wedding right now. After tonight I had only one more night away from him. I turned out the light, pretended his arms were around me, and dozed off.

I'm naked on silken sheets, so cool and refreshing against my skin. I rub my cheek on the pillowcase . . . so smooth. A warm, strong body presses into my back and feels perfect spooned behind me. Ahh, Nate. I burrow my back into him. His left hand glides up my hip to caress my breasts. He kisses me just behind my ear, nuzzles into my neck and hair, and starts to grow large against me. His hand trails down my side, cupping my curves and then pushing lower, past my hair. He explores and massages me there.

The sensation builds. My back arches. I moan and turn to look at him. Oh my God! It's not Nate. It's him. He stares at me again with a surprised look, edged now with curiosity and arousal. "Who are you?" he asks.

I woke up gasping for breath. *Shit.* If I'd had any doubts that I was sharing these dreams, they were over now. *Who is he and what the hell is he doing in my dreams? God! If I hadn't seen him, my body would have happily gone along with the program. What would Nate say?* My thoughts raced as I worried. I took a breath to calm myself, grabbed my iPhone, and started to record.

I described the details of the dream and then added, "It was definitely the same person from the two previous dreams — brown wavy hair, slightly olive skin tone, the same hazel eyes. We recognized each other. I think Harry was right that he's telepathic since he could ask me who I was. I can't recall his voice. There was no tenor, no accent. The words were just conveyed somehow. I'm not sure I could communicate, though I did moan. God, how mortifying. . . . Like the last dream, I think my surprise at seeing him and not Nate ended it. Could he be a bad guy like John or someone else from his group in disguise? Is he projecting himself into my dreams on purpose? It's possible, but I just don't get that vibe from him. My gut tells me he's . . . I don't know . . . kind somehow, but I guess it could still be a ploy. I hope this dream wasn't my fault. I was imagining Nate holding me when I fell asleep."

It was a little after four o'clock when I put the phone down. I tried to relax into sleep again, but my mind wouldn't stop. "Arrgh."

I turned over onto my other side. After about thirty more minutes of trying, I doubted I'd fall back asleep since I kept radiating tension. I lay awake and remembered the dream again and how real it felt, as if he were truly lying next to me, running his hands down my body. I shivered. I was thankful it hadn't progressed any further. I've only had a handful of sex dreams in my life. Sometimes the person was distinct, though often not, but they affected no one but myself. They were pleasant, but mine and only mine. It was kind of horrifying to know I could have sex with a complete stranger in a dream.

Questions raced through my head. *What if it starts out further along next time and I can't stop it, or my body doesn't want to stop it? What if I hadn't seen him? If I'd continued thinking it was Nate, I would have finished what we'd started for sure. God, what would Nate say? He's not going to like this. Should I tell him? Would he understand that this is something I can't control or would it drive him crazy?* I worried for over an hour until I finally gave up on sleep altogether. I practiced yoga, hoping it would settle my mind, but it didn't. I took a shower and then dressed for my day with Diana. I was starting my laundry when I noticed that Nate also had clothes to wash. I added his to mine and hoped it would relieve my guilty conscience.

At ten Diana picked me up for brunch at her favorite café along the 101. "You look tired," she said. "I'd accuse you of having an exciting night last night, but Nate's out of town. You feeling okay?"

"I don't know. I had a disturbing dream."

Diana looked concerned, probably imagining I'd had a vision, and waited for me to explain.

"I had my third shared dream with some guy, someone I've never met. Only this time, we were in bed together and almost had sex."

Diana eyed me dubiously. "You're upset because you almost had a sex dream?"

I described the three dreams to her.

"Why did the dream end?" Diana asked.

"I think because I was shocked to see him. It somehow breaks the connection."

"What would you have done if you weren't shocked and the dream continued? Would you have had sex with him?"

"Not if I could help it! If he were only a figment of my imagination, then I might, but this feels almost real. I'm in love with Nate and living with him. It would be like cheating. What worries me is if my body's already in high gear before I realize what's happening, I might not have the mental faculties to stop next time."

"Why does it matter if you're sharing a dream with another person? It isn't real. You're not cheating. Men have many more sex dreams than women, and they rarely have dream sex with their bedmate. You may never meet him, and you don't have to worry about STDs or pregnancy. How is he different from a figment of your imagination?"

I shrugged my shoulders.

"Even if you share another dream, you don't know if you'll be able to communicate again to find out who he is or where he lives. He's as good as imaginary. I can guarantee you that no heterosexual male would refuse Angelina Jolie or Scarlett Johansson in a dream. I say, seize the day, or guy, for that matter. Good sex, even in dreams, should be relished."

"How do you know the sex would be good?"

She laughed. "Who would dream about bad sex? What would be the point?"

I blushed and sighed. "Why is it that you can talk so openly about sex while I always become flustered?"

"Hello, telepath here. People think about sex all the time. Everyone wants it, most are insecure and worry about it, and some have really warped ideas."

"*All* the time?"

"All. The. Time. Plus, I'm a complex woman, my dear." She glanced in the mirror and covered her lips with gloss. "Experience, a healthy sex drive, and a lack of any moral compunctions about sex all mixed together. *Voila*! Me."

"I wish I didn't have as many hang-ups."

"Honey," she patted my hand, "I have plenty of hang-ups, at least as many as you, but none of them concern sex. I think you can thank your early Catholic indoctrination. Even though you're no longer religious, once a Catholic, always a Catholic, I'm afraid. I was fortunate enough to be raised without any formal religion but still had exposure to Hindu culture, which *created* the Kama Sutra." She got a faraway look and a wicked smile.

"When you're done with *your* sex dream, let me know," I said. She held up a finger for a moment, took a deep breath, then focused on me again. I laughed. "You're sick, you know that?"

She winked at me.

Diana had to focus on the traffic for a bit. A big rig was trying to merge into a space five times too small. When traffic improved again, I just put it out there: "I feel like I need to tell Nate, like I'm being dishonest if I keep this from him."

"How do you think he'll respond?"

"He's not going to like it. He's the jealous type."

"Then, why bother him with it? It's a dream. It isn't real. You can't control it, and at least so far, you haven't had sex in your dream. Each time you were somewhat intimate, you thought it was Nate, right?"

I nodded, still beating myself up.

"Don't blow what you have with Nate. I've never seen you so happy. Besides, how do you know these dreams are truly shared? Maybe you just have an overactive imagination that created some good-looking guy out of the blue."

"I spoke with Harry about the first two dreams before he died. He thought they were unintentionally shared dreams because of the focus on two people and the fact that the guy seemed surprised to see me in the second dream. I think the guy asking who I was last night confirms Harry's hypothesis."

"You don't think John's messing with your dreams again?" she asked a bit warily.

"I considered that, but . . ." I mulled it over for another minute. "I don't know. I had the first dream the night I met John, and the second a few nights later. I think it was the next day when my dreams stopped altogether until after Harry died. It's possible, but this guy seems like a genuinely nice person."

"You like him?" she asked.

"I don't like him, like him, if that's what you're implying, but I feel comfortable with him. Somehow I don't think he'd hurt me. I guess I trust him though I can't say why." I flashed back to what John did to Harry, immobilizing him with his mind and killing him. I had to admit to myself that it was possible that John or someone else could be manipulating me, but I couldn't think of a reason why they would. "To be safe, I've decided I'm going to work on my shielding diligently again to try to prevent any more of these dreams."

"I don't think you should tell Nate."

"But what if it comes out later, and Nate thinks I've been dishonest by not telling him? It doesn't feel right hiding something like this from him, especially if this guy is dangerous and is messing with my head on purpose."

"Ask yourself this: are you telling him because he might see it as dishonest or to appease your guilty conscience? If you're telling him because you feel guilty, that's selfish and probably destructive. If you're telling him so he won't think you're dishonest, that's another can of worms, but it may still hurt your relationship."

We arrived at the breakfast place and put our names on their list. The bicyclists were out in force. I'd always loved watching them on the weekends and respected their dedication. We both observed them quietly while we waited, lost in thought. I think Diana was trying to figure out how likely it was that John or someone like him was intentionally causing these dreams.

We sat down and ordered, still focused on our inward ruminations. "Okay," Diana said. "This is no fun. We need to forget our worries and enjoy the day. The sun is shining. We're going to eat some terrific food and shop for things that Nate will definitely appreciate."

"Agreed."

"I still can't believe you have only a few pairs of matching bras and panties. You're twenty-five, for God's sake! We'll set you up, but we need to lighten the mood first. Did I tell you the story about the embezzling bigamist vice president I exposed a few weeks ago?"

I smiled. "I think you forgot to tell me that one."

Typical Diana, she never gave away all of her tales of adventure at once. She kept some in reserve to unveil at exactly the right moment. Her favorite stories involved arrogant assholes getting their just desserts. She followed the rules and never revealed the names of the people or companies involved, but she loved the gossip and loved her vigilante part in bringing about their downfall.

Her story was intriguing but disturbing. The large number of messed-up people in the world never ceased to amaze me. Money and power seemed to bring out the worst in people. We left the restaurant and headed for the mall. After a few minutes, Diana looked concerned. "Sophia, I could be paranoid, but I think the dark blue sedan two cars back was behind us earlier this morning on the way to breakfast. I noticed it when the big rig entered the freeway. I'm pretty sure it's the same car."

"Sounds like a common make and color," I said. I turned around but couldn't see much through the SUV behind us. I adjusted my side mirror and saw it. It was your average looking car. "Let's leave the highway one exit early and see if the car follows."

Diana quickly moved over to exit and the blue car did the same. That made me nervous. I didn't want to turn around anymore because whoever it was might realize we'd noticed. She took a left, then a right, followed by another left turn, taking a circuitous route to the mall.

"He's still trailing us," Diana said as she looked in the rearview mirror. "It's a guy wearing sunglasses and a baseball cap. He seems tall. I can't make out anything else, and I can't hear his thoughts at this distance with all this interference."

"I can try to astral project, but I've never sent myself into a moving vehicle. It might take a few minutes."

"Don't bother. We're almost at the mall. It's a public place," Diana said. When we turned into the parking lot of the mall, the other car went straight at the light instead. We both breathed a sigh of relief.

"Okay, I probably overreacted," Diana said, but the sinking feeling in my gut and the fact that the car didn't take the most direct exit or route told me otherwise.

"Let's forget about this drama and buy you some sexy clothes."

The next thing I knew, Diana had a saleslady measure my naked body to confirm my exact size. Then, she drowned me in skimpy nighties, sexy bras, and thongs.

"Uh, Diana, could you grab me some normal panties? Thongs aren't my thing. I own a few but rarely wear them."

"Really? I always wear one. I find that I'm not that comfortable in panties anymore."

"Having fabric wedged in my butt crack isn't my idea of comfortable. They also make my butt look huge."

Diana laughed. "You have a perfect body, Sophia. You couldn't make your skinny butt look huge if you tried. I'll pick out some regular panties, but you must purchase at least a few thongs and wear them, especially when you wear your yoga pants. Once you get used to them, you won't want to wear anything else. In my experience, guys find them extremely sexy."

By the time we finished, I'd spent more than ever before on lingerie and hoped that Nate would appreciate it. I was surprised to realize that I enjoyed trying on the negligees. They made me feel sexier, more confident, and I couldn't wait to model them for Nate. We got smoothies and visited a few more stores. Diana bought a new pair of sunglasses and some winter boots, and she convinced me to splurge on a beautiful dress. I noticed, however, that wherever we went, we both continued to look around for anyone suspicious. Neither of us could shake the worry that someone might be watching us.

The rest of the day was spent eating gelato, enjoying a chick flick at the theater, and relaxing at my apartment with take out in the early evening. We agreed to watch our backs more than usual and to let each other know immediately if we sensed anything off. I thought the car incident might be John checking up on Diana and could tell she had the same concern, but we didn't discuss it openly. Since John supposedly cared for her, I hoped he merely wanted to catch a glimpse and see that she wasn't in any danger. Diana had to fly out for London the following day so she left early to pack.

"Thanks for shopping with me," I said. "I'll let you know if Nate's eyes pop out of his head."

"Don't bother. I'm sure I'll find out from him," she teased.

"Ha, ha. Have a safe trip. Promise me you'll be careful." I pulled her into a big hug. She hugged me tightly back, promised and departed.

Nate called later that night. He was enjoying time with his family but couldn't wait to come home. I told him I had a fun surprise for him but refused any details. Before I went to bed that evening, I spent an hour meditating with the GammaBeat. I tried to make my shields more tangible and impenetrable and hoped that my efforts would block the mysterious man from entering my dreams again.

CHAPTER SEVENTEEN

The night passed without any shared dreams. I doubted that my small amount of practice with the GammaBeat was responsible, but I felt hopeful that if I practiced every day for a month, my shields might grow strong enough to prevent anyone from messing with my mind again, whether intentional or not.

The morning proved to be fairly standard. I didn't have a scheduled projection until the afternoon so I started on a military case to track down a weapons stash. The intelligence wasn't that solid, and determining the exact location took me over four hours. When I shared the results with Roger, he asked me about the GammaBeat since he'd noticed me using it over the last few days. I guess I hadn't been as stealthy as I'd intended. I went ahead and told him everything I knew and demonstrated how it worked. He was intrigued and asked me to find out if SDCC could purchase some. I told him I didn't believe it was available any longer but that I'd try to find out.

I had time before my afternoon appointment so I went to the break room for vending machine sustenance and a warm drink. I was dipping a bag of green tea into a cup of hot water, wondering whether I should tell Nate about the dreams or not, when I felt strong arms hug me from behind and a soft kiss on my neck.

"Nate, you're back."

He whispered in my ear, "Did you have any interesting dreams last night?"

"What? No, not particularly," I answered. My hands began to sweat. Fear gripped me that he might know about my shared dreams, but that would be impossible. I turned in his arms and tried not to look anxious. His lips found mine, and that fear washed away, his touch soothing my soul. He wasn't satisfied with sweet, and neither was I for that matter, but when we started to instinctively press our bodies close, I forced us to stop before we got ourselves into trouble.

"We're definitely stepping over the line of appropriate workplace behavior," I teased, catching my breath.

"No one's around." He smiled at me with puppy dog eyes. "I'm only trying to say 'Hello and I missed you' as sedately as I can." He glided his thumbs over my cheeks as he held my face for a final quick kiss.

"I missed you too," I said. We each took a step back, but our hands remained together.

"I can't wait to get you home." His look held a yearning and a deeper meaning.

I also hadn't forgotten that tonight would be our first night *au naturel*. Heat rushed up my neck and filled my cheeks. He smiled and cupped the side of my face with his hand.

"It's a cruel fate that I won't be home until around eight tonight. I have to make up for the time away, but I had to find you before imprisoning myself in one of the projection rooms for the next six hours."

"You're going to project for six hours straight without a break?"

"I'm going to try. I'll be traveling to multiple locations so I'll have some down time while I write up my observations."

"I hope you're not going to come home completely exhausted," I said with a frown.

He laughed. "I'm glad to see you're looking forward to tonight as well. I'll conserve enough energy. I promise. I better get going. Do you mind taking care of dinner?"

"Not at all," I said. He pecked me on the cheek and left to start his work.

* * *

I picked up my favorite Italian food again, but this time I kept the food in the containers and placed them in a warm oven. The food smelled amazing, and I was hungry, but I had a different hunger tonight more in need of sating. I had a hard time deciding whether to wear a sexy bra and panties combo or a slinky negligee and hoped it didn't seem too risqué to be wearing nothing but these when Nate came home. I opted for the negligee with accompanying thong as it covered more and seemed sexier at the same time. A pair of heels completed the outfit. When he walked through the door, I was lying on my side on the couch, propped up on my elbow, coyly twisting some hair around a finger. I made a mental note to tell Diana that his eyes did indeed pop out of his head. He looked stunned. I beckoned him over with one finger, stood up so he could get the full impact, and swayed my hips as I walked towards him.

"Oh, God, Sophia, you look amazing."

I pressed my body against his. "Welcome home," I whispered into his mouth and played at his lips with my tongue. The shock wore off, and he placed both hands on the sides of my face and kissed me as if his life depended on it. His hands slid down my arms and grabbed my hips and lower back, pulling me tightly against him. His hands flowed over my butt and played with the thong. Nate made a deep, guttural sound and started pulling up the negligee. I unbuttoned and unzipped his pants. He was hard and ready. We quickly divested ourselves of the rest of our clothes and lay down on the carpet as we fed voraciously at each other's mouths. When I was on the floor, he started kissing my neck and used his fingers to push me close to the edge.

"Nate, I want you inside me, now!"

"I may not last long. I'm so turned on right now."

"Please," I begged. I didn't have to ask twice. His body fit inside mine like it was meant to be there. The soft velvet of his skin felt perfect. My hips met his, and I tightened around him with each thrust. I couldn't help but vocalize the sounds of my pleasure. His rhythm started to falter as my own reality became fuzzy around the edges. I yelled his name as I went over the top, and I could feel his heat spill inside of me. It felt right, almost magical.

I ran my hands through his hair. "I love you, Nate. I'm so glad you're home."

"I love you too," he whispered, still breathing rapidly, resting his head next to mine.

We lay there in each other's arms not wanting to separate until the chill air raised goose bumps on our skin. Nate fetched our robes. After a quick trip to the bathroom, I made my way back to the kitchen, where Nate was removing our dinner from the oven and appreciating the aromas.

"Dinner smells great. Would you like something to drink?" Nate asked

"Water would be perfect. I'm really thirsty."

"Me too."

We dug into the sublime food. I was famished. After several bites and sips of water, my ability to speak returned. "So, how was the wedding?"

"It was nice."

"Just nice? Did they seem happy together?"

"Yes, but I'm irritated with Brian."

"Why?"

"He kept trying to push women on me. I had a hard time keeping my promises to you about no lap dances and no dancing. At the strip club, he tried to send the lap dances my way time and again. Luckily, I was able to deflect them off onto someone else each time. Then at the reception, he sat Sarah next to me at the wedding party table, even though those spots are reserved for dates or spouses. I can't tell you the number of times he encouraged us to dance. It was as if he knew everything you'd explicitly asked me not to do. I think he was trying to sabotage me. I know he doesn't like the idea of us being together, but I never liked you dating him all those years ago. I didn't try to screw him, and it was his *wedding*, when he certainly shouldn't be thinking about an old girlfriend."

"That annoys me too, but I'm glad to hear that you kept your promises, especially with the odds stacked against you. You have always been too loyal to Brian." I placed my hand on his cheek.

"I don't think you can be too loyal. I think it's something you are or you aren't."

"You should have grabbed me and kissed me all those years ago and let Brian be damned."

Nate placed his hand over mine and squeezed it. "I wish I had." He kissed my hand and let it go so we could continue eating. He was quieter than usual though as we ate.

"I hate to be the bearer of bad news," he said, "but there's something else you're not going to like." Nate shoved his food around on his plate then looked up at me. "Sarah's moving to San Diego next month to work for a biotech company here. She doesn't have any friends or family in the area so I offered to show her around."

"Hmm." I put my fork down. "Do you think she's moving down here to be closer to you? She probably could have found a job in another city."

"I don't think so. San Diego's one of the few biotech hubs. Honestly, she's lucky to have found a job at all, but it's not too surprising it's here."

"Did she make any moves on you at the wedding?"

"No. She said we should dance a few times, but I told her I wasn't interested. Since we were sitting next to each other, we talked, of course. I told her I was living with you. She was surprised but didn't seem upset. Offering to show her around seemed like the nice thing to do."

"Hmm." My gut said she was making a play for him. I carried my dishes to the sink and started cleaning up a little more loudly than usual.

"That wasn't a happy 'Hmm.'"

I didn't answer as I wiped down the counter. I wasn't happy. I was tempted to tell him about the shared dreams so that we could get all of our bad news out at once, but Diana's advice to be cautious held me at bay. I was satisfied that my need to tell him stemmed from concern he'd think it dishonest and not from a need to confess, but I was still afraid that knowing I was having these dreams might throw his jealousy out of whack and hurt our relationship. Again, if he thought I was hiding this from him, he might not trust me again, and what we had would be destroyed anyway.

Large, warm arms wrapped around my waist from behind. I stayed rigid. "Sophia, come on. I missed you. I don't want us to fight. You're welcome to come along when I show Sarah around town, if she ever calls."

"Oh, she'll call," I said. "I can feel it."

"Well, if and when she does, I'll tell you every word she says. I won't hide anything from you. You have no reason to be jealous."

I swallowed hard. My instincts were right. He wouldn't understand if I hid the dreams from him, but I wasn't sure how to bring it up. I stalled by asking a few more questions about Sarah.

"How did you break up? You said that you both felt the chemistry wasn't there, but how did the breakup go down? Did you end things?" Nate put his plate in the dishwasher and then sat back down at the table.

"I initiated it, but she was either expecting it or agreed. She wasn't upset and was fine with just being friends again."

I quit puttering about in the kitchen and took a deep breath to solidify my courage. I leaned my back against the counter and faced him.

"Well, I guess it's my turn," I said. "I have two pieces of news for you as well, and you're not going to like either of them."

I told him first that Diana and I believed someone, probably John, had followed us yesterday. "I know the evidence isn't convincing, but we both had a bad feeling. When two psychics get a bad feeling, there's usually a reason."

His jaw ticked. "What's the other bad news?"

"Do you remember when John prevented me from dreaming?" Nate nodded as I took a deep breath. "Well, just before the dreams disappeared, I had two strange dreams that Harry thought were probably shared. They appeared to be unintentionally shared since the other person seemed surprised to see me in the second dream. I hoped it was some sort of byproduct of John messing with my head. I thought that once my dreams were back to normal, it wouldn't happen again, but I had another shared dream on Saturday night."

The look on his face said he already had an idea as to the type of dream, but he asked the question anyway.

"Is the person you're sharing dreams with a guy or a girl?"

"A guy," I said.

"What happens in these dreams?"

"How much detail do you want?" I asked and could immediately tell it was the wrong thing to say.

"How much do I need?"

"I can give you the gist now, or if you want, you can read my dream journal. It has every detail."

"Give me the gist first, and then I'll see if I want more," he said.

"The first dream was at the Ocean Beach pier, and we watched the sunset together. In the second dream, I thought I was kissing you, but when the kiss broke, we looked at each other and were shocked to realize that we weren't kissing who we thought we were. In the dream on Saturday, I was naked, being spooned from behind by what I thought was you, but again when we looked at each other, it wasn't the person either of us expected. I guess because he's likely a telepath he was able to ask me who I was, but I don't think I could answer him and the surprise of seeing him again pulled me out of the dream."

Nate wasn't looking at me. He was staring fixedly at some spot on the table. "I started trying to reinforce my shields using the GammaBeat," I said. "I plan to keep practicing until I believe no one can get into my head again."

"How is this happening? How do you know he isn't doing this intentionally?"

"Harry thought the guy had to be a telepath and assumed he was unintentionally sharing dreams with me. Although he seemed surprised to see me in the last two dreams, it could be a ruse, I guess. I just don't know."

"Do you find him attractive?" he asked, while scrutinizing my reaction.

I took another breath and let it out slowly. "Well, yes. He actually looks a lot like you, just a little darker, like he has some southern European or Hispanic heritage. He seems a little older than we are."

"Do you have any feelings for him?"

"No, Nate. I don't know him. He's a stranger, but I do have some impressions of him. He seems like a good person. I don't think he'd hurt me."

Nate stared at the spot again and was quiet. I sat next to him and put my hand on his, but it didn't respond beneath mine.

"Nate, you can read the dream entries if you want to know everything, including my analysis. Except for the first time, I thought I was dreaming of you. I'll do whatever I can to make this easier. I knew these dreams would upset you, but I thought you might feel I was being dishonest if I kept them from you. I promise to do whatever I can to prevent them from happening again. Please, please say I did the right thing in telling you."

Nate looked at me, exhaled slowly and squeezed my hand. "You did. I just have so many emotions going through me right now. I'm jealous, concerned for you, and angry at the world. You were right to tell me, though, because honesty is incredibly important to me."

"Can I hold you?" I asked as my voice cracked. A tear started running down my cheek.

His face softened, and he opened his arms so I could sit in his lap. I sat down and put my arms around him as a few more tears trickled down my cheek. I couldn't keep them in any longer after watching his face become hard and feeling a gulf widen between us. I didn't want to lose him, didn't want our relationship to change. He rubbed my back and leaned his forehead against mine.

225

"Sophia, don't worry. We'll get through this. I'm not going to let some stupid dreams come between us, and for the record, I'm not letting anyone take you away from me ever again. You're *mine*. I don't know how I'm going to deal exactly, but I promise we'll figure it out. I am jealous, but I'm more worried that you could be in danger."

"I love you, Nate. Please don't forget that."

"I love you too."

The warmth of his body around mine dried my tears and gave me strength. I wanted to salvage the evening and thought a change of subject might help. "How are your parents?" I asked.

Nate smiled thinking about them. "They're doing great. My dad's still happy at his job, and my mom loves her class this year. She teaches kindergarten and is probably the best teacher in the district. My mom's over the moon right now because she just found out she's going to be a grandma. Ron and my sister-in-law, Stacey, are going to have a baby in May. She's so excited. She couldn't stop talking about it."

"That's wonderful news. I guess that'll make you an uncle."

"Yeah, but it's weird. I can't imagine my brother being mature enough to be a dad." He smiled and pecked my lips. "My parents want to meet you. I'd love for you to come home with me for Thanksgiving. My brothers and grandparents will be there."

"I'd love to, but my mom would be sad if I deserted Thomas and her on Thanksgiving."

After talking through the logistics, we decided to propose to our moms a joined Thanksgiving dinner at Nate's house but would split our time between both families.

"Since your grandparents will be in your bedroom, we should sleep at my house and make day trips to yours. That way, you'll get to sleep with me in the bed I grew up in and see all my old pictures," I tried to entice him.

"I don't think I can resist sleeping with you in your old room, or anywhere, for that matter."

I kissed him and nuzzled his neck. The turn of the conversation had lifted our spirits. "Is there anything else you'd like to do before going to bed? I need to practice with the GammaBeat for a half hour or so." With that reminder, I could see the concern in Nate's eyes return.

"While you do that, I'll unpack and start some laundry."

I didn't inform him that I'd already done his laundry because I looked forward to his reaction. After fetching the headband from my room, I meditated, imagining my impenetrable fortress. When I finished, I turned off the lights and went into the bedroom. Nate was lying in bed reading a book, with the covers concealing him from the waist down. I got ready for bed and then turned off the main light. He was barely maintaining consciousness. The reading light cast shadows across his chest.

"You are so sexy," I said as I let my robe fall to the floor and climbed under the covers with him.

"What?" He stretched and smiled. "I think I pale in comparison to you."

"Nate, why do you love me?"

"You're asking me now?" He could tell I was serious so he tried to restart his brain. "Well, you're kind, sexy, smart, honest, and great in bed, but most of all, you're just you, Sophia. You're *my* Sophia. I feel like I've known you my whole life." He kissed me sweetly. "Why do you love me?"

I looked him straight in the eye and held his face in my hands. "You take my breath away when you stare into my eyes. You're good, smart, loyal, honorable, protective, and amazing in bed. Looking at you half-naked makes my knees go weak. There's a depth to you I just know somehow, like you're a part of me."

He kissed my palm. "My description wasn't nearly as poetic as yours. Forgive my tired, addled mind. Hmm, I want you again, but I'm not up to the challenge tonight."

"It's okay." I reached up and turned off the light. "Just hold me as close as you can." He pulled me into him, and I felt at peace.

"Oh, by the way, thanks for washing my clothes. No one's done that for me besides my mom and not since I was little."

I smiled and snuggled in closer.

CHAPTER EIGHTEEN

I awoke to a ticklish feeling on my arm. Nate was trailing the tips of his fingers up and down. "What time is it?" I asked.

"Around six. I've been watching you sleep for about an hour. You really do look like an angel in a peaceful slumber." He kissed me on the forehead.

"Mmm. Thanks." I yawned and stretched.

"Uh . . . did you have any shared dreams last night?"

"I don't think so." I grabbed my iPhone and checked to see that four dreams were recorded. "I remember these, and none of them were shared."

He looked lost. I put my hands on his cheeks and positioned his face directly in front of mine. "Listen to me. Even if I'm sharing a dream with someone, it's not real. We're real. I love you. I think the last two dreams were sexual because I was yearning for you, and unfortunately, he just happened to join them. What can I do to make you feel better about this?"

"Well, I've been thinking about it, and I *would* like to read your dream journal, if you don't mind. I need to know what I'm up against."

"Nate, you aren't up against anything. I don't think reading the logs will make you feel better, but if that's what you need, I'm fine with it. If you want me to be completely open, I'll do that. If you don't want to hear about them ever again, I can do that too. We should do whatever you think is best for you *and* for our relationship."

"Sophia, I want to protect you from all of this, from the shared dreams and from murderers like John, but I feel powerless. I don't know what to do, and it's torturing me. I can't lose you."

"Don't worry. I can protect myself. I'm a second-degree black-belt in kung fu, and I'm reinforcing my shields."

Nate continued stroking and focusing on my arms. "I'm not sure any of us can protect ourselves from John. The police can't protect us, and he's more skilled than Thomas or Diana."

"We're probably not as susceptible as Harry. All of our shields and psychic abilities are stronger, but then again, John was able to block me from dreaming and projecting. Although he fooled Thomas and Diana, he might not be able to control another telepath. I'd also guess that he can't control more than one person at a time."

"I doubt it will help, but we should tell Detective Jones that John may have been following you two. Maybe when Diana returns from her trip, the police could do something to lure him."

"I think that's Diana's call, but I won't let her lure him alone."

"Of course not."

"So you're okay with us getting involved?"

"I am now. I was hoping that Harry was their only concern, that if you kept a low profile they wouldn't interest themselves in anyone else, but if John was really following you and some guy is invading your dreams again, then it seems like you're involved whether I like it or not."

"You might be right. . . . Crap. I just realized that the police would be in danger if they confronted John. It would probably be trivial for John to control a normal person. If he ends up controlling an officer that's carrying a weapon, it could be carnage."

"So we can't even risk help from the police? Dammit!" He ran his fingers through his hair and sighed. "Well, we can only do what we can do. Diana needs to be on alert, and we all need to be careful. We should be in training, training our bodies and our minds. I'll improve my shields using the GammaBeat, if you'll start running with me. I know you can fight, but I'd feel a lot better if I knew you could run away as well." Some of the worry in his face slipped away at the prospect of doing something constructive to help our situation.

"I'm game, but you'll have to be patient with me. I can't run as fast or as far as you."

"I will be. Thomas is in great shape and can fight. What about Diana?" he asked.

"Diana's never taken martial arts, but she jogs on the beach and does Pilates."

Nate looked at the clock and asked, "Do you want to go running right now? We can run for twenty minutes or so before we have to shower for work."

"Uh, okay," I said. It wasn't exactly how I'd wished to spend the next twenty minutes, but Nate's mood had turned around, and I wanted to do what I could to keep it there. We dressed quickly and ran out the door. When we returned, I was gasping for breath, whereas Nate had barely broken a sweat. I hoped I'd improve enough to make it more of a workout for him, but we could always jog separately. I turned on the hot water for the shower, but Nate stopped me before I took off my clothes.

"Can I read the dream entries now? It might ruin my day, but I want to get it over with. I need to stop wondering and start dealing."

I nodded and opened my laptop. "I group them together by week starting on Sunday night. The first one was on your first day of work, the second the week after, and the last one grouped with last week." I opened the file and found the relevant entries.

"I usually label each dream with a word or a phrase. For these three, my names were beach sunset, kiss, and bed. Do you want me to start my shower while you read or do you want me to stay?"

"I think I'd prefer if you showered. You already look concerned."

I took a deep breath and kissed him on the forehead.

I stepped into the shower and began to run the hot water through my hair. I wasn't sure how long I should stay. It would only take him a minute to read each one, but he'd probably reread them and possibly want some time alone. I was impatient to see his reaction but afraid at the same time. I cut my shower only a tad short so he'd have plenty of time but wouldn't have to wait long if he wanted to talk. I wrapped myself in a towel, took a deep breath, and made my way back into the bedroom. Nate was lying on the bed looking at the ceiling and didn't look at me when I came in. He just kept staring above. I lay down next to him and put my hand on his chest. He grabbed my hand and held it.

"The dreams aren't real, Nate."

"I know. I just don't like that he's touched you and kissed you."

"He didn't physically touch me."

"No, but you felt it. He felt it."

"I thought it was you both times, and I think he believed I was someone else."

"But not in the first dream," he said.

"In that dream, he only put his arm around me. We also weren't dating then."

"I know, but it's the level of trust you felt with him that disturbs me."

I didn't know what to say. "What can I do?"

"Kiss me," he replied.

I kissed him slowly and sweetly, but I soon realized that that wasn't what he wanted. He flipped us, unfastening my towel and pressing me down beneath him, his lips hungrily kissing mine. He was inside me before I realized his pants were down. The quick progress left me somewhat bewildered. Nate had always given me plenty of foreplay, but I did my best to stay in the moment. He rammed me hard and fast. I kept up, meeting each thrust with a tilt of my hips. He collapsed on me with a shudder. I wrapped my legs around him and held him close. After he caught his breath, he sprinkled light kisses on my face.

He looked at me sheepishly. "Kind of fast, huh?"

"Kinda."

"Sorry, that was sort of barbaric. I just . . . I don't know, I just . . ."

"Needed to stake your claim?" He flinched. "Don't worry. Although

I'd prefer not to have too many 'wham, bam, thank you ma'am' sessions, I get it. I do. We're good."

"I love you."

"I know. I love you too."

"So, I guess we have to get dressed now?" I asked.

"Probably."

He leaned his forehead against mine and slowly exhaled. "I know these dreams aren't your fault. I'll try not to let them bother me," he looked me straight in my eyes, "but I'd like you to promise to tell me whenever you have them. If I know you'll tell me, I won't wonder about your dreams when I see you sleeping. I'm still concerned there's a darker purpose. You may trust him, but I don't."

"I promise. Even if I know it'll upset you, I'll tell you." I sighed and hoped to God I didn't have any more shared dreams.

* * *

When Nate and I arrived home from work, his spirits had improved. My mom and Thomas were happy to join Nate's family for Thanksgiving, and we both looked forward to introducing each other to our families.

Around eight o'clock, Nate received a call from Sarah. I strained my ears, listening as hard as I could to his conversation while pretending I was concentrating on yoga poses. Apparently, she had her move-in date and wanted to schedule a time for him to give her a tour.

"Hang on a second. Sophia, would you prefer to show Sarah around on a Saturday or a Sunday?"

Though irritated, I came out of my pose and asked diplomatically, "What do you want to show her?"

"I thought we could drive by the coast, walk around Balboa Park and have lunch. It's kind of far in the future but does Sunday, December 9th, work?"

"I'll check my schedule." I frowned as I toggled through my calendar on my phone. I didn't pretend to be happy about this, and Nate looked tense. I nodded to Nate that the date worked.

"Uh, Sarah, why don't we pick you up around ten o'clock that day? Where are you going to live? Oh, that's not far from us . . . okay . . . I'll text you some time the week before to confirm." Nate tucked his phone back into his pocket and came over to me as I sulked on the couch.

"Please don't be mad at me. I'm only trying to be nice to a friend."

"How did she respond when you said we'd both be showing her around?"

"To be honest, she did seem surprised. I guess she expected me to do it alone, but once she adjusted her view, she seemed okay with it."

I stared at Nate. "Did you love her? Did you tell her you loved her?"

He looked down. "Sophia . . . please . . . let's not do this."

"I guess that answers my question." He didn't offer anything else but instead raked his fingers through his hair and looked grumpily off into the kitchen. I didn't want to fight with him tonight, but I was irked now. Nate liked to call me his, but I felt equally possessive of him. He was *mine*, and I had a gut feeling that Sarah still thought of him as hers. Although my heart ached at the distance rising between us at that moment, I needed some space to calm myself.

I grabbed my iPhone, ear buds and running shoes. "I'm going to jog on the treadmill at the apartment gym. If I'm going to run with you, I'll need to spend some time running on my own. Could you please use the GammaBeat while I'm gone? I'd like to use it when I get back."

I started tugging on my shoes. He continued to brood, suspicious of my overly polite demeanor. I think he knew I was trying to get away from him. Our different styles of dealing with unpleasantness were already showing. He became outwardly angry and somewhat sulky, while I retreated into myself and took a step away from the situation. I left without a backward glance. When I was out of the building, I called Diana. Luckily, she picked up even though she was on London time and still sleeping.

"Diana, I need you to tell me if I'm being ridiculous." I told her everything I knew about the ex-girlfriend and about the small argument Nate and I just had.

"You're not being ridiculous. She probably wants him back. Most women still want the guy who broke up with them as a matter of principle, even if they only get him back long enough to dump him. Sarah's going to be lonely, living in a new city with no friends. She'll want his companionship even if he's not the love of her life. Although she didn't reach the milestone of living with him, they were together a long time, and it sounds like they thought they were in love at some point. She most likely sees you as an interloper and still thinks of him as rightfully hers. You're justified in being jealous but don't let it put a wedge between you and Nate. The bottom line is that Sarah spending time alone with him is a bad idea. I do think you're being gracious in showing her around. Maybe Nate will appreciate your coming, but you can also observe her intentions for yourself."

"Do you think if we meet and become friendly that she won't try to steal Nate?"

Diana laughed at me. "Sometimes I forget you're not a telepath, and then you say something like that. Sophia, most single women can't be trusted when it comes to a man they want. It doesn't matter if you're friends, even if you're close enough that you'd take the time to drive her to the airport."

"Well, that's disturbing."

"Yes, but it's true. I think you're the only friend I'd trust no matter what, which is saying a lot since I can rarely read your mind. You should stop by my house while showing her the coast. I'd love to get my mind on hers. I could tell you exactly what she thinks of Nate."

Usually, I'd think it wrong to spy on someone's thoughts for personal reasons, but because she was likely after my boyfriend, I didn't have any qualms about making an exception. "Okay. I'll try to stop by, but Nate might not be happy about it."

"He doesn't have to know it was planned," she suggested.

"I doubt I can pull that off, but I do think the situation is justifiable. Oh, Diana, you're going to say I'm stupid, but I told Nate about the shared dreams."

"Oh, dear. How did he respond?" she asked.

"He's upset, but I think he'll be okay. He was already better this evening."

"I hope you're right."

"I better go. I'm supposed to be running right now. I'll need to break a sweat before I can go home."

I walked for a few minutes on the treadmill first to loosen my muscles from the morning run with Nate. I was certain that running twice in one day would make me walk funny either tomorrow or the next day, but I needed to back up my cover story for leaving and hoped it would clear my mind.

After a decent run, I was sweatier but less upset when I opened the door to the apartment. Although I felt a twinge of guilt for planning to spy on Sarah's thoughts, knowing her intentions would prevent me from overreacting, which would be better for all involved, right? Nate was sitting on the couch using the GammaBeat but set it down when he heard me come in. His eyes were clouded, missing their usual spark. I don't know what I looked like, but I felt disconnected from him, like I had a palpable hole in my heart. I kicked off my shoes, then sat on the coffee table in front of him. He reached for my hand and gently rubbed the back with his thumb. My heart leapt at the contact, but the aching distance remained.

"Let's not fight," he said. "If you still want to know, I'll answer your questions about Sarah."

"Nate, for our relationship to work, you have to be open with me. You've always downplayed your relationship with her, but since she's coming back into your life, I need to know — did you and Sarah love each other? Did you say you loved her?"

"Well, yes, I thought I loved her for a time, but I know now that I never truly loved anyone until a month ago," he said, eliciting a tiny smile from me.

"How do you feel about her now?"

"I think of her as a friend . . . a friend that I care about. I wish her the best, but I don't want her. I don't love her."

"How do you stop loving someone in just a few months? I don't understand that."

"Well, we cared for each other and had fun together. . . . We had a good sex life," he added somewhat sheepishly. "The relationship was exciting at first, but it became obvious over time that it just wasn't going anywhere. Our feelings weren't that intense. I never wanted to move in with her. Instead of love, I should have said 'care about,' I guess, but there can be different types of love, I think. It doesn't always mean the same thing."

"How is our relationship any different? Maybe what we have isn't a love that will last either. Maybe it's just a hormone-induced delusion like at the start of any sexually satisfying relationship."

Nate flinched, hurt spreading to his eyes. Part of me wanted to take it back, but another part thought there might be some truth to it, so I let it stand. We were both quiet for a few moments, and his sadness and mine tugged at my heart. I had to look away.

He turned my face to him and gently tucked hair behind my ear. "Sophia, you said it for me yesterday. I feel like you're a part of me, like your soul touches mine. You may have had this with Brian, but I've never experienced this with Sarah or anyone else, not even in the beginning. I didn't know I could feel so much, that I could love someone more than I've ever thought possible."

I moved from the table into his lap, brushed strands of hair out of his face with the tips of my fingers and stared into his fathomless dark eyes. They held a depth of feeling that bored into my soul. He was right. What we had was far beyond the ordinary. I had to trust in that. "I love you too, Nate. I told you I've never had this connection with anyone else. I'm sorry I doubted it."

I tentatively touched my lips to his. He was open but didn't respond at first. He seemed to be savoring the contact, slowly absorbing the warmth through his pores. Then, letting out a long sigh, his lips molded to mine, sending an electricity through me. Our kiss became greedy. We needed more. I wrapped my legs around him and pulled him into me. Nate held me against him, stood up and carried me to the bedroom. The kiss didn't pause until he sat down on the edge of the bed. We hastily removed our shirts, pressed our bare chests together and continued the kiss while tugging the rest of our clothes free. Nate moved to the middle of the bed and lifted me into his lap. As he slid inside me, my eyes closed, overcome with the feel of him. Once he'd filled me completely, he focused on kissing and caressing me. The skin he touched tingled. Although I'd read about tantric sex, I'd never experienced it until that moment when it felt like our energies started to mingle and merge. Nate slowly began to move, and my body rocked with his. We broke the kiss to stare into each other's eyes, breathing into each other's mouths and feeling what must have been our lower chakras connect. No emotional gulf separated us any longer. I rubbed the side of my face along his nose, his chin, his neck, his ears. I was marking my territory and had to claim him for my own.

Nate stopped moving and took a few deep breaths. "I need to be still for a few moments or I won't last," he whispered. "God, if I could stop time and hold you like this forever, I would." I framed his face with my hands and kissed him gently, reverently. He kissed me deeply in response but had to pull back, take in slow breaths, fight his body.

"I want us to orgasm at the same time, to experience it together," he said.

He took another slow breath, pulled out a little, and used his fingers to help me catch up. When my moans began to escalate to a feverish pitch, he thrust into me again and again, taking me over the peak with his release. At that moment, my shields vanished, and a sudden warmth enveloped me. It didn't feel like I was projecting, but I seemed to extend outside of my body. I could feel my heart beat, my lungs expand with each breath, and the pleasurable sensations echoing through me, but I could also feel Nate's as if they were my own. Beyond the physical plane, our essences seemed to vibrate together in a state of resonance, reverberating like a song that had been playing for a thousand years.

Time lost all meaning. Afraid to break the magic, we didn't dare move. Then, as quick and sharp as a razor, we were wrenched apart, my shields snapping back into place. Stunned by the abrupt return to normalcy, we breathed quietly. After a few moments, Nate pitched me over onto my back and settled on top of me with my legs and arms still wrapped around him.

"What just happened?" he asked.

"I don't know. It felt like we merged, both physically and spiritually, as if an unseen light passed through us, fused us and cocooned us in its warmth."

"I sensed somehow that we were part of each other, part of a whole long ago that never should have been separated."

"Exactly. God, I love you." I hugged him tightly.

"I love you too." Nate kissed my cheek and laid his head on my shoulder.

I scratched his back and breathed in his scent. "I think I felt my shields fall at the start and return at the end. Maybe we spontaneously projected into each other but in some different plane of existence, like we visited that mythical astral plane together? Though, if that was a projection, it wasn't like my usual ones. People have passed through my projected presence before, but I've never felt what they felt."

"Let's try projecting now before we lose the sensation," Nate suggested.

"Okay."

I closed my eyes, lowered my shields and focused on projecting into him. This time my consciousness hovered above him, around him, within him. Strangely, I could sense his projected presence drifting around as well and tried to merge our projections. I felt something, a sort of tingling may be the best description, but it was nothing like before. We then took turns projecting into each other but still couldn't replicate the experience.

Nate and I wondered whether it had happened because of our shared abilities or because of our connection, or maybe it wasn't that we'd projected, just that we existed at the same frequency for a fraction of time. Whatever it was, it was mind-blowing. It was heaven. I knew without question that Nate had been and always would be a part of me at some spiritual level or atomic scale. By eleven o'clock, we hadn't succeeded in repeating the event. We were drained so I postponed the GammaBeat practice until the next day and settled into bed, spooned by Nate.

"Just so you know. Sarah can't have you. You're mine."

He kissed my shoulder, and I could feel the curve of a smile on my skin. "Without question I'm yours, and you're mine. Happy one-month anniversary, by the way."

CHAPTER NINETEEN

The next week-and-a-half proved much more carefree. Nothing happened that was the least bit concerning. The shared dreams hadn't returned, and no one appeared to be following us, as far as we could tell. Nate and I were also settling into our relationship. During our friendship in college, we'd never had an argument. Overcoming our recent bumps made our relationship feel more resilient. Life even began to seem almost normal again. The only reminder of our lingering issues was our new routine of running in the mornings and working with the GammaBeat at night, but since we were becoming stronger physically and mentally, it wasn't much of a chore.

On Wednesday, we left work early to fly with Thomas to San Francisco for the Thanksgiving holidays. My mom picked us up at the airport. A cheerful, fun, and beautiful woman, she was thirty years older than I was but didn't look it. We shared the same body type and thick, dark hair, but her skin and eyes were darker than mine. She hugged and kissed the three of us as if we were all her children.

"Mom, this is Nate. Nate, this is my mom." I was a little nervous, though I knew she'd love him. She was beyond excited. I think she'd almost given up on me bringing another guy home.

"It's a pleasure to meet you, Dr. Walsh," Nate said. I grinned at his remembering she was a doctor and not merely a previous "Mrs."

"Oh, please, call me Elena. If you call me Dr. Walsh, I'll think I'm at work."

Nate insisted on carrying my bags to the car even though I assured him I could handle it. He was clearly trying to impress my mom, and it seemed to be working as she snuck me a smile and a wink of approval. We packed up the car and headed for home.

"I can't wait to see where you grew up," Nate said, rubbing my hand in the backseat of the car. "I was raised not far away, but I don't know the city well at all."

"I look forward to seeing it too. I haven't been home since the summer. I promise to show you some of my favorite spots."

I think Nate was mildly impressed when we pulled into our garage. My mom's house is a Victorian three-story in the Cole Valley neighborhood of San Francisco. With the pointy, octagonal tower, elaborate trim, scalloped shingles, and wood siding, it always reminded me of a perfect dollhouse.

My dad's mom, Grandma Marie, bought it for my parents when they began their residencies at UCSF in the early '80s. It was a turn-of-the-century home that she'd completely refurbished, updating all of the old systems and making it more structurally sound and earthquake resistant. Since she lived in San Francisco, she wanted my parents to have a home nearby where they could raise a family. Sadly, I never met this amazing woman because she died when my mom was pregnant with Thomas and me, but my eyes and middle name are hers. My mom loved her and kept her pictures, though not my dad's, still prominently displayed after the divorce. She wanted me to see that there's a part of her in me. My mom mentioned once that she didn't think my dad would have lost it and abandoned us if Grandma Marie had still been alive.

When my grandmother died, she left a large inheritance to both of my parents. In the divorce settlement, my mom received more than half of their shared assets because my dad wanted nothing further to do with us, meaning he paid all child support upfront for an agreement that he wouldn't be contacted or burdened with custody. Since the house was paid for, my mom was able to continue working part-time until we were in high school and still pay all of our expenses, including our college educations. She was thrifty, though, and raised us the same way because the money had to last. Until Thomas and I were stable enough for her to work full-time, the outflow of cash exceeded the inflow. Though she now lived alone in this big place, except for renting the lower level, she didn't have the heart to leave the good memories behind.

We pulled our bags out of the car and brought them upstairs into the living room.

"Mom, would you like to give Nate a tour or would you prefer that I do it?"

"I'd love to show Nate around," she said, hooking his arm in hers. I followed to watch their interaction, and Thomas graciously carried the bags to our rooms on the third floor. She told him about Grandma Marie and how she'd wanted them to raise a big family close to her in the city. Nate nodded and made the requisite appreciative comments as she paraded him around the kitchen, office and living spaces. After she finished showing him the main floor, they headed upstairs.

The top floor had four bedroom suites and a terrace that offered wonderful views of the surrounding area. When they reached my room, Nate kept picking up small trinkets scattered about and wasn't paying that much attention to my mom. I grabbed a trophy out of his hands and motioned for him to keep up with her. My mom finished the tour by going back to the main floor and out the back porch.

"The jewel of the house has always been this backyard," she said. "It's rare to have yards this big and green in any city. It's actually as big as the yard I had growing up in Texas. My dad built the kids a fort in one of the trees near the back, and it's still there. Sophia and Thomas spent most of their childhood out here."

"The house is beautiful and perfect for a family," Nate said. "I didn't realize living in the city could feel so suburban. Your yard's bigger than my family's in San Jose."

"We've been happy here," she beamed. "My work, our yoga studio, the martial arts center, and most of the kids' schools are within walking distance. We've rarely needed to drive or take public transportation for our usual activities."

"I bet Sophia and Thomas loved trotting about the city as kids." Nate pulled me into his arms and kissed my cheek.

"They did." She smiled at the memory but then a new glow in her eyes showed how happy she was about Nate and me. "Are you two hungry? I made dinner reservations for seven o'clock, but I picked up a few cheeses and some bread today for us to snack on until then. Why don't the two of you unpack while I set everything up? Oh, and let Thomas know to come down. I bought his favorite cheese."

Nate followed me up to my room and closed the door behind him, grabbing my hand and pulling me close. He kissed me gently on the lips and smiled.

"I like your mom, and I like seeing you in your native environment. I can almost imagine you and Thomas as kids climbing those trees."

"My mom did whatever she could to make sure we had a magical childhood."

He eyed the bed, and his lips began to interrogate my neck. "I recall you saying I could make love to you in your old bed."

"Nate," I laughed. "Stop. We need to head back downstairs. And for the record, I said *sleep* with me in my old bed. I've never actually had sex with anyone here. I was too young and paranoid when Brian visited me. He stayed in the guest bedroom."

He looked at me with those pleading, puppy dog eyes. "Please tell me I won't have to spend the next four nights celibate."

"We'll see. Let's unpack and hurry downstairs."

By the time the three of us returned to my mom, she'd already placed a cheese spread from Say Cheese on the coffee table and was cutting a baguette in the kitchen.

"Would you like me to pour some wine?" Thomas asked Mom, pecking her cheek.

"Please," she said. "Nate, what time should we leave for your parents' house tomorrow?"

"Depending on traffic the drive could take an hour or two. My mom's set Thanksgiving dinner for two o'clock. If it's okay with you guys, I'd like to leave by ten. That way we can help cook and have plenty of time to hang out before we eat."

"That's fine with me," my mom said. "I'm completely ready. I baked an apple and two pumpkin pies earlier today."

"Mmm, so that's what I smelled." Thomas sniffed and grinned.

"That works," I said. "I plan to take you on a jog to show you the sunrise from Tank Hill, but we'll be showered and fed in plenty of time."

Nate smiled and squeezed my hand. "That sounds fun."

Nate and I sat down next to each other on the couch, his arm draping across my shoulders. Thomas and my mom brought over the bread and wine, and the four of us sat cozily and chatted. My mom told Nate a few stories about Thomas and me when we were kids, how because of our telepathic communication we appeared to approach the world with a single hive mind. We were pretty good kids but were almost unstoppable if we concocted a plan, like stealing extra cookies or going on adventures too far from home. If Thomas and I were on a team together, no one else stood a chance since we could seamlessly coordinate our efforts. She also mentioned that others noticed that something wasn't right about the way we interacted and sometimes steered clear of us. Although my mom tried to get us to communicate aloud whenever we were in public or had friends over, we preferred to communicate telepathically. It sometimes appeared as if we were mute while we worked on a puzzle or explored together. Nate was enthralled and kept her busy answering questions about our childhood.

When we'd had our fill of bread and cheese, Nate and I bundled up to walk around the neighborhood for the few hours before dinner. I brought him first to a special work of art in my neighbor's yard.

"When I was in elementary school, the woman who lived here had an artist carve this glorious angel out of an old cypress tree that had to be torn down. She called it the 'Angel of Hope.' Something about her touched me. Whenever I felt sad as a kid, I would walk by here and stare at her for a while. I didn't really pray to her, but I did share whatever was bothering me. Maybe it was simply unloading my worries, but seeing her with her raised sword always made me feel stronger, like I could tackle anything."

We continued our tour until I'd shown him all three of my public schools and most of my favorite places, giving us barely enough time to meet Thomas and my mom for dinner. After the waiter took our orders, my mom explained to Nate how the neighborhood had changed over time.

"A lot of young families have moved in over the last several years. I'm now officially one of the old ladies on the block. I'll have to get a cat soon to complete the picture," she said.

"Mom, you are not old. You're still young enough to date and find someone who will treat you right," I said.

"I know that now, but until recently, I just never saw it as a possibility. I didn't think I'd find someone who could understand us, and I was so concerned with you two for so long. . . . By the time you went to college, I'd forgotten dating was even an option and threw myself into my work. But, you'll be proud of me, Sophia. I signed up on one of those online dating services last week."

I was shocked but excited for her at the same time. *My mom's using a dating service?* I could hardly believe it. "Mom, that's great!"

"I've already received several requests for dates, and some look promising." Mom was as giddy as I'd ever seen her.

"Of course, you did, Mom," Thomas said. "Though if you start getting serious with anyone, I'd like to meet him to make sure he's good enough for you."

"Oh, Thomas," my mom said, smiling. She pretended he was joking, but I knew he was deadly serious and would make certain he met any potential suitors.

When we were in my old bed that night, Nate and I cuddled under the covers while I tried to explain the reasons we shouldn't have sex. In addition to my mom and Thomas potentially hearing unmistakable noises, I thought the fact that Thomas might get an intimate view would dissuade him, but that didn't seem to trouble Nate.

"You've got shields." He turned me to face him and pulled my hips against his.

"But I've never been in the same building as Thomas or Diana when I've had sex. My walls definitely fell when we merged the other night. What if they're compromised every time I orgasm, and I'm just too preoccupied to notice?"

"You'd have felt your shields fall, wouldn't you? My shields are working now. David said they're tough to break." He kissed me behind my ear and started trailing down my neck.

I laughed. "Boy, you're determined. Mmm." I arched my neck instinctively giving him better access. "Just so you know, when I'm really tired, I don't always notice when my shields fall so it's possible they fall other times too, and yours would be even shakier than mine." Nate started kissing down my neck again and had begun to fondle my breasts and tease the peaks. I think he'd stopped listening. I'd certainly lost my train of thought.

My right leg responded of its own accord and wrapped around his hip, opening me to him. I sighed. It was hard to stop my body from doing what it wanted to do. "Nate, please. You know I want you too. I just don't want to embarrass myself in front of my family right now. If it's any consolation, the balance might tip in your favor tomorrow or the next day. I'm already fighting with my body to behave."

"Sorry," he said, taking a deep breath in and letting it out. "I'll be good."

I needed to get his mind off of sex, as he had very nearly breached my resistance. "Tell me what you liked most about today," I said.

"Meeting your mom. She's very sweet and loves you and Thomas so much. I also just liked seeing your world — where you grew up and all the places here that were part of your life, like your angel. I love learning more about you."

I smiled and intertwined my legs with his to warm them.

"So, now that my shields are officially intact according to David. Will you tell me your secret?"

"What secret?" I couldn't think of what he meant.

"When we were talking about social media on the beach near Diana's, you said you'd tell me a secret when my shields were working."

I laughed. "Wow, you have a good memory. I hope you weren't obsessing about it. It's really not that big of a deal. I just didn't want to out Diana."

"I've only wondered about it occasionally. You didn't make it seem important, but it was another motivation to get my shields online."

"Well, you know that SDCC had a total ban on social media when we first started. Diana railed against it, but she eventually complied and shut down her accounts. A month or two later, though, she created a secret Twitter account. I only discovered it because she left the app open on her phone once. Anyway, I've never checked it out myself, but her alias has something to do with the Roman goddess Diana, the goddess of the hunt and moon."

"I guess that doesn't surprise me. She isn't one to follow a rule she thinks is stupid."

"The rule itself isn't stupid, especially for the telepaths. Diana spies on people in person. Having her face searchable on the internet could put her in danger. Since she just needed an outlet to express herself anonymously, the way she skirted the rule seemed reasonable to her. I don't think they'd have reprimanded her for an account that doesn't show her picture or her full name. Still, even though it's technically okay now, I didn't want to rat her out accidentally by telling you before you had shields. I just thought you'd appreciate it as typical Diana."

"I like how the two of you always have each other's backs."

"We have ever since we met. She's like my sister."

"I've got your back now too."

"I know, and I've got yours, and what a mighty fine backside it is." I reached around and squeezed his butt.

Nate smiled into my eyes and kissed my forehead. "Goodnight, babe. Thanks for showing me around today."

I stiffened at his use of the word, "babe," and he noticed. "Can't I call you that?"

"I guess you can. It just reminds me of my dad. My parents used to call each other 'babe.' Brian sometimes called me 'sweetheart,' but I didn't have a specific pet name for him."

"Do you want me to call you sweetheart? It's kind of a mouthful, and I don't really want to use Brian's name for you."

"No, but, out of curiosity, have you ever called anyone else 'babe'?"

Now, he tensed. "Well, yeah. It's just what I say as a token of affection. It's also what my parents call each other. If you want me to think of a name specifically for you, I will."

"We'll see," I said noncommittally.

He sighed and kissed me on the cheek. "Goodnight, Sophia." He pulled my back into him and wrapped his arms around me.

"Goodnight."

*　*　*

My iPhone woke us at 6:15, giving us plenty of time to dress warmly and jog to Tank Hill before sunrise. As we hiked the short distance to the top, we had to watch for thorns poking out from mostly bare blackberry bushes, reminding me of the summers long gone when Thomas and I had picked berries there. We reached the top about five minutes before seven when pink was just beginning to paint the horizon. The view was glorious. We leaned on some rocks to enjoy it.

"What a great place," Nate said.

"Yes, it is. It doesn't give as broad of a view as some of the higher vantage points in the city, but it feels more personal to me. My mom still does Tai Chi here occasionally in the summer. When I was growing up, I used to come here when I needed some time alone or wanted to think. I also had my first kiss up here." I winked at him.

"Hmm. I think you need another," he said, as he leaned over to kiss me. "So," he looked at me suspiciously, "exactly how many boys did you bring up here?"

I laughed. "Just three or four. Brian and I came here when we visited my mom together. I didn't have many serious boyfriends in high school. Usually, I'd get a crush on a guy, and then as soon as he liked me, I'd run away. I don't know if it was embarrassment or self-preservation, but my crush would end shortly before or after the first kiss. I probably just wasn't ready to deal with the hormones or the emotions of an intense relationship at the time. Only a couple of boys made it past my defenses and lasted longer than a few dates. Thomas thought I was ridiculous."

Nate kissed my cheek and settled me against his chest to take in the view.

"Maybe it's the Greek in me, but I always preferred the Greek myths to any other religion. They make the world feel more alive. Right now, Apollo would be starting to race his chariot across the sky. I wish I could actually believe in the myths like a religion. The world would be more magical. We're lucky, though, since we're seeing a little bit of magic right now." I leaned my head back on his shoulder, and he enveloped me in his arms. The entire landscape became pink. The light reflected off the high-rises in the downtown financial district, as if touched by an ethereal presence. We were fortunate that the day was clear, giving an incredible view of the city all the way to the Bay. Looking north you could see the Golden Gate Bridge with the mountains of Marin County in the background. We soaked it all in until the pink light succumbed to the bright light of day.

"Thanks for sharing that with me." He raised us both off the rocks. We held each other for a second and kissed quickly. "Are you up for running some more? It'll thaw us out before we go back to your house."

"Sure, but you'll have to jog slowly on the hills if you don't want to lose me."

By the time we stepped in the door, I was out of breath and sweaty under my warm clothes. Mom and Thomas had started cooking in the kitchen, making eggs, bacon, and potatoes for everyone. We promised to shower quickly and hurry back downstairs.

"Do you think we'll get too distracted if we shower together?" I asked.

Nate smiled at me. "I can control myself if you can."

Although we had a few tenuous moments, we were back downstairs in good time. At breakfast, Nate surprised us when he confessed that he'd never told his family about his psychic abilities and asked that we not bring it up when we visited. Even Thomas raised his eyebrows. Since it was such an integral part of my family, I was shocked that he'd kept his talent a secret. I actually felt a little hurt that I didn't know he'd always hidden what he could do from his family and some worry that he was ashamed of it and by extension, of me, but I think I felt more sad that he didn't feel he could share his uniqueness with his loved ones. My mom assured Nate that we would keep his secret. Nate and I didn't have a chance to talk privately before we left. He could see a mix of emotions on my face. He kissed my ear in the car and whispered that we'd talk about it later.

We had little traffic on the drive to Nate's house, and by eleven, the Barclay clan was greeting us in the front yard. Nate seemed proud to introduce us to his family. His mom was tall and slender. Though age and outdoor activities with her boys had left their marks, she was attractive and had a kind, gentle face. Before I could speak, she pulled me into a hug.

"Welcome to the family, Sophia. I can't tell you how happy I am to meet you. Nate's told us so much about you."

"Thanks for having my family over today, Mrs. Barclay."

"Call me Bev. It's our pleasure. I look forward to getting to know all of you. Come in."

As she greeted my mom and Thomas, Nate's dad, Bob, gave me the brilliant smile I'd always associated with Nate and extended his hand. Bob was an older, darker, and slightly broader version of Nate with the same warm presence. The grandparents hugged us then and insisted we call them Grandma and Grandpa. We filed into the house where the cooking was in full swing. Bev directed us to place our pies on the counter and resumed her position at the helm, clipping her blond wavy hair back into a bun. Nate's brothers, Sam and Ron, and Ron's wife, Stacey, were assisting and introduced themselves as we walked into the kitchen.

"What can we do to help?" my mom asked.

"Nothing, just sit here and tell us about yourselves," Bev said. My mom and Bev hit it off immediately, sharing stories and conversing like old friends.

Nate, Thomas, and I started chatting with his brothers and Stacey. His brothers were fraternal twins, four years older than Nate. All three had the same tall, muscular frame. Anyone could tell they were brothers, but Ron looked most like their mom, with fairer skin, slightly leaner build and dark blond hair. Sam had the dark features of their father, with black hair and an olive skin tone, and Nate seemed like a mix of his two brothers, with a lighter shade of skin and hair than Sam. Stacey was a beautiful blonde, about my height.

"Congratulations, Stacey. I heard the good news," I said.

"Thanks. We're super excited."

"How are you feeling?" I asked.

"Great, only tired now and then. The pregnancy's been a breeze so far. I've had almost no morning sickness."

"How did you and Ron meet, if you don't mind my asking?"

"In college. We were both Computer Science majors at Berkeley. I helped him pass his classes."

"I scored big time," Ron said as he hugged Stacey from behind and placed his protective hands on her still flat belly. "I got brains and beauty. Stacey was the hottest computer geek there."

Stacey kissed his cheek and patted his hands. I liked her. Having majored in Physics, I always felt a kinship with women who ventured into more male-dominated fields.

Nate's dad observed us from the edge of the kitchen, listening happily to the banter, adding an occasional witty or funny comment or putting Ron or Sam in their places in a humorous way when they ragged on Nate too much. Apparently, the two older brothers had always teased Nate mercilessly. You could tell Bob was the strong, silent type, but there was a tenderness in his eyes as he watched all of his family together. His contained emotion made me glad we were celebrating Thanksgiving here. I could see that it meant a lot to him.

Though I wasn't sure how comfortable he'd be, Nate was affectionate with me in front of his family. We were always close, always touching. He either held my hand or wrapped me in his arms, kissing my cheek or hand from time to time. Both moms seemed pleased at how happy we were together and shared conspiratorial smiles.

While we were sitting on the couch in the family room, Sam plopped a large photo album into my lap. "You should probably see what you're getting yourself into." My mom came over to sit on my other side. The first several pages showed us that Nate was an adorable, chubby baby.

"I didn't realize your hair was blond when you were a kid. You're the cutest towhead I've ever seen." As I flipped through more pages, I felt like I was there watching him grow up, seeing this baby change into a cute little boy, then a teenager, and finally a handsome young man. "Nate, you were cute in high school, in that thin, boyish way. I would have definitely gone on a date with you."

"I didn't start to fill out until the end of my junior year and grew about six inches between then and college," he said.

"Who's this?" I asked. Nate was dressed in a tuxedo with a cute girl at his side, taking the requisite prom picture under an arch of balloons.

"That's Tina," Sam answered, "Nate's high school sweetheart."

I raised an eyebrow at Nate, and he quickly turned the page. Sam let out a big guffaw, enjoying Nate's discomfort. Though the teasing was somewhat cute, it was starting to provoke the protector in me. I felt that I needed to come to Nate's defense. "I understand why you're so patient now, Nate. You've had to put up with your brothers' teasing your entire life. Have they always ganged up on you like this?"

"Actually, it used to be much worse," he said.

"We also have videos," Sam continued. I glared at him. Clearly, he didn't get my veiled warning. "Okay, okay, I'll stop picking on Nate, but it's ridiculously fun and so easy. Nate, good for you, you've found yourself a feisty one."

I continued to frown at him.

"Okay. There's no need for the evil eye. I promise to be good now. Scout's honor." Sam smiled and positioned his fingers in the well-known hand signal. I could feel him pulling a smile out of me. He had an impishly jovial personality for such a big guy, and you could tell he cared about his little brother. He might give him hell, but he'd protect him any day.

Bob sliced the turkey, and Thanksgiving dinner was served. Everything was wonderful, and per the ritual, we all ate too much. Bev told us how Nate used to love exploring the wilderness as a child. He collected bugs and learned the species of every bird in the area. He could even recognize them from their song.

"Nate was my shy child," she said. "I think he's innately that way, but I'm certain having two older brothers tease him all the time didn't help. He opened up more when he went to high school but was still my quiet, thoughtful one." I smiled at Nate and squeezed his hand.

Nate had a deep respect for his grandparents and wanted to make sure they knew everything about me, aside from the psychic stuff. In return I got to learn a little about their life stories and Nate's history. After some hot cider, pie, and more conversation, it was time to leave. We hugged all around and headed to my mom's. Thomas drove with my mom in the passenger seat, while Nate and I snuggled in the back. Learning more about his life made me feel even more connected to him. I knew that for the first time I'd soon be making love in my childhood room.

We said goodnight to my mom and Thomas and climbed the stairs. When Nate closed the door to my room, I was already on him, standing on my tiptoes and kissing him voraciously. Nate leaned against the door and pulled me closer. He put his hands down the back of my pants and grabbed my butt, pulling me toward him and playing with the strap of my thong. Nate whispered, "Please tell me you've changed your mind."

"Although we still need to be quiet, I want you," I said. Our clothes were peeled off in a frenzy, and we landed on my bed with a thud. Within seconds he was inside me, moving with a decidedly targeted approach so he could bring me with him. When I started biting my lip to muffle my usual moans, he kissed me to swallow my screams and moved as hard and as fast as he could without vibrating the bed frame against the wood floor. At the end, we were gasping for breath, lying in a sweaty heap.

"Finally, there's something I'm first at," he chuckled and lifted his head slightly to look at me.

"What do you mean?" I asked.

"I'm the first person to make love to you in this bed."

"You are the first," I confirmed.

"And I hope the last," he added and kissed me sweetly on the lips.

I looked at this amazing man and felt a little sad again that his family didn't know what he could do. "Nate, why haven't you told your family you have psychic abilities?" I asked.

"There was never a need to bring it up," he said a tad flippantly. I felt him close off from me a little, erecting some protective barrier.

"They love you. I can't imagine they'd have a problem with it."

He propped himself up on his elbow and brushed some hair out of my eyes. "Maybe it was because of my brothers' teasing, but I just kept that part of myself private. I don't think they have any psychic gifts, and my ability was never obvious. I didn't have any blackouts like you did. I'd just occasionally get sucked somewhere while I was sleeping. No one could tell there was anything different about me, and I didn't let them know."

"Was it hard for you, having no one to share it with?"

"No, not really. At first, I thought the projections were just unusually vivid dreams. The precognitive dreams were never significant so I didn't think much of them either. It wasn't until high school that I realized I had true psychic abilities. I was lying in bed, grounded, wanting to be at a party I wasn't allowed to be at, when all of a sudden, I was there. No one there could see me, but I could see and hear everything. Once I realized what I could do, I figured out how to go to certain places on purpose while awake."

"Where was the first place you visited?" I asked.

He looked a bit embarrassed. "Well, remember, I was a teenager. The first place I intentionally dropped in on was the bedroom of my girlfriend when she was sleeping. Though I knew no one could see me, I didn't stay long. I was scared I'd somehow be exposed as a pervert or a peeping Tom."

"Though I do check up on my family from time to time, I never thought of using my ability to spy on boys I liked back then. Why didn't I think of that?"

"Probably because you had to suppress projecting for most of your life. When I discovered my ability, I was a depraved teenager. After that first visit, I just went to cool places I wanted to see for the most part."

"Was this Tina, the girl from the prom picture?"

"Yeah. She was my first real infatuation and the first person I had sex with. I was obsessed with her at first."

"How long were you together?"

"About six months, I think. I'm not exactly sure why we broke up. We were going to different universities, and graduation was approaching. I wasn't her first, and I'm afraid I may have been a bit of a disappointment in bed back then. I didn't know what I was doing and didn't have much stamina, but the internet became a helpful sexual tutor, and surprisingly, my brothers gave me good advice and didn't even tease me when I asked them about it. I improved over the months with her, but I probably didn't make a great impression."

"Were you heartbroken when you broke up?"

"No. Like I said, it was great at first. We started having sex shortly after we began dating. I thought it was the best thing in the world at the time and thought I was in love with her. But, as time went on, I realized that I liked having sex with her more than I liked her. She was pretty superficial and not an intellectual powerhouse. We didn't have a lot in common. Although she broke it off, I think I was mostly disappointed I wouldn't be having sex on a regular basis."

"Have you ever spied on anyone else?" I asked.

"Please don't get mad at me, but yes. I spied once on another person, on you."

"What? When?"

"That night I had the precognitive dream of us making love. I had to see you, but I didn't have the patience to wait until morning. I projected to your dormitory and found you asleep in your bed. You were wearing a T-shirt and were mostly under the covers. I promise I didn't see anything," he assured. "You were sleeping peacefully, but some of your hair had fallen over your face. I remember badly wishing I could brush it behind your ear. The next day, I'd worked up my courage to ask you out on a date, but then Brian approached, I introduced you, and he took over the rest of the conversation, managing to ask you out on a date himself before the end of it. I was so angry with him, but I couldn't bring myself to confront him, to let him know I had feelings for you. I tried to smother and suppress those feelings, but they never went away. When you and Brian broke up, you were both so messed up that I never considered pursuing you then.

"After graduation, we went our separate ways, but I always had lingering thoughts of you, wondering what you were doing, what your life was like. It wasn't until I realized that Sarah and I had no real future that I finally determined to find out once and for all if we'd be good together. I hoped you weren't already married, engaged, or with someone in a serious way. I quickly did what I could to get a job where you worked and moved down here. God, I'm so thankful it worked out. I don't know what I would have done if you'd been married."

I tugged at his chin to look in his eyes. "Thank you for not giving up on me. I'm sorry I didn't realize what you were going through."

"Hmm." There was pain in his eyes at the memory, but he blinked, smiled, and slid his hands from my hips to my breasts, a potent reminder that I was with him now.

"I love you, Nate." I laid my head on his chest and after a few minutes began to nod off. I willed my eyes open since I had to take my pill. Nate was already out for the count. I forced myself to get ready for bed and then settled back into his arms. I fell fast asleep.

I'm walking through a park with swings, slides, and monkey bars over a bouncy rubber surface the color of the ocean. Two blond children sprint for the swings, and I watch Nate and me run after them. I'm not a part of this dream — I'm an observer, watching myself in something like a movie. My breath catches as I realize this may be a vision of the future. The shrieks of glee and laughter echo in the park. When the kids tire of the swings, Nate and I help them climb the monkey bars and then catch them at the bottom of the slides. Looks of love and devotion pass between these beautiful creatures and us. These are our children.

I woke up, excited to tell Nate about the dream, but he was sleeping too soundly to wake. I hadn't experienced a precognitive dream in a while, but this one had all the signs — it felt more real than a normal dream, and I was an observer. I recorded and analyzed it like any other to stay objective. The dream filled me with joy, and I realized then that I wanted it to be our future.

I looked at Nate in his slumber. I loved this man more than I'd ever loved anyone. *Could my mind be playing tricks on me? Was it really precognitive or did I concoct it from my subconscious desires, from seeing pictures of him as a baby and thinking about Ron and Stacey? Would we pass the test of time?* He'd been in love before, more than once, only to see those feelings fade with the passing months. If the dream was wishful thinking, our relationship could still suffer a similar fate.

Considering the short time we'd been dating, skepticism was completely reasonable, but I wondered how long we'd have to be together before I'd truly believe that Nate would always love me. *Would six months or a year be enough?* Brian's last words still haunted me. *Was he right that I'd never trust anyone to stay with me for the long haul?* I knew I loved Nate more than I'd loved Brian and that our connection was on a deeper and more primal level. *But would my heart ever trust in the future?* I lay awake for the greater part of an hour pondering these questions. *Enough!* I refused to let myself overanalyze any longer. I deserved some happiness and let myself enjoy the moment. The future would come. It always did.

* * *

I awoke to Nate kissing my neck. I stretched and blinked at him, trying to remove the fog from my brain.

"Wake up, sleepyhead. It's early still, but we need to get moving if we're going to have breakfast with my family."

Recalling my dream spurred me to rise. "Nate, I had a dream last night of us playing at a park with two blond children. I think it was precognitive, but I'm not sure."

"What?" he asked. "Really?" His face was ripe with emotion, and the intensity of his gaze upon mine sent shockwaves down my spine. "So, we might have kids together?"

I nodded.

"That's wonderful," he said. He leaned in to kiss me, and we forgot the time, forgot to be quiet, forgot everything but the feel of our skin. Afterwards when I realized where we were again, I was afraid we'd woken both my mom and Thomas.

"Sophia, don't worry. I know it embarrasses you, but everyone knows we're having sex. We're living together and madly in love. There's no question in anyone's mind what we're doing behind closed doors. Let's just hope that our shields remained intact and that Thomas didn't get a first-person view. He's probably seen worse, though."

"Worse than seeing his sister having sex from her lover's vantage point?" I challenged.

He shook his head to get rid of the visual. "I don't want to think about it, but let's pretend our shields contained our thoughts. There's no point in agonizing over it now. Besides, Thomas is smart. He probably reinforced his shields to prevent the possibility of seeing anything. Let's get dressed and hit the road. Maybe if we leave the house before they're up, you won't feel so embarrassed when we return."

On the drive to his house, I played the dream recording. Nate beamed at me when it was over. "Wow," he said. "Do you really think it was precognitive?"

"I think so, but I haven't had one in a while. I may be getting rusty at judging, especially when they're that far off in the future."

"How old did the kids look again?" he asked.

"The boy was probably five or six and the girl about three or four, but I'm not great at telling kids' ages. I haven't been around them much since I last babysat in high school. The girl had blue eyes like me. Do either of your parents have blue eyes? I didn't notice yesterday."

"Yeah, my mom does," he said. "I have my dad's brown Native American eyes."

"Hmm."

"What are you thinking?" he asked.

"Just trying to decide if it was precognitive or simply a vivid dream created by looking at your photo album yesterday. The children looked uncannily like you as a kid except that the girl's hair was a darker blond than yours but not as dark as mine."

"I hope I'm not putting you on the spot, but do you want it to be precognitive?"

"The dream made me happy and excited about our future, but we haven't been together long enough to know if we can last."

"Sophia, I've had feelings for you for more than seven years. I've probably been in love with you the whole time. I never thought it possible to love someone this much, and I can't imagine that will ever change. In fact, I know it won't. I hope your dream was precognitive. Nothing could make me happier."

I grabbed his hand and kissed it. "Me too." Nate graced me with a triumphant smile.

When we arrived at his parents' house, everyone was awake and anticipating our arrival. We had breakfast together as his family talked boisterously about various subjects. Afterwards, Nate showed me his childhood bedroom, complete with soccer trophies, track awards, and lots of science fiction books and comics. Nate closed the door and came at me in a run, toppling me over onto his bed and landing on top of me.

"Nate, what are you doing?" I laughed and could barely catch my breath.

"Do you want to christen my bed like we did yours?" he teased.

"We can't do that. Your grandparents are staying in here and could pop in at any moment. Besides, don't you think it will be a bit obvious when we disappear for twenty or so minutes, make unmistakable sounds, and return looking flushed and disheveled? I wouldn't be able to look anyone in the face again, especially your brothers."

"Oh, I know, but the idea is *so intriguing*," he said, kissing from my chin to my ear. "Promise me that we will."

"Okay. I promise to deflower you in your childhood bed one day."

"Oh, I like that. It sounds kind of kinky." He kept teasing my body with his lips.

"Off," I said. He rolled over to lie beside me, chuckling to himself, and held my hand as we stared up at the ceiling.

"You used to lie here as a boy and wonder about the world and what would happen in your life, didn't you?" I asked.

"Yup."

"I like being here, seeing all of this somehow connects me to your past." I turned my head, looked into his eyes, and smiled.

"Let's go for a walk," he said. "I want to show you where I used to hang out in the neighborhood."

Nate shared with me his favorite childhood park, the place he and his friends would ride their bikes to almost every day in the summer. We then walked by his elementary school and trudged through some woods that used to be much more extensive when he was young.

"How close is your neighborhood to Brian's? None of this looks familiar to me."

"His parents live about a ten-minute drive away. We went to different elementary and middle schools."

"When did you become friends?"

"When we were five. We played on the same soccer team. Our moms became good friends so we played together all the time. When I told my mom I was dating you, she remembered seeing pictures of you years ago and said, 'Oh, Brian's cute girl.' You can imagine how much I appreciated that comment."

We went back to the house and ate leftover turkey sandwiches with Nate's family. Afterwards, we played Scrabble with Ron and Stacey. Nate creamed all of us while Bev watched. Stacey cursed her befuddled pregnancy brain, but Ron told her not to take it too hard because he'd never beaten Nate.

"So, Sophia, your mom said that you got your degree in Physics?" Bev asked.

Nate kissed me on the cheek, smiling. "She's brilliant, Mom."

"I know," she smiled. "I gathered that while talking to your mom yesterday."

I blushed, hoping my mom hadn't been bragging too much. Bev noticed my discomfort.

"Don't worry, your mom didn't go overboard," she said. "Elena just told me that you studied physics and have never made a B in your life. She's obviously proud of you and loves you and Thomas to death. She also said that she and your dad divorced when you were young and that you don't have much contact with him. I hope you don't mind my asking, but is he a part of your life at all? When was the last time you saw him?"

I shifted in my chair as Ron and Stacey pretended to find something interesting across the room. Nate squeezed my hand and seemed to be holding his breath, equally uncomfortable with these probing questions, a typical behavior for her I'd soon discover. "When I was seven, not long before the divorce was final. I haven't seen or heard a word from him since. My mom raised us all on her own."

Bev's brow furrowed. Pity filled her eyes, and she squeezed my shoulder. "I'm sorry to hear that. I hope my question didn't upset you."

"No, I just wasn't expecting it. Don't worry. I'm fine. It happened a long time ago. Talking about it reminds me that I couldn't have had a better mom."

Bev smiled. "She certainly did a fabulous job raising you and Thomas. She said that Thomas is studying for his Ph.D."

"Yes, in Marine Biology, and he loves it," I said, pleased to be moving on to a different subject.

"You and he seem really close. I was watching him yesterday. He's quiet, but he pays attention to everything. He also seems protective of you and your mother."

"We are close, and he is protective. I think not having a dad around made all of us protective of each other."

Bev then eased the tension by entertaining us with comical stories from her kindergarten class. Bob, Nate, and his brothers began dinner, and I sat with Bev and Nate's grandma while Stacey and Grandpa took naps. I could tell Nate's mom had a few more questions for me but wasn't sure how to ask them.

"Sophia, did Nate tell you that I'm good friends with Brian's mom?" she asked.

"He did." My hands began to sweat.

"I hope you don't mind my bringing this up, but she told me something that worried me. She said that she thought you broke off the engagement because your parents' divorce made you afraid of marriage and that you probably didn't intend to ever marry."

Her comment caught me completely off guard. *Had Brian shared his opinion with everyone?*

"I'm sorry I'm being so frank and forward. That's just the way I am. You and Nate seem very much in love. I've just been wondering if there's any truth to what she said."

I swallowed a few times, feeling acutely self-conscious, and finally began to speak. "Well, my dad's behavior did give me some trust issues, but Brian and I weren't right for each other. I wasn't ready to get married back then, and he was insistent. I do hope to marry and have children some day."

I was quiet after that. I didn't know what else to say. Nate was cooking in the loud kitchen and didn't hear our conversation.

"Again, please forgive my prying, but when Brian's mom told me her thoughts, it reminded me of a close friend of mine. She had a similar experience to yours, both with her dad and with breaking off an engagement in college. Unfortunately, she was never able to trust anyone enough to marry, and she never found someone again that she loved as much as her fiancé in college. It's a sad story. . . . Sophia, Nate's a good man. I've never met anyone more honest or loyal. You can trust him."

"I know." I looked into the kitchen at him. Apparently, he'd noticed in the last few moments that we were having an intense and uncomfortable conversation. He was watching us, brow furrowed with a worried look on his face. Since I was certain he'd seen my stress, I smiled at him. He smiled back, but the concern didn't leave his eyes.

"Oh, I should have kept my mouth shut. I've made you uneasy. Please know that I couldn't be more excited that you and Nate are together. I've never seen him so happy."

Nate's grandma, who'd been reading but also evidently listening the entire time, spoke up. "Sophia, my dear, excuse my daughter. She means well, but she can't seem to contain herself if she thinks she can help in any way. Once when she was a teenager, she sprinted three miles to her friend's house because she thought her friend might be choking. When Bev got there, she grabbed a hamburger out of her friend's hand and threw it in the trash. Her friend thought she was insane and didn't appreciate what she'd done to her food, but Bev believed she'd prevented some catastrophe." Bev smiled at her mom and shrugged. I smiled at both of them, and some of my discomfort ebbed. I was pretty sure I'd just discovered where Nate inherited some of his psychic talent.

"There's nothing to forgive," I said. "But if you don't mind my changing the subject, I assume we're going to play another game after dinner. What other board games do you have? I'd prefer to play one that I have a chance at winning. Does Nate always win at Scrabble?"

"Usually," Bev laughed, "unless he has particularly poor luck with his tiles. He's always been an avid reader. I have many other games in the den. Let's see if we can find one where you might have an advantage."

We returned to the family room with the fun and classic, Pictionary. After putting it down, I went into the kitchen to see Nate. His face lit up when he saw me approaching, but I could tell he was still uneasy. I hugged him, and he leaned over me to whisper in my ear.

"Is everything okay? Did my mom say something to upset you?"

"Everything's fine. I'll tell you about it on the drive home but don't worry." He relaxed, but I knew he wouldn't be satisfied until he knew what we'd discussed.

After dinner and games, we said our final goodbyes. On the drive, I told Nate about the conversation with his mom. He was annoyed at her interference and wished he'd warned me about her pointed questions, but I reminded him that she was acting with good intentions and that she deeply loved him. I also shared my suspicion about his mom's potential psychic ability.

"Maybe she doesn't get clear visions or dreams like you do, but I'd bet she gets something. She's also highly intuitive or at least very observant. I swear she almost knew that Thomas was a telepath. Considering her perceptive questions, I was surprised she didn't ask me about work."

"I can explain that. When I visited a few weeks ago, I told them that you and I worked on top-secret projects and that we weren't supposed to discuss them. I asked her not to pressure us for information or put us on the spot. I didn't realize I should have suggested she not ask about other things too."

By the time we pulled into the garage, Thomas and my mom were asleep. We crept quietly up the stairs and into my bedroom. We got ready for bed quickly and climbed in with sleep-laden limbs. Nate pulled me to his chest and wrapped me in his arms. "My family really liked you."

"I liked them too. I'm glad they think you did okay for yourself."

"They know I did more than okay. I'm sure they wonder what you see in me."

"I doubt that. They may not know you have any psychic gifts, but they know you're special." I caressed his hands and sighed. "If the weather's nice, would you like to walk to Golden Gate Park tomorrow?" I asked.

"Sure, but I'd also like to hear you play the piano."

"Okay."

I was almost asleep when Nate's whisper brought me back. "Will you sketch them for me?"

"Hmm?"

"Our kids."

My heart felt like it might burst at that moment, an inadequate vessel to contain such strong emotions. I pulled his hand from my waist to my mouth and kissed it. "Of course, the best that I can."

"Goodnight, my love," he said. I felt his body instantly relax into sleep.

"Goodnight." I smiled at his nickname. I could get used to that one. I snuggled in closer and drifted off as well.

* * *

We set off for Golden Gate Park first thing in the morning and had brunch at a cute café there, followed by a short tour of the significant landmarks. By the time we returned, I could barely bend my fingers, and my ears were completely numb. My mom warmed up some apple cider and chatted with us by the fire. She asked Nate all sorts of questions about his family that must have come to her after meeting them. I enjoyed listening and learned a lot in the process. Afterwards, I spent some time sketching the two children from my dream. I could draw fairly well though I'd never call myself a true artist. Finally I felt that I'd captured their likenesses, and just in time, since their faces were already beginning to fade from my memory. Nate stared at the drawings, as if memorizing every feature, and handled them like precious jewels.

As promised, I played Beethoven's "Für Elise" for him on the piano although I fudged my way through the more challenging sections. When I finished, Nate sat next to me on the bench and placed his fingers on the keys. "I've always regretted never learning an instrument. If we have kids, they should both learn to read and play music." I felt a lump in my throat and smiled. By the way he'd said "both," I knew he was thinking of the boy and the girl from my dream.

As we waited for Thomas to return from visiting friends, Nate, Mom, and I decided we'd all take Muni, San Francisco's public transportation system, to Chinatown for dinner. While on the N-Judah line, I noticed a man slightly under six feet tall wearing a knitted brown cap with ear buds in his ears. After a few minutes, I felt him staring at us in a way that made my skin crawl, but when I looked in his direction, he'd turned his head. I was probably just being paranoid, but something was pricking my senses. Having creeps stare you down on the Muni wasn't that uncommon. I could tell by his height and the glimpse I got of his face that he wasn't John in disguise. At least I could put that paranoia to rest. The man followed us onto the Powell-Hyde cable car and was only about eight feet away, so close that I could hear the rhythmic beating of music escaping his ear buds. He got off at our stop as well but walked away in the opposite direction. *Thank goodness, maybe he just had a hankering for Chinese food as well.*

We ordered family style to indulge in more dishes. I hadn't been home since the summer and missed the food. Though the restaurant scene had vastly improved in the last several years, San Diego still sorely lacked in tasty Chinese food establishments, at least compared to San Francisco. Unfortunately, I tried to make up for the lack in one sitting, but I wasn't the only one who overate. Thomas, Nate, and I were all clutching at our stomachs when we left. I proposed that we walk all the way home to burn off the calories and help digest our food, but because the evening was damp and cold, I was overruled. Right before the doors closed, the same man I'd noticed earlier jumped onto the cable car with us again. Now, I was worried. It could still be a coincidence, but I communicated my suspicion to Thomas. He attempted to listen to the stranger but realized that the man had psychic shields.

Rather than attempt to break those shields and cause a showdown, Thomas thought we should split up at the interchange to see what he would do. I convinced Nate to walk with me an extra stop for exercise instead of making the switch with my mom and Thomas. The man didn't follow us, but Thomas confirmed that he'd joined them on their new train.

After walking a few blocks, I told Nate about the suspicious man. He was annoyed about not being informed immediately but understood that the man might suspect we were on to him if I'd whispered in Nate's ear on the train. Though, for the record, he let me know that splitting up was a terrible idea, safety in numbers and all that. I worried about my mom and Thomas, and the cold gnawed at me while we waited at the stop. When we climbed aboard, though I didn't expect him, I was relieved to see no sign of that mysterious guy on our train.

"He didn't get off at Carl with us. He continued on," Thomas thought to me.

I shared our relief with Nate. He blew out a breath he'd been holding but was clearly irritated with the situation.

"Next time, ask Thomas to tell me telepathically. I don't want to be left out again! I can't help if you leave me in the dark."

"Thomas would have had to break your shields to get into your head without permission, which wouldn't help if we're being stalked by a telepath. You'll have to work with him to be able to let him in without collapsing your shields completely."

"Fine. I'll work with him when we get back to San Diego. God, I didn't even get a look at the guy. How can I watch out for him next time?"

"We'll get Thomas to show you images of him, but he was pretty nondescript. I doubt I could pick him out of a line-up of similar-looking guys."

We arrived home about ten minutes after Thomas and my mom. Thomas didn't think we should tell her about the man. She would worry, which would ruin the holiday family time she'd been looking forward to all day. Besides, it could still be a coincidence, though statistically speaking too many of those seemed to be popping up in my life lately. Thomas and I still hadn't told her we'd been bugged. Unless we thought she might be in danger, we weren't going to trouble her.

My mom was heating up milk for hot chocolate, a family ritual this time of year. She always ordered a special dark chocolate mix from a company in Boston and simply refused to use another brand. The Walsh family took its hot chocolate seriously.

I hugged both Thomas and my mom a little longer and tighter than usual and sniffed the brew my mom was making. "Ah, Mom, I'm mentally looking forward to the hot chocolate, but my stomach is still stuffed. If I don't drink much, please don't be disappointed."

"Of course, I won't," she said, "but we can't start decorating for Christmas without hot chocolate. It wouldn't be right. Thomas and I already brought most of the boxes out of the basement. I know we usually do this the day after Thanksgiving, but you were gone, and I wanted you to be here." I gave her another hug from behind while she stirred.

"Thanks for waiting, Mom. I'll put those two boys to work."

The tree was easy to set up and was pre-hung with lights. As Nate and Thomas fluffed up the branches, I unwrapped and hung ornaments. My mom carried in a tray with the hot chocolates. When I took that first sip, I realized that I was still quite chilled from the trip home. I hadn't paid much attention to my cold limbs while worried about my mom and Thomas. I closed my eyes and was transported back to running around in footsy pajamas and unwrapping presents on Christmas morning. This time of year was always about feeling cozy, warm, and loved by my mom. Nate enjoyed seeing the ornaments we'd created in elementary school and the ones with pictures of us as we grew up. He picked up one ornament and stared. It was a picture of both my parents with Thomas and me when we were about four years old. Although I know my mom still had pictures of my dad stashed away in albums, this was the only picture of him that was ever displayed in our house.

"It's funny," Nate said. "I thought you looked exactly like your mom, but I can see your dad in you, in your skin tone and your eyes and nose. Thomas has his tall build, but I wouldn't have realized that Thomas's face actually looks more like your mom's than yours does."

"You're right," I said. I stared at the picture with him, wondering what my dad might look like almost twenty years later, and then went back to unwrapping other ornaments. Nate hung it on the tree and came over to me, wrapping me in his embrace and kissing me sweetly. He searched my eyes to make sure I was okay.

"I'm fine," I said, "and we have more work to do." When he turned, I patted him on the behind to get him moving. He smiled and raised an eyebrow at me.

"Back to work," I said. "I warned you I was a taskmaster."

By the time we went upstairs to sleep, the tree was fully decorated and some garlands were hung.

When we were snuggling in bed, Nate asked tentatively, "Do you ever miss your dad?"

"Sometimes. I remember him reading to me as a child and how safe and protected I felt in his arms, but I remember more what he said to my mom about not wanting to live with or raise a bunch of freaks."

"I'm so sorry." He kissed my cheek and squeezed me tighter.

"I even saw the woman he was sleeping with. I couldn't understand why she would take my daddy away, how anyone could do that to a child. Since my dad had insisted we be raised Catholic, I saw her as some sort of devil corrupting him. I blamed her as much as I blamed him. They were selfish, self-centered people. I think I miss more that I didn't really have a father, didn't have the comfort of one, than missing him specifically. I sometimes wonder what happened to him, what he looks like now, but I don't want to meet him ever again."

I pulled the covers higher and buried my arms under them. "I know he remarried and had kids a year or two after the divorce. I remember finding my mom crying on her bed one day after school with an open letter in her hand. She couldn't stop sobbing and didn't respond when we came in. It's the only time I ever saw her completely crushed. None of us were good at shielding then. Thomas read her mind, and I read his. She'd just found out that my dad had named his new son Thomas after himself again, as if he were pretending that our family had never existed. I hated him so much then, hated that he'd hurt my mom so much." I remembered holding her as she cried, seeing my strong, happy mother broken, and knowing that I never wanted anyone to be able to do that to me.

"I'm sorry, Sophia, so sorry that happened to you. I wish I could fix it so you wouldn't have that pain."

"I'm okay with it now. It's like an old ache, this little bit of sadness. I'll always carry it around with me, but I've gotten so used to it over the years that most of the time I forget it's even there."

"Well, I'm sorry I reminded you twice today, and I'm even more sorry my mom asked you about him."

"You're both just trying to get to know me better. Like it or not, it's a part of who I am, or at least a part of my past. I understand."

After breakfast, Nate and Thomas hung the lights out front, while Mom and I finished the indoor decorating. Then, we packed and drove to the airport. I looked at my mom, a beautiful, loving, and courageous woman. I wanted to be like her. I wanted to make her proud. I gave her a long, tight hug before leaving her there at the car and flying back to San Diego.

CHAPTER TWENTY

After our morning jog, Nate convinced me to do a round of his punishing burpees instead of my usual yoga poses. Maybe it was our experience on the train, but he seemed to be taking my fitness more seriously. We drove to work early since we anticipated a busy Monday after the long holiday weekend. I needed to wrap up some minor cases before the final scheduled projection for the spying project. I was looking forward to this last projection. Aside from the visit to France, the others had bored me to tears. At the appointed time, I put the GammaBeat on, relaxed and sent my consciousness outward to an executive boardroom in New York City. People were filing intermittently inside as if a meeting would soon take place. A total of twelve men and three women entered before the door was shut and locked. One man took a device that looked similar but not identical to the GammaBeat out of his briefcase and placed it on his head, closing his eyes. *My God, another psychic.* A middle-aged man wearing an expensive-looking black suit with dark hair sat at the head of the table. All eyes focused on him.

He began to speak. "We've come together today to determine a new strategy. As you all know, we suffered a severe blow last week with Alec's death and the complete dismantling of his operation."

I couldn't believe what I was hearing. *Alec? Could it be the same man I spied on a few weeks ago with the picture of a wife and kids on his desk?* I was horrified and prayed that wasn't the case. I missed what the man said while I was occupied with my thoughts, but he suddenly stopped speaking.

"I'm afraid, my friends, that we have a visitor among us. Our little spy has decided to pay us a visit today as well." The others in the room looked nervously around, and then the speaker looked at where I was or where I would be if I'd had a body.

Shit, could he hear my thoughts?

"Yes, Sophia, I can hear you, and yes, your little adventure cost Alec his life. His children no longer have a father because of you." In utter shock, I realized I needed to get the hell out of there. I started to collect myself to project back into my body, but I couldn't break my attachment to the location. Something was holding me there, something dark, cold, and angry. I screamed.

"I'm afraid it's not time for you to depart yet. You will leave only if and when I choose." Panic raced through me. I didn't think someone could trap me in a place away from my body. Suddenly, a vision of Alec building a sand castle with his children flashed into my mind, followed by another of his wife and kids grieving when they were told he'd been killed. *No!* I tried to deflect them, to stop myself from seeing them, but I couldn't.

"You're playing a dangerous game, Sophia. Who hired you to spy on us?"

Our government, the good guys, surfaced in response to his question before I could suppress it.

"Of course, the 'good guys.' Sophia, don't presume to understand what you can't begin to comprehend." I concentrated harder to return. I could sense tears sliding down my cheeks, feel the air in my chest. I focused on the physical, could feel myself getting closer to it, when he forced another flash of imagery on me — an emaciated and tortured Asian man in a prison cell, a car careening into a tree, a person shot to death in an alley. His hold on me was slipping, but then he clawed deeper into my mind to keep me there. My head pounded as if a blood vessel might burst. I pulled away from him with every ounce of power I had and felt my consciousness slam back into my body, thumping in the chair as if I'd fallen or had a seizure. I opened my eyes and saw Nate and Roger standing over me.

"My God, Sophia, what happened?" Nate asked as he pulled me into his arms. "You were screaming and crying, and we couldn't get you out of your projection."

"He tried to keep me there," I mumbled, still crying.

"Who? How?" Nate asked.

"The telepath . . . he wouldn't let me return to my body. He said I got Alec killed. He had two kids." I sobbed into Nate's shirt. Nate was horrified. He removed the GammaBeat from my head and held me tightly to his chest. After the shock wore off, I started to get angry.

I looked at Roger and fumed at him. "Who the hell hired us? Our government or a bunch of assassins? What could Alec have done that he deserved to die without a trial?" I grabbed my head, yelling at Roger made me realize my head was pounding.

"I don't know. Maybe he tried to run when he was arrested? I promise I'll find out whatever I can, but if this telepath he worked with tried to hold you against your will, Alec probably wasn't as innocent as he seemed. Even terrible people have children." Roger lifted my eyelids slightly to look at my pupils and shined his iPhone light in them. "You obviously have a headache, but your pupils are constricting normally. Do you think you need medical care?"

I felt drained, shaky, weak. My eyes and head hurt, but otherwise I didn't think anything was seriously wrong. "No, I don't think so."

"Okay, then I need you to tell me everything that happened now before you forget." He recorded what I said. As I finished, my head began to throb painfully. I pressed hard on my temples to make it stop.

"Sophia, please know that I never realized you could be detained while projecting. I've never even heard a suggestion that any of you could be in danger. Go home and rest. If you need it, take tomorrow off as well. I'll find out whatever I can, and we'll talk soon. Nate, I know that you and Sophia live together, which isn't a problem. You can take the rest of the day off too. She'll need someone to drive her home and watch over her to make sure she's alright."

"Of course," Nate said.

"We'll also need to re-think how we choose cases for projectors. We have to be able to keep you safe," Roger said.

Thomas sensed that something had happened to me and flooded into my head wondering what was wrong and why my shields were down. He saw what I'd experienced and was trying to ask me questions, but with my head pulsing, I couldn't think straight. "Later, Thomas. I'm okay now. I just need to rest." I said this aloud instead of focusing my thoughts at him. It was easier to speak for the time being. I tried to stand but my legs were so weak I fell back into the chair. I clenched my jaw, frustrated by my own weakness, and tried to get up again.

"Shh, Sophia. Relax. I'll carry you," Nate said.

* * *

After we parked in the garage, Nate kissed my shaky hand. I opened my eyes and smiled at him as he pushed hair behind my ear. "You're safe now, my love. I'll take care of you." He carried me into our apartment, tucked me in bed, and brought me a glass of water. I drank as instructed and watched him watch me. His brow was furrowed. I don't think I'd ever seen him look so worried.

"How are you feeling?" he asked, rubbing my forehead and smoothing my hair out of my face.

"Better, less raw, but drained."

"Should I take you to the emergency room? Do you think that headache means you need a brain scan?" he asked.

"No, my head's not pounding as much now. I just need to rest to get my energy back." It was annoying, though, that my hands wouldn't stop shaking.

"I'll get you some juice. You probably need something with sugar in it." Nate must have read my mind and went to the kitchen.

He returned with a cup of orange juice, made me drink all of it, and then lay on the bed next to me. Nate was quiet, moving his hand back and forth over my hip, and staring off into space.

"What are you thinking?" I asked.

"I'm shocked that someone could trap you like that. I always thought we were in a kind of safe bubble. How long could he have kept you there separated from your body? I've been tempted to beat people before, but if I met this guy, I might actually kill him." His fist clenched the covers tightly and then released them.

I held his hand and rubbed my thumb across it to decrease his tension. "I'm here now, and I'm going to be fine. The telepath threatened that he might not let me leave, but I didn't want to hang around to find out. I don't know if he was bluffing or not."

"Thank God, you escaped. I can't live without you." He kissed me gently on the lips and stared into my eyes. "Do you think he could have controlled you, planted something in your head, or harmed you in another way?"

"I wouldn't be surprised if he could, but I don't believe he did. He sent me the images of Alec and his family to punish me, I think, but I don't understand what the other images were about. Besides John, our experience with telepaths has been limited to the benign ones we know. The ones out there who've developed their abilities for nefarious reasons are scary as hell. I wish I could talk to Harry. There must be a way to shield and project at the same time, but I don't know an astral projector who can."

"I wonder if I could have projected there to help you fight him off or distract him. Maybe Thomas could have done something too."

"I don't know, but I'm glad I was wearing the GammaBeat. I think it helped. I know I'm less fatigued when I use it, but I think I'm psychically stronger as well. Thomas might have some ideas about what else we can do. I'll project to him later to see if he can sense me and whether it seems like an unshielded mind to him."

"*I* can project to him later, but until your hands stop trembling, I'm not letting you do anything but rest. If you feel better, you can experiment tomorrow." Nate caressed my shaky fingers. "Hmm, I know it's a little early for lunch, but you should probably eat something substantial." He crawled out of bed, and as I started to follow, he gently pushed me back down and kissed my forehead. "Relax. I'll bring you something."

As I lay in bed taking deep, steadying breaths and trying to still my wobbly hands, I relived how it had felt when the telepath tried to detain me. I became increasingly convinced that if we projected unshielded, we could be susceptible to any mind tricks a telepath could conjure up. We needed to learn to shield and shield well while projecting. Nate returned, carrying a tray with two sandwiches and a bunch of mini carrot sticks. I shared these thoughts with him.

"Considering what you went through, you're being incredibly calm and analytical about it all."

"I have to be. I can't think about being responsible for the murder of a father with two young children. I lost my dad at that age. I know it puts a hole in your heart. I can't deal with that right now. I have to focus on what I *can* do to protect myself in the future."

"That father worked for a telepath who tried to rip away your consciousness. Like Roger said, I doubt he was innocent."

"You're probably right, but I know that doesn't matter to his kids."

After eating, my hands began to steady, and my eyes started to feel very heavy. "Nate, I think I should sleep. Would you nap with me? I need to feel safe in your arms."

"Of course. I'll keep you safe."

"I'm too tired to change, but I'll sleep better if I take off my work clothes."

"I'll help you."

For the first time, Nate undressing me wasn't sexual. It was comforting and caring, like a mother changing her child. He even pulled a nightie over my head and threaded my arms through the holes. He stripped to his underwear, hit the lights, and crawled into bed beside me.

"Nate, I love you."

"I love you too."

* * *

We woke as the sun was setting. I wasn't sure how long Nate had slept, but I'd been out for over five hours. I still felt a little out of sorts but was almost myself.

"How are you feeling?" Nate asked.

"Much better, though I'm still not one hundred percent."

"It's almost time for dinner. Are you hungry?"

"A little. Is that my cell phone?" I heard a ringing coming from the other room.

"It's Diana's ring tone. She's called at least three times. Thomas must have told her what happened." I started to slide out of bed to get to my phone. "Oh, no you don't. I want you to stay here for at least a few more minutes. You were so tranquil while you were sleeping that I could almost pretend this craziness wasn't real. Give me a little more time to hold you, to pretend our lives don't have any more worries than anyone else's."

"Gladly." I nestled my back into him, and although I had a hard time pretending that everything was right in the world, his arms gave me the comfort I needed.

"Do you get the feeling that we're being dragged into something big?" Nate asked. "Do you think the telepath that attacked you was working with John?"

"You didn't sleep at all, did you?" I turned on my side and looked into his face.

"I couldn't turn off my brain. Another thing I thought of was that my friend in the Navy couldn't believe that my military clearance took only one month. From what I've heard, six months is the average. It's like they'd already been watching me in the hope that I'd work for them."

"I think it took about the same amount of time for me. Do you think it was really our government that hired me? I thought I was working for the good guys. It's one of the reasons I love my job, but if they assassinated Alec, I can't see how they're good."

"I don't know. . . . Do you think anyone at SDCC could be involved on either side?"

"I hope not. I know Roger well, and he isn't, but I don't know about the higher-ups. . . . Well, whatever's going on, both sides seem to have serious resources, but what are they fighting over? Do you think they'll leave us in peace now that it's clear we know they exist?"

"I don't know, and I'm worried they might have a score to settle with you," he said softly, ruminating.

This time I could hear Thomas lightly tapping at my shields, which was a good sign. "My shields are working again. Thomas is contacting me. I'll be just a second."

I opened my pathway to Thomas and let my thoughts flood him. I showed him again my escape from the telepath and all the conjectures and worry that Nate and I had. I could sense this time his profound surprise at what the telepath had been able to do. Trapping someone's consciousness wasn't something Thomas had thought possible. He didn't know what would have happened to me if I hadn't broken free.

I closed my connection to Thomas and opened my eyes. Nate was watching me with rapt attention. I relayed our discussion and told him that Thomas would help us find a way to shield while projecting.

Diana's ring tone sounded again, and Nate let me crawl out of bed this time to get it. He pulled on his robe and wrapped mine around my shoulders. As I picked up the phone to talk to Diana, I noticed him calling for pizza.

"Sophia, I've been calling for hours. I've been crazy with worry. Thomas just showed me everything. How are you feeling?"

"Better, just a little tired now."

"Why am I always surprised by the abilities of other telepaths?"

"It's because you don't purposely try to harm anyone."

"At least I don't do anything worse than they deserve," she amended. "Oh, I forgot to tell you that the police got back to me. They found John's car. It was leased from a dealership in Encinitas. None of the information on the application led them anywhere, but they're trying to track down the financial records."

"I doubt they'll find anything. I'm starting to think this is even bigger than we realized."

"You might be right. Thomas said he was going to practice with you and Nate on shielding. When I get back from New York, I'll help too if I can." I could hear the doubt in her voice. "Thomas and I should also try to improve our offensive abilities. It seems like we might need them. God, I'm glad you're okay. I'll call you tomorrow to check on you."

For a few hours, Nate and I tried to conjure back a normal life. Nate insisted I start to watch one of his past favorite shows, *The Office*. A few weeks ago, I'd horrified him when he learned that I'd missed the phenomenon entirely. We ate pizza on the couch like college kids and enjoyed the absurd humor. It was a good distraction, but I couldn't avoid feeling that the world we knew, or thought we knew, was gone forever.

CHAPTER TWENTY-ONE

N ate tried not to wake me when he got up for work the next morning. He didn't succeed, and I punished him by making him snuggle me for a few extra minutes before taking a shower. He tucked me in and kissed me on the forehead when he left. I slept for another three hours and awoke feeling as good as new. The only thing troubling me was that I'd had no dreams during the night or in my nap the day before. I tried to convince myself that it was an aftereffect of my exhaustion, but I couldn't shake an ominous feeling. After brunch, I formally summarized what had happened yesterday and used a secure link to email it to Roger.

I sat down to sketch the people I'd seen in the boardroom, but for some reason, I couldn't see their faces. I remembered the telepath being dark and older — dark suit, dark hair, but I couldn't see his face in my mind. I tried to recall the other people in the room in detail. I remembered that there were a total of twelve men and three women, but their faces blurred together. *Shit!* He did do something to my mind or at least to my memory. Although I couldn't see those faces, the images he deliberately sent me were branded in my brain. I drew the Asian man, whose features seemed likely to be Chinese. Even though his image seemed to be intended as a form of punishment, I felt an inexplicable kinship with him and a deep sadness for his suffering. *Were these feelings mine or the telepath's?* I gently touched the sketch of those eyes so filled with misery. *Who'd been torturing him and why?*

With the GammaBeat on, I tried to project to safe places while focusing on keeping my shields intact, but I found it impossible. The lack of success made me restless so I decided to make Nate a nice dinner. At the grocery store, sales for Christmas decorations were in full swing. Life went on even after waking up in a different world than the day before. I picked up a small potted Douglas fir, some lights, ornaments, candles, and other random decorations. I realized then that I'd never before thought of my apartment as a real home, only as a temporary place to live. I'd always spent Christmas at my mom's house, the only home I'd ever known. Now that Nate and I were living together, my apartment felt more like a home than it ever had in the past. What an interesting change. It made me excited to show him the festive arrangement when he came home.

After decorating the apartment, I worked with Thomas. He hadn't thought much of the lack of distinguishing facial features when I showed him what happened yesterday, but he agreed that if I usually remembered faces well, like the Asian man's, then these memories could have been altered. He also thought it possible that the clear images the telepath sent me could have rendered the other visual memories less distinct. Thomas had no idea how to tell if someone had messed with my mind, which royally pissed him off.

My shields fell every time I projected to Thomas, and trying to raise them after projecting severed my connection to his location. We realized though that raising my shields might be another way to escape if I needed to leave a place, but my gut said it wouldn't have helped me fight that telepath. As we suspected, Thomas could sense me and read my thoughts as if I were an unshielded person standing next to him, but he didn't know how to control me or trap my consciousness. After an hour of trying to hold my mind there and failing, we were both tired and called it a day. I'd never seen Thomas so frustrated.

While I was making dinner, I called Irene to tell her about my experience with the telepath and about possibly being followed by another psychic in San Francisco. There was anger in her voice.

"What do these people want? You must be careful, Sophia. At least we know that Dante, the GammaBeat inventor, is alive. He finally called me and said he always felt that something was wrong about his parents' car accident. He hired private investigators a few weeks ago to help him look into it. When I told him about Harry's murder, he said he thinks they could be connected. He asked me to keep him informed. Can I tell him about what happened to you?"

I technically wasn't supposed to share the details of my work projections with anyone, but I'd already shared most of this one with several people, though I'd never divulged the address or even the city. Besides, someone had attacked me. This was different. This was personal. I neither knew nor trusted Dante, but since he may have lost his parents because of what was happening, I told Irene she could. What I'd told her and what she would repeat were vague enough. I asked her in turn to see if Dante could provide GammaBeats for all of Psi Solutions, even though he no longer owned the company.

*   *   *

As Nate walked in the door, I was draining the pasta. "Welcome, home," I said, looking forward to him noticing the lively decorations. He gave me a kiss on the cheek and waited for me to put the pot down before hugging me tightly.

He spied the decorations over my shoulder and laughed. "Merry Christmas," he said. "I love the cute, little tree."

As we ate dinner, Nate told me that tension was high at work. "There have been whispers circulating about yesterday, but most people don't know what exactly happened. I guess Roger or his bosses don't want everyone to know just yet. He quizzed Jack and me today and had us try projecting with our shields intact. We both failed. Jack is kind of freaking out."

Nate was more concerned with how I was feeling and insisted on pampering me with a bath and a massage. Since he was already on edge about what had happened to me at work, I didn't worry him about my lack of dreams.

*   *   *

I went to work the next day fully recuperated and reported immediately to Roger's office. He was waiting for me with two executives I'd never met. Seeing the three suits together caused the hair on the back of my neck to stand on end.

"I hope you're feeling better," Roger began.

"Yes, I'm fine today. Thank you," I replied. Though not a psychic, Roger picked up on my unease and introduced the two men as the vice president in charge of our division and SDCC's general counsel. Their introduction didn't settle me.

"I want to apologize again on behalf of the entire company for what almost happened to you the other day. We had no idea you could be in any danger, and we will take precautions to protect you in the future. I don't know if it will make you feel any better, but our client confirmed that Alec was a wanted criminal and was killed while resisting arrest. They also asked me to tell you how sorry they were about what you experienced."

Roger cleared his voice as the suits looked on. "I want you to know, Sophia, that working with you has been a joy for me, and you are an essential part of Psi Solutions. We want you and the other projectors to feel safe."

The lawyer chimed in. "We're trying to develop a protocol that will help keep projectors safe, but you have to realize that it will be impossible to remove all risk. We've drafted new rules for evaluating future clients and their projects in order to better protect you, Nate, and Jack. Nate and Jack told us that none of you can shield when you project. We're reaching out to some of our contacts to determine if it's even possible to do both at the same time."

"Nate told us that you thought the GammaBeat may have helped you escape, and I noticed in your report that you observed another psychic wearing a similar device," Roger added. "We've sent out queries to try to obtain GammaBeats for everyone in Psi Solutions. I want to assure you that our biggest priority is keeping all of you safe."

"Can I see the guidelines for screening clients and projects?" I asked.

He handed me the piece of paper from his desk. "This is only a preliminary draft. We value and need your input so please let us know what you think."

The guidelines were still in the bare-bones stage, not yet riddled with legal jargon. I was certain there'd soon be a disclaimer I'd have to sign in which I accepted the inherent risks of my job and held SDCC blameless for any harm I incurred while projecting.

The rules only addressed information disclosure. The clients would provide more details on the projects, and they would have to specify if anyone with psychic abilities might be involved. If so, there were several additional questions they'd be required to answer.

I shrugged. "These seem like a good start, but I don't think we should take on any projects involving psychics. We have plenty of work. You should refuse those projects outright instead of following up with more questions. Until I'm convinced that I can shield myself, I won't take on those projects, and I don't think that Nate or Jack should either."

"That's reasonable," Roger said, and both suits nodded.

"Personally, I don't want to work for Homeland Security again."

"Sophia, they're one of our biggest clients. It's a huge organization. What if we just ban the specific group within Homeland that hired you?"

"Who exactly hired me?"

"I can't disclose that information. I'm sorry, but I can try to avoid projects from them in the future."

"I guess that works. There should also be severe repercussions if any clients clearly lie about the missions."

"Agreed. SDCC should be fine with those stipulations," the lawyer said.

"Sophia, you're important to this company," the vice president finally spoke up. I'd started to wonder if he'd reveal his role in this meeting. "Since we realize now that your job has risks we didn't anticipate, we'll be giving you a $30,000 raise to begin in the new year to show you how much we appreciate you staying with the company after your experience the other day."

I was surprised and unsure how to respond. "Thank you," was all that came to mind. The raise was sure to include signing a hold harmless clause. That was corporate America, but even with the added danger, I still loved my job. I wasn't going to quit. After the brief meeting, I headed back to my desk and read the background on a new case. In spite of my lingering apprehension, it felt good to get back to the grind.

CHAPTER TWENTY-TWO

I awoke with a start and looked at the clock. It was just before two in the morning. "Thank God! We still have time." I shook Nate awake and fully appreciated for the first time how deeply he slept. "Nate, wake up!" I shouted again and again. I threw on the lights and called Diana's home and cell numbers but received no answer. I texted her as well.

Nate finally stirred as I was hastily dressing. "What's wrong?" he asked.

"We have to go over to Diana's now! She's in danger. Get dressed!" I yelled.

"Should we call the police?" Nate asked, willing himself to become coherent. He headed toward the closet and struggled into some sweats.

"It's John so I'm not sure it would help. I had a precognitive dream of Diana being abducted from her house at around 3:30 in the morning. I saw the backlight of her clock by her bed, and then John covered her mouth with a cloth. She thrashed about at first but quickly passed out. He then carried her from the room."

"How do you know it's today?"

"I just have a feeling. Ever since the incident with the telepath at work, I haven't dreamed. It reminds me too much of what happened before Harry was murdered, when John messed with my dreams, only we have some notice this time."

"Her house is a fortress. She's got a locked outer gate and inside security."

"You're right, but somehow he gets in. Jumping her fence isn't a problem. Turning off a security system probably won't be an issue for him."

Nate looked at me with serious eyes and went back to grab the GammaBeat. "I'll drive. Put this on and contact Thomas. See if he can communicate with Diana and wake her. Project quickly to check on her and scope out the place, but if you see John or think he detects you, leave immediately. I don't want another telepath trapping you. I'll keep calling Diana."

Thankfully, unlike with Harry's murder, I wasn't trapped in my head. I was able to reach Thomas and then projected to Diana. She was sleeping soundly, and I didn't see anyone in or around her home. I ended the projection and took over calling her phone. Ten minutes later, we turned the corner to her house and parked directly in front. As I opened my door, a car parked about forty yards away on the cross street raced off without turning on its lights. It appeared to be a large person, but Nate and I couldn't tell anything else, and we couldn't risk projecting to him. We buzzed Diana's gate. After a few minutes of persistent buzzing, the house lights turned on. Diana deactivated the gate security for us and opened the front door. She was groggy, almost in a stupor. "What the hell's going on? Thomas just shoved himself inside my head. He said I was in danger."

I told her I'd had a precognitive dream but didn't elaborate. She seemed to be having a hard time focusing. "What's wrong Diana? Are you hung over? You seem really out of it."

"Sorry. I've barely slept all week. I was so exhausted last night that I took a sleeping pill before I went to bed. I couldn't handle not sleeping another night. I take them occasionally when I'm really jetlagged, and they always knock me out, but not like this." She shook her head in an attempt to rouse herself. "I feel way more out of it than usual. Sorry." She sat down on her couch and tried to will her eyes to be more open.

"Don't apologize. I'm just relieved that we got here in time. I think John left when we arrived."

"John?" she asked, her face immediately anxious.

I told her then about the car and my dream.

"Do you really think it was him in that car?" she asked, wrapping her arms around herself defensively.

"I do."

"It was suspicious," Nate added.

"I guess I should be pleased he didn't intend to shoot me like Harry, at least not immediately," she snarled, "but I'm not involved in whatever psychic bullshit is going on out there. Why would he kidnap me?"

"I don't know, but I'm now convinced he was the person following us when we went shopping. He must be trying to get to you. I haven't dreamed since that telepath messed with me the other day. I assumed it was a result of that experience, but the lack of dreams could have been John trying to prevent me from seeing his plan again. Have you changed your gate and security system codes since John was last here?"

"Yes. I changed them the day the police identified him as someone else. I haven't slept great since I discovered the truth about him, but the sleeplessness I've had lately has been different. It didn't feel like jet lag. My mind simply wouldn't shut down, but not in a jittery way like when you're anxious or up because of caffeine. I just couldn't turn it off."

"Did John know you had sleeping pills?" I asked.

"Yeah, he knew I sometimes took them for jet lag."

Thomas communicated to me that he was parking. "Thomas is here. I'll open the gate." I sensed from him how concerned he was about Diana, one of his best friends as well. He worried that we might not be able to protect her the next time.

Thomas joined us in the living room. "Well, it looks like the plot was thwarted, and you're alright." He squeezed Diana on the shoulder as she looked up at him.

"What should we do now?" I asked. "John's probably gone for the night, but I think he'll try again."

"I doubt the police can watch me 24/7," Diana said. "I could hire a bodyguard."

"Sophia and I think that bringing in people who carry weapons but can't shield might not be a smart idea," Nate said.

"Good point. I could take a leave of absence from work and go home or travel somewhere, but I wouldn't have you guys close. Although I'm not sure what we can do together, I feel safer with you all nearby." Her chin quivered, letting the cracks in her composed façade begin to show. I hugged her tightly, and she finally cried, letting go of all the stress, fear, and insecurity she felt.

After she settled down, she said, "I can't believe I've got a psychic super-assassin after me. If I leave town, do you think he'll follow me?"

"I think it depends on whether his interest in you is personal or professional. If it's personal, he may not be able to follow you around the world," Nate said.

"But if he's located here in San Diego, going to your parents' house in LA wouldn't be a problem. Diana, my gut tells me it's personal, like he wants to talk to you or see you again. He wasn't happy with how things had to end between you. If his interest were professional, I think he'd have accomplished his goal by now," I said. The grimness of that statement hung in the air.

"If he wants to talk, I wish he'd just call me," she said, exasperated and pulling at her hair. "This is freaking me out."

She took a few deep breaths and then began again, trying to figure out a plan of action. "My parents and I are spending three weeks in India with family over the holidays. One of my cousins is also telepathic. She can help me be on the lookout while I'm there. I have only a week here in San Diego before that trip. Luckily, SDCC scheduled all my missions on sight this week since I'm spying on companies SDCC regularly consults with in other capacities. I doubt John would follow me to India. A 6'4" blond would stick out like a sore thumb."

"Until that trip, we can stay here to watch over you, if you'd like. Whatever you need, Diana, we'll do. Just let us know," I said. Nate had gone to the kitchen and returned with glasses of water for all of us.

"I'll think about it," she said. We sipped our water in silence for a few minutes.

"Maybe we should tell SDCC?" Nate suggested. "Maybe they could offer Diana some protection?

"What kind of protection?" Diana asked.

"I don't know, but Sophia said they have some contacts they're tapping into to find out if we can shield while projecting."

"That's true, but I don't know if I trust SDCC as a company any more," I admitted. "I trust Roger, but once you go up the chain of command, I'm not sure where their loyalties lie, with us or their precious clients. The telepath who tried to hold me could be part of John's group, or it could be that John's organization hired me and killed Alec."

"Besides us, do people at work know that psychics have been murdered and other psychics are involved? Do they know that a telepath attacked you and that one of his men was killed?" Diana asked.

"A few know bits and pieces, but I think most know very little," I said.

"We need to tell every psychic we know that there's a struggle taking place that's getting psychics killed," Nate said. "We have to trust somebody. I don't know about the upper echelons of SDCC, but we should inform the people in Psi Solutions. We should explain what's going on and that they might be at risk."

Nate was right. We had to tell what we knew and suspected to anyone who could be in danger. I took a deep breath and looked into Thomas's eyes. Even without telepathy, I could read his mind. Going public made it a lot harder to lie to myself. A part of me knew the moment I saw Harry die that our lives would never be the same. There was no going back. Whether we were participants, targets, or innocents caught in the crossfire, a psychic war was raging.

Diana took a few more sips of water. "I can't ask all of you to stay here. It's ridiculous and dangerous."

"I'll stay," Thomas volunteered. "It won't be that inconvenient for me, and I can keep my outer shields down at night to listen for intruders. I'm also getting better at detecting someone even if they're shielding their thoughts. I can't hear what's in their head, unless I force it, but I know they're there. I've started practicing offensive tactics as well." He had an edge of steel in his voice, a tone I'd never heard from him.

"But then you won't get any sleep," Diana objected. "I don't want you to sacrifice your research and health to take care of me."

"I can get by," he said flatly.

"We can take turns guarding you. We can make sure you're with one of us at all times," I said, patting her knee.

"I'll stay here at night and drive you to work in the morning. You'll be safe there during the day, and Sophia or Nate will stay with you until I can relieve them in the evening." Thomas looked at us, and we nodded in approval.

"We'll watch over you until you leave for India. We can work out a new strategy when you return. You're family, Diana. We'll protect you," Thomas said.

Diana's eyes welled up. A few tears escaped, and she quickly wiped them away. "Thank you."

Diana set Thomas up in the room next to hers while he devised some sort of loud booby trap at the top of the stairs as an extra precaution. On the way home, knowing she'd get the message first thing in the morning, Nate texted Sarah to tell her that something had come up and we wouldn't be able to show her around town that day.

Nate and I woke up late the next morning after our stress-filled night. I contacted Thomas, curious about how Diana was doing. He was tired and making coffee, while Diana was still sleeping. I told him we'd bring lunch and give him the chance to go home and pack a suitcase and his surf gear. Nate hoped to surf with him later in the day. When we arrived with sandwiches, Diana was awake. Her usual happy-go-lucky shine had been replaced with a muted anxiety. Thomas was quiet as he gathered his things to go. I could tell he felt tense leaving even the three of us alone for a short period of time.

Nate suggested *The Office* as a binge-watching distraction, and luckily, Diana was a fan and welcomed it. Since she'd seen the episodes we'd already watched, we began where we'd left off. By the middle of the second show, Thomas returned and joined in to watch a few more episodes. After a while, I noticed Thomas occasionally gazing out at the swell and knew he wanted to surf. The boys then suited up and ran out into the waves like frisky puppy dogs. Covered in blankets, Diana and I chatted on the beach, watching the boys' heads bob in the ocean as they awaited the next good wave.

As we gazed at the ocean, Diana's tight shoulders seemed to relax. Soaking in the sounds of the crashing waves and the moist salt air released some of her stress.

"Thanks for coming to save me last night. I know it could have been dangerous for you and Nate."

"You're welcome, but you don't need to thank me. You're my best friend. I'm just grateful I had enough warning this time. But know this, I may lock all of you up after my next dreamless night."

Her lips curved up a little, but she sighed. "Please tell Thomas how much I appreciate his friendship as well. He waves me off any time I try to thank him. I'm completely disrupting his life."

"You're one of his best friends too. He is selfless and would probably do anything for us, but I'm sure he can handle the lack of sleep and still get his research done. When he was a kid, he couldn't block the barrage of voices and images from people within a mile or two. Most of the time, he could ignore it as background noise, but sometimes he'd go weeks without much sleep, which did affect his health then. Over the years he developed a way to listen and catch some sleep at the same time, but I know he can survive without becoming a zombie for a few weeks."

She seemed lost in thought. "We've all been fools. This brave new world of psychic powers is so much more than we thought. We haven't even begun to scratch the surface of what's possible. I wonder what we might be able to do with the right training. Have you made any progress with shielding while projecting?"

"None. Neither have Nate or Jack."

"Do you really think there's a freaking psychic war going on? Actually, don't answer that. I don't want to know. The more we find out, the more danger we seem to put ourselves in. I'm hoping we can ride out this insanity and get back to normal, happy lives, uninvolved in psychic politics."

"Nate and I hope so too, but I think whatever's going on has just started."

Diana smiled at me. I could tell she was pushing aside her usual instinct to tease. "You and Nate seem to be made for each other. How do you like living together?"

"It's wonderful, Diana. I love waking up next to him every day. I've never been happier. We've had a few blips, but we've worked through them. I can hardly believe how in love we are."

"So Nate's been dealing okay with the shared dreams?" she asked.

"Pretty much. He got over it after a few days, but I haven't had any new ones. I'm hoping they won't return."

"Since you won't hide them from Nate, I hope so as well." We both cringed as Thomas wiped out. He popped up quickly, though, and paddled out again. "I wish we knew why you were having these dreams and who this mysterious person is. I know you don't believe the guy is bad or involved in one of these psychic groups, but I'm not convinced. It's too much of a coincidence that those dreams started when all this craziness began."

"You might be right." I didn't really want to believe that the nice guy sharing dreams with me was purposefully targeting and tricking me. I needed to be able to trust my instincts. If he could fool them, I was in worse trouble than just having to deal with Nate's jealousy. We stared out over the water. It was a cool, cloud-covered day along the coast.

When the boys finally decided to paddle in, Nate walked out of the water with his board tucked under his right arm and shook his brown hair out of his face. My heart skipped a beat just looking at him. When his eyes found mine, butterflies fluttered in my stomach, and our sappy smiles reflected each other. Thomas was at least as handsome as Nate, though with a taller, slightly thinner build and longer hair. If Thomas and Diana had been dating, I would have said then that we were the luckiest girls in the world even with all of our problems.

When the guys finished showering and had warmed up, we walked to a nearby pizza place. A car door slammed hard twenty feet away and set my pulse racing. Fully on alert, we continued to flinch at any surprising sound, even the squeal of a child. Thomas and Diana scanned the area constantly and wore masks of intense focus. Though the afternoon spent breathing in the ocean air rejuvenated us, we hadn't forgotten the danger and were rightfully on edge.

CHAPTER TWENTY-THREE

Since we believed that having one of us with Diana should be enough to keep her safe, Nate and I drove to work separately to give her different options on time of departure. After settling in, I met with Roger and explained that we wanted to inform the psychics we knew about everything we'd learned since Harry's murder and to let them know that someone might be keeping tabs on them as well. To my relief, he authorized me to share certain facts that provided enough information without compromising client secrecy.

Word circulated around the office that Nate, Diana, and I had something to tell everyone in Psi Solutions, and we met in the break room at lunch. Some faces were a bit shocked and worried. Others didn't seem too concerned at all, but most were glad to hear what we knew. We described the surveillance equipment, and I passed around my phone to show the pictures of the GPS tracker attached to my car and a bug from my apartment. After several questions, we all returned to work. Since I'd already updated Irene the night before, I then called Mike from Psychic Investigators and Detective Jones. Detective Jones was intrigued by my story but annoyed we didn't call in John's stalking, though he understood our fear that John could control one of his men with a weapon. I asked him to share the information with Mr. Schwartz, the empath present at my interview. When I hung up the phone, I felt as if a small weight had been lifted from my shoulders. We'd armed everyone with information, the only tool we had at this point.

At the end of the day, Nate and Diana left together to start dinner at our apartment while I had to stay a little longer to wrap up a case. An hour later, laughing, music and smells of searing steak and baking bread greeted me at home. Nate, Thomas, and Diana were happily cooking a gourmet meal together, and they'd apparently been rocking out while making their concoctions. Nate smiled and pulled me into a sort of dance. Taking part in their merriment was pure joy. I savored the moment.

Nate teased me a bit while we were dancing but kept it polite for company. When the song ended, Nate turned the music down so we could hear each other speak.

"It smells great in here. What can I do to help?"

"I think we've got it covered," Nate said. He gave me a long but chaste kiss and whispered in my ear. "Welcome home, my love."

I set the table and poured water for everyone while they finished their various tasks. The dinner was divine and the company even better.

"Do you want to continue with *The Office* or begin the second season of *Game of Thrones?*" Thomas asked.

"I vote we stick with *The Office* for now. It's lifting my spirits," I suggested. Nate and Diana agreed. The humor helped us escape our reality for a time. While watching, I realized that my hands had become used to roaming over Nate, and I had to be careful not to scandalize Diana and Thomas. When they left around ten o'clock, Nate hugged me from behind, moved his hands under my shirt and bra, and kneaded my breasts.

"I've wanted to do that all night," he whispered in my ear. I arched my back, raised my right arm to finger-comb his hair and leaned into him. "Watching TV with guests made me realize how much I put my hands all over you when we're alone."

"I had to watch myself too. It's strange that we don't seem to have that problem anywhere else. I guess this is just how we are at home," I said.

Nate smiled, swept me up in his arms, and carried me to bed.

*   *   *

The rest of the week passed in much the same manner. The four of us spent the evenings together, alternately at our apartment, Diana's house, or eating out at restaurants. At times, we even forgot the unpleasant reason for our constant camaraderie.

On Saturday, we slept a little late and enjoyed a lazy morning. Around ten o'clock, I dropped Nate off to surf with Thomas and picked up Diana to finish our Christmas shopping. I'd already ordered most of my gifts since I hated crowds and preferred to shop online, but I still had to pick out a few presents. Diana needed to buy certain items that her cousins couldn't find in India. Our docket was full, but I hoped to finish by the early afternoon because I did *not* want to spend a full day shopping.

But if I had to shop, there was no better person to do it with than Diana. She was a pro. The constant stimulation never overwhelmed her, and she had a knack for finding the diamond in the rough. My gift to Thomas was a no-brainer, although I wasn't sure he'd accept it. He still drove the same run-down car we shared throughout college. I had enough money for the both of us and wanted to give him a sizable down payment toward the purchase of a new car. The car would actually be a present from my mom as well because her gift would be to pay his car payments until he graduated and got a real job. I only had to find the right key chain to complement the check. I also needed to buy some additional gifts for my mom, Irene, and my grandparents. I'd already ordered a fitness tracker and clothes for Nate, but I hoped to have time to work with Irene soon on a more personal gift I planned to give him.

The mall was festively decked out for Christmas, and holiday music played over the speaker system. Parents with small children waited in a long line for the chance to sit on Santa's lap and tell him what present they wished for most. I loved this time of year. Since Diana had a specific list, we focused on her purchases first, and once we'd completed those, she helped me pick out my remaining gifts. As we walked out to my car, I couldn't have been more relieved that we'd accomplished all of our shopping in only a few hours time.

I popped the trunk, and we placed the packages inside. As I was slamming it shut, arms grabbed me from behind and pulled me into a chokehold. John knocked my keys away before I could squeeze the alarm button. I struggled to reach for his thumb, finger, or any part of his body I could seize to defend myself. He lifted me off the ground by my neck so I kicked and tried to slam my heel into his groin, his shin, his knee, but when the cold barrel of a gun pressed against my temple, I froze. Almost two decades of martial arts training should have prepared me better. I tried to calm my racing heart and breathing and think more clearly. I could still try to disarm him, but I didn't know how readily he'd pull the trigger. Yet, if he planned to take us with him, we might be as good as dead.

"John, please don't," Diana begged, her voice trembling with panic.

"I need to talk to you, Diana. I don't intend to hurt you or Sophia."

Since his voice was calm and convincing, I interpreted it as a sign that he wasn't trigger-happy and attempted to disarm him. Unfortunately, he was better trained, faster, and much stronger than me, and I ended up on the ground, my head smacking hard against the uneven pavement as Diana screamed. A warm wetness began to pool against my ear.

"I wish you hadn't done that. I didn't want to hurt you," he reprimanded in that same reasonable but now slightly irritated tone. I tried to get up, but couldn't figure out where vertical was. The spinning and creeping headache forced my eyes shut for the moment. I had to focus to regain my equilibrium.

"Diana, I promise not to harm you or Sophia again as long as you don't try anything. I need to explain some things to you. Please get in the back of the van, and I'll lay Sophia down." I opened my eyes and tried to concentrate on Diana.

She stared at John for a minute and must have either seen some truth there or the futility of resisting. Diana climbed in as instructed, while John carefully lifted me up and laid me on the hard metal floor. The world was starting to settle, but I couldn't fight him then. He took off his jacket and placed it under my head. When he shut and locked the back doors, we were in complete darkness. The windows were opaque, and a wall separated the front from the back of the vehicle.

Diana put her hand gingerly on my forehead and whispered, "Sophia, can you hear me? You're bleeding from the side of your head. Please tell me you can hear me." Her voice was shaking, and a tear fell from her face onto mine.

"I can hear you," I whispered back. I blindly raised my hand to find hers and felt her grab it. "My head hurts, and I'm still dizzy, but it's subsiding. I should be able to stand soon."

"Can you contact Thomas to tell him what's happened?" she whispered into my ear. We could hear John slam his door and rev the engine. "I've already tried, but I've never communicated with him from this far away. It's not working, and John might be blocking me. Call to Thomas, Sophia."

With the gun against my head, I hadn't thought to reach out to Thomas. *Stupid.* As I opened my connection to him, Thomas was already there about to knock on my shields. He'd sensed that something wasn't right, and he and Nate were paddling in. Thomas explored my mind and saw all that Diana and I were experiencing. He promised to find us and held our connection open so he could see and hear everything. I started to berate myself for shopping at the larger, more distant Fashion Valley mall instead of the local one. It would take them much longer to find us. We'd been sloppy.

Thomas thought to me in a hypnotic tone, *"Shh, Sophia, don't stress. Slow your heart rate. Relax. The bleeding has stopped. The wound in your head is already healing. With your shields intact, John won't know you've contacted me. You're beginning to feel calm and in control. We need to think of a way for you and Diana to protect yourselves."*

We worked out a plan, and I whispered it to Diana. With both of our shields in place and the noise of the drive, we didn't think we'd tipped John off. After about twenty minutes of turns and bumps, John opened his door and walked around to the back of the van. I was already standing. Seizing the element of surprise, I kicked the back door open hard just as he unlatched it and heard a crunch of bone before he fell to the ground.

John's nose gushed blood. He began to stand up and tried to break through my shields, but what I can only describe as a potent stream of Thomas rushed through my mind and attacked John. Because of my link with Thomas, I could feel John's shields like a physical wall. With laser-like precision, Thomas focused his energy on a single vulnerable spot. Diana added her own power, and I sent whatever psychic energy I could along with Thomas. The three of us became a single merged force pushing against his shields. The spot became a hole, and John's mind opened to ours.

Thomas tried to direct John's thoughts and pelted his mind with questions, but a mass of images and emotions from John's life streamed before us . . . *the grand military funeral of his heroic father when he was only a child; his mom's last breath dying from the ravages of cancer as he held her hand in college; saving a young girl caught in the crossfire in Iraq and feeling her pain, her fear, her loneliness, and his own pure joy when she smiled at him in the hospital the next day; the cracks beginning to form in his sanity from feeling so much while being surrounded by despair, loneliness, pain, and death for too long; his "death" from a roadside bomb after pulling most of his men to safety; his awakening to a new life with understanding, teaching, enlightenment and purpose.*

"WHY DID YOU KILL HARRY?" Thomas yelled in John's head over and over again. Finally, some answers came to the fore before John could suppress them. . . . *Harry recruited for a psychic terrorist group, a group waging guerrilla warfare against the established order . . . precipitating economic crises across the globe for over a decade, destabilizing current regimes. . . . They funded his research. . . . In turn, Harry fed them psychic talent . . . former students and mentees . . . had to kill Harry to cut their supply chain, a necessary evil in a war beginning to get out of control. . . .* The feeling of truth in John's thoughts chilled my soul, but I couldn't believe it.

Thomas pushed harder to extract more specifics about John's group, but John became more successful at suppressing his thoughts here. All we gathered was that John was part of a shadowy group of psychics and aristocratic normals, a group that had been pulling the strings in the western world since the end of World War II, not unlike the apocryphal Illuminati.

Blood began to trickle down my neck once again. My concentration flagged, and reality began to blur. Recovered from his initial surprise, John exploited my weakness, focusing his power and training on me.

"Get out of my fucking head!" he yelled. I felt a smack as he pushed us out. The flow of Thomas came to an abrupt halt. I blacked out momentarily and fell to the floor, hitting my head against the cold, hard cement once again. I blinked my way back to consciousness, and though I could feel Thomas still with me, I knew I wouldn't be getting back up to fight this time.

Thomas focused on me now. Though he tried not to share it, I could feel his fear. He began to repeat healing suggestions to me again, but in earnest this time.

Diana grabbed and held my hand. I blinked up at the ceiling of a warehouse lit by fluorescent lights, scattered at such large intervals that the room was quite dim. John left us alone for a minute, either to regain his own strength and self-possession, or because we were no longer a threat to him. I strained to stay conscious by focusing on Diana's voice and the lights above.

John's footsteps came closer. Diana's hand tensed in mine. "How's she doing?" he asked.

"Her head's bleeding again. I think she's barely clinging to consciousness," she said bitterly.

I looked at him. He'd taken the time to reset his nose, stop the bleeding and wipe away the blood. Though still handsome, his nose was swollen, and his eyes looked tormented.

"I'm truly sorry about Sophia. I reacted on instinct when she fought me. She's skilled, which forced me to fight harder than I'd meant to, but she's small," he said, sounding sincere.

Diana stood up, and my eyes followed her. She glowered at him. "What did you expect? You put a fucking gun to her head!"

"I didn't expect her to fight. I thought it would convince you both to cooperate so I could talk to you in person. Christ, if you hadn't told the police about me, I wouldn't have had to do this! I'm not supposed to be here!"

"What do you want? What's left for us to talk about?"

He took a step closer and looked down into her eyes. She stood her ground. "You know what I did, what I *had* to do, but I need you to understand that what I felt for you was real, that what we had together was real. I didn't expect it and didn't even want the complication, but it happened. I fell in love with you. We fell in love." He reached his arms out to her, but she pushed them away.

"How can you say that? We had nothing but lies! Your name isn't even John, for God's sake, and you're a murderer! You used me to murder a friend!" she screamed.

"You don't understand." He ran his fingers through his hair. "I'm one of the good guys. Yes, I've had to kill. I hate it, but sometimes it's necessary. I'm a soldier. I've been trained for this fight, trained to manipulate people's minds, even psychics. I blocked Harry's and Sophia's precognition about my plans and prevented you from sleeping. I've been *trained* to defend the innocent against people like Harry. Death is a terrible thing, but Harry put himself, and *you*, at risk."

"You're mistaken about Harry. He would never work with terrorists or betray anyone. No one tried to recruit me besides the military and SDCC."

"You haven't been approached by them yet because they aren't ready to use you yet. There's more going on than you can imagine. How you and most people believe the world works is an illusion. There's a power struggle taking place, and people are dying on both sides." John reached out for her again.

"Get away from me! I don't know who you are!" She pushed him away with all her strength and started pacing. He followed her.

"*I* barely know who I am!" he yelled, looking frantic. "I don't even remember those visions you saw of my life. I don't recall much of anything before I woke up from a coma seven years ago. I do know that I love you. I will protect you with my life if necessary. I already saved you and your friends. My job was to eliminate Harry and any psychics working with him. I proved that Harry was working alone and that the rest of you weren't involved, but I wouldn't have hurt you no matter what they'd ordered me to do. Diana, please, I love you. I knew you'd find out what I did and couldn't bear the thought of you imagining me a monster. I'm not. I'm just a man fighting a war that I didn't start. God, I need you, Diana. I haven't loved anyone in so long. Please, give me another chance."

"Why? So you can pull me into the war as well?"

"No matter what I do, it may be impossible to keep you out of the struggle and could already be too late for any psychic. It might even get to the point where both sides will either want you or will want to eliminate you." That fact lingered in the air between them.

Diana shook her head, with a mask of grief on her face. "I can't love the person who murdered Harry, no matter the cause. He was one of the kindest men I've ever known. I can't look beyond that, no matter what I felt for you or had hoped we'd have together. It's over. If you really do love me, you'll leave me and my friends alone."

As she finished her last word, John grabbed her and kissed her. She resisted at first but then seemed to melt into him. Diana later told me that her body remembered his and responded against her will, overwhelming her mind and lulling her into the past, but after a few moments, she recalled the current reality and fought once more to be free. He let her go.

"Please, don't ever do that again," she panted, wiping her lips with the back of her trembling hand, but she tried to regain her composure. "Yes, a part of me still feels something for you, based on what we had, but it wasn't real! I could never be happy with a killer. It's not possible."

My eyes started to feel heavy. I struggled harder to keep them open and focus on the conversation. Thomas thought to me that they knew where we were and would be there soon. The word, "soon," flowed out of my mouth. John turned to study me and penetrated my waning shields.

"Your friends are coming," John stated.

"Yes. You should leave us here. We've had our conversation," Diana said wearily.

John's eyes darkened. His face briefly betrayed his inner turmoil and despair but then returned to his confident, professional mask. He stepped forward, almost at attention, and took a deep breath. "I promise to leave you and your friends alone and even to keep you out of this if I can. I'll at least show you that I'm a man of my word. I do love you, Diana, and hoped we could overcome what I *had* to do. I'll go now."

John closed the back doors of the van and then opened the driver's door. He paused, staring at Diana as if he were memorizing her face. "Goodbye, Diana. I wish you the best." He then climbed into the van and drove out of the empty warehouse.

When he was out of sight, Diana broke down into sobs. She sank onto the ground next to me.

"Sophia, I'm so sorry," she murmured. My last thought was that she looked like a wilting flower, and then I fell into darkness.

* * *

The lights were too bright. After blinking several times, the world started to come into focus. I was in a hospital bed with a tube in my left arm. Nate was holding tightly to my right hand, staring down at my fingertips. My head and torso were strapped immobile, with a brace around my neck and a board at my back. I had an excruciating headache. "Nate," I choked out, my mouth dry and chalky.

"Oh, Sophia, thank God you're awake." He brought my hand to his lips. "Thomas and the doctors said you'd be fine, but I couldn't believe it until I heard your voice again." He heard how parched my throat sounded and brought a cup of water with a straw to my lips.

"What happened?" I asked after several long sips.

Nate kissed me gently and explained that I was unconscious when they discovered us. They'd raced me to the hospital where a CT scan showed bleeding in my brain. They thought I might need surgery if the blood continued to accumulate, but when they ran another scan an hour later, much of the blood had already disappeared. No doctor could explain it, but Nate was certain that Thomas's post-hypnotic suggestions and my own psychic abilities had healed me. Apparently, they thought I might walk away with only a concussion, a goose egg with a glued cut on the side of my head, and a few nasty bruises.

After the nurse removed the backboard, I felt more like myself and less like an invalid. Nate had watched me carefully as the nurse performed her duties. I'd already taken to heart his concerned look, but I finally observed his full appearance.

"Why are you wearing hospital scrubs?" I asked.

"Oh, I guess you don't remember," he looked down at himself, having forgotten about them. "Thomas and I were still in our wetsuits when we found you. We laid you down in the back seat with your head on my lap. On the way to the hospital, you threw up all over me. A nurse let me borrow them."

"Sorry about that, but they look good on you." I checked him out and smiled.

Nate sighed in relief. I could see him finally letting go of some of his anxiety. "God, I love you, Sophia. Please don't scare me like that again."

He looked haggard. I was sorry I'd frightened him. "I won't. I love you too." I squeezed his hand.

Snippets of the last conversation I'd heard before I blacked out started to come back to me. "Nate, John's in love with Diana."

Nate's face flushed with rage. "You *cannot* feel sorry for him. He put you in this hospital. He killed Harry. I'd strangle him with my bare hands, if he were here."

"You're right. I just can't help but pity him a little. If you'd seen what we saw of his life, what he thought he was doing . . ." Nate was keeping a tenuous hold on his temper. He was about to lose it so I stopped that line of thought.

"I do hope he leaves us alone, though," I said.

Nate looked out the window as he tried to calm himself.

"How did you find us?" I asked, hoping he'd follow my change of topic.

He turned his head to look at me, and his lips curved a little. "It appears that I can find you anywhere. I concentrated on you, your feel, your scent, and was able to project to you while you were still traveling in the van. I knew exactly which streets to take to find you."

"Thanks for saving me." I squeezed his hand. "You and Thomas are a good team."

"You have no idea," he said. "We are, but it was a miracle we found you without getting into a car accident. As soon as the van started to pull into the warehouse and we knew your final location, we stopped on the shoulder of the freeway, and within seconds I took over driving so Thomas could help you fight. Fortunately, we timed it perfectly and didn't kill ourselves in the process."

A gentle knock on the door announced Thomas. Diana trailed behind him. She was a mess.

Thomas gently kissed my forehead. I could see the beginnings of a tear at the edge of his right eye but knew he'd rein it back in.

"When you first lost consciousness, I thought I'd lost you," he said quietly. "I've never been in anyone's head when that's happened. It was silent and scared me to death. I don't know what I'd do without you." He swallowed hard and tucked hair behind my ear. "Then, I concentrated harder, and I could hear your life still humming along and a few scattered thoughts here and there. You were waxing in and out of consciousness by the time we found you. I'm sorry if what we did to John hurt you, if I forced you to do too much when you were already injured."

"Thomas, don't. I know you'd never hurt me on purpose."

Diana peeked from behind Nate. "Diana, you don't look so good," I teased, trying to lighten the mood.

She smiled a little but became silent and serious again. "You don't look so good yourself. . . . Sophia, how can you ever forgive me?"

"There's nothing to forgive. You know that, and . . . I'm sorry about John."

Her red, swollen eyes proved she was an emotional wreck, but she, of course, tried to rally herself. "What's life without a little heartache? I'd avoided it for twenty-six years. It was bound to bite me on the ass eventually." She paused thoughtfully for a moment. "For some reason, I think John will keep his promise and stay away. Knowing he won't be coming around will help me move on."

I looked at her face. It was the same beautiful face that had smiled at me, laughed with me, and listened to me for so many years, but something had changed. I looked around the room at Nate and Thomas. Something had changed in all of us.

CHAPTER TWENTY-FOUR

On Tuesday, back at home, I awoke almost three hours after Nate had left our bed, with a lingering headache, some mental fogginess, and an aversion to bright lights. I smoothed the sheets on his side and was already looking forward to his return. Nate had spent a night and most of Sunday in the hospital with me. He'd even stayed home to care for me on Monday, but he had to go to work today. The neurologist at the hospital insisted I not project until after the holidays. He thought taxing my mind in any way might hurt my recovery. I also wasn't allowed to drive or do any vigorous physical activity for the next several days and couldn't run for a few weeks at least. Since my quick healing still disconcerted him, the doctor insisted on seeing another reassuring scan before we left town for Christmas.

Diana left on Sunday to spend three weeks in India with her family. The timing couldn't have been better. She needed an escape, and I hoped she might find some solace there. She sent me a text saying she'd arrived safely, but I didn't expect to hear from her again. She needed time. After the holidays, she intended to work with Thomas to see what they could do to improve their offensive and defensive capabilities. Her plan was to heal in India, but when she returned, she wanted to regain some semblance of control over her life.

When Irene knocked on the door to bring me to her house for the afternoon, it was a welcome distraction. She hugged me gently as I opened the door.

"Oh, Sophia," she said, sizing me up. "I am so thankful you are better. I keep calling Thomas for updates on your health. I feel responsible for what happened to you."

"Why?"

"If you had never met Harry, you would not be hurt now."

Her face was inscrutable. I couldn't tell what she was thinking, but I knew Thomas had already told her everything that had happened with John. "Irene, you don't believe what John said about Harry?"

She looked up with fire in her eyes, with a kind of hate I'd never seen there before. "No, of course not, it is nothing but lies!" Her eyes then softened into a deep sadness. "Sophia . . . *you* do not believe it, do you?"

I shook my head thoughtfully. "No . . . but I'm convinced that John did. Someone must have set Harry up." I could tell I didn't put enough conviction into my voice to satisfy her.

"I don't care what John believes," she said, her voice flat. "I knew Harry better than anyone. He was exactly who he appeared to be — a kind, loving . . ." Her voice began to crack, and her effort to hold back the tears filled me with emotion.

"I know. I *know.*" I wrapped my arms around her and rubbed her back, this time making certain she could feel that my belief came from the heart. "I don't know what the hell's going on, but I will always trust in Harry. He would never betray anyone." I wasn't sure I'd convinced her, but when she lifted her head to look at me, her eyes seemed less heavy, like her burden had lightened a bit.

"Do you remember that virus Trevor found on Harry's computer? The one that sent false information to a second virus? Could that have been how they framed him? Did the terrorists set Harry up to be eliminated?" I asked.

"I do not know, and it is driving me crazy." Irene wrung her hands together and then pressed them to her forehead, groaning in frustration. She quieted then to compose herself. "We will talk about this later. Now, I have something for you." She backed out of the doorway a little, moved to the side, and told me to close my eyes. When

I opened them, she held what appeared to be a large framed canvas, concealed by a white cloth.

"This is one of my favorite pieces. Ever since we met, it has made me think of you. Merry Christmas."

She unveiled an oil painting of sunshine, a little girl with eyes closed kneeling in the sand, soaking up the glorious sun. The nearby ocean was filled with strange-looking creatures, some simply bizarre and others quite menacing. Floating along the edges of the sky were more unusual entities. Some were beings, though not angels, that were watching over the girl drawn either by love or curiosity. The power of the sun's rays seemed to be keeping all of these mysterious beings at bay, and as long as the child soaked up those rays, she was protected. The frame accentuated the hues of sunshine in the painting, heightening the impression that the sun and the little girl had created a sphere of peace and safety.

"Irene, I love it." Irene didn't respond but watched my expression as I examined it further.

"Why have I never seen it before? I've never seen at your house or at an exhibition. Where has it been?"

"I have a private room at the house, where I keep my most precious works I do not intend to show or sell. I made this painting about five years before we met, but from the first time I saw you, I felt that somehow in spirit, *you* were this little girl. It has always been meant for you. Maybe it will be a kind of talisman to keep you safe. I only ask that you never sell it."

I hugged her, and tears filled my eyes. "Thank you, Irene. I will treasure it always." I let her go and wiped my eyes. "You'll have to show me where to hang it."

"I insist on it." She smiled and then furrowed her brow in contemplation, intent on finding the right spot.

After using her telekinesis to position the painting on almost every wall of my apartment, Irene frowned. "No place is ideal, but if displayed high enough above your fireplace, the sunlight from that window will not reach it. I do find it ironic that we have to protect the painting itself from the sun. If you want, I brought everything necessary to hang it for you."

To my astonishment, Irene pulled out a large hammer from her purse, as if it were a perfectly normal item to carry.

I laughed. "Please tell me you don't usually lug that around with you."

Irene smiled cryptically. "You never know when something like this might come in handy."

She didn't need a stool. The hammer, nails and hooks flew from her hands, and the painting was quickly hung. Irene sighed, unsatisfied but resigned that no other place would work better. "Sophia, you must promise me that I can hang it in your future homes, wherever you move to, as long as I live. I feel more at peace when my paintings are in the right place."

"I promise."

I collected my things, and we headed to Irene's to work on my Christmas present for Nate. When we arrived, I showed her the sketches. I hadn't yet told her the significance, but I knew she would figure it out.

"Who are these children?" she asked.

"Well . . . they might one day be Nate's and mine."

She cradled my face in her hands, stared into my eyes for a lengthy moment, and then kissed my forehead. "He will love your present."

Irene set me up on her studio table and helped me draw enlarged, faint versions of the original sketches on watercolor paper while at the same time improving the parts I felt were weak. Then, she started me with the watercolors, giving me pointers until I seemed comfortable enough to take over. I'd painted with watercolors in the past but not in the last several months. Though technically difficult, the watercolors should provide a luminous, vital feel and also dry in time for Christmas. Irene sat down to work on an unfinished oil painting as we began to dissect the confrontation with John as we worked.

"Why would the terrorists trick John's group into killing Harry by making him appear to be their recruiter? I still cannot understand what his death accomplishes," Irene said.

"Maybe because he was a leader in the field the terrorists saw him as a threat and assumed he'd stand in their way when they grabbed for power? It's also possible that someone within John's group misled him instead of the terrorists. To play devil's advocate, what if they're not actually terrorists and instead are the *real* good guys? Just because John believes his side is the right one, doesn't mean it is."

Irene looked over at me. "I doubt there is a right side. When two groups vie for power, both often commit atrocities. Innocents become casualties. Which side to support often boils down to the lesser of two evils. If the terrorists set up Harry, they are as responsible for his death as John is, and they deserve their name. I do not see how they can be good, and if the telepath that tried to detain you is one of them, it supports that conclusion, but it is still possible someone else framed Harry."

"Nothing seems black or white any more, but maybe there's a better side."

"I believe that if Harry did work with them, that it was for a good reason and that he kept me in the dark to protect me. He always coddled me."

"He did, but I don't think he kept anything from you."

She wanted desperately to believe me and mostly did, but that fraction of doubt was tormenting her. She put her paints down and leaned against the window, gazing out at her camellias.

"I shared forty years of my life with Harry. I knew his every mood. He was so much a part of me that I almost have to learn how to breathe again. I see something that makes me smile, and I need to tell him. Harry would never have hidden anything from me unless he thought knowing might put me in danger, but even then, I think I would have noticed."

She turned to look at me and narrowed her eyes. "Sophia, I need to make them pay. I plan to go after John and those responsible for his murder." Having finally said it out loud, she picked up her paints and began working again while the silence echoed the enormity of her decision.

I didn't know what to say. I realized then that despite John's warnings of impending disaster, I'd started to hope he might be successful at keeping us out of the remaining power play. "Irene, I don't think that's a good idea. It won't end well."

"Harry had many foundations and institutions fund his research over the years. John said that the 'terrorists' were contributors. I wonder if Harry and Violetta had some of the same donors. If I follow the money, I might learn something. I will have to call Dante."

A chill ran down my spine as I watched this woman whom I'd known for so many years transform before my eyes. I was beginning to realize how dangerous someone like Irene could be when she put her mind to it. Or someone like Thomas. Or even someone like me.

* * *

After Irene dropped me back off at home, I did a healing meditation with the GammaBeat to speed my recovery until Nate stepped through the door. I was sitting on the couch and smiled at him as he sat down next to me.

"How was your day?" I asked.

"The usual, but I miss having you at work. It's not the same. Even if we don't have the chance to get lunch or even see each other, it makes work more cheerful knowing you're there." Seeing his warm, "ah, shucks" attitude did more good for me than a week of meditation.

"I've been looking forward to your return all day." I kissed him deeply and snuggled into his lap. "I talked with Irene today."

"How'd it go?"

"Okay, I guess."

He spied the painting on the wall. "Was that a gift from her? It's incredible."

I scooted out of his lap, and he walked over to the painting to examine it up close. I told him the story of the painting and my conversation with Irene. Nate also believed that John was mistaken about Harry, but he was disturbed that Irene intended to pursue Harry's murderers. That evening, he seemed unusually focused on his own thoughts.

* * *

By Thursday, I felt much better, though I still had an aversion to light and noise, clouded thinking, and a persistent, dull headache that spiked from time to time. I spent most of the day resting and meditating before Nate picked me up in the afternoon for the CT scan at the hospital.

"Did you know today's our two-month anniversary?" he asked in the car.

"No," I said, feeling a little guilty. "Until you mentioned it, I didn't even know what day it was. Happy Anniversary!" I then leaned over to kiss his cheek.

"After the appointment, assuming they're not too backed up, would you like to watch the sunset in Del Mar as a small celebration?"

I squeezed his hand. "I'd love to."

After the CT scan was finished, we were told that the doctor would call soon with the results to clear us to leave town for the holidays. We arrived in Del Mar before the sun even began to set and had plenty of time to find parking, which can be a big hassle there. Nate surprised me by taking out a beach blanket and a duffel bag from the trunk of his car.

"You had this planned!"

"Guilty as charged," he replied.

Nate laid the blanket down on the grass of a small bluff overlooking the ocean. The waves crashed into the cliffs off to our left while they propelled surfers toward the beach on our right. Families walked their dogs and frolicked in the last bit of sunshine for the day. Nate opened his bag and pulled out a container of strawberries, two plastic glasses, and sparkling grape juice since I couldn't yet drink alcohol. He then wrapped a blanket around us so we could snuggle together as we listened to the surf and watched the sun fall into the ocean. As the sun descended, the clouds increasingly reflected pink and orange in wide patterns across the sky that left me in awe. I felt incredibly lucky to be held in Nate's arms, sharing the beauty of the outdoors with him. After the sun finally set, the air cooled quickly. Everyone started to pack up and leave, and I suggested we head home too.

"In a minute." He said and handed me a small, black velvet box.

"Nate, you didn't need to get me anything."

"It's not an anniversary present."

He looked at me then with a searching gaze. "Sophia, we've only been together for two months, but I already know I want to spend the rest of my life with you. I don't want to scare you off, and if you're not ready for this move, consider this an open-ended and unpressured invitation, but nothing would make me happier than for you to marry me."

At first, shock and mild confusion overwhelmed me, but as I began to grasp what was happening, love and warmth flooded my senses. Nate popped open the box to reveal an engagement ring, a beautiful band of platinum, sapphires, and diamonds. "I love you, Sophia. I will always love you. Will you marry me?"

Tears welled up in my eyes, and my mouth went dry. Though I could hardly believe he was proposing, I loved him and wanted nothing more than to spend the rest of my life with him. "Yes, Nate, I will."

Nate grabbed me and kissed me. I poured my heart into that kiss and bathed in his love and his strength. Time stood still. This man was my lifeline, my love. When the kiss finally ended, he had unshed tears in his eyes. My eyes were beginning to overflow. He tugged the ring out of the box, held my left hand, and slid the sparkling ring onto my finger.

As I gazed down at the ring, the symbol of us forever joining our lives together, tears found their way down my cheeks. I was speechless with joy. He kissed the palm of my hand and placed it on his cheek, staring down at me.

"I love you, Sophia."

"I love you too," I whispered hoarsely.

*   *   *

Nate bounced with happiness and relief as we walked back to the car. I was equally happy but bewildered as well. We loved each other and spoke often of being together in the future, but I hadn't expected him to propose then and didn't realize I'd automatically say yes. It seemed that Nate could overcome and maybe was meant to overcome all of my defenses.

Later, when we were eating dessert after a candlelit dinner we'd picked up on the way home, Nate asked me what I was thinking. We'd both been quieter than usual while we ate.

I swallowed my last bite of chocolate cake and set my plate down on the coffee table. I put my hand on his cheek and looked into his eyes. "I'm truly happy, Nate. I love you, but I think I'm shocked that we're getting married. I guess I'm still wrapping my head around the whole idea."

For a moment, his eyes flicked away from mine, but then they returned, earnest. "I'll understand if you want to put off the actual wedding until we've been together longer. Hell, two months ago, I'd have been in favor of taking it slow, but after what happened to you, I couldn't wait a second more to let you and the entire world know my intentions."

I chewed on my lip and stared down at the ring on my finger. "You know what? I don't want to wait." I intertwined his fingers with mine and looked up into his eyes. "This feels right. We're right. The world's a dangerous place. I don't want to waste any more time. I'll marry you whenever you want. Just make love to me, Nathan Barclay. I don't care what the doctor said about physical exertion. I need your hands on me. I need to feel your body against mine."

Nate cradled my face in his hands and kissed me, a kiss that heated my blood and soothed my heart.

"I love you so damn much, Sophia."

He scooped me into his arms, his eyes boring into mine as he carried me all the way to our bed. Nate laid me down and joined me, brushing feather-light kisses on my face and neck and then pushing up my shirt to kiss my stomach. He rested his cheek there and looked up at me with emotion brimming in his eyes. "One day our baby will grow here."

I pulled his face towards me and kissed him. I had to touch his skin and moved my hands under his shirt. In the need for close contact, our hands quickly discarded our clothes. We cherished every part of each other's bodies before we joined and engaged in that timeless rhythm, echoing unspoken promises as much as our vowed commitment.

After hours of gentle and intimate lovemaking, Nate spooned me. I held his arm against my breast and entwined my legs with his. He pulled me closer and nodded off to sleep. I kissed the arm that draped over me. Even though I knew a psychic war was brewing and a sense of foreboding surrounded us like dark clouds before a storm, I prayed that we could sustain this intimacy for the rest of our lives and that we'd live to see those two beautiful children come into the world and thrive.

JOIN MY VIP CLUB

If you'd like to receive a chapter from *Dissonance*, the second book in the *Resonance* series, please join my VIP club email list. Subscribers will also receive occasional *Resonance* prequel short stories and news about the release of upcoming titles. In the next few months, I will be enlisting beta-readers to ensure that I'm writing what you want (there are two potential endings to book 2, and the one chosen will heavily depend on your feedback).

SIGN UP HERE:
http://jennifergreenhall.com

Thank you for embarking on this journey with me!

PLEASE LEAVE A REVIEW!

If you enjoyed *Resonance*, please help me by leaving a review. I would be sincerely grateful. These days, customer reviews can make or break an author's career and cumulatively have more impact than an editorial review. You can be a part of that, and most importantly, if *Resonance* is successful, I will be able to complete the series for you much faster.

Thank you so much!

ABOUT THE AUTHOR

Jennifer Greenhall combines her love for romance, neuroscience and the paranormal in *Resonance*, the first installment of a 5-book paranormal romance and urban fantasy series. Fascinated by the possibilities of the mind, she completed a Ph.D. in Neurosciences and an M.D. at the University of California at San Diego. She also received a B.A. in German and a B.S. in Bioengineering from Texas A&M University where she was selected as one of *Glamour's* Top Ten College Women. Jennifer grew up in a NASA community southeast of Houston, did a short stint in Boston, and settled in beautiful San Diego with her awesome family and two sweet labradoodles.

CONNECT WITH ME AT:
jennifergreenhall.com
Facebook.com/jennifergreenhall
Twitter: @jenngreenhall
Goodreads.com/JenniferGreenhall
Instagram.com/jenngreenhall
Pinterest.com/jgreenhall